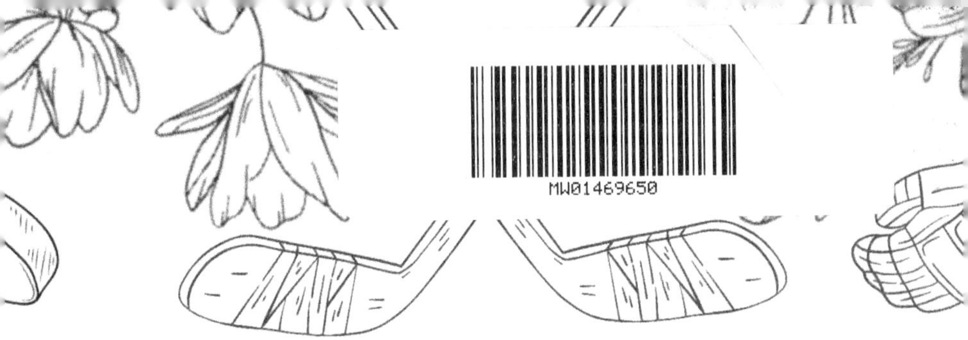

MW01469650

DIRTY Dangles

GABRIELLE DELACOURT

DIRTY DANGLES

BOOK #2 IN THE PUCKHEADS SERIES

GABRIELLE DELACOURT

First Edition | Ebook Publication Date: 3/22/23
ISBN: 979-8-9856984-3-5

Copy Editing by: Colby @colby_bettley
Paperback formatting by: Gabrielle Delacourt
Cover design by: Gabrielle Delacourt
Published by Gabrielle Delacourt

 Created with Vellum

PLAYLIST

No thanks- Alexander Stewart
Cooped up- Post Malone
Gfy- Blackbear & Machine gun kelly
Don't come back- Tate Mcrae
Mine- Noah Henderson
You Proof- Morgan Wallen
Freak Like That- Austin George
Nobody Likes Moving on- SHY Martin
It is what it is- Jamie Miller
Love Somebody- LAUV
You make me- Chelsea Cutler
Better Me Better You- Clara Mae & Jake Miller
Crash Course- Sam MacPherson
Bom Bidi Bom- Nick Jonas
Just friends- Why Don't We
Whiskey on You- Nate Smith
Warning- Morgan Wallen
Make up Sex- Blackbear & Machine gun kelly
Anyone's but mine- Conor Mathews
Think I Might- Cosher
Vegas- Doja Cat
Head first- Christian French
Favorite T-shirt- Jake Scott
She likes it - Jake Scott Russell
Emotions- Ella Henderson
Heartless- Julia Michaels and Morgan Wallen
Monopoly- Mokita & CADE
F**k Flowers– Noah Davis
Just Wait- Emily Vu
Drunk- Conor Matthews

Bae, every time I doubt myself, you remind me of what I'm capable of. I love you more than words.

Hello lovely readers!

Thank you so much for picking up this book and for taking a chance on me as an author.

Before we get into the fun of *Dirty-Dangles*, I want to make a note here about possible Trigger Warnings.

The list of triggers are as follows: neglect/abuse by a parent, discussions of body image issues, disordered eating, depression/anxiety, explicit sexual content, mentions of alcohol and drug abuse by a parent, and mentions of the loss of a parent, specifically to cancer.

If this makes you uncomfortable, I will not be offended if you pass on reading this.

Please note that *Dirty-Dangles* is book two in the PuckHeads Series. Although it is a standalone series, I do recommend reading them in order as other couples and their journey will be spoiled if read out of order.

In addition to these things, myself and my editor are only human. If you find any errors which are likely to happen, please feel free to email me at gabrielledelacourtauthor@gmail.com. I ask that you don't report them to Amazon, as it can result in the book being taken down.

If you enjoy this story, be sure to follow me on social media!

Instagram

Join my Facebook group

My Website

I hope you love Sterling and Jaiden as much as I do.

xx Gabbie D

Dirty Dangles

Hockey slang that often refers to a skilled player making impressive moves to fake out the goalie or opposing player. It is often used as a euphemism for sexual activity.

ONE

JAIDEN

THE FIRST THING I smell when I wake up is a sickly sweet scent. Did someone spray perfume in here?

Something tickles my nose and I swat at it, my eyes still closed. I'm too damn tired for this. Groaning, I turn over, my eyes opening slowly to reveal a woman that looks like a peacock. She's seated on the edge of the bed staring at me, wearing this monstrous blue robe that's covered in feathers.

Blinking several times, I look around, trying to get a sense of where I am. In the morning light, I see that the bed is full of fluffy teal pillows. I look down at my feet and see them hanging off the bed. It's unfortunate that I'm too tall for the bed; it would be comfortable otherwise. *Where the hell am I?*

My mouth is so dry and tastes of stale alcohol. *Fuck.*

"Good morning!" the peacock chirps, her voice too high for the first thing in the morning. *Stella? Samantha? Sarah? Fuck. What the hell is her name?*

Memories of last night come rushing back and I nearly groan. I got so drunk that I couldn't even follow through. It's been the pattern with me lately: go drinking, find a beautiful woman, pass out before I can sleep with them. Check. Check. Check.

My stupid fucking dick is ruined and this damn dry spell is my own fault. I'm supposed to be sleeping *her* out of my system. This wasn't how it was supposed to go.

"Morning," I rasp.

"I made you breakfast," she says, shoving a plate of food at me. The eggs and bacon are laid out in a smiley face, the pancakes topped with whipped cream. Staring down at the plate, I smile back at it.

"Uh, thank you."

She smiles widely, the shoulder of her feathery *thing* sliding down her arm. I get a quick glimpse of her tits and remember why I went home with her last night. I'm more of an ass man than anything, but this woman's rack is honestly a work of art.

I grab the bacon and bring it to my mouth, ripping a piece off with my teeth. When I do, I catch the time on my watch, my eyes going wide immediately. *Fuck. Fuck. Fuck.*

Flying out of bed, I hobble around on one leg, trying to avoid the mess we left on the floor last night. I find my shirt first and then my pants, throwing them on in record time.

I chew the bacon while I tie my shoes, and then look up at the woman on the bed. She's still blinking at me like she's waiting for me to say something, so I say the first thing I can think of.

"Thanks for last night," I say. "And the bacon." With a wink, I rush out the door and sprint down the stairs to the parking lot.

I really need to stop making this a habit. I never take women home to my condo because then women like Miss Peacock would know where I live, and I can't have that. However, it's really not great to be waking up in random women's homes after a night at the bar.

My phone rings in my pocket and I grimace when I see the name on the screen.

"Hey," I say into the phone, pressing it against my ear with my shoulder.

"You're late," a female voice growls into my ear. I don't need to see her face to know the one she's making.

"I'm on my way," I mumble as I throw my car in reverse and

speed out onto the main road. There's silence on the other end until I hear her release a deep sigh.

"This is a really fucking important day for them and you need to be here. Maybe if you weren't sleeping with half of Boston, you'd be here on time." She stops, her voice trailing off. It's almost as though she wants to continue talking but stops herself.

"Did you call me just to bitch at me? Because in all honesty, I really don't want to hear it from you right now. I already told you that I'm on my way."

She scoffs. I can picture the scowl she'll be wearing—the one she wears around me constantly at the moment—and it brings a smile to my face. If I can't make her feel anything other than anger, I might as well continue. I'm glad to be getting some sort of reaction.

"I really hate you," she says, her voice growing more irritated. "I worked very hard on this. Don't fuck it up for me. If not actually for *me*, then for our friends."

"Sterling, I'll get there when I get there. Bye." I hang up the phone, tossing it on the passenger seat. I may be running late, but I'll be damned if I'm not going to stop at my place to shower quickly and throw on a button-up shirt.

By the time I pull up to Roman's home, there are cars lined down the street, and I see Sterling's immediately. Sighing, I stroll through the front doors and right out to the back where the guests are mingling.

It's my best friend's engagement party. It's not a surprise per se, but it's something that Sterling worked tirelessly to put together for her best friend.

Avoiding Sterling's gaze, I wander to where other members of my team are standing.

"'Sup," I say, grabbing Damian's hand and pulling him in for a hug. He slaps my back before pulling away.

"Hey, bro," he replies as I shake hands with the other members of our team. We stand in a circle on the opposite side of the lawn.

"What's happening?"

"Just Sterling being insane," Damian says with an amused

glimmer in his eye. My eyes roll as I laugh. She's been a terror throughout this entire process. The only reason that I can remotely stand to be around her right now is because I have to be. I'm doing it for my friends.

Of course you are, you idiot. Totally doing it for your friends and not because you enjoyed being around her, even if she hates you.

"Speak of the devil," I mumble, lowering my voice.

"Jaiden," Sterling says, "I need your help moving this table."

I stare at her, my brows raised. I can see the muscles in her jaw tense, her posture going rigid.

"Please," she hisses through gritted teeth.

"Of course, Sterling. I'd love to help you, since you asked so nicely."

She shoots me a glare before walking off in the other direction. Her sinfully delicious ass sways as she walks and my dick twitches. Her long legs are perfectly tanned and toned; it makes me want to run my hands up her thighs... I stop that thought before it can go too far.

God, I hate how my body *still* reacts to her. Good to know my almost-fuck last night did absolutely nothing to curb my thirst for her.

"I wish your balls luck," Damian says with a smirk.

"You should be worried about your balls too," Sterling yells over her shoulder and I snicker when Damian holds a hand over his crotch in response.

I say nothing as I walk across the lawn to where she's standing at the end of a table. When my hands grip the end, she lifts, directing me to the rows of other tables. I keep my eyes trained forward, otherwise I'll look down at the cleavage of her dress, sneaking a view of her breasts which were shaped by God himself. *I'm too damn horny for this right now.*

We set it down and almost instantaneously, she conjures a floral arrangement from somewhere I hadn't seen, and places it on the table.

Without a second glance, she walks back inside the house. I hate to admit that I watch her ass again the whole time. It's the only view of her ass I get nowadays. All she ever does is walk away from me, or glare at me with waves of hatred rolling off her.

I don't know why I'm even here. I love my brothers more than anything and I'm happy that Wyatt has found love with Dakota, but I feel unwelcome here.

These are my friends and my family, but over the last few months, I've felt less and less connected with them. Almost like I'm on the outside looking in.

I can tell that Sterling's been trying really hard to keep that fake ass smile plastered on her face, but I know her well enough to see right through it. She doesn't want me here either.

Running a hand through my curly hair, I sigh. It's easy to turn away from her gaze because I hate myself as much as she does.

How did we end up here?

If only I had kept my dick in my pants, maybe this wouldn't have happened. Instead, I'm standing at my best friend's engagement party, feeling like an outsider.

"Enjoying all of that self loathing you've got going on?" Roman crosses his ankles as he leans against the fence. He eyes me with an expression that looks an awful lot like amusement. *Asshole.*

"I shouldn't be here," I say. "She's practically burning through my flesh with her eyeballs."

"She's a force to be reckoned with, that one. I'd hate to be on her bad side," he chuckles.

It's almost as if he's enjoying this. I glare, pushing off the wall and standing at my full height. I can feel myself shutting down. This is not a conversation I want to have right now. That woman already occupies more of my headspace than I'd like her to. As if Roman sees this, he eyes me, his face softening.

"Jai, I know this has been hard for the both of you. I'm here if you want to talk, or just verbally spar. Whatever the hell you need."

There's sincerity in the statement, yet I still struggle to take him up on the offer. I've felt more like a burden than a friend or a brother these last few months. I settle for a nod, but he doesn't look convinced.

I sigh, crossing my arms. "I'm fine, Rome. But I promise I will come to you if I need it. So, can we please just drop it now? Jesus."

His jaw clenches slightly, but he nods, finally letting it go.

"Where's the couple of honor anyway?" I say, changing the subject. Roman looks at me out of the corner of his eye.

"In the house somewhere. Sterling is due to grab them any moment." His hand runs across his jaw as he looks around. Without wasting another moment, I wander across the lawn until I wind up by the refreshment table.

My fingers grip the handle of the lemonade spout as I pour the sour liquid into my cup. Bringing the cup to my lips, I take a sip as someone sidles up next to me. I see their feet before I look up and meet a pair of bright gray eyes.

"My wife seems to think that you're struggling over something, son." Gray blinks at me, a small smile playing at the corner of his mouth. *God, here we go again.*

Am I a walking billboard for mental distress right now?

"I may be the father of the soon-to-be-bride, but I've considered myself a surrogate father to the three of you boys, four if we're counting Damian, since we met." He shakes his head as Damian flirts with several women across the lawn. "Tell me what's on your mind, Jaiden."

I snort, nodding my head. "It's nothing I can't handle." It's a lie in the worst form; I haven't been able to handle this situation for months.

"Well, if or when you can't, I'll be around." He looks at me a moment before patting me on the shoulder and walking away.

Is this an intervention? A way to make me feel less alone? What they don't realize is that it's making me want to retreat further. I've been faking it for months. Why does everyone give a shit all of a sudden?

I chance a glimpse at where Sterling is standing with our friends.

Her long brown hair is falling over her shoulder in a waterfall of waves. I flick my eyes away before I'm caught staring.

Roman has meandered over to the group, his daughter on his hip. She's getting too big to be carried like that, but she insists on it, so of course we can't deny Princess Lily.

Roman gesticulates wildly with one hand while Lily laughs at his side. The ladies laugh, Sterling smiling at him with reckless abandon.

Something like jealousy rushes through me at the ease of their interaction. We used to talk like that, with ease and confidence. Now, though, I walk on eggshells when I'm around her. It's my own fault, but even then, I don't share the same hatred for her that she has for me.

Almost as though she could feel me staring, Sterling looks up at me, that gorgeous smile quickly replaced by a scowl. *I want her to smile for me again.*

She taps her wrist absentmindedly, her face still angry. I used to love pinning those wrists above her head, forcing control out of her hands. Literally *and* figuratively. Maybe she's remembering those moments, too.

When I nod at her, she disappears into the house again, returning a moment later with the couple-of-honor.

I can't help but smile as I watch the two of them walk into view. Dakota looks happy, but there's a note of discomfort there. Over the past year, I've learned how much of an introvert she truly is. Wyatt loves to be the center of attention, so I find it ironic how the two of them found each other.

Wyatt's bright blue eyes are watching Dakota with such admiration that it makes *me* emotional. He holds their hands out to the crowd, the band around his finger the center of attention.

Wyatt is my best friend, and I'd do anything for him, but that won't stop me from giving him shit about being the proposee. That man *gets off* on Dakota stepping up and taking charge. For such an alpha male, he sure does like being the submissive sometimes.

I smirk at Roman, grabbing the inflatable diamond ring and

walk towards him. The moment I get down on one knee, I already know that Wyatt knows what's happening.

Extending the ring to Roman, I look up at him with my best gooey eyes. "Roman, my love. Will you marry me? Make me the happiest man alive!"

"Oh, fuck off," Wyatt says from the side, his expression more humorous than angry.

"What?" I ask, feigning innocence. "I'm just taking a page out of Dakota's book."

Wyatt drops Dakota's hand, his face serious now. His eyebrows raise at me as he charges in my direction.

I shriek in a rather unmanly way, rushing to my feet and running toward the grass.

"You're going to make such a beautiful bride, Wyatt," I toss over my shoulder, laughing.

Wyatt tackles me to the ground a second later, his fist rubbing against my scalp as I shove at him. He's got me in a headlock and I don't even regret it for a moment.

It's when I can feel the temperature drop several degrees that I freeze. *The Ice Queen is nearby.*

"Boys, it's a party—not a wrestling match," Sterling says sternly.

I scramble to free myself from Wyatt's grip and retreat to the opposite side of the backyard—far away from her. My balls are safer when Sterling's not around.

Months ago, I began feeling those *adult* feelings for Sterling, but I was too much of a coward to follow through. I have a tendency to hurt the people I love most, so I might as well not let anyone get too close.

My mind wanders as Roman runs through his speech. He talks, but I find myself looking at Sterling. Like a planet in her orbit, I gravitate toward her, walking slowly as the words flow out of Roman.

Before I can think about what I'm doing, I'm standing in front of her, my eyes looking down. I don't know what expression I'm making but from the way she's looking at me, there may be an element of vulnerability there.

"You did a great job with this party, Silver."

Her eyes narrow at me. "Don't call me that. You lost that privilege months ago."

I sigh, my expression morphing into one of irritation before I can stop it. "Yeah, *Sterling*, I did. I ghosted you. If you wanted to continue"—I wave my hands at her—"whatever it was we were doing, maybe you shouldn't have gone behind my back when you took the job." The words are out of my mouth before I can stop them. It's too late to take them back now.

I'm vaguely aware of all the eyes on us, but I don't care. This woman infuriates me. I've kept my mouth shut and I've worked hard to keep the peace, but I'm *done.*

"How *dare* you say that to me, Jaiden? This is your doing. I had the audacity to get a job? I was pursuing my *dream*, you asshole!"

"I *never* said that, and you know it. Why do you have to be so dramatic?" I raise my voice at her, my hands balling into fists to keep from slamming them down on anything near me.

Sterling throws her head back as she screams. Everyone is staring at us now. Dakota and Wyatt are walking toward us, but I keep my eyes trained on Sterling.

"You know what? I fucking *hate* you, Jaiden Thomas. I hate you so much! How dare you call me dramatic!" Sterling looks around us, and the moment her hand slams into the cake, I see Dakota lunge for her.

Her cake-filled hand comes flying at my face, smashing the strawberry filled sponge right into my nose and mouth. I stumble backwards, spitting cake onto the ground at my side, my eyes full of rage.

This woman is maddening; the worst kind of crazy. Why the hell did I even think it was a good idea to get involved with her? She's made my life absolutely miserable these past couple months. I've *tried* to be around her. I've really tried to make it work for my friends, but right here in this moment, I only feel defeated.

"You two," Dakota hisses, her voice portraying nothing but pure anger, "inside. Now."

I don't think twice before I storm away from Sterling. I vaguely register Damian handing me a towel and I wipe my face clean with it.

Once we're inside, I stand by the kitchen table, my hands shoved into my pockets. I wish I could disappear. I want to escape this place, and to separate myself from my friends. It would be easier for everyone if I just left.

"Can the two of you help me with something?" Dakota's looking at me with a soft smile. I know her well enough to see that there's more to it than just sweetness. She's plotting and I don't like it.

Sterling frowns, her eyes narrowing. "Uh, sure."

I just shrug, willing to do whatever they tell me so that I can get the hell out of here as soon as possible.

"Great. Since the two of you ruined my cake, I'm going to need a new one. Can you grab the cake mix and frosting please?"

"Sure?" Sterling side-eyes Dakota before she walks into the pantry and I can't help but feel like this is a trap. I follow her anyway. The door closes firmly behind me and I sigh, a feeling of dread pooling deep in my stomach.

"Chair, please," Dakota says before I hear the scrape of a chair and the rattling of the door knob.

"Dakota!" Sterling yells. "Don't do this. You can't!"

"I can and I will!" she yells back. "You two are making everyone around you miserable and today is my last straw. This is supposed to be a party and it's *my fucking birthday.* Until the two of you can work out your shit and agree to behave, I'm not letting you out of there. And before you complain—there's enough food and water in there for weeks. And there's also an emergency bucket."

"Dakota," I groan. Every bit of fight I had left is gone now.

"Don't you dare try and fight me on this. Enjoy the pantry. Come, *fiancé,* we have a party to attend." The sounds on the other side of the pantry door are quiet, telling me that they're all leaving us. It's barely a moment before Sterling turns her feral gaze back on me.

I lean against the door, my arms crossed over my chest.

"This is *your* fault." She shoves her hand against me, her touch sending a pulse right to my dick.

I don't give her a reaction, but I'm freaking the fuck out inside. As much as I want to be pissed, to be angry at her and to hate myself for what I did to her, I can only think about how fucking beautiful she is when she's angry.

It was a mistake to come today. I can't be near her without losing my head. I want her *so* bad, but I've denied myself for this long, I can't give in now.

"I know," I mumble, defeated.

"You are such an asshole, Jaiden Thomas. I wanted to fucking date you. Was that what scared you away? Or was it because you wanted to continue getting your dick wet with other women?" She continues rambling, her eyes digging into my soul with the pain of the last few months. "I'm not tied down easily, Jaiden, and yet I wanted to be with you. But you ran. You took the easy way out and this is all your fault." I try to keep a grip on my emotions, but I can feel the way my control slips the more she speaks.

"There are things you don't understand, Sterling. Things I don't want to burden you with. It's easier this way."

People don't understand. I may have my friends, but I often feel alone. My father was absent, my mother sick for a majority of my adult life. I've been alone for a very long time.

The only reason that Wyatt and Roman are in my life is because they forced their way in and refused to let me push them away. It's what I do: I push people away. When I need them the most, I push and push until they're gone.

So, yeah, maybe it's my fault that I'm lonely, but I refuse to risk the shit that comes with *loving* relationships. It's easier this way. Lonely is easier.

"You didn't even have the decency to talk to me. You owed me at least that, Jaiden. Do you not respect me enough to talk to me? I deserve so much better than that."

"I know. I'm sorry. I freaked out and—"

"No, Jaiden. You don't get my time because I am worth so much more than this—than you. I waited for you to talk to me. I put the ball in your court when it happened and you're choosing to do this *now*? *Months* later? Fuck that. I'm done, Jaiden. If there was a chance for us, you ruined it."

She shoves at me, her hand pressed firmly on my chest now. She heaves, her eyes locked firmly on mine.

I feel the tension then, the tether between us threatening to snap.

With her hand still pressed into my chest, I feel as her fingers weave into the fabric of my shirt. Her nostrils flare, the muscles in her jaw flexing, and I can't tell if she wants to pull me closer to her, or shove me away.

"Are you sure about that?" I ask, my voice raspy. God, I'm so fucking turned on when I have absolutely no right to be. This is *dangerous.*

"Yes," she says in a sultry huff. "I hate you so *fucking* much."

"I hate you too," I breathe.

I take a step toward her, and she backs away. She takes another step, her back hitting the wall behind her. She looks up at me, her pupils blown and beautiful.

"But every time I'm around you, I think about the way you came around my cock, and those breathy moans you gave me each time I traced your body with my tongue." I lower my mouth to her ear, my hand now pressed against the wall to steady me.

She releases what sounds like a whimper as I nip at her ear.

"I think about you all the fucking time because I'm a goddamned idiot. No matter what I do, I can't seem to get you out of my head, Sterling. How about you? Can you get me out of your head?"

Her nostrils flare again, the shallow bob of her throat giving her away. After the smallest shake of her head, she replies. "No. And I hate you for it."

"I hate me too," I say, my voice barely audible.

I turn my head to her face, my lips gravitating toward hers. My eyes flick between her's. I want her to stop me, to push me away and to tell me fuck right off, but she's not.

Instead, she looks needy, her nipples peeking through the thin fabric of her dress.

I close my eyes as my mouth descends on her lips.

It's a feral kind of kiss, filled with hate and anger. She kisses me back just as ferociously. Our tongues battle for dominance and eventually I win.

My hand twists into her hair, pulling her head back so that I can kiss her neck. She moans, pressing into me.

My free hand moves from the wall to slide down her backside until I grip her ass. I could run my hands up her bare thighs forever. Every inch of her skin feels like velvet, and it taunts me. I lift her with my arm, and she brings a leg around my waist, holding tight to me as I force her head back, making my way down her neck and chest with my tongue.

I slip a hand into the top of her dress, rubbing her nipple over the lacy fabric. She pants, her lips moving to my neck. She bites and I growl, bucking my hips into her. At this angle, her core rests right on the crotch of my pants. My cock is already rock hard and pressing against the zipper of my jeans. I want to free it and drive it right into her, but I don't. Instead, I continue teasing her nipple until *she's* grinding on *me*.

"What do you want?" I ask, slipping down the fabric of her lace bralette and tugging at her nipple with my fingers.

"Please," she gasps.

"You know how this goes, Sterling. You get nothing if you don't behave."

Follow the rules, sweetheart.

"Fuck. You," she spits.

"Ah, there's the brat I know so well." I pinch her nipple–*hard*–

and she whimpers. "Are you going to be a good girl and tell me what you want?"

That all too familiar flare of her nostrils gives her away, but she nods. "I want you to fuck me, Jaiden. Please put me out of my damn misery."

I don't waste a breath as I remove my hand from her hair. One hand holds her up, the other slowly inching to her core. Sliding a finger into the crotch of her panties, I push them aside before running a finger through her slickness. She's dripping for me and it has me harder than ever.

As my finger dives into her pussy, I swallow her moan with my mouth. She pants into me, grinding on my finger. Adding another, I pump into her, curving my fingers to hit her G-spot. She's wound so tightly that it takes barely a minute before she's gasping into my shoulder.

I feel her pussy clench around my fingers, and I can't help the satisfied smirk at the fact that *I'm* doing this to her. I still as she rides out her orgasm, her perfect moans filling the space of this small pantry. I need my dick inside of her right now.

My hand slips from her to undo the button of my pants and free my cock. Suddenly I'm thankful for my choice to forgo wearing boxers today.

The head lines up with her entrance when I freeze.

"Are you still on birth control?"

"Yes," she pants. "Are you sure none of your stupid fucking puck bunnies have diseases?"

"There are no puck bunnies," I growl into her ear, and she shivers.

Driving up into her, I groan as her head falls back, a breathy moan coming from her.

"Jaiden," she gasps. "*Fuck.*"

I pump into her, slowly at first. When my pace increases, she rolls her hips on me in just the right way. I feel myself losing control, the need to fuck her senseless almost overwhelming me.

She pants as our bodies slap together, boxes of food falling off

TWO

EIGHT MONTH'S LATER

STERLING

FUCK good vibes and happy thoughts.

Over the past several months, I've been on a mission to transform back into the hot ass bitch I used to be, but sans the attitude. I'm trying to be calm, even-tempered and sensible.

That's a joke, right?

It's not working very well for me at the moment.

The air rushes out of me in a quick huff, my lungs constricting as I try to gulp in air.

"Why the fuck do you both do this to yourselves? Isn't yoga enough?" I hunch over, my breathing slowly returning to normal. Though that doesn't stop the burn in my chest as I breathe.

Lani and Dakota look over at me, their eyes full of amusement. We just ran five miles, and for some ungodly reason, they both still look like they could walk the New York fashion week runway. *How?*

"I, for one, have to keep up with Wyatt's stamina, so running helps." Koda gets that glimmer in her eye as she says his name. I fake gag, but in reality, a part of me is jealous.

My best friend's engaged to a hockey player. Not just any hockey player; an all-star, Stanley Cup champion hockey player. Did I mention he's hot? He and all of his friends are so attractive, it makes my chest hurt.

One of his friends in particular can go to hell, but that doesn't take away from the fact that every time I look at him, my pussy throbs. *God, I fucking hate him.* Jaiden Thomas can go straight to hell for what he did to me.

I loathe everything about him: the way his lips quirk when I frown; the way his eyes glimmer when I curse his name; and most of all, how he invades every corner of my brain.

I didn't want it to be like this. When I slept with him that first time, it was supposed to be as casual as scratching an itch. I guess that's what I get for sleeping with the one man I knew I shouldn't have. Then I slept with him again, and again and again until it was no longer something I wanted but *craved.* Then right when everything fell apart, I looked into his eyes and felt my body physically *ache* for him. So, of course, I had to fuck him again... And I haven't been the same since.

But I am a new woman—good vibes and calm, happy thoughts only.

"I have no excuse. I just love running." Lani flips her now sunset ombre hair over her shoulder. I don't even remember what her natural color is. I've seen her rock every color of the rainbow on her head. Colorful hair has become her brand.

"Well, I hate you both. I can't run five miles and survive it." I crouch to the ground, my hand braced on the wall of the coffee shop. "You run here every morning?"

"Yep," they say in unison.

"But you own a tattoo studio that has a coffee shop and bookstore too... Why run to get coffee at someone else's shop when you could sleep in?"

Koda laughs, her eyes watering. "Silver, I love you, but I thought *you* were the one who wanted to do this whole good vibes, healthy mind and body thing."

I roll my eyes at her, and she laughs harder. "I do, but running? Why did it have to be running?"

"The weather finally permits outdoor activities and running is good for the heart," Lani says, her hand planted on her hip. She's wearing a cute athletic set, the black cheetah print glinting in the sunlight.

There's a look in her eyes that tells me she wants to say more, but she stays silent. She's been having problems with her boyfriend *Lame Dane*, and I know it's taken a toll on her emotionally.

"Lots of things are good for the heart, like sex and smutty books," I counter, looking up at them from where I'm crouched on the ground.

"Speaking of things good for the heart..." Koda looks at me, her eyes hesitant.

"Say it."

"We're having a family dinner next weekend when y'all come back and we'd love to have you there."

"Is *he* going to be there?" I ask, keeping my voice light, but inside, all that *live, love, laugh* energy is dying. Standing, I look at her at eye level again.

"He's a part of the family, so yes. I'll continue to invite the both of you no matter what."

I sigh, trying to keep my emotions in check. It's past time for me to move on, but even though we were never quite together, I feel like I've been going through the worst breakup of my life.

"I'll think about it," I say. "It depends on how much he pisses me off while I'm with them."

"When do you leave?" Lani asks.

"Tomorrow. We'll be gone for a week. We have home advantage so I'm hoping we'll be back here for a while, assuming we'll continue on in the finals."

"I think we've got an excellent shot," she replies, looking over at Dakota. "Wyatt is killing it this season."

"He's always killing it, thank you," she says with a wink.

"Those boys are a force to be reckoned with, that's for sure."

I've never stuck with one team. When I became a photographer, I wanted a piece of all of them, but now that I'm with Boston, it would be cheating to root for another team. It's pretty damn lucky that Boston is a great team. We're in the finals again this year and I hope they carry us all the way.

Being a hockey fan is exhausting sometimes. I've never had more anxiety in my life than when I started watching hockey. Now, I have friends that I care about on this team and it's even more anxiety-inducing seeing the people you care about get thrown around like rag dolls. It's a full contact sport, so they signed up for this, but damn. Not to mention, I get way too invested in who wins to sleep well at night.

"Let's get coffee and then I suppose I can have Wyatt pick us up so we don't have to run back." Dakota raises an eyebrow at me and I practically fall to my knees again. She's speaking my love language, and it makes me so happy that I'm weak in my damn knees. I can't even blame the stupid running for this, either.

"Yes, fuck. I could kiss you right now. Please have your knight in shining armor rescue us. *Please*," I say, drawing out the word.

Dakota laughs, shaking her head. "Well I've got good news. While you were dying, I texted him. He's on his way."

I swear I feel a happy tear slide down my cheek. "Have I told you that I love you today?"

"Nope. Go ahead, say it again."

Lani bites her lip to keep from laughing and I hate how beautiful they look right now. Maybe after all of this good vibes tour, I'll look like a damn supermodel after running five miles.

Ha, yeah right.

GAME ONE DOWN, FOUR MORE TO GO. THE GUYS ARE celebrating, throwing water around like it's raining.

The testosterone levels in this building are astronomical, so I take this moment to excuse myself. I got my photos for the day and I'm ready to hide away before they walk out for press.

I don't know when this became my routine. It's easy to avoid

Jaiden when I'm the first one out and hidden away until I'm needed again.

With my equipment slung around me, I retreat to the hallway and into the small office in the locker room. Pulling my camera off me, I kick my feet up on the desk, my heels hanging off my feet lightly. We all have a dress code to follow in order to keep the team and staff looking cohesive. Usually I have no problem wearing heels, but after taking up running, my feet are a mess.

Who am I kidding? *I* am a mess.

My feet fucking hurt and I'm tired of seeing his stupid face all the time and *still* feeling something. I wish I could just turn my emotions off, or at the very least truly hate him.

Footsteps echo down the long hallway and I straighten, trying to look at least slightly more professional than I did a second ago.

A knock sounds at the door, and I look over to see Noah leaning in the doorway. "Got a minute?" he asks, his eyes looking at my heels. Noah is the head of public relations for the team. We work closely often and I've found it easy to be around him. *Thank God.*

I nod my head twice, kicking my feet off the desk before I swivel in my chair to face him.

"What can I do for you?"

"I–Uh," he studies me for a moment and I quirk my mouth in a half smile as I watch him struggle.

I tilt my head, my finger toying with my lip subconsciously as I look at him. "You okay?"

"Great," he says, lowering himself into the chair across from me. His hand rests on his chin as he watches me, his eyes lingering on my lips for a moment. "There's something I wanted to ask you," he says, his voice now hesitant.

I raise a brow at him, my lip rolling between my teeth.

"Fuck it," he says through a breath. "The guys are going out to celebrate and I'd love to take you out for drinks, with them... but also separately."

"Noah James, are you asking me out on a date?"

He shakes his head at me, his eyes amused at my tone. "Yes, Sterling Bexley, I am. Can I take you out for drinks? Maybe some food too, if you're up for it."

I look between his eyes, searching for any hidden intentions. Noah is hot, I won't lie. He's built, and tall—though not as tall as the players. Those suits he wears hugs his body tightly, making me believe he's got some muscles hidden beneath the material.

"Okay," I say.

"Okay?"

"Yeah. Let's do it."

He grins at me, a little dimple appearing on the side of his mouth when he does. "Great. I'll swing by your room to pick you up?"

"Sounds like a date." I wink at him.

He smiles again, rising from his chair and nodding at me before he leaves my office.

This is happening. I'm dating again.

A flicker of anticipation runs through my body as I lean back in my chair.

I'm going on a fucking date.

Kicking my feet off the desk, I right myself before walking back out into the corridor and waiting for the team to arrive.

As we wrap up the events of the evening, I catch Noah glancing over at me several times. I can't help but smile down at my feet.

"What are you smiling about?" A hand nudges my arm, and I look up to see Damian wiggling his eyebrows at me. His ginger beard is trimmed and styled. It suits him. He's had it long and wild during most of the season as a part of his superstition. I think I prefer him with it all trimmed and cropped closer to his face—it makes it easier to see his handsome face.

"Oh, nothing," I lie.

"Right, well, maybe that look would explain why our PR manager has been eyeballing you all evening."

I look up at him, my eyes wide, and he laughs. I roll my eyes as I shake my head. "Is it that obvious?"

"A bit," Damian says, adjusting his suit jacket. Today he's in a green velvet suit that compliments his coloring spectacularly. "That, and Jaiden looks like he's constipated as hell."

I laugh, my hand coming to my mouth to cover the sound. "He does look constipated," I agree. "Hope he's okay."

"Yo, Jaiden! Your butt good, bro?" Damian yells it across the room and I lean forward laughing. Damian looks down at me, his eyes smiling.

Jaiden just glares, flipping him the bird before he turns away.

"Thanks for that," I say, wiping the tears from my eyes. "I needed that laugh."

"Glad to be of service," he says with a salute. "You comin' out with us?"

"Yes, and no."

He raises his eyebrow, and I press my lips together to keep the full smile at bay.

"You'll see."

He nods slowly. "This better be good."

I LEAVE MY HAIR DOWN, MY NATURAL CURLS FLOWING down my back. My feet still hurt, so I choose a pair of high-top sneakers to wear instead of heels. As I finish the knot, a light knock sounds at my door.

Grabbing my denim jacket from the bed, I stop to check my outfit in the mirror before I rush to open the door.

The door swings open, my eyes meeting a casually-but-not-too-casually dressed Noah. His eyes rake over me slowly before a smile crosses his face.

"You look stunning," he says.

"Thank you." My cheeks heat at his compliment.

He's wearing blue jeans, his gray shirt hugging some hidden muscles beneath it. I appreciate the sight of him. He's attractive enough.

"Ready?"

I nod, stepping out of my room and closing the door behind me. His arm rests on my back as we walk through the hallway of the hotel.

"No heels tonight?"

I laugh, my eyes shooting to the side to look at him. "No, definitely not. I've taken up running and heels are making me feel unstable."

"Running, huh?" He guides me through the lobby doors, the desert heat surrounding us immediately.

"Yep. I'm trying this new thing with fitness and shit. My best friends run, so I thought I'd try. It's not going well for me." I laugh, turning right onto the main street and down a ways until we see the neon sign for the bar.

"I admire you for trying. I prefer doing other things to get my cardio in."

I try not to read into his comment, but my core reacts. It's been so long since I've gotten any action. It's not that I can't—it's that I'm desperately trying to change my ways.

"Yeah, well, when you have to hear about your best friend and her fiancé's *stamina,* it makes me really want to keep up with them." I raise my voice as a car passes so that he can hear the end of my statement. The loud honking comes and goes as we walk right to the door.

He laughs, his eyes widening. "Is this Wyatt's fiancé?" He leans in closer so that I can hear him.

"It is."

Noah opens the door to the bar, the myriad of voices filling my ears. Several of the team members are gathered around the bar, drinks in hand.

"Ayeeee!" several people call. "Sterling's here!"

I scan the room looking for any sign of the guys. It looks like they're not here yet, so I relax a bit.

"What about me?" Noah says and people boo at him. I laugh, smiling at several of the team members.

"Can I buy you a drink?" Noah rests his hand on my back again and there's a possessive edge to it. It sends a weird feeling to my stomach.

"Rum and coke, please." I slide onto a barstool by the counter as Noah orders two drinks.

"Your drink, milady." He slides the glass in front of me and I grip it tightly.

"Why, thank you." I give him a smile that I think is sexy, but who knows if it actually is. I haven't been on a date in so long that I don't remember how to do this.

"I'm going to run to the bathroom." He taps my shoulder before stalking off toward the back of the building.

I nurse my drink, taking a sip every few minutes. The team all mingles with each other and I can't keep up with the chatter between them.

When I feel a hat being placed on the top of my head, I look back, seeing Damian standing over me.

"Sup, cutie?"

"Ya know, the hat kind of completes the look I'm going for," I say, lifting it up and turning it around before putting it back on my head. "High tops and a backward baseball cap: I'm official."

Damian laughs, "You're right. Keep it." He winks at me before taking the seat beside me.

I watch as Jaiden walks past me, his eyes looking me over before he talks to the bartender.

"Silver," Roman says, "You look lovely tonight."

"Why, thank you, kind sir. So do you."

He smiles before he walks toward the other members of his team.

"So, what's this thing I'm hearing about?" Wyatt asks as he slides into the seat next to Damian.

"Just wait." I wiggle my nose at them and they laugh.

"You're kinda evil," Damian says. "I love it."

"Yeah, you do."

Noah returns a moment later, his smile growing when he sees

the guys next to me.

"Hey, guys! Keeping the lady company?" He slides his hand down my back before he reaches to grab his drink from the counter in front of me.

Damian cackles beside me, his eyes going wide. "Oh, you little devil," he says.

I smile at him, lifting my shoulder to my cheek and batting my eyelashes.

"Damian completed my look," I say, standing up from my seat and doing a little turn.

My black dress has a slit up the side, almost to my hip. It's just the right amount of dressy and casual. I'm very thankful that I packed it for this trip.

Noah practically eye-fucks me when I stick out my ass a little. "It's perfect."

"Don't look now," Damian says, his voice low.

I don't follow direction well, so I glance up just in time to see Jaiden clapping Noah on the back.

"Hi *friends,*" he says, through his teeth. An incredibly fake smile crosses his lips and it takes everything in me not to snort.

"Hey, dude." Noah responds, his face not as smooth as it was a moment ago. He's leaning forward from the force of Jaiden's smack. "Good job on the ice tonight."

"Thanks." His voice is clipped as he looks right at me. I don't want to hold his stare but I do it anyway. "What are you two doing together?"

"Noah here asked me out on a date," I say, blinking at him innocently.

"How unfortunate," he says, his voice barely audible.

I choke on my drink, sputtering coughs until Damian claps me on the back. When I recover, I glare at Jaiden.

"What was that?" Noah asks.

"I just said how fortunate. She's a good lay," he says, winking at me before he walks away.

Jaiden-1, Sterling-0

I fucking hate this twisted game we're playing—neither of us seem to be winning. My teeth grind together as I attempt to keep my mouth shut.

It's always this roundabout with us. I think that I've got the leg up, but somehow he bests me. For once, I want the upper hand.

"Sorry," I say to Noah. "I'll be right back." I jump out of my seat, running after Jaiden.

"What the fuck is wrong with you, Jaiden?" I hiss, trying to keep up with his pace. He continues to walk through the bar and down the long hallway.

"Nothing is wrong with me," he says, his voice even. It pisses me off more.

"Then why the *fuck* did you do that?"

"Do what?" he asks. He continues walking and I push past him, turning my body so that I block his way.

"Why are you trying to ruin my *date*?"

"I wasn't trying to ruin your date," he replies, his face bored.

"Yes, you were," I say, pointing a finger into his chest. "You don't have a right to care, Jaiden, much less to act like a jealous ex."

"Is that what I'm acting like? Oh, sorry, I was going for a *protective friend* vibe." He raises an eyebrow at me. I growl in frustration, throwing my hands down at my sides.

"Don't fuck with me, Jaiden. This is my life and I can do what I want with it. If you wanted me, you would've chosen me *months* ago." I jut out my hip, pointing my finger harder into his chest. My eyes narrow and I glare, *hard*.

"If I remember right, you walked out on me in the pantry."

"Yeah, after you practically pushed me away, spewing bullshit about how you're not going to change and it's better this way. You don't get to do this."

His face remains blank and it's making me feral, and he knows it. He glares at me and I see the moment his control snaps. He shoves me backward and I yelp quietly. My back presses into the door behind me. It's dark and I've been talking quietly enough that hopefully no one could hear.

His hand presses on the handle, opening the door and guiding us out into the Vegas heat. Once my back is pressed firmly into the wall behind me, I look up at him, my breathing ragged.

"Do what?" he asks, his voice husky. "Be jealous because the past eight months have been hell for me? Ruin your date because seeing you on a fucking date in the first place reminds me of how badly I fucked up? You can still go back. I'm sure Noah will be so *nice* to you."

"What is that supposed to mean?"

"It means that you like it rough and that you're a brat that needs to be tamed. I highly doubt that Noah will cut it for you."

"Wanna bet? Maybe I want a nice guy. At least they'll have the decency to talk to me before they cut me off. You don't know me anymore, Jaiden."

"I think I know you better than you think." He leans in close, his lips brushing against my cheek and I swear I stop breathing for a second. "Go back inside, Sterling. Take Noah back to the hotel and sleep with him all you want. I know exactly what you like and I can promise you that you'll leave and have to finish the job yourself."

I can't speak. I can barely breathe, but I keep my eyes locked on his. His hot breath caresses my cheek and in a weak moment, I get the urge to kiss him.

His hand comes to my hair, his fingers running through the long locks. "I like your hair like this." He yanks on it slightly exposing my neck to him. I don't know why I let him do it.

"Go back inside, Sterling." He releases me, turning away and walking down the street. I watch him walk away, the growing frustration building in my chest. I want to scream, but instead I run my fingers through my hair.

He likes my hair, huh? *We'll just have to do something about that later.*

Clenching my jaw, I squeeze my fists tightly before releasing them and pulling the door open. When the cool breeze from the AC hits me, I shiver lightly. I don't know if it's the AC, or the fact that I'm turned on. *Fuck him.*

Wyatt is talking with Damian when I return, the two of them arguing about something. I catch the tail end of it when I place a hand on Damian's back.

"He left?"

Damian's face softens slightly. "He mumbled something about work, but I called him on his shit. I think we scared him away."

"Fucking Jaiden," I say, sighing as I take the seat next to him. "I have to work with Noah still and he didn't even stay to talk to me?"

Wyatt laughs quietly and I narrow my eyes at him. "If it makes you feel better, Damian here made him feel terrible for being a pussy and leaving." Wyatt shrugs and I laugh.

"Appreciate it." I look around the bar, and suddenly I really don't want to be here. "Should I talk to him?"

"Only if you want to. You don't owe him anything."

"I'd think I'd like to at least try. Clear the air, at least, since I have to see him frequently."

Damian nods in understanding, and I release a breath at the softness on his face. Who knew Damian was going to become one of my best friends during this process.

He looks at Wyatt, sending him a nod before turning back to me. Those boys have a language of their own. "I'll walk you back," he says, extending his hand to me.

I eye it a moment before taking it. "Thank you."

He guides me through the bar, leaving the noisy bar for the busy street. It's not late by any means, but I feel like this city never sleeps. It's nearly midnight on the East Coast which means I can't even vent to my best friend about Jaiden's stupidity. That will have to wait until tomorrow.

"So…" I say as we walk down the street. "Go on any dates lately?"

He snorts, his face turning to look at me. In the light, his amber eyes look almost golden, like the street lights turn his gaze into liquid gold. He's attractive, and he knows it. It sucks that my heart is attached to another. *Fuck you, heart.*

"We both know I'm not the dating type." He shakes his head and I laugh.

"You could be. You just choose not to." I look up at him, pursing my lips and widening my eyes in my best sassy face.

He raises an eyebrow before nodding and humming.

"I'm right," I say, turning my face back to the street, my feet walking slower than normal. I'm enjoying the warm night air. The bright lights all around us create an ambiance that I adore. It's aesthetic and very… romantic? Well, it would be if I were actually dating someone.

Damian nods his head to the left before pulling me into the hotel lobby. We walk in silence down the hall and around the corner to the long strip of doors.

"Thanks for walking me," I say. With my free hand, I fist bump his arm. "You're a good guy."

He snorts a breath through his nose. "Yeah, or I'm terrified of Dakota and what she'd do to me if I weren't protective of you."

I throw my head back as I laugh. "Yeah, my best friend can be scary if she wants to be."

My tongue slides across my lower lip as I look up at him. I just watch him for a moment until the slam of a door draws my head in that direction.

Jaiden stands down the hall, his eyes narrowed at us. His glare is murderous and I can't figure out why until I look down. I hadn't even realized that our hands were still joined.

"Sup, bro." Damian nods his head at him and I can't tell if that makes the situation worse or not. Jaiden's nostrils flare before he turns, stomping in the opposite direction.

I groan, my hand releasing Damian's quickly before I can think better of it. "Does he hate me?" I say under my breath.

"No man reacts that way toward someone they hate. He's practically sweating jealousy," Damian replies, running a hand through his hair. He nudges his chin down the hall. "Go talk to Noah, and if you need me to beat his ass, I'm only a text away."

I give him a half-ass smile as I turn and walk down the hall toward Noah's room.

Wish me luck.

THREE

STERLING

AFTER THREE KNOCKS, I'm ready to give up, until the door swings open. I look up to see a disheveled Noah.

"Oh, wow. Okay. I was going to explain to you, but I *really* don't want to now." I turn on my heels, walking away from him.

"It's not what it looks like," he says, his voice breathy. I barely turn, glaring at him and he sighs. "Okay, fine, it kinda is."

"So, you ditch me after I tell you I'll be back, and go find some girl to sleep with instead? You work fast." My tone is icy, "Not that it matters to you, but I came back."

"Look, Sterling, you're cool, but whatever happened between you and Jaiden... I'd rather stay out of it. That fucker is scary when he wants to be."

"Fine. Thanks for the drink." I flip my hair over my shoulder and walk away.

"That's it?" he calls after me.

"That's it," I yell, probably a little louder than necessary. When I make it to my room, I shove my key into the lock, opening it quickly before I slam the door behind me.

Releasing a growl of frustration, I fall onto the bed face first. The bedding muffles my scream and I'm thankful for it. *Men. Fucking. Suck.*

I pull out my phone and type a quick message to Damian.

Me: Permission to fuck Noah up.

I barely wait a minute before my phone vibrates in my hand with his reply.

Damian: That bad?

Me: That bad.

Damian: Company?

Me: Naw. It's fine. I'll talk to you on the plane tomorrow.

Damian: 10-4

I laugh, tossing my phone across the bed. Pulling off my clothes, I drop them to the floor in a small pile before walking to the bathroom. My makeup washes off with ease. I'd planned on getting this makeup *fucked* off, but I suppose this is good too. With my teeth brushed and flossed, I pad back to the bedroom and climb under the covers.

Sleep doesn't come easily for me. Instead, I spend most of the night tossing and turning.

My frustration over Jaiden is mind-boggling. We'd barely been *together* for three months, but those months... I was happy. Maybe he didn't feel the same way. I don't want to continue feeling like this. I just want Jaiden *fucking* Thomas to go away. Maybe then my heart will stop thumping every time I see him.

My eyes flutter shut and I finally succumb to sleep.

What feels like mere minutes later, my alarm blares by my ear. I groan, rolling over to turn it off. I've got an hour to get ready, pack and be down for breakfast before our flight. Let's not forget that I'm due earlier than everyone else so that I can take photos of the boys. I'm their personal paparazzi.

Why did I sign up for this again?

I use every minute of that hour to get ready and packed for the day. Everything but my gear and carry on is loaded onto the bus. The boys still aren't out so I wander over to the breakfast counter. The coffee is shit, but hell, I'll drink it because I wouldn't survive today without it.

My hands fumble with the creamer and sugar, pouring small amounts into my cup, when I feel someone behind me. I stiffen, my body knowing exactly who it is.

He smells like lime and cedar. I'd know that smell anywhere, and I hate my mind for committing it to memory. It's the smell of his deodorant that admittedly still lingers on some of my clothes.

I refuse to look at him, to give him my attention. It's a fight to ignore his presence when everything in my body is *begging* me to look. Reaching across the counter, I grab a stir stick and put it into my cup. My coffee transforms from a dark brown to a milky color in seconds, the sweet smell wafting up my nose. Stirring exactly seven times, I pull out the stick and tap it on the lip of my cup.

Jaiden makes a funny noise beside me, and I look at him from the corner of my eyes. His curly hair is disheveled and out of place. Looking down, I disguise my perusal of him as a study of my feet. He's dressed in joggers, sneakers and a tee. He looks... *sexy.*

No. Admiring him is absolutely *not* allowed.

"What?" I say, keeping my eyes down. My hands grip my coffee tightly, the heat making my hands burn. Maybe it's my punishment for being a dummy with men.

"Seven," he says.

I turn my body to him fully now, my eyes squinted as I look up at him. "Huh?"

"Seven. You stir your coffee exactly seven times." He licks his lips, bringing his coffee cup to his mouth and taking a drink.

I watch as his throat bobs with each swallow. It shouldn't be attractive, but it is. His rings press into the cup, making my mouth go dry. When his eyes meet mine again, they're darker. It should intimidate me, but instead, I feel my core flutter. I curse it almost immediately.

He turns, leaving me alone again, except this time I actually *feel* alone. I hadn't been looking forward to his presence before, so there was nothing to miss. Now I'm reminded of the addiction I felt for him. How long will it take my heart to move on and to forget the way he made me feel?

This is the worst form of torture.

Sighing, I sling my camera over my shoulder and wait for the guys to load onto the bus. The whole time I wait, I feel this pit in my stomach. *Stupid boy.*

I'M ONE OF THE LAST PEOPLE TO BOARD THE PLANE. ALL the players have long since boarded. Walking through the narrow pathway, I avoid the gaze of Noah as I pass him.

There are two seats left. One next to Damian and the other next to Jaiden, who is slouched in his seat, his glasses perched on the edge of his nose and a book in his hands. Walking past him, I slide into the seat next to Damian, his amber eyes twinkling at me as I slide my bag under my seat.

"Noah's balls are still intact," I say, my voice low. Damian snorts beside me and I smile down at the floor.

"It appears so," he says, his voice laced with humor. His phone pings and he fishes it from his pocket. When he looks down at it, there's a small smirk that toys at the edge of his lips. He types in a quick text, his fingers flying across the screen.

"Ew. Please tell me you're not sexting right next to me." I nudge his elbow and he laughs. A couple people look at us but I don't even care. Wyatt and Roman are sitting behind us and I feel Roman lean into the gap between our chairs.

"I wouldn't put it past him," he says, and I laugh.

"I'm *not* sexting. It's just Lani. She's designing a tattoo for me."

"You know she has a boyfriend, right?" I cross my arms, an eyebrow raised at him.

"Yeah, and? She's just designing a tattoo."

Wyatt snorts behind me, and I point a finger at him. "Back me up."

He shakes his head, his face scrunched as he laughs silently.

"She's a perfect angel baby. Don't mess with my friend, Damian." I stare at him until he concedes.

"It's just a tattoo, Silver."

"If you say so." I turn away, closing my eyes and resting my head against the seat. I'm exhausted and I hope I can get some sleep on this flight.

"Want to tell me about Noah?" Damian says, his voice low. There's a hint of teasing in his tone and my eyes snap open.

"Shut it, LeDuke. Can't you see the lady is getting her beauty rest?" My eyes close again as I wait for his response.

"Didn't sleep well?" I peel an eye open just in time to see his wink. There's a fat smirk on his face and I want to wipe it away.

"Could've been better." I breathe deeply, my chest relaxing with each breath.

"Not enough activity for you?"

What is with him?

As if in answer, his eyes glimmer, shooting sideways slightly and then back at me. I look down the aisle to see Jaiden's hand gripping his book so tightly it looks like the pages are close to ripping. He's baiting him, and something like an evil laugh sputters out of me. I slap my hand over my mouth, my eyes going wide as I look at Damian for help. He leans in, his grin wide like he just told me the best joke of his life.

"It's fun, ain't it?" His voice is low.

"What?" I whisper.

"Pushing his buttons. He's been unusually calm for months. Within the last twenty-four hours, I've seen him show more emotion than he has in ages. It's quite entertaining."

Because clearly, I don't understand what the hell he's trying to get at, my face scrunches in confusion as I look at him. "Why is it entertaining for you?"

"Silver, I'm a no bullshit kind of guy. If Jaiden can't be straightforward with his thoughts and feelings, it's not unlike me to—" he waves his hand at me in a straight line—"give him a little nudge in the right direction."

The corner of my mouth turns upward. "I'll keep that in mind." My eyes close, my head resting back against the seat. "Now let me sleep. My mind wouldn't shut up last night."

Damian laughs. "As you wish."

I FUCKING *LOVE* TENNESSEE. THE VIBES HERE ARE immaculate. It's beautiful and the music is superb. Lani would love it here. Damian looks like he's enjoying himself too. Everywhere we go, he's bobbing his head to the music.

It's the night before our game and we've got the night off. Damian suggested wandering around Nashville, so that's exactly what we're doing. Jaiden tagged along, but he's been a grump the whole time, hanging back like he's not a part of the group.

When we hear music blasting from a bar down the street, I practically run, dragging Damian behind me. Okay, maybe not dragging, because he's totally happy rushing into the bars with me.

A young couple sit on the stage with a small band behind them. The music coming from them is *unreal*. As we stand there listening to them, I feel chills shoot up my arms. Pulling my phone out, I call Lani, the phone held close to my ear.

"Hey, gorgeous," she says upon answering.

"Lani!" I yell over the noise. "Listen to this. You'll love it!" I hold the phone out so that she can hear the music. It's a pop country song and something about it just hits me in all the right ways.

Their voices compliment each other so well, the sounds of them blending like magic. I learned terms like that from Lani.

When I bring the phone back to my ear, I hear nothing but silence. "Like it?"

"Fuck, Silver. That's ear porn."

I laugh, muscles flexing as I wheeze. "I *knew* it," I reply. "Good shit."

"Definitely. If you can get a name for me, I'd love to add them to my playlist."

"Anything for you, babe." I end the call, shoving my phone back into my pocket.

Damian looks over at me, his smile so wide. "I already texted her the name."

"Way to steal my thunder, dude." I punch him in the arm lightly and he laughs again. The punch is seriously pathetic. I'd barely make a dent against this six-foot-something hockey player. In fact, I probably look real scary walking through the streets with four gigantic men flanking me.

"Onward," I say, pointing my finger out the door and grabbing Damian's sleeve.

He shakes his head, but follows me. Wyatt and Roman are talking outside. I don't see Jaiden but he's probably around somewhere, creeping in the shadows.

"Having fun?" Wyatt asks. He's leaning against the wall and I can see why Dakota fell in love with him.

"Totally. This is the most fun I've had on this trip. I'm sad Koda and Lani aren't here."

Wyatt gets this dreamy look in his eyes at the mention of Koda. I fake a gag and he laughs.

"What?" He throws up his arms and shakes his head.

"You went all gooey-eyed for a moment." I smile, my hand now resting against the wall.

"What? I can't get gooey over my fiancée?" He raises an eyebrow, and Roman snorts behind his back.

"Oh, you can, dude. Just keep the bedroom eyes... in the bedroom?"

"How boring is that, to just keep it in the bedroom?" Wyatt questions with a sly grin. We all make sounds of disgust before laughing.

"Remind me never to sit anywhere in your condo," Damian says from my side.

"I slept on your couch," I say with a grimace. Wyatt just smiles this dopey smile and I can't be angry at him. He's made my best friend more happy than I've ever seen her and that's all I could ask for. I also know he'd do anything to protect her.

"Speaking of couches, where's Jaiden?" Damian looks around his eyes scanning the street.

"He went into the bookstore down the street. I haven't seen him since."

"Bookstore?" I ask, my eyes squinting in the direction his eyes search.

"Yeah. Koda's been giving him some fantasy recommendations and he's read through most of the series already. I guess he wanted to find the last book." Wyatt looks down, his foot knocking a rock off the curb.

I swallow, that ember of attraction blazing bright again. I knew he was a casual reader, but the fact that he took a recommendation from my best friend... It's attractive as fuck and it has no business being so.

Damian nudges my arm, his eyebrows raising. "You good?"

I nod. *Yeah, I'm okay in theory, but I'm sick.* Sick of this wedge between my friends and sick of these stupid lingering feelings for Jaiden *fucking* Thomas.

FOUR

JAIDEN

WHY DID she have to wear that dress? That fucking dress with a slit up her thigh so high it leaves barely anything to the imagination. It hugs her body tight in all the right ways. I want to run my tongue up her thigh just to get a taste of her skin.

Can someone die from jealousy?

I've been doing *fine*. All was fine and dandy… until that fucker Noah. Maybe I was just biding my time, hoping that I could get my shit together long enough to claim her as mine, but ho-fucking-ho, I can't.

I can't give her what she wants. She wants *more* than just sex. She wants the emotions, the feelings, and everything in between. That would require access to the ugly and broken parts inside of me. I'd rather not be ripped wide open for people to see; definitely not someone I care about. It's easier for her opinion of me to remain how it is than to allow her to see the darkest parts of me. The sting of rejection is something I'd like to avoid at all costs. *Fuck that.*

Settling for staring at her in that fucking dress while I self-loathe is the safer option. She's so damn gorgeous. Sterling Silver in the flesh is a whirlwind that came crashing into my life. It's enough for me to just be around her at a distance. Even if she's sitting on the lap of one of my best friends.

I could punch his nose in... Or I could *accidentally* deck him on the ice.

That's *my* girl... but then again, she's not mine. Like she so often tells me, I lost that privilege months ago when I let her walk away from me.

Her laughter filters through the small building and I'm ready to bash my head into the wall nearest me. The raspy way she laughs is angelic and I hate her for it.

This is the worst kind of torture. I'm punishing myself with her presence. Traveling with her across the country for weeks at a time is endless torture. My cock certainly hates me. I've rubbed him raw for months. Palmala has never gotten so much action. It's the way my mind wanders, thinking about the ample curves of her body or the way she sounds when she comes.

Fuck. I feel myself growing hard in my jeans, and I twist in my seat to hide the bulge. She laughs again, Damian grabbing her waist as she leans forward to grab her water from the bar. That *fucker.*

Downing my soda, I slam my cup on the bar and rise to a stand. I *have* to get out of here immediately, so I shoot the guys a look a rush out the door. I'm halfway across the street when I hear someone calling my name, but I don't stop. Instead, I jog back to the hotel and right into the gym.

Tugging my shirt over the head, I toss it to the side and turn the treadmill on full blast, running until I'm panting, sweat dripping down my back. My legs jump off the track, the feeling that I'm still running making me wobble.

Walking it off, I grab my shirt and toss it over my shoulder, feeling the cool air of the AC blast me the moment I walk underneath it. It makes me shiver, but it's a welcome feeling to the frustration I was feeling earlier.

When I turn the corner to my room, I see Roman and Wyatt leaning against the wall by my door. *Nope, not today, Satan.*

My body tuns in the opposite direction, but Roman's voice stops me.

"Don't do that, Jai."

I stop, still facing away from them. "Do what?"

"We're your *family*, Jai. We don't want to attack you."

"I don't want to talk about it," I say, turning slowly.

Wyatt shakes his head, throwing his arms up in surrender. "Fine. Then don't talk about it, but don't shut us out."

My eyes narrow at them, my lips pursed. That's all I do for a minute, just stare them down until I huff a breath. "Fine."

I unlock the door, leaving it open for them to follow me in. They busy themselves while I shower, but when I exit the bathroom with a towel draped around my waist, I find Wyatt splayed across my bed.

"It's like college all over again," he says, patting the bed.

I snort, shaking my head. "Eager to sleep with me, Wyatt baby?"

"Definitely. Since Dakota can't be here, I'm lonely at night." He laughs, grabbing a pillow and hugging it as he flattens down onto the bed.

Roman gags in his seat across the room, and it only causes me to laugh harder. "You two were always in a bromance. I'm curious how I stuck around so long."

"Admit it. You love us."

"I do," he says, shaking his head. "I couldn't have raised Lily without the two of you."

"Damn right," I say. "Best. Dads. Ever."

"Y'all are uncles. Don't forget it. *I'm* the best dad ever." Roman points his finger at us and Wyatt wheezes. He smashes his face into the mattress before raising back up onto his elbow to look at us.

"What? Jealous that Lily loves us more than you?" He says it through laughs which makes it funnier.

"Sometimes," Roman says, his voice low and I cough a laugh again.

"Naw, man. She loves you the most. Now Dakota and Sterling... You should be afraid of them," Wyatt deadpans. The way he says it with such a straight face sends me laughing again. This time I'm not alone; Roman loses it too.

This is the most present I've felt and most fun I've had in a long time. I've been distant from my friends for months and it feels good to just be in this room and feel *normal.*

"I'm afraid that she's going to start drawing on the walls and ask to give me tattoos. Your fiancé is going to create a monster."

"She's been very impressionable lately," Wyatt says, and I look between the two of them.

"Yeah. She's doing this mimicking thing. I can't say anything remotely questionable around her or she'll repeat it." Roman lifts his leg over the other, resting his ankle on his knee. He grips the arm wrests like he's afraid and I smile. I can't imagine what he's feeling raising a daughter. It's a different adventure altogether, but we all love her. She's our buddy and our pride and joy. I love that kid with a fierceness I never knew possible.

"So, are we talking about Sterling yet?" Wyatt raises an eyebrow at me.

"Nope," I say, popping the *p*.

"Not a thing?" Roman probes and I shoot him a glare. I'm silent, looking between them with my lips pursed. They're waiting for something, *anything,* but I don't know what to offer.

"How did it get this bad?" Roman asks from the chair. My shoulders slump and I sigh. I walk to the dresser, pulling on shorts and a tee before sitting on the bed with Wyatt.

"I never talked to her after I spoke with y'all that day. I'd meant to apologize, but instead, I just went on ignoring the problem until it festered. She blew up on me when I finally tried to apologize, saying it was too late. I think, at that point, she'd confided in Dakota and I was toast."

I twist a curl in my finger and pull it down in front of my face. When I look over at Wyatt, he looks sad almost.

"I've only really heard Dakota's side and some of Sterling's when they talk on the phone or she comes over for dinner, but man... You gotta do better if you want to fix this."

"You genuinely look pained every time you look at her," Roman says. "I gotta admit, though, the butt comment from Damian almost made me shit myself with laughter."

Wyatt, chimes in with a mumbled *oh yeah,* their laughter filling the room.

"Yeah, yeah. This is my own personal hell," I say.

"Look, man," Wyatt says, looking at me from across the bed. "She's hurt because she feels disrespected. You have to remember that you were friends before anything. She's not only lost whatever you two had together, but she lost her friend. And from what I saw, y'all were pretty damn close."

He's right. She was as close to a best friend she could get. Any time I had free, I was calling Sterling to do random shit. Everything moved so fast because, like usual, I thought with my dick instead of my head.

"Dakota is oblivious to the fact that the two of you are still fighting. Is there a reason for that?" Wyatt's eyes narrow at me.

I glare back at him, but he doesn't break. "Not a clue. Maybe ask her *best friend.*"

Wyatt's eyes widen at that. The truth is that after the pantry incident, we both wanted this to go away. So much so that we avoided each other for as long as possible. Maybe it was stupid of me to make a scene with Noah, but I couldn't just stand back and watch.

"What the hell is going on between her and Damian?" I ask, keeping my voice casual.

Roman and Wyatt exchange looks before their mouths quirk up. "Dunno," Wyatt replies.

"Right," I say, rolling my eyes. "I'd like to sleep now, so that means get the *fuck* out of my room. There's the door," I say, pointing to it.

They laugh on their way out the door and I swear I hear Wyatt telling Roman that I'm almost as bad as Sterling, whatever the hell that means.

I dream of Sterling in that damn dress. My cock is solid when I wake and I think of her when I fist it in my hand, jerking myself to completion under a cold spray of water. That insufferable woman is driving me mad. I want to hate her. I want to despise her. It would make this easier, but the hard truth is, I don't hate her. Not even a little bit.

FIVE

STERLING

"*BRRR*, IT'S COLD IN HERE."

Damian rubs his hands over his arms as we walk through the private air strip. I look over at him, but barely register his words. Instead, I'm in my own head.

It's the last game of this round in the finals. Everything is riding on this. Whether we continue onto the finals or not is decided by how we play tonight.

I'm a hockey fan first and foremost. This is my team now and, *fuck*, do I want them to win. It was incredible to make it to the finals two years in a row, but to win? That would be the icing on the cake.

"Sterling, you good?" Damian nudges my arm and I shake my head as I look at him.

"Oh, hi. Yes. I'm fine. What did you say?" I blink up at him and he looks at me with a slightly stunned expression.

"It lost its impact the moment it left my mouth. Are you sure you're okay?" He continues walking by my side and I appreciate it. He's been almost like my protector throughout this whole trip.

"Yeah. I'm okay. I just want the team to win today."

"Ah, she slipped into hockey mode." He laughs, crossing his arm over his body to move his bag up his shoulder.

"It's an illness," I confirm with a small laugh.

"We'll do fine. Everyone is nervous. Who knew we'd tie with our competition?"

I shrug my shoulders. *Not me.*

Wyatt's pace picks up ahead of us, his long legs carrying him through the building until I spot the streak of white blond hair colliding with him. He wraps his arms around her middle, lifting her into the air and spinning them both around.

Dakota's laughter reaches my ears and I can't help but smile.

"Welcome home, baby," she says to him, and I fake a gag.

"You two are just *so cute.*" I shove a finger into my mouth like I'm gagging again and she sticks her tongue out at me.

"Don't shit on my parade." She kisses Wyatt and he laughs into her mouth. They are really fucking cute. Good thing I can hide my jealousy behind fake disgust. *I want that.*

"Yeah, yeah. Hurry up. You're taking me home." I follow in the direction Damian walked until I see the line of cars.

"I can drive you home, ya know," Damian says, leaning against his Charger Hellcat. It's a beautiful car and I've yet to ride in it. I curse myself because *damn* is that offer tempting.

"No, it's okay. I need to talk to Koda about this trip anyways."

"Alright. Text me when you get to the rink. I'll walk with you." He ducks his head as he sits in the diver's seat of his car. The engine revs a second later and the wink he sends me should be illegal. Damn I love that car.

"Thanks, D."

"I'm honored that you chose me over a sports car," Dakota says from my back.

I look over my shoulder at her. She's walking hand-in-hand with Wyatt and they're fucking adorable.

"Yeah, well, you're lucky I love you."

The car turns over when she hits a button on the key. She's driving Wyatt's Bronco today which only solidifies their relationship status.

We all climb into the car, Wyatt tossing our bags into the trunk before walking around to the passenger side. When Dakota pulls the car out of the parking lot, she looks in the rearview mirror at me.

"So, there's something we wanted to talk to you about."

I look up at her, sliding forward in my seat so that I can look between them as she drives.

"Hit me." I rest my elbows on the middle console as I lean forward.

"Wyatt and I have been talking about the wedding a lot more lately and we think we want to keep it small." The car turns onto the main road, Dakota's arms crossing one over the other.

Wyatt looks back at me, his eyes excited.

"Okay. Small is good."

"And I want to have it in Canada." She smiles into the mirror and I think I know where she's going with this. "I called your mom's assistant the other day and the lake house is available for the whole summer. We could have it there."

"I fucking *love* that idea, Koda. I know you've always loved the lake house. We have some great memories there." I wiggle in my seat with excitement and she laughs. "You're good with that too, Wyatt?"

"Whatever makes my girl happy. It's beautiful, but most importantly, this is her day more than it is mine, so I'd pay anything to make this happen."

"Oh, that won't be necessary. My parents may be dicks, but there's no way I'm letting them charge you. Koda is my family. Plus, that house is going to be in my name soon anyways."

"Wait, what?" Koda glances back at me through the mirror again, the car coming to a slow as we pull into the condo parking structure.

"Mommy dearest wanted to sell the home, so I told her I'll take over ownership."

"Wow, that's huge, Silver!"

It is. It's the least my parents could give me considering they're barely even parents. I don't say that, though. I know Dakota will see it written on my face. She's the only one that knows the true struggle I have with my parents.

"Just tell me what you need and we'll make it happen." I clap my hands as she pulls the car into a spot near the elevator.

"You're the best," she says as she unbuckles her seatbelt. "Now tell me everything about you and Damian."

I shoot Wyatt a look and he shrugs his shoulders, his hands flying up to his sides. I laugh, my head shaking.

"Oh boy. There's nothing happening between Damian and me."

Dakota narrows her eyes at me like she's seeing through my bullshit and I glare right back at her.

"It's just a way to piss off Jaiden. It's nothing," I concede. "I swear."

Accepting my answer, she bites her lip like she's trying not to laugh before opening the driver's door to climb from the car. I follow her out of the car, my legs asleep from the weird position I was sitting in.

"You're telling me more about that later, but until then, go home and take a nap before tonight." She pulls me into her arms, her head resting on my shoulder. This is why she's my best friend.

DAMIAN GREETS ME OUTSIDE OF THE RINK, HIS MAROON suit drawing attention to him immediately. As always, he looks stylish as fuck. However, instead of staring at me in that flirty way he usually does, his eyes are wandering over Lani who walks by my side. *Oh, this is bad.*

Okay, not bad really, but inconvenient for me. I was just starting to get under Jaiden's skin.

"Ladies," he says, holding the door open for us. "You both look incredible." His eyes linger over Lani a little longer and I snort quietly.

Lani is dressed in jeans and a Yellow Jacket's jersey. There's no specific player's name on the back, but it might as well read LeDuke. I nudge her with my arm and she looks at me sideways.

"What?" she whispers.

"That man likes you," I say, keeping my voice low as Damian walks ahead of us.

"What? No, he doesn't." She blushes and I chuckle.

"Yes, he does. He was just eye-fucking you."

She sighs, looking down at the ground. "Yeah, well, that's unfortunate for him."

It's my turn to look at her sideways. "Unfortunate how?"

"Just because my boyfriend of five years currently sucks, doesn't mean I can flirt with a *gorgeous* hockey player." Her voice gets mushy as she says the word gorgeous.

Well, that answers my question on whether Dane actually gives a shit about her again. He's been completely absent recently and rarely ever home. I know it's taking a toll on her confidence—not to mention the fact that she's dedicated *years* to this man. They started dating right after high school.

"Yeah, about that. I guess I should tell you something."

Lani's head turns, her eyebrow raised.

"Not about Dane," I say and she visually relaxes. "I've been kinda messing with Jaiden over the last week and Damian's been helping me."

"What do you mean?" She steps to the side to avoid the crowd of people as we walk into the tunnel.

"Damian noticed that Jaiden was... extra pissy, I guess, when he flirted with me. So, we made it a thing. I obviously enjoy being with Damian because he's great, but it's been this unconscious thing we've been doing to get under his skin. Jaiden wants to play games with me, so I'm finally back on the board."

"I mean, that's very on brand for you," she says with a laugh. "You two push each other's buttons already, but it seems like he just couldn't give a damn lately."

"That's what's been so confusing. How can I be so wrecked

over this, but then I'm trying to move on and he suddenly cares? It's irritating." I adjust my camera harness as we walk further, handing Lani my other camera case. "Just act like you're helping me today, that's all you need to do," I say with a laugh.

She nods, releasing a laugh and pulling the zipper closed on my case before she pulls the strap over her head. "You got it, boss."

The sounds of cheering drown out our conversion as we make our way toward the glass. I have a designated area where I take photos in our rink; it allows me to get the best shots of the game. I genuinely think that this is the best job I could be doing. It's every hockey lover's dream to be up close and personal with the players.

As the introductions are made, our fans boo at the competitors and it brings a wicked smile to my face.

The pressure is high tonight. I can feel myself tremble with anticipation. This is the tiebreaker that we need to move on.

"Let's do this, boys!" Lani yells from my side. I smile wide and she winks at me. *I taught her well.* She's an incredible heckler and I couldn't be more proud of her.

I look over and see Dakota walking down to the glass. She nods at me, before sliding into the seat next to Lani.

"Sup, bitch?" I grab her ponytail and twirl it between my fingers. Her eyes close and I snort.

"Please continue playing with my hair. It's heavenly."

"I would, but I have to work," I say, dropping her hair and sitting by my camera. She whines but it's quickly replaced by cheering as the players skate by the ice. Wyatt stops by the glass in front of Dakota, knocking against the glass.

They have this ritual before home games. He comes to skate by the glass and they play a game of rock, paper, scissors. Usually she loses, which pisses her off, but she'll do it because she loves him. I laugh when Wyatt throws his hands down after losing this time. He blows her a kiss before skating off and I mumble *ew* which is quickly reprimanded by a small knock to my arm.

"Hey! You're lucky I photograph this every time."

"Fine. I guess you can live another day." She blinks at me innocently right as the announcer's voice booms through the stadium.

Wyatt and Roman are on the ice, kicking off the first period with a bang. I think that we've got a good chance, but it's truly anybody's game at this point. I move my camera, the shutter clicking as the players fly across the ice.

I stand up when a player slams into Wyatt after he successfully steals the puck. The ref doesn't make a call, causing several people to scream—including the tiny human next to me.

"Hey, ref! Does your mother know you're fucking us?" Lani screams as the refs skate by, and I can't help the laugh that comes out of my mouth. I can't tell if Wyatt heard it or not, but I swear I see the hint of a smile as he skates backward past my lens.

In the second period, I see Jaiden and Damian skate out onto the ice. I catch Jaiden's eye a few times and it sends an unwelcome flutter through my stomach. He has no business being that attractive in his gear. *Fuck me.*

Lani screams as Damian flies down the ice, the puck quickly passing to another Yellow Jacket player and right into the net. The crowd goes wild. We're tied and I can feel my heart beating so quickly. *Come on, boys!*

"Get off your fucking knees, ref! You're blowing the damn game!" Lani stomps her feet, the crowd screaming behind her. I laugh again until I hear my name.

"Sterling," someone says from my right. I look over to see Noah walking toward us. I roll my eyes and turn back to the ice.

"I deserved that," he says, shoving his hands into his pockets. "Look, I just came to apologize. What happened in Vegas was unacceptable and I didn't even give you a chance to explain yourself. That was uncool of me."

"Excuse me," I say, holding up my hand to him. "Explain myself? You wanted me to *explain myself*? You're the one that left *me* to go get your dick wet. If someone should be explaining themselves here, it's you." I narrow my eyes at him.

He pales slightly, probably not expecting me to call him out on it. *Guess what, bud? I'm not one of those pushover girls you're probably used to going out with.*

"I hope that we can at least be cool since we still have to work together."

That's what he chooses to say? *Wow.*

"I don't know. I haven't even heard the apology yet." I raise a brow at him and he laughs. I don't know why he's laughing. I don't see anything funny.

"You're right. I'm sorry. I shouldn't have done that to you. Forgive me?" He pulls a hand from his pocket and extends it to me.

I smile sweetly at him, taking a step forward. Avoiding his hand completely, I grab his tie and wrap it around my fist, yanking him toward me. My lips brush his ear as I speak, my voice low and vicious.

"I could ruin your life, Noah. I could make *every day* of your life a living hell. We see each other at work every day and I promise you that if you ever cross me again or pull shit like that one some other sweet girl, I'll ruin you. You should be afraid of me because I'll turn every single pair of tits in this building on your ass. If you want to keep your balls intact, I'd think about that next time, 'kay?" I press a kiss to his cheek sweetly and just as I'm going to release his tie, I hear Lani's raised voice beside me.

"Sterling!" Lani yells a moment too late. Her voice is panicked, and I realize now that it was a warning.

A player of the opposing team is smashed into the glass, Jaiden's shoulder ramming into him.

The loud crash has Noah flying backward, jumping away from me. His face is white as a sheet when he looks through the glass at Jaiden, who sends him a death glare before skating away like nothing happened.

"What the hell is his problem?" Noah asks, running a hand down his suit jacket. His voice is shaking and it sends a shiver of glee through me. I almost laugh, but I don't.

"They used to bang," Lani says. "And now that she's trying to move on, he's acting like a jealous, possessive ex because he's still into her but won't admit it." She grins up at me, her eyes flicking back to the ice before she screams at the players again. Dakota shrugs, her laughter barely contained.

"I hate both of you," I say under my breath.

"You love us," Lani says, her eyes still on the ice.

"Well, that explains a lot, I guess." Noah moves farther away from me, his eyes wandering.

That gives me an idea. I look at Dakota then back at Noah. "Oh, speaking of, you saw how Jaiden acted just now?"

Noah nods, his brows drawn up in confusion.

I smile a little more viciously this time. "Imagine how he'd behave if I told him what you did to me in Vegas." I twirl my hair around my finger. "I have no control over that man, so he'd do *whatever* he wanted to. You know how violent hockey players are, right Noah?"

The color drains from his face completely and it brings me *so* much joy.

"Anyways, I accept your apology. Thanks for being so considerate. Run along now." I shoo my hands at him to leave.

"I'll see you around, Sterling." He turns quickly, practically running in the opposite direction.

"Yeah. See you around." I drop the sweet act, my face cold and angry now.

The fuck was that with Jaiden? Was that intentional? What the fuck is his problem? Why the hell does he care now?

I shake it off as I sit down in front of my camera again.

"What sweet nothings did you whisper to Noah?" Dakota asks, her brow raised at me. Of course she'd know that I'd threaten his balls.

I refuse to let anyone get away with treating me like that. I'm not a doormat, nor am I someone who is okay with letting a man treat me like second best. He wanted to go on a date with me and left in the middle of it to go fuck someone else. Sue me for refusing to let him get away with it. Maybe it'll scare him into being more considerate of the sweet women who work with the team.

"I threatened to ruin his life and chop his balls off." I smile at her and both Lani and Dakota laugh, their heads thrown back. I stare at them for a moment before finally releasing the laugh I'd been holding back.

We laugh for several minutes until I wipe stray tears from my eyes. It's then that I lock eyes with Jaiden across the ice. I know it's him. There's a piece of me that thinks I'll always know where he is and which pair of silvery gray eyes are his.

I miss him. I miss the feelings I felt with him and for this moment, I'll allow myself to feel it because today is goodbye. I'm done.

It's not looking good for us. The guys are working hard to move the puck but this team is good—better than we'd anticipated. The energy is tense again, the fans screaming at every miss. They've made several attempts at the goal but each time it's blocked almost effortlessly.

With the clock counting down, I feel a spike of anxiety when the opposing team scores another point. We've got two minutes left and I'm not confident. To keep from stressing, I focus on my photos, moving my camera down the ice and capturing photos of their movements. I'm happy with what I've shot so far.

Jaiden captures the puck, shuffling it before passing it off to Roman. They move the puck down the ice with amazing speed.

Five...

Roman passes the puck, our forward pushing onward.

Four...

Jaiden obtains the puck, skating around the defensemen charging toward him.

Three...

The puck is passed again, my eyes barely able to track it.

Two...

Jaiden hits the puck into the offensive zone in an attempt to make a goal.

One...

At the last minute, the goaltender slides, knocking the puck out of the way, and crushing my team's chances at the Stanley Cup.

Zero...

The buzzer sounds, the voices drowning out the loud screams from my friends. My eyes track Jaiden, his knees sliding across the ice as he watches the other team celebrate. He looks pissed and my black heart hurts for him. The others surround him, but I know he isn't budging. I know him well enough to know that he's taking the blame for this loss, and there's nothing they can say to change that.

SIX

JAIDEN

WANT to know the best way to nurse a loss? Alcohol. And the best way to cure an aching heart? Alcohol.

Alcohol is the answer to a lot of my problems nowadays. It's a cure all, but only for a moment.

When my mother passed away, I found the cure to my problems at the bottom of a whiskey bottle.

Loss is something I'm rather unfamiliar with. I never knew my father. He's a name and an unknown face in a sea of people. He wasn't here, so he deserves no part in my life. He wasn't here when my Ma got sick. He wasn't here when she went through her cancer treatments each month. He didn't care that I had to sit by and watch the first love of my life wither away and die.

Fuck cancer.

She was too young to die. She had so much life left to live and yet she suffered while my sperm donor was traipsing around the country somewhere without a care in the world.

Fuck him for reaching out to me last spring. I don't owe him a thing, but if that were true, why does a piece of me want to face him? I want, no deserve, answers for everything he's done in the past.

The bar grows louder, my teammates talking at my sides. I'm in my head a lot more lately. I haven't been like this since my Ma's passing.

I've withdrawn from my friends, my only solace being hockey... but sometimes even hockey isn't fun anymore. Not when I have to see her stupid, *beautiful* face all the goddamn time. Especially not now that we've lost our spot in the finals.

I stare down my glass, swirling the whiskey-coke around, enjoying the way the ice clinks against the sides.

"Don't look now," Luca, my teammate, mutters at my side.

The guys have been ogling every woman that walks through the doors of this bar. Even the ones they already know. I usually wouldn't spare a glance, but something in my gut draws my eyes in the direction of the door.

Ice floods through my body the moment I see her. Not just *her.* She's with Damian, his arm slung around her shoulder. It doesn't even matter to me that his other arm is slung around Lani's shoulders too.

I should stop watching her, but instead I watch them walk together. He leans into her, speaking quietly into her ear. When he pulls away, she laughs, her eyes smiling in that oh so familiar way.

I school my features into cool indifference, but my body is burning red hot inside. I can barely control my reactions around her anymore. Ever since I saw her with Noah that first day, all I seem to do is lose my mind any time she's near.

I have no business feeling this way, and yet it feels like a knife is being twisted in my gut every time she's around. It shouldn't hurt this much, but it does.

They pass me, almost in slow motion, and Sterling's beautiful blue green eyes meet mine for a split second before she turns away quickly, laughing with Damian...my *friend.*

The urge to pull her to me, drag her out of this bar and press her against the walls behind the bar, to slam my lips against hers...it's insurmountable. I want to show her that she belongs to me, that she's *mine.* But that's not the truth. She's not mine. I ruined that for myself months ago.

Rushing to my feet, I toss a twenty to the bartender, and trudge through the crowd, stepping out onto the busy street. I vaguely hear people calling after me, but I don't care enough to stop and listen. It's not until I hear *her* voice that I finally stop.

"Jaiden," she pants, her arm reaching for mine. I pull away from her, unable to look at her fully. I can see from the corner of my eye that she's hurt by my actions. I regret it straight away, but I won't tell her that.

"Are you okay?" Her eyes assess me with an intensity that sends me staggering backwards. Before all of this happened, it was those eyes that intrigued me the most. She's always had the ability to see right through me, and that was the scariest thing about her. She *saw* me, and that wasn't something I wanted. *No one* sees me. Not in the way she did. It was only a few months but hell, she did it.

My jaw clenches as I fight the urge to push her away again.

"I'm fine." *I'm not.*

"Are you sure you're okay?" She takes a tentative step toward me, her hands tucked into her jacket.

She looks beautiful. She changed after the game into a more casual outfit. When I'd smashed that player into the glass, she was wearing slacks and a low cut button up. Her badge hung between her breasts— as if I needed any more reason to stare at her. Now she's dressed in a sky-blue shirt that hugs her breasts and a black leather skirt which accentuates her delicious curves that I grew familiar with.

God, I want to hold her.

"It's not your fault, you know."

There it is, the thing I was afraid of.

"It is." I turn away from her, my legs carrying me across the street. She runs to keep up with me.

"It's not, though." She pants as she runs. "Jaiden, stop."

"No!" I keep walking. "Go back inside, Sterling. I can't do this with you right now."

"Do what? Care? Is that what's happening? You're finally starting to care that I'm moving on?"

"Please, *don't.*" I turn to look at her, my gaze heated and my voice firm. "Don't." I hold up a finger to her and I can see the way her jaw clenches.

Her nostrils flare, her face angry as she bows. "As you wish." She turns, flipping me the bird over her shoulder and running in the opposite direction.

I throw my head back, my fists clenched before I release them and jog to my Jeep. Yanking the door open, I climb into the car and slam the door shut behind me.

My fist pounds against the steering wheel, the impact shooting pain up my arm.

"Fuck!" I yell into my empty car. "Fucking *fuck*!"

I hate this so damn much. She threw me a bone *again,* and I fucked it up, *again.*

My chest heaves as I stare forward, the parking lot filled with cars now.

I need to leave before I do something I regret. Shoving my key into the ignition, I start it, revving my engine before I peel out of the parking lot with reckless abandon. The star-speckled sky is my only companion tonight.

ROMAN TOSSES BROWN SUGAR INTO THE CART ALONGSIDE the other ingredients. At the end of every school year, the teachers host a graduation party for the kids to celebrate the end of one grade and the beginning of another. Roman's baking cookies. Well, I suppose *we* are baking cookies, but that's besides the point.

I walk down the aisle to the chocolate chips, my finger trailing down the shelves. Grabbing a bag of caramel and chocolate chips, I turn, tossing them into the cart. Roman eyes them, nodding his approval and continuing down the aisle.

I'm looking at vanilla when Roman's phone rings in his pocket. He pulls it out, a concerned look crossing his face.

"Hello," he says, the phone pressed against his cheek with his shoulder. He pushes the cart toward me and I take it. "Yes, this is Lily's father."

I watch him as his face shifts from concern, to anger, to urgency. "Wait, this happened when?"

My eyes go wide when Roman nods his head toward the check out. *We'll come back for the rest later*, he mouths to me and I nod.

"And my daughter is alright? She's safe, correct?"

I'm close enough to hear the mumble of a *Yes, sir.*

"Keep her in the classroom please. If that's where she feels comfortable, keep her there. I'm on my way."

He pauses, listening to the voice on the phone.

"No, I'll have words with them later. Bye." He shoves the phone into his pocket as I finish putting our items onto the conveyor belt.

"What happened?" I look at him from the side, his face more worried than before. Anything that involves his little girl is urgent—that girl is his whole world.

"The aids had to break up a fight on the playground. I guess some kids were pushing Lily around. She wouldn't say why they were fighting, but the nurse had to patch her up after one of the kids shoved her."

"One of those brats *shoved* our girl?"

Roman nods. He's just as pissed as I am. His hands fumble with his wallet, handing the cashier money before we take the bag and rush out the door.

I'm barely in my seat before Roman is pulling out of his parking spot. Within minutes, he's pulling up to the school and unbuckling himself from his seat.

I watch as his irritation and fear grow. His baby was hurt at the hand of someone else and it's not exactly appropriate to fight some kid; Roman isn't used to not being able to fix everything all the time. Not being able to protect Lily from other children has always been one of his worst fears.

"Where's my daughter?" Roman says, his voice louder than normal.

Several of the office staff stir, their faces a mix of concern and fear as this six-foot-eight hockey player and papa bear rushes through their office building. I'm thoroughly entertained.

A young woman stands, her face unfazed by Roman.

"I'm assuming you're Lily's father?"

He nods, his eyes narrowed at her.

"Great. Well, how about you calm down before I take you to her. I won't tolerate yelling in my classroom."

"Your classroom?"

"That's correct. She's in my classroom." She crosses her arms in front of her and I nearly laugh. This tiny woman is standing up to Roman and it's almost comical.

She's a gorgeous tiny woman, by the way. Her almond eyes narrow at Roman, almost like she's sizing him up.

He sighs. "I apologize for my outburst. I'm Roman Wilkes. I'd like to see her now, please."

"That is much better." She extends her hand to Roman. "Miss Sharpe. I'll be her second-grade teacher next year."

"Nice to meet you, Miss Sharpe. Can I see my daughter, please?"

"It's *may I see my daughter, please*. And yes, you *may*. Follow me." She turns on her heels, leading us down a long hallway until she stops in front of a door.

"Lily?" Roman says, peeking his head through the door.

Lily's head pops up from a table in the corner of the room, her face red and puffy. She stands immediately, running toward us.

"Daddy," she cries, colliding with his legs.

"Hey, Bug." He lifts her into his arms, holding her tightly to him. "¿Qué pasó, mija? ¿Por qué lloras?" *What happened, babygirl? Why are you crying?*

I know it's serious when Roman slips into Spanish. It's his way of privacy even when there is none, so I take a step back, allowing them their moment.

"I'm okay," she says into his shoulder. She starts crying again and I swear I feel my heart break a little. "They pushed me, Daddy. She said I'm not cool because I can't skate like them."

"That's what this is about? Skating?"

"That's exactly what it was about." It's not Lily's voice that answers. It's the teacher's this time. *Miss Sharpe.* "A bunch of the kids here are starting skating lessons and since Lily is not one of those, there was a fight on the playground. They're excluding her from playing with *the group.*" She throws up air quotations when she says *the group.*

"That's bullshit," I say, and Roman shoots me a glare over his shoulder. "That's poopy," I repeat. "Don't repeat that, Lily."

She laughs, a smile forming on her tear-stained face.

"Ve con tu Tío Jai," Roman says, putting her down. She runs to me, and I lift her onto my hip, holding her tight to me like a precious gift. She runs her fingers through my curly hair, that smile of hers growing.

"Your hair's messy, Uncle Jai. Are you sad?"

I cough, looking at Roman with wide eyes. He laughs and I can't help but laugh too. "I'm okay, Princess. Thanks for being concerned, though."

"You know... I still love you, even if you're a loser." She kisses my cheek and I chuckle.

"Love you too, Lily."

"What exactly happened? They were talking to her about skating, my daughter wasn't included and then they fought?"

"They started shoving her around in a circle, basically passing her from person to person until she fell."

Roman turns to Lily. "Did you shove them back, baby?"

Lily shakes her head no.

"She's not allowed to do that," Miss Sharpe cuts in.

"Yes, she is. She's my daughter and she should be allowed to protect herself. If there is a *group* of kids shoving her around, you expect her to just take it?"

"We teach gentle communication here—"

"Where was the gentle communication when she was being *shoved*?"

"Mr. Wilkes, I can't condone violence in my classroom."

Lily nudges me, her eyes full of mischief. "She's pretty, isn't she?" She winks at me with such exaggeration, I can't help but laugh.

"She is," I whisper.

"She's my daughter and I can parent her how I want. She should be allowed to defend herself. It's bullying if a whole group is ganging up on her. It's bullying even if it's only one. What is being done about those children?"

"This is my classroom and my students, and therefore, we go by my rules. And I promise you that action is being taken."

Roman nearly growls. "Fine, but she has my permission to shove them back. I won't punish her for that." He turns to me and Lily. "I'm signing her out early. Let's go."

I lock eyes with the teacher for a moment. Her eyes are squinted in frustration, her hand resting on her temple. I almost feel bad for her, but she stood her ground well. Roman's generally a nice guy, but when it comes to his daughter, there's nothing that will stand in his way. She is his first priority.

Sending her an apologetic wave, I turn with Lily and follow after Roman.

"Byeeee, Miss Sharpe. See you soon!" Lily waves over my shoulder and I hear the faintest laugh as I walk out of the door.

My voice could go hoarse from the amount of cheering I'm doing tonight. Our little girl is receiving an award for exemplary performance in all of her classes. It's not *that* big of a deal, but it is to me. I've watched that little girl grow up to be the incredibly intuitive and smart girl that she is today. She certainly didn't get her smarts from me.

Sterling sits several seats away from me, but despite the distance, I can still *feel* her. She giggles when Damian leans in to say something and just like *that,* the happy mood I was in disappears.

That fucking dick.

I don't even know what's happening between them, but everything about it pisses me off.

She laughs again and I move my head to glare at her.

"What?" she hisses.

"Can you shut the fuck up? I'm trying to support my little girl here."

It's childish and I know it, but that's what she fucking does to me. I want to scream at her all the damn time. Because if I didn't scream, I'd probably pull her into the nearest corridor and fuck her silly until *she's* screaming my name.

"What are you? The fun police?"

"No," I say with an immature glare. "Just shut up. I'm trying to listen." At first I think I've gotten through to her, that is until she mocks me, over exaggerating the motion of zipping her lips and throwing away the key. It's a stupid game we're playing and it doesn't help that Damian laughs.

Rolling my eyes, I turn my head back to the stage, trying to wrangle my bad attitude. It doesn't improve much though, not even when the ceremony ends and I follow my friends outside to wait for Lily.

The sun's nearly disappeared and I watch the street lamps around the school flicker to life. It's a calming sort of feeling to watch the transition from day to night. As someone who desires control in every area of my life, it's somewhat comforting to experience parts of life that I have *no* control over.

"What's your problem?" Sterling asks, interrupting my moment of peace. Who needs peace anyway? Apparently not me. Ever.

"My problem? What's yours? You've been a real *bitch* lately." The moment the words leave my mouth, I regret it.

A hollow laugh leaves her and fear pulses through me for a moment. Anger I can handle, but whatever emotion just crossed her face was something more evil. It's something I've only seen directed at other people thus far, and I'm not sure I'm ready for it to be directed at me.

"A bitch...me? That's rich coming from you, Jaiden." She breathes deeply and I know she's gearing up for a fight.

"First, you ghost me, making me feel like absolute shit for taking the job of my dreams. Then you fucked me in a pantry after *months,* just to remind me once again why we can't be together, and how my wants and desires mean *nothing* to you. And *now* you've ruined the one date I've been on since you, and you have the audacity to call *me* a bitch? For what—trying to move on? For trying to be happy without you? You're giving me emotional whiplash, Jaiden," she growls.

"Of course, it's all about me. You wanted more than I could give you, Sterling. What about that don't you understand?"

"I understand just *fine*, Jaiden. You're emotionally unavailable and fucked up, but that doesn't mean you can ruin *my* happiness too." The angrier she gets, the louder her voice becomes. I don't want to match her, but I can't help myself, not even when I *swear* I hear someone yelling at us to stop. I'm too angry to listen to them.

"Well, don't go rubbing it in my fucking face," I yell. I'm about to say something else when I hear soft crying. Lily runs past us, swiping at her face.

Roman glares at me as he runs after her and I finally take in the full scope of the situation. She must have heard everything.

"Great fucking job," Wyatt says, his arms crossed over his chest. "I hope you're happy."

"What?" I croak, seeing Sterling's spine snap straight beside me. Damian walks up to Wyatt's side, looking between Sterling and me.

"She stood there asking you to stop yelling at her Aunt Sterling and when no one listened to her, she burst into tears." He shakes his head, huffing a breath. "This"—he gestures between us—"has gotten way out of hand. There's clearly way more that's happened between you two that needs to be resolved. You're hurting the people around you because of it."

I feel gutted, my stomach sinking and leaving a sick feeling in its wake.

Lily is my world. I'd do anything for her and yet I just watched her running away with tears in her eyes that were caused by me.

"I didn't mean for her to hear that," I say, my voice weak.

He shakes his head in a disappointed dad way and it makes me shrink further. "Family dinner is this weekend," he says. "I'd advise y'all to sort your shit out before then."

He looks right at Sterling. "Not a word of this to Dakota. She's stressed enough as it is with wedding plans. I don't need her trying to *fix* whatever is happening between you two. It's not her job to make you both pull your heads out of your asses." Wyatt huffs again, his face devoid of emotion. "Lily looks up to you, Jai. We're her family and she needs us to set examples for her. I don't mean this to hurt, but I'd never want her to date someone who treats her the way you just treated Sterling. I don't give a shit about what's happened between you two; no one deserves to be treated like that."

He walks away leaving me to hang my head in shame. With how quiet Sterling is beside me, I know she's probably feeling similarly. We're silent until she looks up at me with a slightly pained expression.

"I don't want to be friends with you, Jaiden. I don't want anything to do with you. I only have to see you because of where I work and because of who my friends are. Outside of that, you mean *nothing* to me. I'm done. Stay out of my way." She shifts on her feet a couple times before I hear the soft click of her heels as she walks away, Damian following after her.

Is this what rock bottom feels like? It's gotta be. I've disappointed my family and I've ruined my one chance at happiness. I could've been happy with her. Maybe there was a chance for me to have what Wyatt has with Dakota, but I went and fucked it all up.

God, the fuck is wrong with me?

SEVEN
STERLING

MY CELL PHONE rings twice before I answer the call I've been dreading for the last few days. It takes all of my effort to muster up any semblance of happiness into my voice when I speak.

"Hey."

"'Sup, bitch," Dakota says, her voice teasing.

"Not much. Work's been interesting, to say the least." I kick my feet up onto my desk, heels and all, before opening the top drawer in my desk and pulling out a lollipop.

Dakota speaks as I pull off the wrapper and pop it in my mouth. "Well, it's a good thing Wyatt's making tacos tonight, isn't it?" She's very chipper and I want to match her energy, but ever since the fight with Jaiden, I've just felt *lifeless.* My heart aches in ways it hasn't before. He was more than just a fuck buddy to me, and I'm pretty sure he knew it too. Maybe it's my fault for falling to him when I knew deep down that a relationship with him wasn't going to happen.

"Tacos, you say." I pull the lollipop from my mouth with a pop. My office door is wide open and from this angle, I can see Noah leaning against a wall, his newest victim blushing at whatever bullshit he's spewing.

"Tacos," Dakota confirms. "Please tell me you're coming? Lani and I need a gossip sesh before dinner."

It's really tempting. I do miss my best friends desperately, but since the fight, I've felt myself retreating a bit. After thinking for a moment, I sigh.

"Fine," I groan. "I'll be there, but only if I get first dibs on whatever dessert y'all have planned for after."

"You got it, babe." I can hear the smile in her voice and it almost brings a smile to my own face.

"Okay, well, I've got a rogue Noah to scare. I'll see you tonight." I blow a kiss into the phone before hanging up and slipping the sucker back into my mouth.

As I kick my feet off my desk and stand, I let the click of my heels signal my arrival into the hall of the fifteenth floor offices.

Noah's eyes snap up the moment he sees me leaning in the doorway.

"Oh, hi, Sterling." He stands straighter, the new secretary turning to look at me.

"Hey," I say, eyeing him curiously. I'm still angry at him and I'm really not in the mood to look at his face today. "Why are you here, Noah?"

He opens and closes his mouth a few times. Good to know he's still scared of me. "After lunch, we're due at the rink for a meeting with the team. We're running small promos for end of season content."

"Great," I say under my breath. The last thing I need is to spend more private time with the guys.

I open my mouth to say something else, but I'm stopped by the sudden appearance of Damian in his Yellow Jacket's tee and joggers. It looks like he's just come from practice because he's juggling a puck in his hand, his orange and black stick in the other.

Damian spots Noah, an evil gleam in his eyes a moment before he props the puck on his stick and sends it flying across the hallway. The sound it makes as it hits the back wall makes me flinch.

I look in confusion at the wall and then back at Damian and

Noah who's now gripping his ear. The secretary's eyes are wide, her mouth agape and I have half a thought to laugh.

"The fuck, man?" Noah stares angrily at Damian.

"It's your ear today, Noah, but the next time you piss me off, I won't miss my mark." He leans in, whispering loud enough for me to hear. "I don't forgive easily. You're lucky my girl over there left you with just a verbal warning. I, on the other hand, won't be so kind. Got it?"

He nods frantically, scurrying away.

"Ready for lunch?" Damian winks at me and I shake my head at him.

"Let me grab my purse."

DAMIAN ESCORTS ME INTO THE RINK. I HADN'T REALIZED how much I actually needed that lunch break until I was on it. Damian didn't relent until I was laughing over my gyro. It helped my mood a lot, that is until Jaiden decided to push past us, his shitty mood palpable in the air. I shouldn't be affected by it, but I am. The anger at his mere presence rubs off on me, making my body tense. I really thought that I could be mature about this. I thought that I could see him and deny the way my heart squeezes painfully every time he's near me.

By the time Noah walks to my side, I'm a grouch all over again and not even trying to hide it. I can feel him staring at me and I know he's judging me.

"What?" I snap.

"What's up with you today?"

"Nothing." I bite my tongue, trying to breathe through my frustration. I'm such an idiot for involving myself with yet another coworker. I can't fucking wait for this season to be officially over. "I just don't want to deal with this shit today."

He scoffs. "I didn't feel like losing an ear today, but here we are."

"You didn't lose an ear, Noah. You just pissed off the wrong people."

He mumbles something under his breath and I freeze.

"What did you just say?"

He looks at me, slightly panicked.

"*What* did you say, Noah?"

He huffs. "I said, you're kind of being a bitch today."

I see red, and with how hard my teeth are clenched, I'm surprised I haven't cracked a tooth. Every bit of control I have left snaps, the floodgates of my bad mood now open and ready to destroy.

"What is with people calling me a bitch lately?" I say, my voice nearly a screech. I don't give a shit who hears. "I'm sorry for having *feelings* that aren't happiness and fucking rainbows, and for not being afraid to stand up for myself."

"All I wanted was to sleep with you without any complication, but clearly *you* are way more complicated than I'd thought."

My nostrils flare in anger and I stomp toward Damian. "Give me your stick, Dame."

"Why?" He looks at me, his eyes swimming with amusement.

"I want to smack him with it."

"That's assault," Noah says, but I can hear the way his voice shakes slightly.

Good. Be afraid, fucker.

"You won't let her hit me? Right?" His voice cracks on the word *right* and I look back at him before turning my angry gaze back on Damian.

"Give me the stick. He called me a bitch. I'm so *fucking* tired of men thinking it's okay to call me a bitch."

"Why do you need the stick?" Wyatt and Roman stand behind Damian now, their expressions amused at my display of aggression. Jaiden's got headphones in and his back to us, and I want to scream at him too.

"I don't want to get my hands dirty," I say with a huff. "You know what, fuck it."

I turn back to Noah, clenching my fists when I'm suddenly scooped up and lifted off the floor. I flail around, yelling insults at Noah, the last of my patience melting away before I feel the hot tears stream down my face. Damian carries me caveman-style down the hall and into the locker room. By the time he sets me down, I'm crying, my body shaking with the pent up feelings and rage I've felt over the last few days.

He kneels before me, his thumbs wiping the tears away. "Did you know that oftentimes other emotions will manifest as anger when we don't know how to process them?"

I blink at him several times, my eyes still wet with tears. When I shake my head, he continues.

"My mom told me that when someone hurts us, our emotions can run wild. After my ex cheated on me, the only way I knew how to process my hurt was through aggression. It made me a damn good hockey player, but it also fucked with my reputation on the ice." He looks up at me, his lips pursed. "Jaiden hurt you, and he continues to hurt you, so you're lashing out in the only way you know how. I don't blame you for being angry—hell, I'd be angry too—but this isn't the way, Silver. You deserve a man who will value you, but you have to heal before you can get that."

My lip quivers as I look at him, the kindness in his voice causing fresh tears to fall. "I think I loved him," I admit. "Or at least close to it. Am I not good enough?" My voice breaks and his face softens.

His hand brushes over my hair, moving it from my face. "You are more than enough, Sterling. He was just too afraid to deal with his own shit to cherish you. Maybe one day he will, but he needs to get there on his own time."

"I miss him." It's that confession that breaks me the most. I didn't mean a word of what I said earlier this week. I do want to be friends with him. His friendship is one of the things I miss the most these days. I'm still angry, *so* very angry, but maybe I can admit that there's more than anger lingering under the surface.

"I know," he says. He smiles sadly at me, letting me calm myself until I'm okay enough to do my job.

I'm a big girl. I can do this.

TACOS ARE THE BEST THING IN THE WORLD, BUT WYATT'S tacos are next level.

I was bribed by tacos. *Tacos.* I'm stupid enough to agree to something as simple as tacos to sit through an entire *family dinner* with Jaiden in the same room.

He could barely look at me yesterday, so why would he even agree to come tonight? I saw him. He wanted to talk to me but he pushed me away all over again. I won't lie; it fucking hurt. It hurt almost as bad as it did the first time.

Dakota's been spewing something about exciting news and waiting for everyone to be here to talk about it. I guess that's why he's being forced to come too. At least I won't be the only miserable one here.

Shit. Good vibes and happy thoughts.

I'm *not* miserable. I am perfectly content and all sorts of happy. *You liar.*

Groaning, I set the table, laying out napkins and silverware for everyone. Dakota and Wyatt are hosting tonight. I guess it's better this way because I feel more comfortable in my best friend's home anyway.

When a knock sounds at the door, Dakota practically floats over to open it. "Coming," she yells.

I see the sunset hair before the door is fully opened.

"Hey, babes," Lani says, pulling Dakota into her arms.

"Hey! Where's Dane?"

Lani sighs, her shoulders shrugging slightly. "Work."

I shoot her a look from the table and she shakes her head. *Oh, my sweet girl.*

Damian shoves past the women, walking right into the kitchen with Wyatt. "Smells like *heaven.*" He slings an arm over Wyatt's shoulders and leans into him. "Who knew Wyatt could be such a good housewife?"

"Ha ha," Wyatt says sarcastically, pinching Damian's side. "Every man should know how to cook."

"Damn straight," Roman says, walking through the door. He places a covered plate on the table then pulls me into his side. "How ya doin', pretty lady?"

I laugh, shaking my head at the bit of country that comes out in him every so often. "Hanging in there," I say.

"Good." He releases me, making his rounds with his friends. As the others talk, I walk toward Lani.

"Want to talk about it?" I take her purse and place it on the floor by the couch.

"Not really. He's been avoiding me more and more, and it's just... Something feels wrong. I'll tell you about it later."

Nodding, I hold her hand.

"'Sup, ladies?" Damian plops into the seat beside me. His arm slings across the back of the couch, as he leans into us.

"Girl talk," I say, my eyebrow raising at him. The corner of my mouth lifts when he's momentarily stunned. "Kidding. Nothing juicy happened yet."

He laughs, his fingers finding my hair and running through my long ponytail. "Now that we're officially off for the season, I've asked Lily to teach me to braid." He winks, and I nearly groan as he pulls at the long strands of my hair. He's been very attentive to me since my meltdown at the rink.

The vibe changes in the room the moment the door opens. Jaiden walks in, his still wet curls draped in front of his face. He looks delicious and I hate my body for reacting to him. *God, I miss him so much.*

His eyes lock on mine and whatever he sees makes him angry. That's when I realize Damian's hand is still entangled in my hair. I freeze. I promised I'd be on my best behavior tonight and we're already starting off rough.

It doesn't phase Damian one bit. He continues playing with my hair, his eyes watching Lani. *This is going to be so fun.*

"Dinner's ready," Dakota calls from the kitchen. I don't move when the others begin pulling out their chairs and sitting around the table. When Damian releases my hair, I walk to the table, my eyes watching Jaiden. He doesn't spare me another glance.

I don't listen to the conversation that flows across the table. Instead I focus on my food, taking small bites and savoring the flavor. It's easier than listening for his voice in every conversation, feeling overly aware of his presence.

"So, Sterling, how have you enjoyed this season?" Roman shoves a taco into his mouth as he looks at me.

I blink several times, processing his words. "I've loved it. This has been a dream come true for me."

Jaiden snorts, his taco halfway to his mouth. I tense, the freakout from earlier still fresh in my mind.

I glare at him, my food forgotten. "Got something to say, Jaiden?"

"Nope," he says, keeping his eyes off my face.

I continue talking. "I've been able to meet so many incredible people and, of course, I love hockey, so what's not to love?"

Jaiden snorts again, his eyes watching me this time.

I clench my fists under the table and I feel Dakota tense beside me.

"Well, go on then. Say what you want to say." I look at Jaiden with what I hope is a look of indifference.

"I don't want to say a thing." He takes another bite of his taco, chewing deliberately as he stares.

"Jaiden," Wyatt warns, his voice low.

"That's the second time you've interrupted me with your snorts. I know this isn't about the job, Jaiden. It's about the fact that you aren't man enough. Stop passing off blame onto me. I took this job because I wanted to."

He slams his hand down. "No, you took this job to prove a

point. You made a decision and I respect you for it. What I think doesn't matter—you're going to do what you want anyways."

"And so will you!" I yell. "I was doing what I thought would make me happy. I thought that you cared about me, but I guess I was wrong."

"Yeah, I guess you were," he says.

"God, I fucking hate you," I say, tossing my napkin on the table and rushing to a stand. "*Fuck* you!" I point a finger at him and he stares down at it.

"Okay, that's enough," Dakota yells. "Just stop you two." She stands, her eyes filled with rage.

Jaiden tenses as she looks between the both of us. "We are a *family*. You—" She points to me—"are my best friend and I love you, but Jaiden is Wyatt's best friend and Roman's best friend and Damian's, *I think,* and the two of you fighting over this stupid miscommunication is making everyone miserable. I shoved the two of you into that pantry last summer because I thought it would help you *talk*." She throws her hands up. The room is completely silent as she talks, her voice filled with authority.

"Jaiden, I love you, but you suck at communicating. Sterling, I also love you, but you can hold a grudge like no one's business and clearly the two of you didn't talk like I thought. You are some of the most stubborn people I know and it's infuriating. Either you both were merely tolerating each other, or this has been going on the whole time and I just didn't see it. I love the both of you and I want you both at my wedding, but if you can't be in the same room without fighting, I don't think that's going to happen." She shakes her head and I feel my stomach sink.

Dakota has been my best friend since I was a kid. She's my everything and I'm suddenly feeling like the worst friend in the world.

"I was going to wait to announce this until *after* dinner, but here we are. The two of you better get your shit together and fast. We're going on vacation for the whole summer. I spoke with your parents, Sterling, and we'll be at the lake house. It'll be a great bonding experience for us. I expect you both to be there. I guess then I'll decide who's staying for our wedding because I certainly won't allow this to happen on my special day, and I refuse to have one of our friends babysit the two of you. We leave in a week." She looks at everyone before she sits back down.

I shouldn't smile, but I want to. The way her steam has ebbed like she's run out of energy to confront us, it's one of the reasons I love her. It was my job to finish that, to continue on for her when she couldn't, but instead I'm on the opposite side of it. It sucks.

"I did warn you," Wyatt says, his face neutral. It's silent for several moments until Roman speaks.

"Lily is packed and ready to go," Roman says.

"You knew?" Jaiden asks, his voice hoarse.

"Of course he knew," Dakota says. "He's got a whole ass person he needs to prepare besides himself. Plus, school ends this week, so I very well couldn't make plans without him knowing."

She shakes her head like it's a ridiculous notion. She picks up a taco, shoving it into her mouth.

I stare down at my plate, unsure of what to do now. I'm embarrassed and ashamed. This whole situation is stupid. I couldn't deny myself the attraction I felt for Jaiden and that really didn't work out for me.

I wish my stupid heart would behave. This is my best friend and she is more important than anything, so I will do anything to fix this. With my appetite fully gone now, I can't bear to be here another minute like this.

When Damian breaks the silence, I slide from my place at the table.

"I'm sorry for my behavior." I look right at Koda, hoping my eyes show my sincerity. "I'll be packed and ready to go. I have some things I need to take care of." I look at Wyatt, sending him an apologetic look. "Thanks for dinner."

I run, actually *run* from the condo and down to my car. I hate running, but it felt like an appropriate time to utilize it.

Say goodbye to the old Sterling. It's time that I make some changes.

"THANKS FOR MEETING ME," I SAY, SHOVING MY HANDS into the small pockets of my leggings.

"You're my best friend. Of course I'd come, even if I was *very*, very pissed last night." Dakota looks at me, her eyes filled with nothing but sincerity.

"I'm really sorry." I feel the prickle of tears at the corners of my eyes, but I push them away. "I've been a bad friend and I wasn't even thinking when it all happened... He just—*ugh*—he gets under my skin."

She looks at me, her lips pursed and her eyes slightly sad. "Why didn't you tell me it'd gotten this bad, babe? That wasn't any normal fight last night."

"No, it wasn't," I admit. "I'm so *damn* hurt and I just... I don't know."

She pats my arm, a determined look crossing her face and if I had half a brain, I'd think she's been plotting. "Actually, I have something I wanted to talk to you about. I know after last night this may seem out of left field, but I was talking to Wyatt after everyone left and we have an idea."

"Okay?" I try to keep the apprehension from my voice, but I know she hears it.

"I promise it may sound crazy after everything, but I think it could work." She eyes me and I nod, urging her to continue. "So, this thing with Damian was just something to piss off Jaiden at first, but what if you made it a *real* thing?" She throws up air quotations when she says *real*.

"*What?*" Is she crazy?

"Hear me out. Wyatt told me that Jaiden's been nothing but stoic and he's withdrawn a lot since whatever happened between you two." She waves her hand in a circle toward me. "And when you started dating again, he changed. I think his jealousy is pulling him from whatever place he retreated to, even if it's not the healthiest method. He won't talk and it's sort of like a...backwards reverse psychology intervention."

A stunned laugh flies from my mouth. "You're serious about this." It's not a question, it's an observation.

"I am. Everyone would be in on it—except Jaiden, of course—but I think it could work." She blinks at me as she waits for my response.

"I just really don't want to get hurt, Dakota. Not again. I really liked him and—"

She holds her hands up. "If it becomes too much for you, stop at any point. Obviously your happiness is most important to me above all else, but we really want to help Jaiden." *And you* was the unspoken implication of that sentence.

I breathe deeply, my heart beating wildly in my chest as I consider her plan. After several moments, I speak, my voice weak.

"Okay. What do you have in mind?"

She squeals. "Ah! Really?! This is going to be so fun," she says, jumping up and down, just like she did when we were kids.

"Okay, okay, calm down, crazy lady," I say with a smile. "Can I make a request?"

"Anything," she says, her eyes wild with excitement.

"I've been thinking about making some identity changes for a while now. Would you come with me?"

"Of course. We can talk about the plan while we do it."

"I CAN'T BELIEVE I'M FUCKING DOING THIS," I SAY, MY hands clenched around Dakota's so tightly I think she's losing circulation. "Why am I doing this? A tattoo is fine but, holy *fuck*—" I grip her hands tighter as the needle pierces my nipple.

"I thought you were supposed to be the brave one," Dakota says, her voice teasing.

I breathe deeply as the woman laughs lightly, her hands stilling as she inserts the jewelry into the tip and slides it back through my nipple. "I still bleed, Dakota." I grit my teeth as she twists the diamond onto the other end of the piercing, another wave of pain shooting through me. "I'm brave, and still a fucking wimp when it comes to needles," I finish when I can breathe again.

"Great job," the piercer says. "You did amazing, and you look sexy as hell too."

I look down at my freshly pierced nipples. They do look fucking hot.

"Thanks," I say, releasing Dakota's hand. "One down, one to go." I look at Dakota, my eyes conveying the slight fear I have of this next change.

"It's gonna be great," she says, smiling wide.

"I hope so," I mumble. *I fucking hope so.*

"I GET THE FEELING YOU JUST WANTED AN EXCUSE TO ride in my car," Damian says as he revs the engine, the car rushing forward down the long empty road.

"I did, but I also have something to talk to you about."

He looks at me from the side before slowing the car down and pulling off onto a side road. When he's fully stopped, I turn to look at him again, my body fully facing him.

"I have a proposal for you and you're going to think I'm crazy, but I swear, I'm not." I purse my lips as I wait for him to show any reaction.

A single eyebrow raise is what I get and I'm not disappointed. He runs a hand through his auburn hair, his back leaning into the door so he can face me.

I sigh, rubbing my hand up and down my jeans to calm my nerves. *Just spit it out.*

"I want you to date me," I say and immediately regret it. I sputter, trying to explain but instead, I feel like I'm looking ridiculous.

"What I mean is, I want you to *fake* date me. Dakota has this whole plan and she thinks that if we come out as an—" I throw up air quotations—"*official couple*, that it'll drive Jaiden to finally communicate his feelings. She said the guys are going to be working on him from the other side, but I told her I would at least try." I bite my lip as I look at him. Who knows if he even really finds me attractive enough to 'fake date'.

He eyes me before he leans forward, his body shaking with laughter. "Okay, that is *not* what I thought you were going to say. It is *so* much better." He laughs, his body continuing to shake with the intensity. His hand smacks the steering wheel and the horn honks.

I can feel my cheeks heat with embarrassment. *You're a bad bitch, so act like one.* I start to speak when he holds a hand up.

"Of course, I'll date you. I'll be your whore any day. But I have a question for you."

"Uh—Yeah?"

"Do you want to do this to help Jaiden or to piss him off? Or even to win him back? I'd like to be aware of your intentions so I can play my part properly."

My eyes widen at his bluntness. "I mean… I do want to help Jaiden. I still fucking hate his guts, but a piece of me still has *feelings* for him." I shiver. "I do enjoy pissing him off, though."

"Okay, then. I'm down for some dirty dangles."

I laugh, my body shaking unexpectedly. "Okay." I confirm. "We may need some rules though."

"Rules?" His mouth quirks upward, a mischievous smile crossing his face.

"Yes, rules, Damian. I'm not having sex with you, but I also am not above leading Jaiden to believe we are."

"Okay, no sex, but we can fake it. What else?"

"PDA is fine, but only if we've done it before and we're both comfortable."

He smirks before leaning in and smacking a rather unromantic and wet kiss on my lips. I'm disappointed to admit I felt nothing. I haven't felt any sort of vagina tingles or sparks of chemistry since my time with Jaiden. *Damn him.*

"There. Now our first kiss is out of the way. What next?" He wipes his lips and I frown at him which only causes him to laugh.

"What are the sleeping arrangements when we get there?" I tap a finger on my leg, my heart beat rising as I worry more about sharing a space with Jaiden.

"Whatever you want it to be."

"This is so much easier than I had anticipated. Uhm, I guess that's it for now, and if I think of anything I'll... text you?" I bite my nail—an old habit of mine—and turn to look back to the road.

"Sounds like a plan, *fake* girlfriend." He winks, turning over the engine and lurching the car forward again.

I lay my head back, enjoying the freedom of allowing someone else to be in control for a moment. It's a wonderful feeling to experience the speed of the car, the worries of the day dissipating.

There's two things left on my list that I've been avoiding. It's time to kill two birds with one stone.

DAMIAN PULLS UP TO THE CURB OF THE SALON, MY BODY shaking with anxiety by the time I make it to the door.

As I pull it open, I spot Lani seated on the couch. She waves at me as I walk toward her.

"Hey, babes," she says, pulling me into her.

"Hey! Thanks for being my emotional support for this." I give her a squeeze before releasing her. "Let me check in and I'll be back." I walk to the desk, giving the receptionist my name before walking back to the couch where Lani is sitting.

"I have something I need to talk to you about," I say, biting my lip lightly. This conversation can go any direction and it honestly scares me. "So, look, I know you're with Dane and you've been having problems, and I don't know what's going on with that fully but I want to be considerate of your feelings." My hands run through my long hair for the last time, my anxiety spiking a bit.

"Dakota talked to me already," she says, her eyes not giving away any of her feelings. "And honestly, I have a boyfriend so I can't be jealous. Damian is great, but it's inappropriate for me to tell you no. Plus, I'm inviting Dane with us. I think it'll be good to get away together." She smiles lightly and something tugs at my heart.

"Are you sure? I will call everything off. I just want you to be comfortable."

"Definitely. I'm with Dane and that's that." She nods, her tone set with finality.

I grab her hand and give it a squeeze. "Okay, then." I smile at her right as the hair stylist calls me back. "It's time," I say with anxiety.

Goodbye, long hair. You've been good to me.

EIGHT

JAIDEN

I'M DREAMING. I swear to the God above that I'm dreaming as I pull my Jeep beside Wyatt's Bronco. This is not at all what I was expecting when Dakota was raving about a lake house in Niagara-on-the-Water.

What the fuck do her parents do? The moment I think it, a beat of frustration rushes through me. That's a detail for a relationship, one I never earned because I'm a *coward.* I don't even know why I never asked. Even as a best friend, I should've asked about something like this.

She'd always been touchy when it came to her parents, and I'd gotten the idea that they neglected her. But even so, I feel angry at myself for never asking.

There's not many things in my life I regret, but after our blow up over dinner, I felt the regret flood in at full force. It took a long time to decide to actually come. And it took even longer to come up with an apology that didn't sound rehearsed. I think I owe her at least that. Maybe I can even afford to be nice to her. We're stuck in this place for three months and this is *her* home. She'll be unavoidable, so I best make peace now.

We're going to have *so* much fun. I roll my eyes at my own sarcasm as I dismount from my Jeep.

I take a moment to admire the house. *House? More like a mansion.* The exterior is a mix of wood and rough stone, giving it somewhat of a modern log cabin feel. Though that really doesn't do it justice—this is something straight out of a magazine.

The tire on the back of my SUV rattles as I slam the trunk shut, my duffle bag and suitcase gripped tightly in my hands. I'm thankful that Wyatt and Dakota are currently the only ones here. I've got another hour or so to be free of Sterling.

Unwanted jealousy rushes through me at the thought of her driving up with another man. That's what he is right now—another man. *Some best friend he is.*

I curse myself for the feeling, but unfortunately, jealousy is pretty much all I've been feeling these days. I'll brush it off much like I always do.

When the front door swings open, I blink letting my eyes adjust to the lighting. It gives me a moment to look over the interior of the house. It's much like the exterior: the wood and stone; the quadrants of the home split by the staircase to the second story; a smaller one going down to what I'd assume to be a basement or lower level. There are so many windows, making this place a lighting dream. Its openness makes it feel welcoming; I suppose that will change once ice queen Elsa walks through those doors.

Walking around the staircase, I drag my luggage with me. Dakota and Wyatt are sitting on the back deck, their heads barely visible over the reclining chairs. Dropping my bags, I walk through the door to the enclosed porch and out onto the back deck.

They look like they're having a moment and I don't want to interrupt, but *wow*.

"Holy shit," I mumble, keeping my voice low to avoid attention.

It's truly incredible. I can't help but take in the view of the water and the dock that extends far out into the water. To think that people live in places like this all the time is wild. I've always lived in big cities, and this...this is incredible. It's truly a luxury to be away from that city feel for even a moment.

My lungs fill with fresh air and I close my eyes, enjoying a moment of peace.

"I know," Dakota says, her voice breaking me out of my moment. She's got her head rested on Wyatt's shoulder, their entangled hands resting on his thigh. They're the picture of love, and it's disgustingly cute. "I'm getting married here," she says with excitement.

"You came here when you were younger?" I walk into view, nodding to Wyatt before I sit on the edge of the chair next to them.

"Yep. Sterling invited me for the summers when her family was here. It was usually just me and Sterling left to get into trouble, but sometimes her parents joined us. I have a lot of good memories here." She looks over at me, her eyes slightly glassy. I can see how much this place means to her. I wish I had something like it—a place that holds happy memories.

The rickety trailer I grew up in is the farthest thing from a keeper of happy memories. We never had a home. It was always the trailer and roach infested apartments.

I'm lucky I made it to college. Kids from my neighborhood have the reputation of becoming nobodies. It's why I refused to let that follow me.

Having a multi-million dollar contract for hockey doesn't feel real sometimes. My ma worked hard, and we got by, but I look back often and see how far I've come. I spoiled her as much as I could while she was alive. It was my honor to give back to the woman who gave *everything* to me.

I sigh, looking firmly at Wyatt. "I never got to apologize to you both. I'm sorry for how I behaved at dinner the other night, and I promise to be on my best behavior during this trip."

Wyatt and Dakota exchange a look, their eyes glimmering before they both look back at me. "It's all good, bro," Wyatt says. "But we appreciate it." He kisses the top of Dakota's head before standing. "Let me show you to your room."

He leads me back through the double doors and into the house until we reach the stairs. He points up the stairs and down the hall.

"Dakota and I are sharing the master. Lily is set up in the kids' room next to Roman's." We continue walking through the maze of rooms. He points into another room. "Lani and Dane are in this room and their bathroom is across the hall."

Peeking my head inside as we pass, I notice that the rooms are all themed differently, alternating between water and wilderness decor. Either her parents or their decorator knew what they were doing. Even I can appreciate the effort that went into the decor.

I hardly notice when we turn a corner and pass a movie and game room. *Of course a place like this would have a built-in movie theater.*

We've made a full loop now, stopping in front of the smaller staircase before taking the steps two at a time down toward the basement. I lift my suitcase to avoid it scratching the stairs.

"How many levels does this house have?" I watch my feet as we walk, being sure to not miss a step. It isn't until the ceiling lowers that I nearly miss ducking my head to avoid the dip.

"Three and a half. There's a half loft on the top floor. It's like it was added after the original building of the home." Wyatt descends the last stair and takes a left. "This whole floor loops around in a circle, so it doesn't matter which way you go. Damian is here, Sterling's in this room, and this is you." He points at all three rooms as we pass them. It's only then that I realize that I'm between Damian and Sterling. Why the hell did they put me between Damian and Sterling's rooms? *Fucking hell.*

I look down the hall before following him into the room he pointed out as mine.

"What's down there?" I ask, pointing toward the lone door under the balcony. It's out of the way enough to be obscure, but obvious enough to draw me in.

"Oh, you'll love this." Wyatt sets my bag down on the floor by my bed, waiting for me to do the same, before leading me down the hall toward the door.

"The previous owners were parents to a hockey player. They

used to spend summers here, I guess." He pushes the door open to reveal an indoor hockey rink.

Oh, hell yes.

"We're supposed to stay away from the ice in the off season," I say, ogling the indoor rink.

"Yeah, well, a couple of times won't hurt." He raises his brows at me, and I laugh.

"I guess you're right. What Coach doesn't know won't hurt him." I wink before shoving my hands into my jogger pockets.

It's a small rink compared to what we skate on normally, but it's large enough for the four of us to skate comfortably. I've never seen something like this, and I'm truly in awe.

Wyatt turns to me, still holding the door open. "By the way, we made meal plans so that everyone's cooking during the week. Considering this is bonding time, family dinners sounded good. We already went into town and grabbed food, but feel free to get whatever you need."

I eye him with a little bit of apprehension. Family dinners again already, huh?

"I'm making tri-tip on the grill tonight for sandwiches. Do you mind helping?"

I shake my head. "Not at all. Are we doing that now?"

"You've got a bit to get settled first. I want to start before everyone gets here, though." He nods back toward my room and I thank him before retreating to my room.

The moment I close the door, my eyes swing to the bookshelf built into the wall on the opposite side of the room. The shelves break around a window, a reading nook built beneath it like a bridge between the shelves and the window. There's no way that this room was given to me without thought. With my current reading addiction, the nook is perfect for me and it even looks long enough that I could stretch my legs out.

Making quick work of unpacking my things, I close the door to my room and wander through the rest of the home until I eventually make my way outside. It would be easy to lose myself to this place. It's beautiful in every way possible.

"Enjoying the view?" Dakota walks to my side, staring out onto the water.

"It's gorgeous. I can see why you'd love it here."

"Can I ask you something?" She looks up at me, her arms crossed in front of her.

She looks so small from this angle. It's no secret that she's been vertically challenged since the moment we met, but standing next to her makes me feel like a giant—though I often feel like a giant in general. There's a small percentage of the population that's as tall as my friends and me, and unfortunately that small population does not frequent Boston. *No, the weather is not different up here. Yes, I have large feet and hands, and you know what they say about men with big hands.*

"Go ahead."

"Did you mean to hurt my best friend?"

I freeze, my blood running cold at the bluntness of her question.

"No, I didn't. It was my own stupidity that got in the way," I say honestly.

"Then how did it get this bad?" The corners of her mouth pull into a frown. She's not angry, but I can see the pain there. She's the peacekeeper and the lover of the group—conflict doesn't sit well with her.

"Can I tell you something? Please don't say anything to Sterling. I need this to be something I tell her."

"Of course. I hope you know that I'm always here to talk and listen, Jaiden. You protected me and helped me, and I'll do the same for you."

I sigh, feeling the swell of emotion in my throat. "The week everything went to shit, I got a letter from my father. He abandoned us when I was little, but my mom never failed to remind me that I was just like him. It wasn't meant to be an insult or harmful, but it came off that way." I kick at a rock, aiming for the water. "Anyway, he reminded me where I come from and that I may be some hotshot hockey player, but I'm still that loser whose father left him. That's even after everything I did to set him up with a new life after his addiction forced him out of his job and left him homeless. I'm still this bastard child to him.'" I pause, kicking another rock. "I don't think I'm capable of giving her what she wants."

"You're not your father, Jaiden. I've seen you do incredible things. And I think Sterling would understand this better than you think."

"That's what scares me," I mumble.

She pats me on the back. "Just...be careful with her heart when, or if, you decide to talk with her. She's not as brave and confident as she lets on."

Before I can say anything more, she turns and walks away, leaving me alone with my thoughts and the cool breeze of Niagara-on-the-Lake.

"UNCLE WYATT!" LILY SCREAMS AS SHE RUNS THROUGH the back porch and out onto the grass where we're grilling.

"What am I? Chopped liver?" I flip the meat on the grill just as Lily collides with Wyatt's legs before he picks her up and spins her around.

"Hey, beautiful girl," he says, beaming at our niece. This man is absolutely meant to be a father.

"What about me?" I ask, giving her a pouty face. Wyatt releases her and she runs toward me.

"Careful!" Roman yells from a distance. "No running near hot things!"

"Hi, Uncle Jai!"

The smile she gives me is the best thing ever. After upsetting her, I'd apologized profusely until she'd ran away only to return with homemade brownies she and Roman had made. It was a solid peace offering and I definitely didn't deserve it, but that's just who she is.

I grip her waist and lift her above my head to fly her like an airplane. Her little giggles fill the air and I find it comforting.

"More! More! More!" she yells when I put her down.

I chuckle, picking her up once again. "I gotta watch the meat, sweet girl, but real fast, okay?"

She nods profusely before I spin her around again. When I finally set her down, I see Lani standing next to someone I don't recognize.

"Go ahead," Wyatt says. "I'll bring the food inside. It's almost done."

Lily holds my hand as she pulls me back toward the house. I look up at the porch, my eyes squinting as I try to get a better view of the two women.

It's only when she turns that I realize who it is. Her hair is a pale silvery-blond, cut short, right above her shoulders. When she turns fully, I see a panel of chestnut, the last bit of the Sterling I knew, resting at the front of her head and a small strand under her left ear. It's like a harlequin checker that covers half her bangs, maybe to remind her of where she came from or who she once was. The woman standing before me is different, besides that single strip of brown.

I stand, staring at her in awe. She's Sterling by name, but now she's also Silver at heart, owning the nickname she's so fiercely protected. Silver is someone she reserves for people she loves, and I used to be one of those people.

Yeah, maybe she's Sterling Bexley legally, but right now, I only see Silver, the woman I hurt. She's absolutely beautiful. My heart clenches in my chest as Lily drags me forward.

It's only then that I see who's hand is joined with hers. A rush of jealousy and red-hot anger rushes through me once more.

NINE

STERLING

RAGE IS the only description I have for Jaiden's face. It's lit up by pure rage. He doesn't even try to hide it.

Lily drags him toward us, and panic rushes through me. This was all fun and games before, but now it feels very real. It might still be a game to Damian, but to me…The stakes feel different now.

"Auntie Sterling," Lily screams, releasing Jaiden's hand and barreling toward our group. That girl runs on pure energy. I don't know how Roman keeps up with her. She's got total golden retriever energy, making everyone feel special by the way she greets you.

I drop Damian's hand and squat to the ground so that she runs right into my arms. When she collides with me, I fall backward lightly, but Damian's legs step behind my back to support me. I look up at him in thanks, then pepper little kisses on Lily's head.

"Hey, princess. I've missed you."

She squeals in delight. *So much squealing.* "You look so pretty," she says, running her hands through my hair.

"Why, thank you. So do you." I hold her hand, guiding her to do a little spin for me. She's decked out in ripped jeans and a baseball tee. She's adorable and I want to be her. This kid is more stylish than us all.

When a shadow descends over us, I look up to see Jaiden staring down at me. I breathe deeply as I wait for words to come out of his mouth.

"Your hair looks nice," he says. It's the first kind thing he's said to me in a while and it hits me like a ton of bricks.

"Uh, thanks. It was time for a change." *And you said you liked my hair long.*

Everyone has dispersed around the porch or back inside the house, Lily slipping from my hand and running toward her dad and Dakota.

Rising from my crouch, I blink as the light meets my eyes again. I look around for Damian and see him talking with Wyatt. *Thanks for abandoning me.*

"I had eight hours of a drive and I was thinking—"

"Oh, there are thoughts in that brain of yours?" I quip, and the corner of his lips turn up. I'll count that as a win.

"Yes, smartass, I do think. Occasionally. I'm not always an idiot. I was thinking that we should call a truce."

I narrow my eyes at him. Is he serious? "Oh, Jaiden. Sweet, naive Jaiden." I run a hand down his arm and his head dips to watch my fingers. "There's no way I'm making it that easy for you."

A sexy smirk crosses his face and I swear I feel my pussy flutter. *Fuck me.*

"Good," he says, leaning into my ear. "I wasn't expecting it to be easy." His hand slides up my back and into my hair. His fingers swirl there and I momentarily forget where I am. Is this my off switch? Someone playing with my hair?

"It's still long enough for me to pull while I fuck you from behind," he whispers into my ear.

It's totally out of pocket, but damn, does it make me feel something. "I wasn't aware you wanted that," I say, my voice weak.

He doesn't answer, just pulls back to look me in the eye. It's almost like he's allowing me to see inside his brain, but I want him to say the words. That's what this game is all about.

"You should let go of me now," I say, stepping away from him slightly.

"And why's that?"

"Babe!" Damian yells from a distance and I turn to look at him. I can see the amusement on his face and I wave at him. He nods his head toward the dock and I hold up a finger, turning back to Jaiden.

That mask has slipped back over his face. He's cold and indifferent. It upsets me to see him like this. I think I preferred it when, like a moment ago, I could see the burning jealousy.

"Eight months I waited for you," I say, turning away from him. I hope it hits where I want it to.

Walking away, I feel my heart tug in the opposite direction. My stomach twists as I step into Damian's arms. He places a kiss onto the top of my head as we walk out onto the dock. It takes everything in me not to turn back, but instead I continue walking with my fake boyfriend, the hope stirring that maybe, just maybe, Jaiden will finally want *me.*

DINNER IS TENSE, TO SAY THE LEAST.

Jaiden doesn't speak... *much.* Instead, he stares at me, his grip tighter than usual on his fork as he shovels the mac salad into his mouth. I catch a glimpse of the sharp point of his incisors each time he chews and my stupid brain can't stop thinking about running my tongue across them.

It's still long enough for me to pull as I fuck you from behind.

How fucking... *hot.*

No.

Not hot. Definitely not hot.

Okay, it was *really* fucking hot, but I need to get it together. I have a 'boyfriend' now. *Act like it, bitch.*

I look across the table. As little bits of chatter pass between us, I watch Lani and Dane. He's a blond-haired, blue-eyed man. Dane is unimpressive, if you ask me and I've always felt like they've looked rather mismatched. She's all color, her punk rocker look her biggest identifier. Lame Dane on the other hand... At first I enjoyed his company, but lately, that stick has been shoved so far up his ass I don't know where it got lost.

Even now as we sit at dinner, he barely converses with the group.

"So, Dane. How's work been?"

He looks up from his food, his face neutral as he eyes me. I lived with this man for months while my apartment was under construction—you'd think he'd be nicer to me.

"It's fine," he says. "Busy."

I swap glances with Dakota before I catch Lani elbowing Dane. I know she wants him to participate, but he looks like he really doesn't want to be here.

I sigh, taking another bite of food.

"Uncle Wyatt!" Lily says from the other side of Jaiden.

The whole table stops to look at her.

"Yes, Bug?"

"Did you hear that my daddy got into a fight with my teacher?" She smiles, blinking several times.

Roman claps a hand over his mouth as he chokes, coughing. Dakota brings her lips together to stifle her laughter and I lock eyes with her. She snorts and I can't help but giggle a bit.

"He did?" Wyatt asks, barely stopping his laughter from escaping.

"Yeah. My classmates were being mean to me and then Daddy came in to rescue me, but he and Miss Sharpe fought because Daddy has power issues."

It's me who laughs this time. I bring my shirt up to cover my mouth as I laugh into it, attempting to hide my face.

"Where did you hear that I have power issues, Lily?"

"Miss Sharpe. She was saying it to a TA when she thought I wasn't listening."

"Oh, I'm going to have to talk to that woman when we get home," Roman says, and the whole table bursts with laughter.

"He's met his match," Jaiden says through broken laughter.

"You were there?" Wyatt asks. He swipes at his eyes and Dakota hands him a napkin.

"We got the call while we were shopping for the cookie ingredients. I got a front-row seat for the show."

"Man, why didn't you tell me? That's epic."

Jaiden freezes, looking at him, unsure of what to say. It's awkward for a moment until Lani jumps in and changes the subject.

The conversation picks up again. I lock eyes with Jaiden, not paying attention to the chatter around us much. Damian's hand slips over my thigh, his thumb rubbing circles there. I'll admit that it's weird, but not because of the affectionate way he's touching me. It's because of the new pretenses in which he's touching me. We're supposed to be a couple now and I feel like I'm doing a shit job at acting like it.

When dinner is done, I sit in the movie room with Dakota and Lani. The guys are in the game room playing some new video game that they bought.

"How hard was it to get Dane to come with you?"

Lani sighs, her head rolling slightly before she looks at me. "I'll be lucky if he even stays a month. He's just so not into this. I thought it would be good for us to have the time all together. Plus, I really want him to get to know the guys." She looks out of the door toward the back of the home. Dane sits alone on a chair, his laptop pressed to his lap as he types away.

I'm suddenly thankful that she's here with us instead of sitting out there with him. I've needed time with my girls desperately, and I'm mad that he's ruining her time here.

She leans her head onto me and I pat her shoulder before running my fingers through her hair. Dakota clearly feels left out so she leans onto my other shoulder and I laugh.

"Can you believe Lily outed Roman like that over dinner?" Dakota stifles a snort and I look over at her.

"I totally can. I think Lily is smarter than we all give her credit for." I think about the way Roman turned bright red at Lily's proclamation. It was incredible.

"That girl is totally blunt. I love it." Lani slaps her leg as she laughs.

"I need to tell you both something," I say, leaning back into my recliner to look at both of them.

I recap my interaction with Jaiden earlier and they both stare at me, momentarily stunned. Suddenly, they're both laughing uncontrollably.

"Oh, he's got it so bad," Dakota wheezes, leaning forward and almost falling from her chair.

"I fucking knew it," Lani shrieks along side her.

"Knew what?" I wail.

"He wouldn't last a fucking moment not saying something to you. You look so fucking hot, how could you not?" Lani wipes tears out of her eyes.

"He really said that to you?" Dakota's mouth quivers as she looks at me, trying to hold back her laughs.

"He did. And it was really fucking hot," I admit.

They burst into laughter again. "You kinky bitch," Dakota says.

"Like you can talk, miss hockey-stick-headboard-and-dick-piercing." I glare at her, my face fighting a smile.

Dakota wheezes. "The dick piercing is so fucking great."

"I wouldn't know."

"Ha! And you never will. He's mine." Dakota points her finger at me. She moves closer to boop my nose and that's when I finally lose it.

"Why," *wheeze*, "the fuck," *wheeze*, "did you *boop* my nose?" I shake my head at her and she just laughs, kicking her legs up into the air.

Lani slides off her chair when she tries to do the same, and it sends us into another fit of laughter.

"Woah! What the hell is happening here?" Jaiden and Wyatt

stand in the doorway watching us. Damian appears behind them, resting his arm across Wyatt's shoulders.

"How do we get them to stop? They're so damn loud." Jaiden frowns, crossing his arms over his chest.

"There's a whole damn house for you to occupy. Find a quieter spot," I say, but Dakota falls forward, laughing as she wheezes.

She yanks on my hair as she falls and I laugh harder. "Did that work?" she asks from the floor.

"Are you drunk?" Damian asks.

"Not even close," I say, but I don't miss the way Jaiden's eyebrows raise at me, his eyes darkening slightly.

I'm so fucked.

TEN

JAIDEN

FOOTSTEPS SOUND across the hall and I curse myself for leaving my door open. Lani and Dane have already retreated to their room, so the only two people left to return are Sterling and Damian. Unfortunately for me, it definitely sounds like two pairs of feet.

I shouldn't be listening in, but I can't help it when I hear her voice. After all these months, I can't seem to get my body or heart to behave. My fucking head is the only one whipped into shape. My body, though? It reacts to the sound of her voice, to the nearness of her every time she enters a room. It's some fucking shit, honestly.

You're too late.

Yeah… We'll see about that.

"You sure you don't want to sleep with me?"

I don't want to spy, and I *know* I really shouldn't, but if I lean my body just a bit to the right, I have an almost perfect view of them. As I lean, trying not to make any noise, I can see Damian leaning against the door frame.

"I'm sure. I need to decompress from the trip. I'll see you in the morning." Sterling leans in, rising onto her tiptoes to meet his mouth. They kiss, and I hate myself for watching them. She doesn't bite his lip, though, or twirl a hand into his hair. Instead, she just kisses him in a way that screams vanilla. *I never thought of Damian being vanilla.*

When they pull apart, Damian turns his face in my direction, a smug look across his face.

I ball my hands into fists before climbing off the bed, stomping to the door and slamming it shut.

"The fuck?" Sterling says from the other side of the door. "Real mature."

Idiot.

Day one: Sterling-1, Jaiden-0.

If this is how it's going to be, I'd better prepare for battle. Truce, my ass.

THE SUN BARELY PEEKS THROUGH THE BLINDS IN MY room before I'm up and out the front door. Sweat drips down my back as I run along the lake. It's beautiful at this time of the morning, the light glistening off the calm waters of Lake Ontario.

What I've learned in my short time here is that many of the homes sit right up against the water. There's enough space between them for privacy, but they're close enough to be considered neighbors.

I don't know how far I've run, just that I've seen several properties, many of which house people sitting on the porch, watching the sun rise.

When I finally turn around and head back in the direction I came from, I peel off my shirt, letting the breeze cool me down. The sound of the rocks crunching beneath my feet fuels my run, urging me on. It's not until I see bright sunset hair that I realize that the women are up, too.

Dakota and Lani step into a yoga position with such fluidity that it looks like they're synchronized. When I see Sterling helping Lily, my heart clenches.

They laugh as Lily wiggles around a bit before moving into the next pose.

I try not to stare, but it's hard not to. Sterling's ass is right in my line of sight, her hand stabilizing Lily even as she does her own downward dog pose.

My pace slows by the dock. I'm panting lightly and end up walking until they're no longer in my view. The sounds of the waves crashing distract me before I hear the creak of the dock behind me. I turn and see Wyatt walking toward me, with Roman following close behind.

"Hey, man." Wyatt says, his hand gripping his coffee mug. Before I can reply, he nudges my arm with the spare coffee in his other hand. I take it gratefully, letting the steam hit my face.

"Mornin'" I reply, turning back to the water.

"We're hitting the golf course today and the ladies are staying here. You down?"

"I guess. I was thinking about going for a swim."

"Got the rest of the day for that," Roman chimes in. He looks back at the women, checking on Lily. They're still doing yoga on the back lawn, laughing whenever someone falls.

"Or the rest of the summer," I mumble, and Roman nudges my arm.

"That's the spirit," he says, the smile audible in his voice. "The course opens at ten. Be ready to go." He turns, leaving Wyatt and me alone.

"How are you doing?"

"My head's fucked," I admit with a sigh.

"Why?" He runs a hand through his hair, pressing it back as he looks at me.

"I can't do this whole relationship thing. People I care for get hurt, and losing my mom fucked me up. And the shit with my dad... But—" I groan, rubbing my hands down my face.

"But?"

"I can't get that damn girl out of my head," I say. "*But* now she's moved on with Damian. Fucking *Damian.* He's never been in a relationship the whole time I've known him."

"I think he's gotten tired of the bunnies." He crosses his hands across his chest. "Why now, after you had months to figure this shit out?"

"Seeing her moving on makes her statement that I've lost her seem all too real, and I don't want it to be. I guess I had to experience it to kick my ass in gear."

"So, what? You want her now? Like a relationship, or just as a fuck buddy again?"

I purse my lips, shaking my head. "I just want her. But I still don't know if I can give her what she wants."

Wyatt grabs my shirt from my hands and whacks me with it. "You're an idiot. Stop saying that." He whacks me again and I shield myself with my arms.

"Hey!" I yell, stepping away from him.

"You keep saying that you can't give her what she wants, but that's just an excuse not to do the work. Relationships are hard, and you just gotta commit to putting in the effort to *make* it work." He wraps my shirt around his hand. "Look, man. I know that losing your mom was hard for you, but that's life. People die, relationships end, people get hurt, but how would you know without taking the risk? Is she worth the risk to you?"

Is she worth the risk? Is Sterling someone I'd risk my sanity and comfort for?

I've already risked my sanity for her.

"Yeah," I mumble. "She is."

"Then do the fucking work. Don't be an idiot." He smirks before he whacks me again and I grab the shirt and yank it from him. He chuckles when I smack his ass with it.

"I deserved that."

"Yeah, well, I also deserved it. What the fuck am I supposed to do?"

Wyatt winks, turning away from me. "You'll figure it out."

Piling out of Wyatt's Bronco, the guys chat, laughing about the way Damian tossed his club across the course in a true rookie move. It was quite entertaining and comforting to learn that fucker isn't good at everything.

I still glare at him, despite the fact I want to laugh. I thought we were friends. Doesn't it go against bro code to date your friend's ex? Well, I guess she isn't really my ex.

I'm about to pull Damian aside to talk when I think better of it. Maybe this is a conversation for another time. It's barely been a full twenty-four hours of vacation.

The guys walk into the house and I follow them until we see the ladies sitting on the floor of the living room in a circle. There are piles of colorful beads surrounding Lily, her arm decorated in beaded bracelets.

"Daddy!" she exclaims, her eyes lighting up.

"Boys," Dakota says. "Please sit. We have presents." She's got stacked bracelets going up her arms, almost as if she were going to a rave.

"What do we have here?" Wyatt asks, leaning against the frame of the living room.

"We made bracelets for each of you. Lily has her own, and then we decided on special bracelets from the adults." She gestures to the couch. "Sit, please."

I remain standing for as long as possible, waiting for the others to get comfortable until I sit at the edge of the U-shaped couch.

"Go ahead, Lily." Dakota presses a hand to her back as she stands.

She's carrying a stack of beaded bracelets as she walks toward Roman.

"Daddy, this ones for you. They're good luck charms so that you will win." Her little hand extends, dropping a bracelet into his palm. He examines it, smiling before he pulls her into his arms and plants a kiss onto her cheeks.

"Thank you, babygirl. I love it."

She stops in front of Damian, handing him a bracelet next.

"Thank you," he says. "How did you know I love music?" He winks before showing the bracelet to Roman. I can see the little wiggle of the charms she added.

"I'm smart," Lily says matter-of-factly. She's not wrong. That girl is intelligent as hell.

Walking to Wyatt, she hands him his bracelet and I see the rock-paper-scissors charms on his bracelet. It brings a smile to my face. This girl has my whole heart, and for being so young, she gets us.

The thought sends a pang through my chest. I've been doing wrong by Sterling. I don't want Lily to see her Uncle Jaiden being an asshole; I want her to be proud of me. Roman was right about leading by example.

Wyatt thanks her, pulling her into his arms and kissing her head. She giggles as she disentangles herself and stops in front of me.

"Uncle Jaiden," she says as she hands me my bracelet.

I look down at it, laughing when I see the pair of fairy wings. "Thanks, princess." I kiss her forehead, slipping my bracelet over my hand and onto my wrist. "I'm never taking it off."

Dakota slips another bracelet into Lily's hand. "Don't forget this one."

I peek over at the bracelet as she slips it onto Wyatt's wrist. He releases a full belly laugh, leaning back into the couch as he laughs.

I gasp in mock outrage. "I *knew* you had favorites," I say as Lily giggles.

Wyatt is sporting a new bracelet, one that reads *Bestie* across the front in square beads.

"I'm offended. Very hurt, Lily. I thought I was your favorite." I pretend to cry and she leans over, placing a kiss on my cheek.

"They made me do it," Lily says, pointing her hands to the girls behind her. They're all standing with their hands shaped in halos above their heads.

"That is the perfect segue into our bracelets for you," Sterling says with a wicked gleam in her eyes. "Lani, you can go first."

"Since Dane is working, I made your bracelet, courtesy of Silver." Her cheeks turn pink as she slips the bracelet onto Damian's wrist.

"BDE," he says with a chuckle. "Damn right."

"I would know," Sterling says with a wink, and Damian smirks.

That lightness that was there a moment ago is replaced by something darker. Green jealousy creeps through my blood as I watch their exchange.

"This one's for you, my love," Dakota says, stepping between Wyatt's legs and kissing him. Sterling gags and I catch her eyes before she looks away from me.

Wyatt throws his head back laughing.

"Are we wrong, though? You totally have bi-wife energy," Lani says from the side and we all laugh.

"You do, bro," I say before he narrows his eyes at me. "Best bride ever." He looks like he wants to whack me again so I scoot away from him and he laughs.

"Please tell me you didn't teach my daughter the meaning of this!" Roman's eyes go wide as he looks at his bracelet.

The whole room erupts in laughter as we see the *DILF* bracelet on his wrist.

"It means Daddy is a little fun." Lily's eyes look concerned as she glances around the room. The girls snicker as Roman sags in relief.

"Yes, baby. That's *exactly* what it means."

I'm thoroughly entertained until Sterling stops in front of me and drops a bracelet into my lap. It reads *clown* in big letters with a shrimp charm beside it.

"What does this even mean?" I mumble.

"It's because that shrimp dick should really be a circus attraction." Sterling says it low enough for only Wyatt and I to hear. Wyatt coughs, covering his laugh, but I only glare up at her with heat in my eyes.

"I didn't know this was a roast," I reply. "But you of all people know that isn't true."

"Do I?" She shrugs, turning away and handing a bracelet to Dakota. "For you, babes."

Dakota clutches her wrist to her hand. "It's perfect." She extends her wrist to Wyatt, showing her the *SMUTSLUT* bracelet.

He laughs, shaking his head, but I don't get the joke.

"It's a thing," Lani says to me. "We read smut, so it's like a girl tribe. Don't question it."

I nod my head. *Got it.*

They continue exchanging bracelets between them, the ladies laughing at each other's words. Lily's says *babyface* and she wasn't a fan, claiming that she is indeed a big girl.

"You're growing up too fast, Bean, but you're right. You're practically an adult at this point." Roman pulls her hair away from her face as she sits in his lap. She raises her chin at his comment, seemingly content with his answer.

Sterling's says *HOEDOWN* with a camera charm and she bursts into laughter when she receives it. "Y'all know me so well," she says.

I can't believe we're bonding over beaded bracelets.

"Best for last," Sterling says as she gives Lani hers.

"What does it say?" Lily asks from Roman's lap.

"BFB," Lani says, smiling.

"It means best fucking bitch," Sterling whisper yells, and Roman slaps his hands over Lily's ears.

"She repeats *everything,* y'all. I really don't need her teacher yelling at me for her calling her friends BFB's."

"Sorry," Sterling laughs, her eyes squinted and her cheeks full with her smile.

I think back to my conversation with Wyatt this morning. It's that smile that I miss the most. I miss when that smile was because of me, something I did, whether it was knowingly or just because we were together.

It was so easy with her before, having her sit on my lap in the bar or her legs draped across me as we watched movies. It was never that easy with anyone, until her. With her, I was just Jaiden and not some hot-shot hockey player.

I watch her as she laughs, Lani playing music and dancing around the room. It isn't until Damian stands and sways with Sterling that I'm reminded of the work I need to do. I don't know what the fuck she wants, but this summer isn't going to be all fun and games. If she wants Prince Charming, then Prince Charming I will be.

ELEVEN

STERLING

HUSHED VOICES CREEP through the hallway as I walk out of my room. It's coming from Lani and Dane's room and I don't want to snoop, but I can't help myself.

Lame Dane has been keeping to himself all week instead of spending time with the group. At this point, I've all but forgotten he even exists, which is honestly fucked up. Lani deserves better and I'm angry for her.

The voices rise, Lani huffing a defeated sounding *fine* before yanking the door open. I startle, turning my body like I wasn't snooping, but when I turn back to her, I see her swiping at her face.

"Hey," she says, a sad smile filling her face.

"You okay?" I walk to her side and lean my head on her shoulder.

"I'm fine. I'm just frustrated. I wanted him to come and be here with all of us, but instead he's holed up, working on whatever he can find."

"Want me to yell at him for you? I will, and I won't even feel bad about it."

She laughs weakly. "No, it's okay. I'll manage."

I grip her hand, weaving our fingers together. "If you change your mind, you know where to find me."

We walk out onto the deck, the outdoor volleyball court set up in the sandy area. Dakota and Wyatt are already on the court, passing the ball back and forth. I elbow Lani, winking at her as we walk closer.

"We're gonna kill this. The boys are going down."

"No fraternizing with the enemy," I yell at Dakota when she leans up to kiss Wyatt. He looks slightly dazed when she pulls away from him. I don't miss the way he squeezes her ass before she walks away. God, they're sickening, but I'm so damn happy for her.

"Ready to kick some ass?"

"Definitely." Dakota kicks some sand around, evening the surface.

"Alright, gang! Ladies versus men, with Lily and I as the refs. Make sure to keep it clean, please." Roman looks at all of us intently, that fatherly stare telling us all to behave.

"Got it, Coach," I yell with a mock salute. Roman rolls his eyes before pulling the whistle over his head.

I call the girls into a huddle. We stick our heads in, wrapping our arms around each other's backs.

"When do the shirts come off?" Lani asks.

"We'll strip on a signal. If we need the advantage, just tug at your ear and we'll strip. Make sure the signal is received, though. We need it to be a statement."

The girls both agree.

As we pull out of the huddle, we smack each other's asses for good luck, then assume positions.

"Alrighty then. Team names. Ladies?" Roman sits in his lifeguard chair looking down at us.

"Ball Busters," I reply with a smirk.

Roman coughs a laugh before turning to the guys.

"Team name?"

"Safe Sets," Damian supplies, winking at me.

I bring my fingers to my eyes then turn them on him. "Watch yourself, hottie. I'm comin' for you."

"Yeah, you are," he replies, and I swear I see Jaiden's fists clench.

Roman blows his whistle right before Dakota serves the ball. Damian sets it to Wyatt who hits it over the net and right to me.

It goes back and forth for a while, until the guys score a point. When Dakota serves again, Jaiden misses the ball, giving us a point.

The competition ramps up, the guys scoring another point as I dive to save the ball but miss it only by a hair.

Dakota growls and I laugh. That girl hates to lose.

"Wyatt Lane, the future of our relationship rests in this game. You better hope I win."

"Not a chance, babe," he yells. "I love you, though. Better win fair and square."

"I don't like you right now," she says, her head shaking.

We go again and again, the score tied before Lani and I collide into the net trying to save the ball.

"Fu— Fudge," I yell, kicking sand up.

"It's okay, babe. You're not a loser...yet." Damian winks and I glare back at him.

"Watch yourself, Damian."

Jaiden serves the ball, Lani jumping for it and setting it up.

"Got it," I yell, slamming it over the net.

"That's out," Roman yells.

"Oh, come on!" Dakota yells. "It was not."

Roman purses his lips and shakes his head. "It was."

"I hate losing. It's really unfair to be up against professionally trained athletes."

"It's not our fault you ladies are short."

"Excuse me," I say, slapping a hand onto my hip. "I'm not short. You all are just freakishly tall."

Jaiden smirks, slinging his arm over Wyatt's shoulder. Roman's got all of them beat by several inches, while the others all rest around the same height.

Lani raises her hand on my left. "I am definitely short." She laughs, her sunset hair brushing in front of her face when the wind blows.

"You're fun-sized," Damian says. "Fun-sized is best."

I have half a thought to yell something at him, but I don't. I watch Damian, my eyes sliding across the room until I see Jaiden watching me curiously. He raises an eyebrow and I turn away from him, tugging at my ear when I turn. Both Lani and Dakota nod.

"First team to twenty wins. Current standings are: Ball Busters have thirteen points, and Safe Sets have fifteen."

"Great," I hear Dakota mumble and I laugh.

Pulling my shirt off, I reveal my royal blue bikini. It makes my tits look amazing and my skin look radiant. I haven't seen it with my new hair, but by the way that Jaiden's jaw nearly drops to the floor, I think it looks pretty great.

"Damn," Damian says, looking between us. "That's not fair."

"Totally is," Lani says, smiling, her burnt orange bikini complimenting her hair beautifully.

Dakota's wearing emerald green and Wyatt looks about ready to end the game now. I'll be surprised if he *doesn't* waltz over here right now and sling her over his shoulder.

"Fuck," he says, running a hand through his beard. "I'm out, give them the win." Wyatt smirks as he trudges toward Dakota.

"Don't you dare," she screeches. "You said to win fair and square."

"And you did," he says, his voice deep. I step out of his way.

"Says who?" she asks, her hand pressed firmly on her hip.

"Says me." His voice is a growl now, and it sends a rush of jealousy through me.

I want that. I want that so bad.

Slinging her over his shoulder, he runs toward the water as she squeals.

"Wyatt," she yells and we all laugh.

I mentally take a picture of this moment, remembering the way my best friend looks so happy, her cheeks pink and her hair wild. It sparks an idea, and I smile toward the water.

"I guess we're swimming," Roman says from the chair.

Lani takes off toward the water after them, the guys quickly following.

"You coming?" she yells.

"No. Go ahead."

Walking to the deck, I lay my towel out onto the chair and sit down. I grabbed my camera earlier, hiding it beneath the chair, so when I loop the strap over my shoulder, I snap a few photos of Dakota and Wyatt. When I'm satisfied, I sit it aside, laying back, my arm slinging over my eyes to protect them from the sun. My body is warmed from the gentle kiss of the sun.

I love this.

Their voices fade as they play in the water. It isn't until a shadow blocks the sun that I peel an eye open. Jaiden stands over me, slipping into the chair beside me.

"Not in the mood to swim?"

"Nope." I close my eyes again, breathing deeply. There's silence for a moment before he speaks again.

"So, shrimp dick."

"What about it?" I don't open my eyes to look at him, instead I pretend he isn't there, like maybe he'll go away if I can't see him.

"I distinctly remember you telling me I was your biggest."

Sighing, I look over at him then. I can't deny him because he's right.

"Maybe I was lying." I bite my lip, hoping he won't spot my lie.

He eyes me curiously. "So, you've slept with someone bigger than me since we were together last?"

"Why does dick size matter?" I huff, my cheeks growing hot.

He leans over, his breath hot against my neck. "Because I take pride in being your best, being someone who sets the precedent for all your lovers."

"Why, Jaiden? So that you know that every person that comes after you sucks? I thought we were supposed to be in a truce. You want me to talk about my sex life? How about you talk about why you ghosted me, because *it's better this way* isn't a good enough answer for me. And if you can't offer me a better answer, then sure, let's discuss how Damian beats you in the dick department." I shrug, pursing my lips. "Maybe he'll even let you measure."

Jaiden's eyes darken with frustration as he shakes his head. He opens his mouth to answer but I cut him off.

"Did you care for me even a tiny bit? Because I was falling for you. *I* cared for *you.*" I admit it against my better judgment.

He's silent, looking out at the water where our friends are fooling around. I follow his gaze to see Damian lifting Lani into the air and tossing her into the water. She's laughing and smiling, and I'm happy for her. This trip has been hard for her with Lame Dane being an asshole.

"You're okay with that?" Jaiden asks, watching them.

I look at him, then back at our friends.

"Yep. Totally fine."

"You sure y'all are in a committed relationship? That looks quite flirty from where I'm seated."

"Oh, yeah. Totally committed." I play with my fingernails, not giving him much attention.

"Right," he says, the suspicion clear in his tone.

My stomach drops as I watch Lani and Damian. I need this fake relationship to work. But at the same time, I can't even remember why I'm fake dating him. It's not like Jaiden is going to talk to me. Even if he does, what do I get out of it? Do I want to be with him again?

I don't know what I'm doing.

"I wouldn't treat you like that," he says as he stands.

"But you fucking did," I spit at him, letting my frustration get the better of me. "I didn't even do anything wrong. I just had feelings and I didn't even admit them to you, and yet somehow, we ended up here."

"I caught feelings too, and that's the scariest part." He turns, walking away from me.

I seethe. What the *fuck* is that even supposed to mean? I wanted him and he wanted me too.

He continues walking until he stands at the end of the dock. I don't even think as I stand, my feet carrying me out toward the dock. *Towards him.*

The wood creaks beneath my feet as I stomp, my emotions the only thing driving me. He had feelings. Not the crazy possessive feelings a dominant man like him feels—he had *real* feelings. At least that's what it sounds like.

He wanted me too and he still did that to me.

How do you just stop talking to someone you care for? I don't understand—and I desperately want to—but right now, I'm just fucking angry. So fucking angry that as I reach Jaiden, I shove him with all of my strength.

"The fuck?" he yells, his body flying until he reaches the water, making ripples as he goes under. When he returns to the surface, he shakes out his hair like a wet dog and I glare, turning on my heels and stomping back toward the house.

"Don't ask." I can hear the firmness in my voice as I pass Dakota.

I keep walking until I reach the house, not stopping until I walk into my room. Ripping my phone from the charger, I wander into the bathroom, furiously scrolling through it.

I'm fuming, my eyes barely registering anything on the screen as I lower myself to the toilet seat.

When the bedroom door slams, I jump to my feet. Jaiden storms into the bathroom, dripping all over the place.

His eyes are so dark, and his shirt sticks to his body in a sinfully delicious way. My eyes trail across his broad shoulders and that perfectly tanned skin of his. His muscles ripple under the wet shirt and I feel my body clench. I shouldn't be eye-fucking him right now; I'm angry at him.

He growls at me, ripping the phone from my hands and slamming it on the counter.

"What?" I ask, my eyes wide as he shoves me backwards.

"You wanna play? Let's play, *Silver.*" He turns the water for the shower on, shoving me backwards until I'm standing under the cold spray. The water drips down my face and I shiver.

His hand tangles into my hair, his grip tightening to yank my head back to look up at him.

I gulp, my heart beating so fast as he leans down to meet my ear.

"Be angry, Sterling. I deserve it. But do *not* come at me when I can't see it coming. If you can't play by the rules, there will be consequences. Clear?"

Consequences.

I don't say anything, my body frozen under the slowly warming water. I couldn't care less about the temperature though. My body feels so hot from his near proximity. I squeeze my thighs together, my core heating as his breath hits my cheek.

"Words, Sterling," he goads.

"Clear," I say, my voice husky.

"Good girl," he praises, and I nearly melt. I stare into his eyes a moment, the silvery gray color of his irises deepening the longer I stare. I want to run my finger over the small freckle that sits right underneath his right eye. It's barely visible most of the year, but now that we've been in the sun, I can see it much clearer.

He's so close to me, his lips barely a breath away. I want... I don't know what I want. Do I want him to kiss me? Do I want him to punish me with his tongue? I shake off those feelings. I can't want these things. He's not *mine*.

He leans into me, teeth nipping at my ear, before he releases me. I feel a sense of loss immediately. I miss his hand tangled in my hair, his body heat warming me. *Fuck.*

"Your *boyfriend's* looking for you." He turns, leaving me alone in the bathroom once more.

It's then that I know for sure that he's suspicious of me, or maybe that's my own insecurity talking, but that's a problem for later. Right now, I'm so turned on I can't breathe. My body feels alive with electricity, like a simple touch could set me on fire.

I lean my head back onto the tiled wall of the shower, my hand slipping into my bikini bottom. My fingers circle my clit, my body jolting with the feeling of it.

I whimper quietly. I don't even fucking care that my bathroom door is wide open.

My breathing quickens as I press hard against my clit, a finger slipping into my core, curling in just the right way. I moan, my body tightening with the pressure.

Circling my sensitive nub again, I feel myself shatter and clench around my fingers. My toes curl, the water dripping down my body as I pant.

When I come down, I slump into the wall, trying to catch my breath.

“Oh, god. You’re so totally screwed,” I mutter to myself.

So very screwed.

TWELVE

STERLING

I STILL HATE RUNNING. I hate good vibes and positive thoughts. It's such a lie when it comes to running. How am I supposed to have good vibes and positive thoughts when I feel like I'm dying inside?

I pant, a burning feeling in my chest and throat as I slump, my arms resting on my knees. I'm about to fall over when I hear the back door slam, Jaiden running right toward me. Thankfully he doesn't see me, so I right myself, popping out my chest and running with what I hope is practiced elegance.

He eyes me as he passes, his gaze roaming over my form. I see the corner of his mouth lift as he continues to run right past me.

When I'm sure he can't see me anymore, I fall into the grass, heaving air into my lungs.

"Fuck," I groan into the cool grass.

"You good?" Damian's voice is laced with laughter and I don't have the energy to look up at him to respond, so instead I lift my arm above my head with a thumbs up. He chuckles, crouching to the ground by my face.

"You know, you don't have to torture yourself with running to get him to notice you. He stares at you when you simply exist."

I look up at him then to see the sincerity on his face. My

stomach flutters. I don't know if that should excite me or not. Even if it were true, it's not like he'd act on anything because he's a fucking wimp.

"I don't know about that." I kick my feet, trying to make my body language appear less stiff.

"I do," Damian says, lowering himself to the grass in front of me.

"This isn't ruining your relationship, is it?" I feel a bit of guilt about the cold shoulder Damian's gotten since this whole thing started.

"Nah. We'll be fine. He needs this kick in the ass."

"It feels like it's kicking me in the ass more than him. Even after everything, those feelings for him won't go away and it continues to hurt me." I pull up blades of grass, twisting them.

"Where's that overly confident girl I know? The one that's become my best friend over the last year." Damian slides a finger across my cheek.

"Being here is hard for me. It's a reminder of the ways that I don't meet everyone's expectations, and how I'm apparently not enough for Jaiden to like me back." The words taste sour coming out of my mouth. I hate the truth of them, the insecurity I've buried deep down now seeping out.

"Hey, it has nothing to do with you and everything to do with him. He's got shit he needs to work through and whether he likes it or not, he fell for you too. That asshole is afraid to love, and everyone but him knows it. We just need him to see what he's missing." His eyes look between mine and I smile at him. Damian presents as this playful hard ass, but he's got layers. Like an onion.

There's this mischievous gleam in his eyes and I can't help but laugh.

"How are we doing to do that?"

Damian leans in, his lips meeting my ear. "Act natural, and pretend I'm saying something funny."

I chuckle, running my hand down his arm as he mumbles the stats to the Stanley Cup Finals.

I feel *his* presence a moment later, his stomping footsteps audible as he nears us. He glares for a moment before rushing past us, up the deck and through the back door.

"He'll snap eventually. He's too possessive to keep away for long." Damian pulls away and I laugh.

"*Right*." I say, my voice oozing doubt. "I thought we were doing this to get him to communicate and open up." I wave my hands into the air as I accentuate the words *open up*.

Damian chuckles, his amber eyes squinting. "Naw, girl. We're trying to get your boo back. He deserves a little torture, though." He jumps to his feet and salutes.

I laugh, dropping my head to the grass again before rising to my feet and dragging myself into the house.

When I enter the kitchen, I see Dakota's hands wrapped around Wyatt's waist as he pushes food around in a frying pan.

"Gross. PDA." I walk to the table and shove a piece of bacon into my mouth, chewing it slowly.

Jaiden, who's seated at the head of the table sipping his coffee, watches my mouth with growing intensity. Just for funzies, I decide to flip him off before I leave the kitchen. Of course, I have to sway my ass a little more than usual because why the hell not.

DAKOTA APPEARS IN THE FULL LENGTH MIRROR BESIDE me, her long hair curled down her back. She's wearing a black tie-front crop top and black, floral maxi skirt. She poses in the mirror, her leg slipping from the slit of her skirt.

I turn from the mirror and grab my black Sonoma hat from the bed, turning to place it onto her head.

"There. It completes the look." I boop her nose, smiling at her. She laughs, her hand coming to run through my freshly curled hair.

I run my fingers through the other side, my fingers freeing from the thick locks too quickly. It's taken some getting used to, but I think I'm finally feeling better about how short my hair is. Before this big chop, it had been a long time since I cut it last. Long hair was always a staple I'd become attached to. It was the one thing my mom actually liked about me.

Dakota frees her hand from my hair, her fingers coming to my chest. She fiddles with the button of my dusty blue dress. I look down to watch her as she undoes another button, leaving the plunging neckline gaping.

"I'm jealous your tits look like that without a bra," she says, tucking the fabric into the belt at my waist. Finally, adjusting my cream hat that matches hers, she looks into the mirror again.

"We look hot," I say.

"Hell yeah, we do." She kicks her foot into the air, her strappy heel visible.

I'm happy I was able to convince her to wear the heels. She would've gone for her Doc's and not that I don't love her style, I wanted her to be dressier for our adventure today.

I turn around, looking over my shoulder at her. "Check my butt. Mother nature hit today out of the blue. Gotta love irregular periods while on birth control."

She looks at me, giving my ass a little smack before giving me a thumbs up. "All good. Just tap me if you need checks tonight."

"Thanks," I say, smoothing my hands down my sides one last time.

"Car's leaving in five," Wyatt yells down the hall. "Hurry up, ladies."

"We're coming," Dakota yells back. She smiles at me before walking out of the bedroom. I hear her footsteps retreat, but I don't make a move to leave just yet.

When I hear the door next to mine close, I grab my purse from the bed and step out into the hallway, nearly running right into Jaiden.

"Excuse me," I say, letting the shoulder of my dress slip a bit.

Jaiden's breathing stops, his eyes darkening as he looks at me.

Looking up at him, I breathe his scent. Notes of cedar and lime fill my nose and it's intoxicating.

He swallows, stepping aside so that I can pass him. It takes me by surprise and it takes everything in me to keep my face neutral.

"You look exquisite," he says, finally breaking the silence. His verbiage sends a chill down my spine. Not beautiful, not perfect, not even pretty. He called me *exquisite.*

"I know." I turn away from him, the smirk I dawn only for myself breaking free. I feel beautiful today and there's nothing he could do to take that away from me. Not tonight.

We load into the car and I'm surprised when Jaiden slides into the seat next to me.

"You're not taking your own car?" My eyebrows scrunch together, my heart beating faster. I'm not prepared to sit through an entire car ride with him pressed up against my side.

"It just makes more sense. Saves gas," Wyatt says from the driver's seat.

"Says the professional hockey player with a gas guzzler," I mumble and Jaiden snorts beside me. I look at him sideways and he shrugs.

"Don't knock my car," Wyatt says over his shoulder.

"I, for one, love the Bronco," Dakota says, sliding into the seat next to me.

Great. I'm in the middle.

"You're lucky it's surprisingly roomy back here." I roll my eyes as Wyatt backs the car down the driveway.

"We could've taken the Hellcat," Damian says from the passenger seat.

"I'll never say no to a ride in the Hellcat."

Crossing my legs, I settle into the seat, not caring to press my dress down even as it rides up my thigh.

Jaiden leans against the door, his head resting on his elbow as he stares out.

This town has my heart. Niagara-On-The-Lake is incredible, but I'm a little biased. When I was a kid, my nanny took me into the

American side of Niagara falls while my parents worked, but the Canadian side has always been my favorite.

This place is filled with so much history. The nineteenth-century architecture has always been one of my favorite things about coming here. I could stare at the buildings that line downtown for hours, enjoying the history built into them. I would build a whole home inspired by this town.

As we enter downtown, I see a line of classic cars parked alongside the buildings. A horse drawn carriage pulls a group of people through the streets of the town. It's extremely picturesque. A dream, really.

As a kid there wasn't too much to do, considering it's filled with wineries and boozy spots, but now I can enjoy the adult pleasures of this town.

One of hockey's greats, Wayne Gretzky, has an estate here with a winery *and* distillery. That's where we're going today.

The Bronco pulls into the parking lot of a large gray building with glass windows overlooking the scenery.

The hockey fangirl in me is freaking out, even though I've been here before. It doesn't stop that giddy feeling I get in my chest.

Jaiden climbs from the car, his hand extended to me. I look at it suspiciously before taking it. He helps me from the car, immediately releasing me.

"I'm really sad Lani isn't here for this," Dakota says, walking to my side.

"Me too. Stupid Dane." I mumble it, but I know she hears me. She nudges me lightly, her chuckle following.

I'm so glad I'm not the only one that hates him. He's been miserable this whole vacation.

I loop my arm through Dakota's, walking with her toward the whiskey bar.

Our heels click on the cement as we walk through the property. I should've brought my camera with me, but Dakota made me promise not to *work* while we're here. Little does she know, I've got plans.

We're greeted by several people before we find a table that seats five.

"Oh my gosh, the boys need to try poutine," Dakota says to me as she looks over the menu.

"Absolutely," I confirm and she smiles.

"Isn't that basically just cheese, fries and gravy?" Damian says it and I glare at him in return.

"You take that back," I say with my eyes wide. "Don't disrespect poutine like that."

Jaiden lifts a hand to his mouth, covering a laugh with a cough.

"Am I wrong, though?" Damian's hand runs through his auburn hair and I can see the hint of teasing in his eyes.

"I think we need to break up," I say, my face serious.

"Babe," he says, reaching over to take my hand.

I glare at him and he laughs.

"I take it back. I'll even let you feed me the first bite." He winks and I snort.

"Fine."

The waiter returns to take our order, setting drinks in front of all of us. I look over at Jaiden's old fashioned. *Classic taste.*

I stare out, looking at the waterfall, the soft music dulling my thoughts until I hear Damian cough. I meet his gaze, my eyes questioning until he extends his hand to me.

"May I have this dance?"

THIRTEEN

JAIDEN

WATCHING her dance with another man, not to mention one of my best friends, is a specific kind of torture. The more time I spend with her, the more I realize that Sterling was, and is, the girl of my dreams.

It's that attitude that does me in the most. Her inability to behave and her will to fight back. I've never felt safe enough to exert my dominant side with sex before. The puck bunnies just wanted to sleep with a hockey player. My face or my name didn't matter, only my status as a professional player. It wasn't worth it to express that side of myself, not until her.

She made me feel safe, accepted the praise and fought back, making my job hard. *I love that.* She's beautiful and talented, and the way she made me feel...*fuck.*

Why did I throw it all away? Why am I afraid of love and commitment?

I don't know how to fix this and it physically pains me.

Talking to her would be the simplest option, but of course, that's not going to happen. Not yet.

"I'm going to take a piss," I mumble, not caring to wait for reactions before I rise from the table and walk away.

There are portraits of Wayne's family throughout the halls. It's like a memorial, of sorts, for hockey fans. The accomplishments he achieved and the precedents he set for players like me. I cross my arms over my chest as I stare up at the photos.

"Hockey fan?" A female voice asks from my back. I look to my right to see a woman looking at the wall.

"Uh, yeah. You could say that," I say with a chuckle.

She smiles, her hand tucking into her pocket. "I always wanted to play hockey."

I raise an eyebrow at her. "Did you ever?"

"No," she says, shaking her head. "I suck at skating." She laughs and turns to me.

"Ah," I say. "It's a learned skill, that's for sure."

"I'm Darla." She extends her hand to me and I take it.

"Jaiden. Nice to meet you."

"You too. What team do you play for?"

I laugh, shaking my head. "That obvious?"

Her eyes squint as she smiles. "You kind of scream hockey player, but it was a lucky guess."

"Funny you say that. Out of all of my friends, I never thought that I would be the one that gave off the hockey player vibe."

"Well, take it as a compliment then." She looks over her shoulder. "Well, I'll let you get back to your browsing. Your girlfriend over there looks about ready to burn a hole through my skull."

"Oh, she's not—" I start to say, but she's already walking away. I train my eyes toward the table to see Sterling staring at me, her face a mixture of irritation and...maybe jealousy? It confuses me, but it also sends a satisfied feeling to my stomach.

I turn back to the wall for a moment before walking off to the bathroom.

When I return, Sterling is seated with her face away from me. She stares out at the fountain, her body language completely closed off.

Damian leans into her, mumbling something and she nods her head, speaking quietly to him.

When he turns back to his seat, he meets my eyes for a moment. We haven't talked, and I miss it.

"How ya been, man?" I throw him a bone, hoping he'll take it.

He blinks, the corner of his mouth lifting. "Fine. A little sore from our loss, but good. You?"

"Oh, just dandy," I say with a little smile.

His mouth quirks again, his right eyebrow lifting.

The waiter comes to our table, setting down the food. I immediately look at Sterling and see her still staring off into the distance. I can't get a read on what she's feeling. Even when she's angry, her temper is usually on the explosive side. She's not one to shy away from speaking her mind and that's what is most confusing about this.

"Can I try your poutine?"

She turns her head, her eyes almost empty. I can see that mind of hers working, like she's trying to see any ulterior motives. After what feels like an eternity, she nods her head.

I shove my fork into the poutine and make sure to get a bit of everything. Holding my hand under the fork, I bring it to my mouth and take a huge bite.

Both Dakota and Sterling watch me expectantly. I have half a thought to fuck with them, but I can sense the thin rope keeping this moment together.

"I stand corrected," I say, swallowing my bite. "It's damn good."

There's a hint of a smile on Sterling's face. It'll do, *for now.*

Damian moans over his poutine and I snort. He makes it sound like a heavenly experience. There's been only one time in my life where I've experienced anything close to that, and it was with his *girlfriend.*

The rest of the night feels off, and by the time we pile back into the car, Sterling is shoved so far back into her shell and I don't know what to do. This is so unlike her. *What the fuck?*

Dakota, Wyatt and Damian talk quietly, my ears drowning out the sound of their voices.

Sterling's head rests on Dakota's shoulder, her eyes closed and her breathing even. She's beautiful as she sleeps, and I can't help but discreetly watch her. At one point, I catch Dakota watching me carefully.

For a moment, I see the fierceness behind her eyes, her unsaid message loud and clear. *Hurt her, and I hurt you.*

What she doesn't know is that seeing Sterling hurt now feels like a stab to my own heart. Maybe that's why I'm so on edge with her behavior tonight.

The car pulls up the long driveway, and when we stop, Wyatt and Damian climb out immediately, Wyatt opening the door for Dakota.

She pats Sterling's head lightly. She doesn't stir.

"I'll stay with her," I say quietly.

"Are you sure?"

"Yeah." I pull Sterling toward me, her bodyweight coming to rest on my arm.

"Thanks," Dakota says, before climbing out of the car.

Damian's eyebrows raise as he looks at me.

"We'll be fine," I confirm, and he shakes his head before walking away.

The sound of Sterling's breathing fills the small space. I feel an odd sense of peace at this moment. It feels almost serene, a reminder of the way things used to be.

She felt comfortable enough to fall asleep with her head resting on my shoulder, or her legs slung across me. It was safe to have her seated in my lap, or my arm wrapped around her.

I breathe in deeply, her honey and cinnamon scent filling my nose. She always smells like the perfect blend of sweetness and spice. It's quite ironic, considering she's the farthest thing from sweet.

"I'm sorry I hurt you," I say, even though she's not listening. "I didn't deserve you. You were too good for me. I'm fucked up in more ways than one, and I couldn't bring you down with me. But maybe everyone's a little fucked up and I shouldn't have let you go so easily."

Against my better judgment, I lay my hand on her head, stroking her hair lightly.

"I want to be better for you. Just give me time. I swear I'll let you go if that's what you want. If you want to be with my best friend, then so be it. It'll fucking hurt like a bitch though."

She stirs and I look down to see her eyes still closed.

"I'm scared," I breathe. "You scare me."

Her chest rises and falls with each breath and I'm thankful that she's asleep. There's a note of vulnerability in my voice that I'm not ready to share yet. I sit there for several minutes, the silence of the car deafening. When she finally stirs again, she blinks several times, her full dark lashes framing her beautiful eyes.

"Hi," I say.

"Hi," she says, her voice husky from sleep. "Are we home?"

"Yeah. Everyone went inside already."

"Oh," she says, wiping her eyes gently.

My heart clenches as I look at her. *I want her.* I don't just want her body, I want *her.* That thought scares me.

"Are you okay?"

"No," she says, sitting up and pulling away from me.

"Why?" My voice is weak and I don't expect it to be.

"It's nothing." Her tone is closed off, her eyes downcast. I get the urge to wrap my body around her, but I don't think she wants that.

"Tell me," I say. "Please." It's a desperate plea for communication.

She sighs, her eyes finally meeting mine. "Even when we were *together*," she says the word like she doesn't know the meaning of it. Were we ever truly together? *Yes.* "It was never easy like it was with that girl."

I blink at her several times, confused. "What?"

She releases an irritated breath. "You were talking with her and smiling like it was the easiest thing in the world. We weren't like that."

I should be happy that she's jealous, but instead I'm irritated and angry.

"I don't want easy," I say, my voice firm. "I didn't sign up for something easy with you." I toss my hands up. "You're loud and vulgar and so fucking blunt. I hadn't expected it to be easy when I was dying to fuck you. In fact, you made it so damn hard for me and yet I continued to pursue you."

"Then you just gave up like I was nothing. A lot of confidence that gives me," she scoffs.

"Why are you jealous anyways? You've got a *boyfriend* now, Sterling, or have you forgotten?"

Her mouth gapes. "I haven't forgotten," she huffs.

"Are you sure? For a woman with a boyfriend, you're not quick to deny my touch. It was almost too goddamn easy to get you to submit. Not to mention that touch between you and Damian is few and far between. Oh, and not once have I seen you sneaking from his bed in the morning. Is he so boring that you aren't fucking like rabbits every night?"

Her cheeks redden, her nostrils flaring. I can't help the smile that crosses my face as I see the fire lit in her eyes.

"You know what? Fuck you. Who are you to judge my relationship?" She turns to exit the car and I fly out of my door, rushing to meet her.

"Relationship," I repeat with the same note of skepticism from earlier.

"Yes," she spits. "Relationship, Jaiden. You know that thing I wanted with you, but you couldn't hang." She stomps towards the house and I rush after her.

"Where are you going?"

"Why do you care?" she throws over her shoulder.

"Because I do," I say quietly.

She swings the front door open, and I continue to keep pace with her, making sure to close the door behind me. I follow her through the house, up the stairs and down the hallway to our rooms.

She stops in front of Damian's room, pounding on the door. "Damian," she calls loudly.

The door opens a moment later, Damian's shirtless form appearing in the doorway. "Are you okay?" he asks, but his words are stopped by Sterling crashing her lips into his. She kisses him with fervor, but there's a driving force behind it.

I grow more suspicious the longer I watch. It looks platonic. Is that just me seeing what I want to see?

"Sterling," Damian says between kisses.

"Hmmm?" she asks, her eyes peeks open to see me staring.

I roll my eyes. "Gross. Get a room," I say, walking past them.

Damian pulls away and looks between us. He smirks, his hand sliding up Sterling's back then down to her ass. "Mmmhm. What a great idea, Jai." In one swift movement, he pulls Sterling into the room, slamming the door behind him.

"Seriously?" I groan.

"Definitely," Sterling says from the other side of the door.

FOURTEEN

STERLING

"SIT THERE AND LOOK PRETTY," I say as I shove Damian toward the bed. I'm so fucking tired of Jaiden's shit. He was being so sweet. It took everything in me not to cry at his words. *I'm fucking scared too.*

But there's no *fucking* way that I'm letting him have this one. He wants to see a relationship, then that's what he's gonna get. Fake sex and all.

"What happened?" Damian asks from the bed, his grin wild and filled with mischief.

"He's onto us," I whisper.

"What?" Damian whispers, but it sounds mocking and I roll my eyes at him.

He laughs, his body now propped up in bed like he's waiting for me to mount him. *Not gonna happen, bud.*

"Just pretend we're having sex," I say as I jump onto the bed and make as much noise as possible.

"Oh my fucking god," I gasp, louder than necessary.

Damian slaps a hand over his mouth, his laughter barely hidden. "Fuck," he says, drawing out the word, and I laugh as I continue jumping while Damian methodically knocks against the wall.

"Yes. Just like that." I moan, my hands running through my hair to make it look messy. "Jesus fucking Christ. YES!" I bite my lip to keep the laughter at bay.

Damian shoves his head into a pillow as he wheezes.

I can hear Jaiden pound on the wall beside us. "Shut the fuck up," he yells, and I snort.

"I'm gonna come," I yell and Damian grunts. It's the stupid face that he makes that causes me to lose it. I bounce on the bed, my body rebounding and colliding with him. He holds me tightly.

"Yes, Damian, yes. Please. Fuck." I call out, my eyes watering from laughing.

"I really hope sex with Jaiden wasn't like this," he whispers and my cheeks grow hot.

"It was somehow a lot less fun." I smirk, patting him on the head.

"I highly doubt that." He pauses. "Think it worked?"

A door slams and I'm almost certain it's Jaiden's door. I hear the heavy footsteps pound down the hallway until the sound disappears.

"I hope so," I say with a laugh. *Take that, sucker.*

"What did he say?" Damian moves his arm behind his head, leaning back to rest against the wall.

"He said we don't touch and," I pause, my cheeks heating. "There was an incident after I shoved him in the water."

Damian's face falls, but not with disappointment. He looks ready to punch someone.

"He didn't hurt me. I promise."

"I'll beat his ass if he does," he says, and I know he means it. I lay across his bed, looking around his room. "You're welcome to stay if you want. Could even take one of my shirts for good measure." He winks and I laugh.

"Thanks. Do I get to pick?"

In answer, he nods, extending his hand to the room. I pick a shirt and escape to the bathroom to slip it on. Folding my clothes neatly, I set them on the chair before jumping back onto the bed.

For the next couple hours, Damian and I watch the first two

Lord of the Rings movies. He tries to argue with me about certain details, but I won't have it. By the time the third movie starts, Damian is passed out.

I smile at his relaxed form. I hadn't realized how much I'd been craving friendship like this. There are no expectations, I can simply be Sterling. At one point, it was easy to be myself with Jaiden.

Without waking him, I creep from the bed and open his bedroom door quietly. I shouldn't have to creep through my own house, but that's what I find myself doing.

As I round the corner to the kitchen, I see Lani seated on the porch, her hands pressed against her face. I slide the door open, and slip into the seat beside her.

"Are you okay?" I reach for her hand, running my thumb over her palm.

She chokes out a laugh. "Honestly, no." I see her tear-stained face and it sends chills down my spine. "I'm miserable, and seeing Dakota so happy... *Fuck*."

"I know," I say with a small laugh.

"I'm so damn happy for her, but it reminds me constantly of how miserable I am. I'm on one of the best vacations of my life, in a new city, and my fucking boyfriend can't give me the time of day."

I run my free hand along my neck as I sigh. The stars in the sky illuminate our faces and I can see the pain on hers. It pains *me* to see her this way. Lani is my ray of sunshine, the bubbly and beautiful, best fucking bitch. I *hate* that Dane has stolen her sunshine.

"Can I ask you something?"

She nods, her lip pulled between her teeth as she swipes at a freshly fallen tear.

"Why do you stay with him?"

She looks out toward the water. Her amber eyes look radiant under the light of the night sky. I just wish that there was happiness instead of sadness on her face.

"I've dedicated so many years of my life to him. He's all I know and it's scary to think that this might be coming to an end. I don't even think he finds me attractive anymore."

My jaw drops as I look at her. "You? Not attractive? No fucking way. I'd wife you up in no time. He's stupid if that's true."

She laughs weakly. "Thanks, babe." She sighs, her grip tightening around my hand. "I don't know what to do."

"Well, I've been meaning to ask you. I want to plan the best wedding ever for Dakota. Do you think helping with that would keep your mind off it? I could certainly use your creativity."

"Yeah. I'm down to help," she replies. "Are we DIY'ing shit?"

"Most definitely. That's going to be the fun part. Almost as fun as spending Wyatt's money." I wink and she laughs.

"I love you," she says.

"I love you, too. Don't forget it. I'll beat Dane's ass in the morning. Just for funzies."

She rolls her eyes, but there's a bit of hesitance there. I won't *actually* beat him up, but I really want to.

"Get some sleep. I'm going to grab a snack then slip back into bed."

"Yours, or Damian's?" she asks and I double take. It's the way she says it that gives me pause.

"It was all fake. I swear," I say in a rush.

She purses her lips. "I know. I really hate myself for even feeling an ounce of jealousy."

"Don't say that." I return to the chair, placing my hands on the back. "This has been going on for months. Dane doesn't deserve you. When you're being neglected and treated this way, I don't blame you for feeling the way you do." I pause, looking down at my feet.

"I know you're right, I really do, but I feel so guilty about even having anything remotely close to feelings for someone else."

"I get it. I do. If you're this miserable, I think it's time to think about your future and whether that includes Dane or not. And I swear to Persephone that I'll end it with Damian if you want to pursue something. I hate seeing you like this." I grip the chair tighter. I'm so fucking scared, but I'd much rather have my friend than a fake boyfriend.

She sighs. "I can't think about that right now, but I promise that you'll be the first to know." She reaches for the mug and holds it tightly. "Are you sure though? This whole thing with the two men is..."

"Exhausting?" I ask, and she laughs.

"Yeah, that."

"I think our ruse is coming to an end anyway. It's been fun while it lasted," I joke, but on the inside I'm freaking out. I don't know how to behave around Jaiden without Damian. He's been my buffer and without that, I'm scared.

It's not over yet.

JAIDEN RUNS OUT OF HIS ROOM SANS SHIRT AND PANTS, his face angry. "Sterling!" he yells, and I continue to eye him from my place in bed.

I know what I did, but I won't give him any inkling of that. Instead, I watch him as he approaches me. His chest is on full display and for the first time in a while, I let myself admire him.

The summer has been very nice to him. He's tanner than usual and he's more muscular than I remember. God, the way he's angrily prowling toward me is making my panties wet and it has no business doing that. I'm supposed to be angry at him.

"The fuck, Sterling? Saran wrap on the toilet seat, seriously? Is that the best you got?" He sneers and my brow raises in response. The way he says my name is way sexier than it needs to be.

I want him to say it again.

I hadn't intended on stooping to this juvenile level, but here we are. I was so angry at him after we were *nearly* there. I could've seen myself being friendly with him and then he had to open his mouth and ruin it.

"I don't know what you mean," I say, pulling my Kindle from

the side table and turning it on. If I'm going to be here a while, I might as well get some reading done.

"You will," he says and it sounds more like a promise than anything. The floor creaks as he turns on his heels and I watch through my lashes. Only when he's gone do I allow myself to breathe. A part of me wanted him to stay, to threaten me with something, and that part of me is disappointed. Maybe I'll have to work harder to get a reaction from him.

The next morning I get up early, starting the coffee machine and waiting patiently for Jaiden to stumble into the kitchen. I've pre-made coffee for Lani and Dakota, hoping they'll avoid the massacre that's going to occur if my devious plot pans out.

My book's splayed out on the table and I skim the pages as I sip my latte. Eventually Dakota and Wyatt come down the stairs, arm in arm, and I greet them before they go on their run. It's getting really hard to wait patiently; the anticipation nearly has me shaking. I want to see his face scrunch up and his eyes flick to mine in that way it always does when he's angry. I'm swimming in dangerous waters, but that's exactly where I want to be.

After an hour, I've all but given up until I hear the distinct sound of his footsteps. Roman and Lily come down a moment before him and I sit up straighter, the grin peeking at the corners of my mouth dangerously.

Jaiden yawns, ignoring me with perfect ease. He's got headphones in and he's dressed like he's going for a run.

I try to focus, even as Damian walks to my side, placing a kiss on my cheek.

"What are you up to?" he asks, his eyes flicking between mine. I look away quickly, watching Jaiden dump three heaping spoonfuls of *sugar* into his coffee.

I allow myself to smile for one second, tilting my head in Jaiden's direction before holding my book up to hide my mouth. Damian quickly pulls the seat out beside me, swiping my coffee and taking a long sip from it.

Jaiden stirs three times, his back still to me.

"Are you going swimming with us today, Auntie Sterling?" Lily bounces on her toes beside me.

I sigh, looking at her with a smile. "Absolutely. I wouldn't miss it." It takes everything in me to keep my attention locked to her, but at the last minute my eyes flick in Jaiden's direction.

"Do you want to play mermaids?" Lily spins around, her hair in a long braid. "Daddy said he'll play with me."

"I did?" Roman says and it's in that exact moment that I realized that there would be collateral damage in my war. Brown liquid spews all over Roman's gray t-shirt a second before he could step out of the line of fire.

Jaiden sputters, coughing and choking on the salty coffee.

"Jesus Christ!" he yells after he stops choking on coffee. "Sterling," he growls and I shiver at the sound of it. It shoots right down my spine and to my core. It's a sick, twisted game I'm playing. I shouldn't be horny at the way he growls my name, or at the way his eyes promise punishment. I have to swallow thickly several times to regain my composure enough to speak.

"Gotta go." I slip from my chair and practically run from the kitchen and out the back door.

SEVERAL DAYS PASS BEFORE JAIDEN RETALIATES. I LEAVE my room only to be showered in ice cold water. My ass hits the floor so hard I let out a yelp. Ice floats in little puddles around me and I growl, splashing it at his door.

His chuckles haunt me that night, forcing my hand between my legs until I'm panting and whimpering curses that may include his name.

Two weeks. *Two* damn weeks continue in much of the same way. The only difference is that there are many more instances of collateral damage than before. My retaliation to the ice bucket was an oiled floor. Jaiden was *supposed* to walk out and slide across the kitchen, but instead Lani ate shit and I begged for forgiveness in the form of tacos.

Many unsuccessful pranks later, I have no doubts that the house is beyond angry with us. It's why I'm sitting on the couch, my hair stained purple from the *stupid* purple depositing shampoo Jaiden switched for my toning shampoo. There were many more pranks, but once Jaiden screamed at me when Lily tried to offer him a plate of shrimp, it was all over. She burst into tears and I don't think I've ever been on the opposite side of Roman's angry stare. I shrink five sizes in my seat as he glares.

"Good fucking God." He looks between us. Lily is wiping her tears away, his arm firmly on her shoulder. "This was all fun and games, but I'm so sick and tired of your—" he freezes, looking down at Lily for a moment. "Lily, can you please put on your earmuffs? Daddy needs to yell at your aunt and uncle."

She giggles a snotty sounding laugh before plopping her hands over her ears and humming.

Roman, seemingly satisfied, looks back between Jaiden and me. I feel like a teenager being scolded after sneaking out. "I'm sick and tired of *both* of y'alls shit. I'm tired of looking over my shoulder and being worried I'm going to be sprayed with piping hot coffee because *someone* switched the sugar for salt." He glares at me and I purse my lips, looking at my feet. "Just *please*, can you either go bang it out or fight like normal people?"

My mouth hangs agape at his words. Did he seriously just tell us to go bang it out?

Jaiden's brows furrow and I see his fists clench in his lap.

"We can't fight if we're not talking," I say, my voice clipped.

"Can you please tell Sterling that we're not talking because she thought it was a good idea to dump itching powder into *every single pair* of boxers I own? I refuse to converse with a *terrorist*." He crosses his arms over his chest.

My jaw tightens and I glare at him. "Well, you can tell *Jaiden* that it was low blow to turn my hair fucking purple." I lift a piece of my hair up to show the room, even though it's only the four of us until Damian and Wyatt walk in through the back door a moment later.

"You can tell Sterling to go fuck—-"

"Children!" Roman yells. "I've had enough. I don't know how to punish adults, so I'll tell you each to go to your fucking rooms and sort out your shit. This war is *done.* If I catch either of y'all pulling another goddamned prank, I'll lock you both out of the house until the two of you *talk.* Do you want that?"

"No," we say collectively.

"Good." He points at us. "*Behave.*" As he leads Lily away, I play with my thumbs, a growing frustration building in my chest.

Jaiden's looking at me with a hint of desperation. I've seen that look before. It crossed his face when he admitted to me that he cared and that he was scared. He stared at me like he wanted me to see inside his mind.

Well, too fucking bad I can't read minds. He's just going to have to admit everything to me, for real this time.

"You're punishing me," he says, his voice lifeless.

My eyes squint as I look at him. He's got his mask firmly in place and yet for the first time, I see a hint of sadness shine through.

Everything in me screams to hang onto my anger. It's the only thing I have left of my walls. Once the anger is gone, there's only rawness and desire left. I am not ready for this to be over.

"I'm angry," I admit. "You wanted me too, and yet you still hurt me."

"I did."

It's those two words that have my heart pounding in my chest. It forces me to stand to my feet and leave him be. I'm not ready for this, to accept the raw vulnerability in his voice. It sounded awfully like acceptance, like maybe he's ready to move on from this. But that begs an even bigger question...

Am I?

FIFTEEN

JAIDEN

THIS FUCKING book is blowing my mind. I've been knee deep in this fantasy series for weeks now. I picked it up on a recommendation from Dakota, and I'm so glad I did.

It's not particularly smutty, which is something I'd expected from a self-professed *smut slut* like Dakota, but I'm enjoying it nonetheless.

I'm learning.

I'd heard that this author likes to throw some twists into her books, and I'm wholly captivated by the one she just threw at me. If this character fucking dies, I'm going to throw the book at Dakota. *Gently.*

I slip the bookmark between the pages when I hear someone sliding the backdoor open. I haven't quite allowed myself to stop looking over my shoulder every time I hear someone coming. The prank war may be over, but I'm still paranoid.

"Hey," Damian says as he slips into the seat next to me. He leaves his legs hanging over the edge, almost like he's not committing to staying long.

"Hey."

"We good?" He looks at me, a small smirk creeping at the corner of his lips. He's an arrogant, unapologetic prick sometimes, but I love him for it. His intentions are usually good.

I roll my eyes before responding. "Yeah. We're good."

"Great, because we're on dinner duty tonight and we need groceries." He chuckles and I shake my head.

"Yeah. I heard. Wyatt wants to take the boat out this week for the Pride thing on the water, so he asked that we grab beer and food for the cooler."

I stand to my feed and pull my sweatshirt from the back of the lounge chair. "I'll drive?"

Damian nods before walking through the slider door.

Roman is seated at the table with Lily in his lap. She's telling the group a story about some movie they watched while we were at dinner last night. She's so expressive, her hands waving wildly as she talks about her new favorite animated movie.

I want to hug my little munchkin. She's perfect and I never want her to grow up. I want her to stay just like this.

"We're headed to the store. Anyone need anything?" I pluck my keys from the dish on the kitchen island.

"Alcohol and chocolate," Sterling says from the hallway. I hear her footsteps, but I don't see her until she rounds the corner.

I narrow my eyes at her. She's wearing an oversized band tee that screams Damian. Her hair is slightly mussed, but she still looks incredible.

I want to react, to go caveman on her—to claim her like my body is screaming to. Instead, I nod politely and walk out the door before I do something I regret.

"We'll be back before the cornhole tournament," Damian says as he stalks after me.

Kicking the front door closed behind me, I grip the grocery bags tighter in my hands. The house is mostly empty beside Damian and myself.

He sets the bags down onto the island and retreats back to the car for the remaining groceries. As I unload, the sounds of voices travel through the screen door. I peek out, seeing Dakota and Sterling practicing for the tournament.

Sterling's silver hair blows into her face right as she throws the bean bag. It hits Dakota's leg and they both break out into laughter.

"We're going to suck," she says, and I smile as I watch them.

Dane's moping in the corner like usual. I'm actually surprised to see him today. Usually he's locked himself into the room, doing whatever the hell he chooses to do with his time. It's not like we're on vacation or anything. He could sit outside and work, but he remains out of sight most of the time.

Grabbing the beer, I crouch to the ground, loading the cool bottles into the chiller. Loud footsteps storm past me with a flash of orange hair. Her face is angry and my body tenses as I watch her storm from the room and out the screen door.

"How long?" Lani yells.

Damian walks through the front door at that moment, his eyes wide. I shake my head and he rushes to set the bags down before following me out the door.

"How fucking long, Dane?" She's gripping a phone in her hands, the screen lit up.

"What are you talking about?" he asks, his voice raised. It's weak, lacking conviction.

I briefly see Damian and Sterling lock eyes. She looks panicked, her hands balled into fists at her sides.

"How long have you been cheating on me, you idiot? Or are you going to deny that too?" She shoves the phone at him. "Apparently she felt the need to tell me how much of a horrible boyfriend you are to me and how you've chosen her. There are screenshots, Dane. Proof." She shoves at his chest.

I think about stepping in, but something in my gut tells me to wait.

"What—"

"You know what? I don't care," she throws her hands up, then rips the phone from his hands. "We're done, Dane. You've been making my life miserable. You're making my *friends' lives* miserable by being here and staying away like a recluse. I thought you'd actually try, but I guess you just decided to sext your side piece the whole time." She huffs, her jaw tensing. "*Eight* years, Dane. Eight fucking years I've wasted with you and you do *this* to me? Please, just fucking leave."

Lani turns away, her eyes red from tears.

Dane stutters for a moment, looking shocked, but then like a switch is flipped, he storms off.

"You're a fucking bitch, anyways," he mutters loud enough for both Damian and I to hear. He rushes past me and knocks Damian's shoulder. It doesn't do anything. Damian barely moves from the impact. That puny, cheating, fucker does nothing next to a six-foot-four hockey player. He forgets that Lani is currently surrounded by professionally trained *fighters.* That is exactly what we do right? We fight on the fucking ice.

I reach my hand out to grip his shirt. He stops retreating and looks over his shoulder at me, his eyes blazing, but I currently give no fucks.

"Sterling, he called your best friend a *fucking* bitch," I yell over my shoulder. A moment later footsteps sound on the stairs.

The feral way she approaches sends blood south, *way south,* and I decide to worry about that later.

"Dane, let me make a few things clear." Her sickly sweet voice almost makes me smile. "One, my best friend is not a bitch. She has dedicated years of her life to you and you can't even be decent and offer up an apology. You don't deserve my ray of sunshine. Second, move the fuck out of the apartment. If you're still there by the time we get back from our vacation, I'll call the fucking cops, my dad's lawyer, and these guys—" she nods to Damian and me "—so please be afraid. We don't want to see you or hear from you. Lastly, I hope your dick shrivels and falls off. Get off my property; you're no longer welcome here."

Sterling's eyes flick to mine, the intensity swirling within them. I smirk lightly before releasing his shirt. He doesn't expect it, so he collides face first with the floor. The indignant, very unmanly shrieking that comes from Dane is almost comical. He scrambles to his feet and rushes through the house.

Damian looks barely restrained. They might think I'm stupid—Sterling and Damian—but I'm not. I see the way Damian looks at Lani. Maybe it's because she was unavailable that he tied himself to Sterling. Either way, that's why I did it, why I stopped Dane from leaving. Had Damian crossed that line, there'd be no turning back for him.

If this is what makes Sterling happy, then so be it. I won't let him ruin this for himself.

Lani runs off a moment later, but when Damian takes a step forward, Sterling's hand shoots out to stop him.

"She needs her girls," she says, her eyes watching him. Her hand slides up his arm before she pats him and rushes after Lani, Dakota following behind closely.

I stand there a moment, unsure of what to do. I breathe, speaking to Damian's head. "If you hurt her, I swear I'll smash your nose in. If you even have an inkling of feelings for Lani, promise me you'll end it with Sterling before you pursue her."

Damian turns to me, his eyes boring into mine. He's shorter than me, but only by an inch. I don't give a shit though. He's playing with hearts, and one of those hearts belongs to someone I care for deeply. I'd do anything for Sterling. I may be a stubborn idiot, but after these past few weeks, I can't deny myself that. I want her and I'd do *anything* to make her happy. Even if that means letting her go, finally.

He doesn't speak. Instead he nods, walking into the kitchen and busying himself with the groceries.

This is so *fucked.* I grip at my chest, my eyes finding Roman who's standing with Wyatt by the grill.

"What the fuck?" I ask, my heart pounding.

They walk to my side, Wyatt clapping me on the back lightly. "Awh, is that cold dead heart coming back to life?" He smirks and I laugh lightly.

"Is this what Sterling felt when I ghosted her? Caring for someone and realizing they won't be yours?" My voice is weak.

"You may be surprised, man. Don't give up."

I shake my head, my hand still gripping my chest. *Feelings are fucking scary.*

I dare not say the word out loud. The four letter word my mother used to say to me. The one that reminded me that even while she was dying, that four letter word kept us together, *whole.*

Fuck me.

SIXTEEN

STERLING

GASPING BREATHS IS the first thing I hear when I round the corner toward the boat house. Lani's crouched low to the ground, her head between her legs.

"Breathe, babe," I soothe, my hand running across her back as I kneel beside her.

Dakota comes to her other side, her eyes focused wholly on Lani.

"I—can't—breathe," she gasps out, and I grip her face between my hands.

"Lani, look at me. Breathe with me, okay? In—" I take a deep breath in, my eyes locked on hers "—Out. Again." We go through the motions until she's calmer.

Lani's golden brown eyes peek open, tears falling from them. My heart breaks for her. Lame Dane was an asshole and she didn't deserve that. I should've decked him when I had the opportunity. Jaiden was giving me the chance, but I couldn't do it.

Lani deserves better and I won't stoop to his level.

"I don't know what to do now," she says, her arms reaching behind her as she lowers herself fully to the ground. "I need to go home and deal with this, but I don't want to see him."

"You don't need to deal with this right now," Dakota says, her fingers intertwined with Lani's. "We're on vacation and you do not need to deal with him, not if you don't want to."

"I told him to get the fuck out," I interject. "Of the house, and of the apartment. He should be gone by the end of summer and if he isn't, I swear I'll kick his ass out myself. You've got a whole team of people on your side, babe."

"Wyatt said the team will take care of everything. It's going to be okay."

Lani nods her head several times. She's still breathing heavily but it's much more even now. Her bright cheeks are tear-stained and I reach out to brush away the stray tears from her face.

"I can't afford that apartment on my own," she cries. "Not right now."

"Actually, you can," Dakota says. "Become an artist. I'll continue paying you as my receptionist, whatever you need, but start taking on clients. I'll teach you everything, anything."

"But we don't need to worry about that right now. Dane can pay for it. It's the least he can do. If not, I'll move in with you. You've got options." I pause, looking at her to gauge her reaction.

"Don't go," I say. "Stay here with us and enjoy your vacation. If you really need to go, then I'll respect that, but stay a while. You deserve this so much. We all do."

Lani shakes her head, sighing. "I don't know."

"I know you may not want to go out, but there's this incredible bar not far from here. We can make one of the guys be DD, and get wasted like we used to. I'll even dance the night away with you. It'll be like old times. If you really want to leave after that, then I'll let you go. Just have fun with us tonight."

Dakota smiles. "We had a lot of fun together in our bar phase." She wiggles her shoulders in a mock dance move and I laugh. Lani's smile is back when I look over at her.

"Okay, fine. I could use a drink right about now."

"Hell yes," I say with a smile. "Let's get wasted."

It's a Thursday night in June. I'd anticipated it to be quieter and less crowded, but of course there's a crowd. We're drawing a lot of attention to ourselves by walking in with an entourage of hot men.

That'll really draw attention to three girls. Bring hot men with you and you'll get all of the jealous stares. I nearly roll my eyes when I feel the glares starting.

I follow Dakota to the bar, ordering drinks for the table. When we return, I set the tray down, grabbing a shot glass and holding it out.

"To new and better things," I say, before tossing back the shot of tequila. The liquid burns going down my throat, and I shake my head as I swallow. Dakota laughs at me, shooting back her own shot and coughing.

"God, that's horrible. Why did you choose that? I want my fruity drink." Her face scrunches as she sips some water.

I lock eyes with Jaiden as he licks his hand, rather seductively I may add, and shoves a lime wedge into his mouth. I gulp. It's the way he watches me that stuns me. I don't even feel ashamed for staring back.

His tongue runs across his full pink lips and I watch every second of it. My fingers twitch. I want to run my hands through his curly hair, across his longer stubble.

I blink, heat coursing through my body. When he stopped Dane, I felt a myriad of emotions. I hadn't expected arousal to be one of those. Seeing the guys get violent on the ice is one thing, but off it is a different experience.

Dragging my eyes away from him, I look to the dance floor right as "Get Low" by Lil Jon blares through the speakers.

"Are you thinking what I'm thinking?" Dakota asks, her eyes gleaming. She looks at Lani, grabbing her hand and dragging her behind us.

I practically jump onto the dance floor, my ass grinding on Dakota. Her hand grips my hip, the other raised in the air as we dance. I pull Lani to the front of our train and she laughs when I smack her ass as she walks.

I couldn't care less that people are staring. This is our moment to dance away the shit of the past year. As I drop it to the floor, my eyes lock with Jaiden's.

The look on his face is something unlike anything I've ever seen before. Keeping eye contact with him, I dance, my body swaying and moving with the beat.

I barely register that the songs ended and the next one's started. Dakota bends to the floor right as the lyrics to "Low" by Flo Rida blares through the speakers.

Like they're watching a show, the guys sit back until they can't anymore. Wyatt is first to break, his arms wrapping so tightly around Dakota's waist that she laughs in glee. They dance together, his arms gripping her as she grinds and sways.

Damian is next, but instead of coming for me, he grabs Lani's arm, spinning her around and right into his chest.

I watch as she laughs, then stares into his eyes. It feels like a private moment, so I dance by myself, closing my eyes and vibing.

I feel so free. The alcohol flows through my body, giving me some of that overwhelming confidence back. It's not until I feel the light touch of a hand on my waist that I open my eyes. I'd expected Jaiden, but instead I'm looking into the bright brown eyes of Roman.

"Since Damian isn't doing his job," he says into my ear, spinning me around to face him. I smile, a laugh passing through my lips.

"Thanks," I say. We dance until I'm sweaty and smiling like a fool. I pull away from the group to get another drink. As I'm ordering, a familiar face fades into view. I smile as she walks toward me, a matching smile crossing her face.

"Hey, babe." She kisses my cheeks, her arm resting on my shoulder. "You look incredible."

"Why, thank you. So do you! What are you doing here?"

She laughs, her black hair dropping from her shoulder to her back. "Vacation. Same as you, I'm assuming." She waves over my shoulder, I'm assuming to Dakota. "Is that her fiancé?"

I look over at the group to see Wyatt's arms wrapped around Dakota's shoulders. She's watching us with a smile.

I nod. "Yeah. That's Wyatt. I don't think you've met Lani, and the other idiots are Wyatt's friends."

"They're cute together." Her eyes wander over the group.

"Well, since you're here... Care to dance with me?" I wink and she shakes her head.

"Still the same Sterling, I see." She drops her hand from my shoulder and reaches for my hand. "Let's dance."

SEVENTEEN

JAIDEN

WHAT'S WORSE than seeing the woman you lo—*really like* dance all seductive like on the dance floor? It's seeing her dance with her best friends and now your best friends too. Roman swept in like a knight in shining armor while I was too busy watching Damian and Lani.

What the fuck is happening? I feel like my head's going to explode. She doesn't seem to care, nor does anyone else. Am I on a game show? Am I being punked?

Just when I thought it couldn't get any better, Sterling walks off the dance floor and returns with a gorgeous *woman.*

The way they're dancing together sends more jealousy through my body than I felt with Roman or Damian. What the hell is wrong with me?

Dakota is watching them with a look I can't decipher.

Instead of moping, I toss the rest of my drink back and make my way to the group. My body warms and I can really feel the alcohol now. My lips loosen when I drink and I really don't want to say something stupid.

"You should come to Pride this weekend," the woman says to Sterling. I didn't mean to eavesdrop, but here we are.

"Do you have to be gay to go to Pride?" I ask it loud enough for everyone to hear.

Sterling freezes, her head whipping to me. "What did you just say?"

My eyes widen. "I was simply asking if you need to be gay to go to Pride."

"No," she says, her voice firm. "You don't." She turns back to the woman, their conversation lost to me.

"Do you know her?" The question is directed at Dakota.

She nods, her eyes meeting mine. "That's her ex-girlfriend, Z. They dated for a couple years, but the distance became too much."

"Wait, Sterling is gay?" This time I regret the words out of my mouth.

The silver-haired beauty whips in my direction again. This time, her companion is abandoned as she walks toward me. I look to Dakota, but she shrugs her shoulders, her body leaning into Wyatt who gives me a *good fucking luck* look.

"I'm bisexual. You got a problem with that? I'd think about your next words very carefully, Jaiden."

"No, I'm just surprised." That only seems to anger her more.

"Why are you surprised? You barely took the time to get to know me. I wanted to share these things with you, but you didn't want that with me."

I stutter, the alcoholic haze over my brain preventing me from formulating a proper sentence.

"Honestly, forget I asked. I want to go home." She turns away from me, walking back to Z.

"Zahraa, I'd love to see you at Pride this weekend. Do you still have my number?"

I watch, my hands clenched at my sides as they exchange numbers, Z giving me an apologetic look.

"Nice to see you again, Dakota," she says. She nods to the rest of us before leaving.

"I'm riding with you, Damian." Sterling doesn't spare a glance as she walks out the door of the bar, leaving the rest of us standing awkwardly.

"Did I say something wrong?" I ask.

Dakota pats my arm as we walk toward the front of the bar. "Her parents were assholes about it. Still are, quite frankly. Just give her some time."

My heart clenches at her words. I don't know much about Sterling's parents. They're some rich financial moguls in Toronto. I haven't heard much about them, and suddenly I'm angry on her behalf.

I didn't mean to upset her. I can only imagine how she feels. If her parents rejected her, she may be afraid of others doing the same.

I climb into the passenger seat of Wyatt's Bronco, the seat already adjusted for a man of my height. He pulls the car out of the parking space, the only conversation between Wyatt and Roman.

I'm really fucking this whole thing up all over again.

I can't find Sterling when we return to the house. Her room is empty and no one's seen her. As everyone trickles back to their rooms, I stay in the living room. I need to know she's okay before I can sleep.

With my book in hand, I spread out on the couch. After an hour of reading, my eyelids feel heavy, my book slipping from my hand.

I barely remember falling asleep until the slight click of a door wakes me. My eyes open adjusting to the dark. Light from the moon pours in but it's barely enough to see Sterling's face fully.

"Why are you out here?" she asks, her voice quiet.

"I wanted to make sure you were okay," I reply, moving my legs from the couch to allow her to sit.

"Oh." She slides into the couch, her legs drawing close to her body. She looks small and vulnerable right now. I want to reach across the space to intertwine our fingers.

"Look," I say at the same time she begins to speak.

She sighs. "Can I go first?" She blinks, her hands gripping at the cushion. I nod.

"I'm sorry I blew up on you." She leans forward, her chest meeting her legs. "When I came out to my parents, they treated me with disgust. They have a high social standing and an image to uphold. When their company decided to become more LGBTQ+ friendly, suddenly they were flaunting their bisexual daughter, and I guess I just expect people to react similarly to them. I'm sorry."

I swallow, my chest rising as I look at her. "I don't care that you're bisexual, Sterling. In fact, I think it's kinda hot knowing you're not afraid to date who you want. I admire that, but I also understand why you were quick to react." My fingers twitch as I stop the urge to reach for her. "I wouldn't react that way, but I probably should have waited to talk to you when we weren't drunk and in the middle of a crowded bar."

She laughs quietly. "Yeah. Maybe drunk conversations are not the best."

"Can I ask why y'all broke up? Clearly, I don't know how to have a good relationship with past flings or whatever." I hope it comes off as a joke and I feel a sense of relief when she laughs.

"We've been pretty terrible, haven't we?" She nudges her elbow at me.

"Yeah. I'm pretty sure our friends want to kill us more often than not." My heart pounds at the ease of our conversation. It feels familiar and comfortable. I don't want it to end.

"We started dating before Dakota and I left Toronto, but the whole long-distance thing is really hard for me. I'm a needy bitch and even though I was traveling a ton at that point in my career, I didn't have my place in Canada and I refused to take money from my parents. It took a toll on our relationship, but fortunately she was really cool about it. She got married last year. I'm super happy for her." She twists the ring on her finger a couple of times before she looks up at me. She doesn't speak, just looks at me like she's solving a puzzle.

"I miss you," I say under my breath. "And I'm sorry. I really fucked up and it's taken me this long to realize that I miss your friendship more than anything. The fucking was nice too, though." I wink and she lightly punches my shoulder.

The fucking was better than nice. It was a spiritual experience.

I'm not dominant with most of my partners. I give them what they want and go on my way, but with Sterling it was different. She allowed me to be who I am, to push the limits of our sexual relationship. She gave as much as I did, and took for herself when she needed it. It's unlike anything I've experienced before. She wanted to please me as much as I wanted to please her. It was like an unspoken language between us. The bedroom became the one place that she could relinquish control, albeit very stubbornly—it wouldn't be Sterling without the stubborn, bratty attitude.

Her lip rolls between her teeth as she looks at me. I can visibly see the way she softens, her eyes studying me. A look passes her face the moment she meets her resolve.

"I miss you too, and I'm only a little bit sorry for making your life hell. You hurt me, Jai." *That damn nickname.* Coming from her lips, it shoots straight to my heart. "But I can see you're trying to fix things. So...maybe you can call me Silver again." She raises an eyebrow, the corner of her mouth lifting.

My eyes go wide in mock surprise. "I've earned the right back? You like me enough to let me call you *Silver*?"

"I guess you're alright." She runs a hand through her hair and I watch every second of it.

"Can I ask you a question?"

She nods, blinking. "Yeah." Her voice is quiet, weak almost.

"Do you like women more than men? Like why date men when you had someone like Zahraa? You looked so comfortable around her."

"Why?" She watches me again like she's decoding me. It's terrifying, but for once I don't want to shut her out.

"Why what?"

"What does it matter if I like women more than men? How does it affect you?"

I groan, throwing my head back. *It doesn't.* "I want to learn how to be enough for you, and I worry I won't ever be that." As soon as the words are out of my mouth, I regret them. I don't know what to do. I can get up and walk out of the room, or I can pretend like it never happened.

Her voice breaks through my internal panic. "You would've been enough, Jaiden. I could've been happy with you. I wanted to settle down and to be yours. You *are* enough," she says, and my throat closes up.

I'm so fucking lost to this girl. All along, I'd been falling for her, even while we fought.

"Thank you." It's the only thing I can think of to say. I want to make her promises, but right now I can't. I'm a work in progress and that's enough for me. I hope it's enough for her too.

"Friends?" I ask, grabbing my book from the floor.

She smiles, her eyes glittering in the moonlight. From here, she looks almost ethereal. The silver strands of her hair are illuminated, and I want to kiss her, to devour her. Not like I used to, but in a way she deserves. But I can't. She belongs to another man.

Though I want her to be *mine*.

EIGHTEEN

STERLING

AS SOON AS I wake up, I toss my blankets off of me, sliding my legs from the bed. I'm wearing a large t-shirt and I can't be bothered to wear anything else.

My mind wandered over the events of last night with an intensity I can't describe. I normally don't fixate as heavily, but with this, I couldn't make it stop, and I need to talk to someone about it *desperately*.

Ripping my door open, I take two big steps to Damian's door, my fist pounding on the heavy wood.

When it finally opens, Damian's hair is askew, his eyes barely open. "What?" His voice is groggy, the word barely formulated.

My palm comes to his chest as I shove him backwards into the room, kicking the door closed behind us. He stumbles and sits back onto the bed.

My body is alight with anxious energy, so I jump into his luscious bed, pushing the blankets around until they're covering me slightly.

"I need to talk to you," I say, my voice higher than normal.

Damian rubs at his eyes, the usually cocky man slowly coming back to reality. "Okay?"

"Jaiden and I talked last night, and I told him that he can call me

Silver again." I blink at him several times waiting for him to register the enormity of the situation.

He freezes, his head tilting as he looks at me. "Oh, *fuck.* Okay? And then what?"

"Well, he told me that he missed me and he asked me about my bisexuality and said something about wanting to be enough for me and I couldn't stop thinking about it. I still can't." The words spill out of me so quickly, I can hardly stop them.

"So, you're friends again, and Jai slightly admitted that he likes you in a stubborn Jaiden sort of way?"

I nod aggressively.

"Okay, how do you feel?"

I twist my hands in my lap. "I don't know. I don't know where to go from here."

"What do you want?" He pushes his hair back. I appreciate the way he gives me his full attention, his amber eyes watching mine.

"I think I want to test the waters of being friends again. I'm finally feeling like myself again and I don't want to mess that up."

"I'll support you through it all. He fucks this up and I'll beat his ass." He leans in, kissing the top of my head. "Now get out of my room so I can shower."

I laugh, my stomach clenching with the full force of it. Standing, I smile at him before opening the door and slipping through it.

My heart stops when I see Jaiden standing in the hallway. His lips purse as he looks at me. His eyes wander down my body. There's an almost sad look that crosses his face as he gives me a nod and continues walking past me.

I should stop him. I feel my arm reaching for him, but I yank it back. *Not yet.*

I shuffle back toward my room, a sense of determination coming over me. I've got shit to do.

Lani grips my arm as we walk through the crowd. Pride has been incredible. I'd forgotten how liberating it is to be around people like me.

Dakota's seated on Wyatt's shoulders as we walk further into the madness. I look up and smile at her, seeing her green eyes full of delight. She'd protested at first, but Wyatt insisted on carrying her. Of course, the massive man would make carrying her look easy. I can barely run down the street, but he's walking with ease with a whole human on his shoulders. I know Dakota's not a fan of crowds, so I appreciate Wyatt being so in tune to her needs.

There's a sense of peace within my soul. Seeing all the rainbows and myriad of different Pride flags brings a smile to my face. What makes me happier though, is that all of the guys are decked out in rainbow. Jaiden is shirtless with little rainbow pasties and rainbow booty shorts. When he came out of his room dressed like that, I nearly choked.

I sneak a peek at him, the muscles of his sides on clear display. I look a little too closely at the single angel wing he has tattooed on his side, the feathers opening up onto his rips. There's sweat dripping down his back from the heat, but I couldn't care less. He looks absolutely delicious. I could run my tongue up his abs and back down to his perfect v... I shake my head.

Get your head out of the gutter.

Wyatt, Roman and Damian are all matching with their rainbow shorts and a muscle tee with an ally flag on the front. We've gotten lots of stares, but I'm used to it by now. Any time I went anywhere with Jaiden, there were eyes on us at every moment. He's hot and he knows it. I was confident enough then to see that his eyes were solely on me. Now, I don't know what he wants.

Friends. We're friends.

The crowd disperses slightly as we near the side streets where we parked.

I look back at the parade once more before looking forward again.

"Hey," Jaiden says from my side.

"Hey," I say, smiling up at him. It's weird being friends with him again, but it feels like a sense of rightness has returned to my life.

"Wanna ride back with me?" He raises a brow and I snort, nodding my head.

"Sure. I do miss the Jeep." I lick my lips as I feel Lani squeeze my arm. When I look at her, she's smirking at me and I nearly roll my eyes. *Yeah, yeah. I know.*

Right as we near the end of the street, I catch sight of a sign that reads "Take a Duck, Don't give a Fuck." There's a giant rubber duck on the sign and I nearly collapse.

"I fucking love ducks," I say, slipping my arm from Lani and rushing toward the booth.

The booth is decked out in different kinds of rainbow rubber duckies, each with a different flag. I jump up and down as I look at them, the person behind the booth smiling.

"Take one," he says, his eyes smiling.

My fingers run across the different ducks, and I pick the one with the bisexual flag on it. I start to turn away, but suddenly I'm struck with an idea.

"Hey. Do you happen to have more of these ducks?"

"Tons." He leans down to grab a full bag of mixed ducks. "Here—take a bag. I'll be wrapping up soon anyways."

I take the bag from him right as Jaiden appears at my side again. "Thank you!"

He nods politely before looking back at the crowd.

"What's with the ducks?" Jaiden asks.

"You'll see," I say with a conspiratorial wink. I practically skip to the line of cars.

When we reach Jaiden's Jeep, I look over at Damian. "I'm riding back with Jaiden. Don't expect us right away."

He doesn't miss a beat, a small smirk toying at the corner of his lips. "Bring her back safe," he says, hitting the auto start button for the Hellcat. The car roars to life and a familiar sense of glee fills my belly.

"Should I be scared?" Jaiden asks, unlocking his Jeep.

"Absolutely. This is going to be so fun." I can't help the borderline evil giggle that escapes me. I've wanted to do this for so long.

"Where to?" he asks, turning the engine over. As the car roars to life, a rush of excitement runs through my blood.

"Just drive through town for a bit." I grip my bag of ducks tightly in my lap.

The drive is mostly silent until we pull up to a stoplight downtown. A bright blue Jeep pulls up to the side of us and I grin.

"Dakota is always too weenie to play this with me." I pull a duck from the bag and unbuckle my seat belt.

"Silver! What are you doing?" Jaiden's voice is slightly panicked when I rip the door open and jump from the car.

"Duck Duck!" I yell, sitting the duck on the driver side mirror before diving back into the car. "Go!" I scream, and Jaiden hits the gas, propelling us forward.

"What the fuck was that?" he asks with a laugh.

"It's called *Duck, Duck, Jeep*. Jeep drivers will keep rubber ducks in their cars and throw them into the windows of other Jeeps or leave them on the mirrors or windshields of the parked Jeeps around town."

"I've had a Jeep for years and have never been ducked." He flicks a curl from his face, keeping his eyes trained on the road until we pull up to another stoplight.

"Well, you're not hanging with the right people then. Dakota has been ducked *so* many times and I die every time. She's got a small collection in her glove compartment."

I see another jeep parked on the side of the road and I don't even need to ask Jaiden to pull up to the side of it. Their window is open, the person sitting on their phone.

My eyes meet Jaiden's before I toss the duck through the window and he yells "Duck Duck!" as we peel away.

His laughter flows through me like a drug. I never want to forget that sound. It's rich, like the best kind of cheesecake, and deep enough to make my belly flutter with arousal. I'm struck with a memory of Jaiden laughing into my ear as we lay in bed together. It was memories like those that hit me when I hated him the most. He made me laugh like no other. He's got this cache of dumb jokes that are so stupid, I couldn't help but laugh.

His hand reaches across the center console to rest on my leg and I don't resist it. His thumb draws small circles on my thigh, the feeling incredibly comforting.

"Wanna hear a joke?" He pulls up to another car and I toss the duck softly onto the hood.

"Sure," I say with a laugh.

"Where is Peter Pan's favorite place to eat?" He turns to look at me briefly before looking back at the road.

"Where?"

"Wendy's." He purses his lips waiting for my reaction and I barely resist a moment before a very unladylike snort erupts from my nose.

"That's so dumb," I wheeze. "But it's *so* funny."

He chuckles again, his hand tightening on my thigh as he accelerates up the long driveway of the lake house.

I take a moment to appreciate it. This home is incredible, and everything I've always wanted.

"I want to make it up to Wyatt and Dakota for being such a bitch these last few weeks by planning the best wedding ever. She deserves that much."

"Just tell me what you need." His hand lingers for a moment longer before slipping from my thigh and gripping the steering wheel as he climbs from the car.

I sit and stare a moment, taking a deep breath. Things are finally looking up for me.

I *want* him. I don't just want friendship—I want to date him.

Maybe it's time I step up my game.

NINETEEN

JAIDEN

LILY SCREAMS the moment we walk through the door. Her little legs carry her quickly toward me and I squat before she collides with my chest.

"You just saw me a couple of hours ago, Princess," I say into her hair with a laugh.

"Yes, but I missed you, Uncle Jai. All of the adults got to have fun while I sat with the baby." She scowls and I look over her shoulder at Dakota who is shaking her head.

Dakota's brother, Dallas, and his wife, Casey, are here with their kid, Hunter. He's gotten so big since I saw him the last time. He walks, stumbling a little, with his arms outstretched toward Lily.

"She's got a new fan," Casey says from beside Dakota.

"Daddy says I can't date until I'm thirty." Lily crosses her arms across her chest.

"Well, it's a good thing Hunter is way too young for you right now," I mumble. Silver jabs my side and I laugh, looking up at her.

"Now, since everyone is home, we were thinking about setting up a movie out back. Care to join us?" Dakota looks around the room and I nod when she locks eyes with me.

"Koda, we've got a whole ass movie room and you want to do it outside?" Silver shakes her head as she walks to the girls, pulling

Casey into her arms and speaking quietly to her. They laugh before releasing each other.

"Yes, I absolutely want to do it outside. In case you've forgotten, this vacation was my idea." Dakota points to herself and for a moment, I see the similarities between Sterling and Dakota. Although they look nothing like each other, there are moments when I can see the proof of the decades of friendship they share.

I'm still watching Sterling when I feel a tug at my shorts. Lily looks up at me with this shit-eating grin on her face.

I lift her into the air, her soft giggles filling the space as I prop her on my hip. Her small hands come to my face as she brings her mouth to my ears.

"Do you love Auntie Silver?"

I nearly choke, covering it with a cough as I look with wide eyes at her.

"Uhm, why would you ask that?" I sputter with the least bit of swagger. My niece is a savage.

She giggles, her hand running across my short beard. "Because you look at Auntie Silver like Uncle Wyatt looks at Auntie Koda." She smiles sweetly before continuing. "Daddy says sometimes I'm too smart for my own good."

I boop her nose and she scrunches her face with laughter. "You're scary smart." I turn my head to watch the women talking again.

Do I love her?

I don't completely remember what love feels like. I remember the hurt and the loss of losing someone I love, but the actual feeling of love itself? Casual love, like the love I have for my brothers or for Lily, I know that feeling well. Romantic love is a different story.

"I don't know, Princess," I say honestly.

She blinks at me, her head turning like she's solving a puzzle. *What is with these women reading me so well?*

"Auntie Silver doesn't look sad anymore." She says it matter-of-factly. My heart clenches. "She was really sad."

"Was she?" I choke out.

"I heard her talking to Auntie Koda and she said that some guy was mean to her, and then she cried."

"I'm a dick," I say under my breath as I put Lily down.

Wyatt walks into the house and summons everyone out back. He takes one look at my face and I can see the moment he realizes something is wrong. It doesn't take long for everyone to walk to the back, the house emptying.

He walks to me, his eyebrows raised and his hands shoved into his pockets. "What's up?"

"Lily told me she overheard Dakota and Silver talking about"—I throw up air quotes—"some guy that was mean to her and Silver was crying."

Wyatt's eyes soften. "Man, it's in the past. Y'all seem to be doing okay now."

"Yeah, but I made her cry. I'm not that guy, and I became that guy because I'm a fucking idiot." I follow Wyatt to the fridge. He cracks open a beer and hands it to me.

"Our niece saw it, which I'm assuming is the hardest part for you to grasp."

My tongue runs across my lips as I think. "I can't do that to her again."

"No," he says, his voice firm. "You can't. Partially because Dakota will have your head on a platter, and partially because you both deserve better than that. You're in a good spot right now. You finally look happy again."

"Well, my balls aren't being nailed to the wall every time I speak, so that's an improvement." I laugh, but it's not a true laugh. I'm panicking on the inside.

"Yeah, don't do that." Wyatt eyes me seriously and I swallow. "If you like her, commit. No more of the internal panic, wishy-washy bullshit. I can promise you that she can handle a lot more than you think."

I huff a breath. "Okay."

Wyatt fist bumps my arm. "It's going to be okay."

After today, I can believe that.

EVERYONE'S SEATED ON THE BOAT EXCEPT FOR SILVER and Lani. We're tied to the dock as we wait, the boat bobbing in the water.

Leaning my head back, I let the warm sun kiss my skin. I may have dozed off for a moment, but when I hear voices, I slowly blink my eyes open.

What my eyes see should be criminal. Silver is walking across the dock in a see through sarong, the neon yellow bikini underneath on full display.

She looks edible, the neon bringing attention to the glow of her golden skin. Her silver hair is tied back, the bits of brown and silver of her bangs hanging out of the small bun.

It's the way her hips sway and the carefree smile on her face that does me in. I cough, crossing my legs to hide the quickly growing stiffy in my swim trunks. *Fuck me.*

"Hey, boys! Happy July first," she says, and I don't skip a beat, reaching my hand up to help her into the boat.

She watches me as she steps into the boat, then looks down at her small hand in mine. I feel the air freeze around us.

I realize then that I'm not just starved for touch. I'm starved for *her* touch. Her spicy-sweet smell hits me and I breathe deeply.

"If y'all are done eye fucking over there, can we get this boat moving?" Damian chuckles and I look over my shoulder to glare at him.

"I wasn't," I say but he shakes his head.

"All good, man." He raises a hand, a small smirk on his face.

Silver laughs, sitting next to Dakota and Lani on the padded stern of the boat. Wyatt revs the engine, pulling away from the dock and out into the open water. When we make it to a clear spot of the lake, he hands the controls over to me as he straps into his wake-boarding gear.

"Ease me into it, Jai. I'm a little rusty." He winks at Dakota before leaning back into the water, his board lifted and his hands gripping the handle.

"Got the flag?" I look at Damian and he nods. I flip him a thumbs up before easing the boat forward. In the mirror, I can see Wyatt get up immediately.

Dakota sits up, watching him show off.

"Rusty my ass!" I shout and Dakota laughs.

"Get it, baby!" she yells. I doubt he can hear her, but who fucking cares. I'd be excited to have a beautiful woman cheering me on too.

After a while, I turn the boat and Wyatt releases the handle, Damian throwing up the orange flag.

We circle back until Wyatt climbs onto the back of the boat. "Who's next?"

We each take turns wakeboarding after Wyatt. When it's my turn, I wipe out trying to jump the wake. Everyone laughs but I don't miss the slight concern on Silver's face.

When I climb back into the boat, Wyatt ties the tube to the back after hooking the boards back onto the rack.

Lani, Sterling and Dakota jump onto the tube in a fit of laughter. The life jackets nearly drown them, but it's necessary.

Wyatt takes it easy at first, then suddenly the tube is bouncing wildly across the water. I can see the smiles on their faces as Wyatt drives, sending them flying. I look forward for a moment, and my heart stops when I hear a blood curdling scream.

I look back and see one person missing from the tube.

"Turn the boat around," I say. Wyatt doesn't hear me so I raise my voice. "Wyatt, turn the fucking boat around!"

He looks at me and sees the panic in my face. He nods, slowing the boat and circling back. I see Sterling bobbing in the water, her hand gripping her life vest tightly.

I rush to the back, gripping her and raising her onto the low step. She winces when I touch her.

"Take me back home." Her voice is low with a hint of pain.

"Are you okay?" I ask and she shakes her head.

"I'm fine." Her eyes look red, and there's something about the way she says it that makes me believe that she's the exact opposite.

Dakota and Lani climb back onto the boat once the rope is secured to the back once again. I see Dakota whispering to Sterling, her head bobbing as they talk.

Wyatt takes us back to the dock quickly. We're barely secured to the dock before Sterling storms off the boat, not caring to remove her life jacket first. Lani says something, but I don't hear it.

"Is she okay?" I ask Dakota with a hint of panic.

She shrugs lightly. "I think she's hurt."

My blood runs cold. *Hurt. She's hurt.*

"I'm gonna go," I start to say and Dakota smirks.

"Go ahead."

I jump from the boat and sprint down the dock toward the house. I slip on the hardwood floor when I rush through the back door and down the hallway to the stairs.

My heart pounds, my head spinning when I approach her room. Shouldn't Damian be doing this? Shouldn't he be freaking out over her safety? He's her boyfriend, not me. Why did everyone just let me go, running after her in a panic?

I shake my head, knocking on her door. "Silver! Are you okay?"

"I'm fine," she yells, but I can hear the shake in her voice. She's crying.

"I'm coming in," I say, just as she yells a weak *no.* I don't listen though. My woman is hurt and I need to help her.

I see her standing in the bathroom with her hands gripping her chest tightly. There are tears streaming down her face as she paces.

"What happened?" I ask as I approach her slowly, watching as her eyes go wide.

"I said I'm fine." She moves her hand from her chest to swipe at her face and that's when I see blood.

In two steps, I'm in front of her. "Show me," I command. "Show me where you're hurt."

She shakes her head, a beat of panic crossing her face. "I can't."

"Silver." My voice is firm, and I leave no room for discussion.

She sighs before removing her hand from her chest again. I see the pool of blood seeping through her bikini top. She turns away from me, showing me her back. "Untie me, please."

My hands shake as I loosen the strings of her top. I shouldn't be turned on right now. I shouldn't be enjoying the feel of her skin beneath my hands—but I am.

She whimpers, her head looking down before turning to face me again. She blinks, the tears falling from her eyes.

My jaw clenches as I take in the sight of her. "Fucking hell," I breathe.

Her arms grip her waist tightly, but it does nothing to hide the jewelry that decorates her nipples. My eyes lock on the thin bar through her nipples, two diamonds glimmer on either side of it.

"This is new," I say before meeting her eyes. She grimaces, her chest rising and falling as she breathes.

"I had a moment of courage, and you had just pissed me off," she says with a weak smile.

I point at her chest. "This is because of me?"

I look into her eyes, trying to keep my gaze from her breasts. It's nothing I haven't seen before. I've seen those little vines decorating her collar bones and the crescent moon on her sternum. So why are these *damn* piercings doing something to my insides?

She shrugs. "Kinda. I wanted an identity change, so I had them pierced." Her lips purse slightly before they quiver again. "I think it snagged on my life vest when I fell off the tube. It fucking hurts."

"Okay. What do you need me to do?"

After I helped Sterling clean herself up, I left her to rest in the room. She was still upset when I left and although I barged into the room, I didn't want to overstay my welcome. We're just now getting back to normal and I don't want that to change.

Walking out onto the back porch, the others are sitting around the fire pit. I close the door behind me and make my way toward them.

"Hey," Dakota says, smiling. She hands me a s'more and I take it gratefully.

Shoving it into my mouth, I take the seat next to Damian.

"Is she okay?" he asks, his voice low.

"Yeah. She's sleeping." I lean forward, resting my elbow on my thigh. The warmth from the fire reaches me, warming me from the slight nip in the air.

"What happened?" Damian takes a bite of his s'more and chews it slowly.

"I don't know how it happened, but her piercing snagged on the life vest and aggravated the healing skin."

He's silent for a moment, his eyes looking forward. "Piercing?"

I look over at him, the red in his beard illuminated in the light of the fire. "Yeah. Her nipple piercings."

He meets my eyes and I see the surprise cross his face before it's replaced by something else. "Oh, yeah. Well, I'm glad she's okay."

I stare at him, my eyes squinting. "You didn't know," I say plainly.

He shrugs. "Forgot." He gets up from his seat and grabs another s'more from the stack.

He forgot about the sexiest nipple piercings on the planet. How does a man with a penis forget about that? I blink into the fire for several moments, my mind swimming.

I run through the events of the past four weeks. So much of this didn't make sense to me. Their lack of touch and the friendly nature of their relationship is just the foundation of my suspicion, and now Damian just forgets about something as large as this. I thought they were sleeping together.

When I look up from the fire, I lock eyes with Dakota. She's watching me, her eyes almost devious. My gaze wanders across everyone around the fire and suddenly I feel hot, my vision blurring red as the pieces *finally* start falling into place.

TWENTY

STERLING

MY BODY IS TRAPPED within a blanket, and I'm wrapped up like a burrito. Jaiden tucked me in before he left and the sentiment behind it makes my stomach flutter with attraction.

I don't want to leave the comfort of my bed, but the urge to pee is so strong that I can't remain much longer. After arguing with myself for several minutes, I finally unwrap myself from my comfort and slide from the bed.

I'm washing my hands when the bedroom door slams, loud footsteps stomping through my room.

My breathing hitches when I see Jaiden standing in my room, his eyes furious. "What. The. Fuck?" he asks, stalking toward me. I back up, my skin kissing the wall of the bathroom.

"What?" I ask, my voice panicked.

"What?" he asks, his voice exasperated. "That is the question of the evening, isn't it?" He towers over me, his chest heaving.

"Uh. Yes?" I frown at him, my body shivering from the nearness of him.

"Tell me, Sterling, why Damian didn't know about your nipple piercings?" He tilts his head. "I distinctly remember the overly aggressive sounds of *sex* coming from his room."

I steel my expression, unwilling to admit the truth to him. "He's never seen me *fully* naked." It's the best lie I can come up with.

"Huh. Is that so? I think you're lying to me." He leans in, his hot breath caressing my neck. I gasp when his hand grips my wrist and raises it above my head.

"I'm not." My voice wavers.

"Then tell me to stop," he says, his free hand sliding under my shirt and sliding up my belly. "Tell me to stop because you have a boyfriend."

His fingers trail the underside of my breasts and I suck in a sharp breath at the sensation. Heat shoots right to my pussy and I whimper involuntarily.

"Tell me to stop, Sterling." The command is clear in his voice. I don't want him to stop. My body is on fire for him, my skin sensitive to his touch.

"No," I say with a gasp. I writhe against him as his fingers stay in one spot. I want him to move, to touch me all over.

His gray eyes narrow, his full lips so close to me now. I suck in a breath, the earthy smell of him filling my nose.

"Okay, then." He pulls his hand quickly from my breast, his eyebrow raising at me. I protest, my eyebrows drawing together and he *tsks*. "When you behave, I'll give you what you want."

"We broke up," I say, with a huff. "He likes Lani."

"No shit. Anyone with eyes can see that, but that's not the truth." He pulls away from me and I feel cold.

Like a child, I stomp my foot, my eyes glaring at him. "What do you want me to say?" I snap at him. I fight back, poking at his need for control.

His pupils dilate "I want you to tell me the truth."

My spine straightens as I stand up taller. My toes come right to his as I tilt my head in challenge. "Make me."

He smirks before his hand comes to my hair, a handful gripped into his fist. He pushes me back, his other hand coming to my neck and his thumb resting on my jaw. "Tell me it's fake. Tell me that I can kiss you; that this whole fucking time I've been killing myself because you've moved on, when in reality, it was all fake. I was ready to let you go."

I nearly cry at the vulnerability in his voice. He was ready to let me go. Why does that thought send my body into a fit of anxiety?

"It's fake," I admit. My voice is quiet, lacking the defiance from before.

"Why?" he asks, his hand tightening in my hair. It sends a pulse of pleasure through me.

"I can't tell you." I blink at him, hoping my eyes convey the truth. It feels manipulative and sticky, but in actuality, it was a cry for attention from *him.*

He growls, his hand ripping away from my throat. He shakes his head as he walks around in a circle.

"And everyone knows? You've been faking this whole time?"

I nod.

His jaw tightens and the heat from before is gone. Instead, it's replaced by insecurity and confusion. I fear he's going to run away from me.

He meets my eyes again, his face softening. "Okay, here's what is going to happen. I'm going to run this shit off because I've been an idiot in the past and I refuse to do that again. I *want* to talk to you and—" he rubs his hands down his face— "*Fuck,* I want to do so much with you, but right now I need a minute. I promise you that I'll come back."

I bite my lip, the creep of anxiety crawling up my skin. "Okay," I say, my voice lacking confidence. I fear that he'll hop in his car and drive away. I'm scared that being this close again will lead to tragedy once more. *We're this close.* I can't suffer the loss of him again.

He sighs, his lips pressing to my forehead. "I'll be back." And then he's gone, the door closing behind him.

I shut my eyes before walking to my bed and grabbing my phone. My fingers fly across the screen as I type out a text to the girls. It's full of vulnerability and fear, and for once, I'm not afraid to show it.

Me: I need you.

TWENTY-ONE

JAIDEN

IT'S NOT the same as skating on a hockey rink, but it's pretty damn close. I shouldn't have packed my skates, but I did. Maybe I knew that this moment would come, and that I'd need the peace that skating brings me.

I skate across the small indoor rink, dribbling the puck as I move.

"What is with you guys and escaping to the ice?"

I freeze, looking up from the ice to the door. Dakota's standing there with her arms resting across her chest.

She looks like she's just rolled from bed, but she still looks as fierce as ever.

"It's safe," I reply. "It's always been safe."

She smiles, walking toward the bench at the side. When she sits, I skate to the side, leaning over the railing.

"Hi," she says, her brows raised. It's a peace offering, and I know it.

I sigh, my shoulder's sagging. "Hey."

"It was my idea," she blurts.

I frown, my arms resting on the side now. "Okay..." I say, unsure of how to proceed.

"Look, I love you like an older brother and you're one of my best friends, but you're an idiot. No offense," she laughs, and I can't help but free the smile that toys at the corner of my lips.

"None taken," I say with a chuckle. "Please, do go on insulting me."

She rolls her eyes. "You both were so miserable and anyone with a set of eyes could see that you both had some sort of feelings. Maybe manipulation of the situation wasn't the best choice, but hey, I was the fixer of my family." She shrugs, her lips forming a thin line. "Making you jealous was just one part. With Sterling, she needed the safety net of having some sort of project and challenge. She needed to believe that this was to help you, and it was an easy shove."

She looks at me as the silence grows around us. "Also, Sterling manipulated shit when it came to my relationship, and it was only fair that I returned the favor."

Sterling was a mastermind behind many elements of Wyatt and Dakota's relationship. She practically shoved them together, and although I know Dakota needed that shove, I don't like the feeling of manipulation. Wyatt and Dakota are meant to be together, but I don't know if I can say the same for myself and Sterling. Then again, there is no one else I want her to be with. Maybe that's just my crazy possessive feelings talking though.

I point my finger at her, but it lacks conviction. "I can't believe I have been a pawn this whole time. I hope you know I've been a perfect gentleman despite what my brain has been telling me to do."

She scrunches her nose in disgust. "Jaiden. I don't need to know your dirty thoughts about my best friend, thanks." She locks eyes with me, her chin raising. "It worked, didn't it? You're friends again."

"Yeah, yeah," I grumble. "We're sort of talking again."

"Good. The foundations need to be better this time. Not just sex. I'll cut your balls off if you hurt her again, Jai. I'm serious." She stands, and even though she's small, I'm terrified of her. "Go talk to her. Be honest and then"—she waves her hand around haphazardly — "don't wake the whole house. I'm going to wear ear plugs."

"Dakota Easton, did you just tell me to go fuck your best friend?"

Her eyes go wide, her face turning red. "I really dislike you right now, but yes. Please. You're irritating everyone with your sexual tension." She shakes her head. "I'm leaving now." She practically runs from the indoor rink like her butt was on fire.

I can't help but smile after her.

I sit down, unlacing my skates, before walking down the hall and into my room. As I set everything down, my body panics. I don't know what to say to her, or how to have this conversation, but I just need to trust the process. It's the only thing I can do.

When I sneak into Sterling's room, she's curled into her pillow, her hair sprawled out in every direction. Her face is red like she's been crying and I want nothing more than to capture her in my arms. Something like this would've scared me away before—the raw emotion and the vulnerability of the situation—but she's worth the risk.

Pushing the blanket's aside, I climb into the bed beside her, my arm wrapping around her and pulling her close to me.

A small groan leaves her mouth before her leg wraps around my body. My cock twitches in my shorts, but it's not the time for that. A beautiful woman's body is wrapped around mine, I can't help it.

Her warm breath hits my chest and I'm content like this—with her wrapped up safe in my arms, and for this moment, she's *mine.* I stare at the wall, thinking over what needs to be said when I notice the breathing has stopped. I look down to see her watching me.

"What are you thinking about?" she asks, her voice quiet.

"There's so much I need to say to you, and I was thinking about how I'm going to say it." I move my hand to her face, brushing the silver strands of hair from her cheek.

"My ears are open." She blinks, waiting.

My heart pounds in my chest. I need to lay it all out there, to bare my heart to her. It's fucking *scary,* but it must be done.

"Let me start by telling you that these aren't excuses. I was an idiot and I'm owning that now, but I need you to understand what was happening in my head at the time shit hit the fan."

She nods, urging me on.

"My mom was my best friend, and the only family I ever had. In high school, she got really sick, but hid it from me because she didn't want me to worry, and at that point, I had my sights set on going pro in hockey." I take a breath, closing my eyes to focus on the words. "Everything was fine for a while and then I went to college for a minute and when I came home before being picked up by the AHL, I found her unresponsive on the floor."

Sterling gasps softly, and I run my fingers through my hair to soothe her.

"I saw her deteriorate quickly from that point, until one day she was just gone. It was the hardest thing I've ever been through. You remind me a lot of her. She was spunky, opinionated, strong as hell, and refused to put up with anyone's shit. She had to be with me as her son." I laugh, remembering the way she would jut out her hip and point at me with that damn wooden spoon in her hand. She was this tiny woman, and I towered over her in middle school, but she scared the living hell out of me.

"Anyway, I guess I've been broken since she passed. It's easier to not get attached than to worry about losing someone important to you. But that happened to me already...with you. I freaked the hell out, Sterling. You scare me more than my mom did. Everything about you scares me: the way you just see right through me, and how being friends with you was the easiest thing I've ever done. So when I felt myself getting attached, I ran. Not to mention I'd gotten a letter from my fuckhead father that same week, and it was a reminder of the man I could turn into."

Sterling's eyes flick between mine, and I'm scared to see the reaction to the words coming from my mouth.

"Running was easier than confronting this"—I wave my hand between us, and she laughs.

"You're an idiot," she breathes. "You're *such* an idiot. I would've waited, Jai. I would've been patient with you, but cutting me out altogether hurt me *so* much."

I grip at her waist, the fear of her leaving creeping at the edges of my mind. "I know, but I'm here now."

"Yeah," she says, her mouth twisting slightly. "Thank you for telling me."

My throat tightens as I look at her. "What now? I'm leaving this up to you."

She bites her lip, her eyes avoiding mine. "I don't know if I trust you just yet, but I want *something,* even if it's casual for now. I need to know you're not going to do that to me again."

Casual... fine. Casual is fine for now. Not at all what I was expecting, but okay.

"You're in control."

Sterling gasps, mockingly. "Jaiden Thomas giving up control? Never thought I'd see the day."

"Shut your mouth, or I'll shut it for you." I'm teasing, but the excited gleam that crosses Sterling's eyes goes right to my cock.

"I'm not opposed to that." She sits up, her eyes watching me as she pushes me so that I'm flat on my back. Bringing one leg over me, she straddles my waist, and I pull her mouth to mine.

She tastes like candy, a lingering sweetness on her lips from earlier. I want to taste every inch of her, to remember the way that her body reacts to me, but instead I slow my pace, urging my tongue into her mouth and deepening the kiss.

Her hips rotate on my waist, and I groan. *Wicked, evil, little thing.*

"We play by my rules in the bedroom, sweetheart." I bite her lip, and she moans, pressing her chest deeper against mine. I can feel the piercings and suddenly I want to explore them. My hand grips her ass, holding her to me as I flip her onto her back.

Releasing her mouth, I pull the stretchy fabric of her shirt down, exposing her breasts. She's so beautiful, a woman crafted from every fantasy. I palm her left breast, my thumb rubbing over the jewelry decorating her nipple. With the first flick of my tongue, she writhes against me, her soft moan filling the room.

"*That* is how you sound during sex, not that horrendous moaning you did with Damian." I suck her hardened bud into my mouth, loving the way that she reacts to the sensitivity of it.

"Please," she gasps.

"Please, what?" I growl into her breast, and she shivers.

"More, give me more. I *need* more." She bucks into me, and I chuckle. I want to please her, but I also want to torture her. I want her to feel my anger and my jealousy from the last couple weeks. She needs to know the way she makes me feel, and the way that I feel about her. She played games, and now it's my turn.

I release her, rising from the bed without a word. I can hear the indignation in her small whimpers of protest, and I nearly turn back, but I need her to behave.

She glowers at me from the bed and I only stare until she huffs, raising a brow.

"Good," I praise. "Take off your panties." I stand at the foot of the bed, watching her as she slides the thin fabric from her body.

"Now what?" It's her tone that brings a wicked smirk to my face.

"Shirt," I say, crossing my hands over my chest. I pull my own from my body, tossing it to the floor. Her eyes rake over my bare chest and it brings me a sense of satisfaction.

As she settles, I grip her legs and yank her to the edge of the bed. She yelps, and I silence her with a look.

"Here's how this is going to go: I need you to not wake the whole house, so when you're good, you get to come, and when you're not, I walk away. Got it?"

She nods furiously, and I chuckle.

"Good girl. Now, spread your legs for me."

I kneel before her, my fingers running through her folds. She's soaking, but I'm not surprised. I massage her, seeing the way her body arches to my touch. My cock is painfully hard, but tonight isn't about me. I'm sending a message. *Mine, and only mine.*

My face comes to her core, the flat of my tongue running across her clit. She moans, her legs tightening over my shoulders and around my neck. With my hand, I massage her opening, not yet entering her.

"*Jai*," she gasps as I flick the sensitive bundle of nerves with my tongue. She tenses, my finger sliding inside of her, letting her adjust to the intrusion. It doesn't take long before I'm adding a second finger, my tongue still working her.

She's quiet—for the most part—and I praise her, rewarding her with a third finger. I watch her, her head thrown back and her chest heaving, as I work her closer to a climax. She gasps, her body tensing. That's when I know she's close, and precisely when I stop my movements, pulling my hand from her and slipping my fingers into my mouth.

She growls, her head shooting up to look up at me. "Jaiden, what the fuck?" Her voice is breathy and flustered, and I hate to admit that it turns me on knowing I've worked her up like this.

I smirk, pulling my fingers from my mouth. "You don't get what you want until I say so."

"Jaiden," she growls.

"No," I say. "You and Damian played with me for weeks, and now I have control. Don't worry, sweetheart, I'll take care of you... eventually." I smirk again and she glares at me.

"I fucking hate..." She breaks off her protests with a moan as I bring my mouth back to her clit, my movements more aggressive than before. She whines when my fingers slide back into her at an achingly slow pace. It's fun teasing her like this. I *know* her body, and the control I have right now has me hard as fuck.

I move my fingers, hitting her g-spot and making her cry out. Her legs tighten, and she presses her pussy harder into my face. I laugh, flicking my tongue across her clit. It takes less time than before to get her to the point right before release, her body tightening around my fingers before I remove them, leaving her gasping in frustration.

"Why?" she complains. "I've been good."

"Have you?" I taste her, slipping my tongue inside of her. My hands grip at her ass, raising her pussy to my face. She tastes incredible, just like I remember. She's an addiction, and I don't have it in me to care about the danger she poses to my heart.

"Yes," she gasps, her hands gripping the bedding. "*So* good."

"You danced with him, Sterling. You let me believe you were sleeping with him. You let his hands touch you, and it wrecked me. I've never seen green before, but with you, I want to rip you away from any man who lays eyes on you."

Licking my lips, I let my fingers do the work, bringing her to her peak and stopping before she can come.

She shakes, her eyes watering as I look at her. "*You* ran, Jaiden. Not me. I *wanted* to move on, but it was only ever you."

"Well then, this will serve as a reminder that you were only ever mine to begin with, and I don't plan on letting you go ever again." I flick my tongue against her, feeling her writhe against my face. She cries, her body shaking as she reaches her peak, her body denied the release once more. A frustrated scream leaves her mouth, and I silence her with my tongue. "If you want casual, fine, but you're *mine*."

She pants, her body tensing.

"Say it, and I'll let you come."

She whimpers, her legs shaking around me. I feel her tense, and I'm ready to pull my mouth from her pussy when she finally speaks.

"I'm yours," she whispers. "Please."

It's a broken plea, and I can't deny her anymore. With a single flick of my tongue, she topples over the edge, her body squeezing my fingers tightly. I help her ride out her orgasm until she relaxes on the bed. It's then that I hover above her, capturing her mouth with mine. Her face is wet with tears and she tastes like salt, but I don't care. She's mine, and that is all that matters.

TWENTY-TWO

STERLING

"I WANT to keep this between us for a while," I say as Jaiden pulls his shirt over his head.

He looks at me with apprehension, and I want to ease his mind immediately.

"I'm not ready to share you just yet. I just want this to be for us. Plus, I really don't know what this is yet. I need to learn to trust you again."

His eyes soften as he walks to me, his hands settling on my shoulders. "I get it," he says. "I'll follow your lead."

I reach around, grabbing his ass and squeezing before releasing him. "We're gonna be late," I say as I strut away from him. When I look over my shoulder, I see him staring at my ass and I couldn't be more proud.

I have a feeling that my life is about to get a whole lot more fun.

Jaiden drives me, Lani and Damian to the Great Canadian Midway while the others take Wyatt's car. I'm honestly slightly terrified to be coming here with the two most competitive people I know. I predict lots of screaming and groaning while we're here. This is supposed to be fun, but I already know that Wyatt and Dakota are going to turn *everything* into a competition.

It's worth it though, to be with all of my friends in one place. I hadn't realized how much I needed a vacation. I'm feeling a little inadequate and undeserving of their friendships, but I shove those feelings aside.

"Who's ready to have some fun?" Wyatt grips Dakota's hands between his and claps them together. They're walking like one of those cute couples that are *so* in love. His arms are wrapped around her shoulders and his body draped over hers as they walk. I still envy them slightly, but for the first time during this whole vacation, I have hope that maybe I'll have that for myself.

As we walk through the doors of the Midway, Lily's eyes go wide, her cheers of excitement bringing smiles to all our faces. She's truly the cutest kid, and that's saying something coming from me. I'm not someone who ever imagined myself having children. After the way I was raised, I don't think I could subject a child to that kind of life.

Of course, I had everything I needed, I suppose, but I wanted my parents to give a shit about me and they didn't. I don't know how to raise a child because my parents never actually raised me.

Damian pulls me from my thoughts, his elbow bumping me softly. "There's something different about you."

"What?" I turn my face to look at him as we walk.

"You're, like, giddy or something." He smirks, and my face reddens a bit. *Did he hear us?*

"Nope. Totally normal. The same 'ol Sterling."

"Right," he says with a laugh. "Come play this game with me." He leads us toward a racing game.

Out of the corner of my eye, I see Jaiden staring at us, his face calm on the outside, but I see the possessive gleam in his eyes. Lily tugs at his shorts, urging him in the opposite direction. He licks his lips before walking away with her and I shiver at the memory of his mouth all over my body last night. *Not the time, nor the place.*

I sit in the chair beside Damian, my hand gripping the steering wheel. I feel hands touch my shoulders and look up to see Lani.

"Hey, babe," I say with a smile.

"Please beat his ass, girl." Her nose wrinkles and I laugh.

"Oh, I plan on it."

"Woah, my girls ganging up on me? I'm hurt." He slips our coins into the game, starting the intro music.

"Your girls?" Lani scoffs, and I smirk. The words don't quite meet her eyes though. I see the sparkle of hope.

My eyes find the screen again. We choose our cars, then suddenly the game starts. I fall behind at first, but that's okay. The car drifts around a turn, and I see Damian's car ahead of mine. What he doesn't know is that Dakota's brother taught me everything I know about racing games. He may not look like it, but Dallas is a car snob.

My foot presses on the console gas pedal, then suddenly I drift through the next turn, speeding right past Damian. He makes a strangled noise, and I laugh, continuing through the track. The seconds count down and I rush through the finish line ahead of Damian.

He throws his hands up and Lani laughs a loud *ha* at his loss. He glowers in response. Lani and I lock eyes before high fiving. I *love* winning.

When I look up, I see Dakota skipping toward us with a shit-eating grin. "Did y'all win too?" She does a lil dance, her eyebrows waggling.

Lani and I laugh before nodding. "Yeah. Damian here is going to lick his wounds for a while."

"Yeah, yeah," he says from the side, but it's all fun.

"Well, there are chances at redemption for the losers. We're doing laser tag. I put us all on the list." Dakota shakes her shoulders.

"I feel like that is a very dangerous game to play with you."

"Oh, it is," Wyatt says from behind. He places his hands onto Dakota's shoulders, massaging them a little. "She made a kid cry last time."

Dakota scoffs. "I did not."

I can't help but laugh. There's not a scenario in my head where Dakota *doesn't* make a kid cry playing laser tag, and it has me wheezing just thinking about it.

She turns to glower at Wyatt, but he only bends to kiss her head. "We start in twenty minutes," he says, before pulling Dakota with him toward a skeeball machine.

Damian walks away with them and I stay behind with Lani.

"How are you feeling?" We walk slowly toward the back of the arcade. I briefly see Jaiden with Lily and Roman. They're crowded around a whack-a-mole game.

"As much as it sucks, I think I'm okay. I feel like I've been grieving the end of our relationship for a while now."

I sling my arm over her shoulder, hugging her to my side. "He didn't deserve you, and I'm glad you're still here."

"Me too. Can't let a man ruin my vacation." She winks at me and I roll my eyes.

"Exactly."

We file into the briefing room a few minutes later. A young girl hands us off, leaving us be until the attendant can run us through the rules and provide us with the gear for the game. This whole experience reminds me that we're never too old to have fun. I'm surrounded by four large men who look more excited to play than Dakota, and she's nearly bouncing on the balls of her feet with anticipation.

I sit in the corner while we wait until a man walks through the side door. He scans the room and smiles at us as he introduces himself. As he runs through the rules and instructions, I vaguely register the fact that his eyes keep coming back to mine, for way longer than necessary. It isn't until he points to me that my heart pounds.

"Do you mind if I use you to demonstrate how to put on the equipment?" He smiles *almost* innocently, but not quite.

I don't look at Jaiden as I walk to the front of the room. "What's your name?" he asks.

"Sterling," I say quietly.

"Pretty name," he says with a wink. "Okay, Sterling, arms up please."

I do as I'm told, and he places the vest with a sensor over my chest. My cheeks heat as I feel the burning from across the room. When I look up, Jaiden is glaring at the man, his jaw clenched. The others don't see the intensity of his reaction, but I do.

"Now the straps come across like this, and you tug so that they're tight against your chest." He grabs the gun from the wall and hands it to me. "There's a switch here, and I'll have half of you flip them when you pick your teams."

He holds his own gun and points it at my vest. "Now if you were a laser, you'd be set to stunning," he winks, his cheesy line forcing me to hold back a scowl.

Is he seriously hitting on me right now?

He laughs at his own joke, the rest of the room making weird noises of fake laughter. I look at Jaiden again and he looks about ready to burst.

"When you get shot, your vest will light up like this"—he shoots my vest and it turns red—"and you'll have a thirty second lull until you can shoot again. Once that happens three times, you're out. Got it?"

Wyatt nods, his face amused.

"Great. Who are the team captains?"

Jaiden steps forward, his hand raised as he watches me. I can feel the tension rolling off him. "Wyatt and I are the captains."

"How very high school of you," I say under my breath and Jaiden glares at me. I know I'll be in trouble for that one later and the excitement has my thighs rubbing together.

"Okay, great," the attendant says. "Go ahead and pick your teams."

"Sterling," Jaiden says, and I walk toward him.

"Babe," Wyatt says, and Dakota smirks. "We get to be on the same team for once," he says, kissing her cheek.

"Damian." Jaiden surprises me, holding his hand out. "And Lani."

"We've got Roman and Lily then." Wyatt points at Lily and she giggles.

They gear up, and then we're being ushered into the dark room, illuminated only by the black lights and neon colors throughout the room.

Through the loudspeaker, we're given a countdown and asked to spread to our sides of the room. I follow Damian through the darkness until I find our zone. I don't see Jaiden anywhere, so when the buzzer sounds, I rush forward, hiding behind anything I can.

My gun is held in front of me as I clear the area. I want to go for Dakota first. She's insane and I know I need to take one of the golden duo out. She'll hate me, but it'll be worth it.

The sounds of lasers go off in the distance, and I duck behind a shelter. My heart beats wildly when I hear Wyatt and Damian. I'm about to round the corner when a hand wraps around my mouth and I gasp.

"Shh," he says, his breath hot against my ear. I shiver as his fingers brush against my hip as he guides us backward.

As his hand releases my mouth, I turn to look at the incredibly handsome face of Jaiden *fucking* Thomas. I dare not forget he exists for a moment.

"What are you doing?" I hiss.

"Reminding you of who you belong to." His lips crash against mine, his teeth biting lightly on my lip. I moan, leaning into his warmth.

His hand grips my ass, squeezing as I get lost in his touch.

We're breathless when we pull apart. "We're gonna get caught," I whisper.

"That's exactly the point," he says, his middle finger flicking up toward the ceiling. I follow his hand to see a security camera. At first I'm stunned, but now I can only laugh.

"You possessive fucker," I say, placing a firm kiss on his lips before pulling away again. "Come. We've got a team to demolish."

"Oh, you're evil. Poor Lily."

TWENTY-THREE

JAIDEN

STERLING CLIMBS INTO THE KAYAK, her butt firmly seated while I push us out into the water. The others are already out on the water.

Dakota watches me with her eyebrow raised before smirking. "I haven't heard any fighting lately, so that must be a good sign." She tosses the comment over her shoulder and Sterling points at her back.

"We're passionate people. I'm sure we'll find something to fight about. Just because we're friends again doesn't mean I won't purposely piss him off." She looks back at me right as I climb into the kayak.

"I'd like to see you try," I say, my voice a bit growly. I can see her shiver as if the idea of misbehaving excites her. *Fuck, this woman is going to kill me.*

When I'd paired up with Sterling, I was expecting some odd looks, but at this point, I think our friends are starting to watch us less and less. I think we've proven that we can get along well enough. Maybe she's right and we'll fight again, but that fact doesn't scare me anymore.

We paddle out into the lake until we follow the water to a

narrower passage. The sun blazes down on my back and I take a break to wipe the sweat off my forehead.

Sterling fans herself, settling the paddles across her lap while we rest.

"This is beautiful," she says. "I've always wanted to do this, but my parents weren't much into adventures." She smiles, but it doesn't reach her eyes.

I want to know more about her family, and why she is the way she is. I know she came from money, but there's a tug in my heart every time she talks about her childhood.

I was poor, but my life was really full. I may not have been able to do the Disney World trips or the vacations like my peers, but I was happy.

"My mom used to take us camping every summer at the lake. I have some of my best childhood memories on the water."

"We didn't really do vacations. If we ever came here, my parents were still working and I was handed off to my nanny." She sets the paddle down again to tie her hair back. The hair sticks to the back of her neck. I watch the way her arms flex—I hadn't realized how muscular she was.

"What are you doing back there? Paddle faster." She laughs when I splash water at her.

"Have you been working out?" I ask, my eyebrow raised when she turns to look at me.

"Yeah, see, when you ghosted me, I went on this bender of good vibes and health shit. I took up running and I've always worked out, but never like this." She flexes her arms and kisses her bicep. "I'm sexy, right?"

I lean forward, my lips brushing against her neck. "Very." I run my tongue up from the base of her neck, stopping to nip at her ear. She shivers.

"Jaiden," she hisses. "Our friends are right there. Keep your hands to yourself."

Dakota says something in the distance and I look up after them.

"They won't see anything. They're too far ahead. Plus, I could do far worse considering the only thing separating us is that skimpy bikini bottom."

Her breath slows as I lean back, paddling us farther through the narrow channel.

"What are you thinking about?"

The water rushes, the kayak moving with the waves. I rest in the silence, feeling the breeze cool my skin.

"I'm thinking that I really fucking missed you, and now I can't stop thinking about your mouth."

"What about my mouth?" I really want to touch her, to pull her into my lap and to slide that piece of fabric to the side.

"The things your mouth does to me, and your fingers brushing my skin."

"Mmhm," I say, my eyes locked on our friends. They're all moving at their own paces, the pairs talking amongst themselves.

She turns to look at me again, her cheeks pink and her skin flushed. "I'm thinking about how I haven't slept with anyone in months because no one makes me feel like you do."

My cock springs to life at her words. I need to be buried *so* deep inside her. Some primal need takes over, my mind roaring to take care of her, to please her.

When the water rushes again, my body moves with it, the kayak tipping with the force.

"Jaiden," she screams, her arms holding on tightly to the sides.

I go first, the cool water hitting my skin as I slide from the kayak. I catch the paddles as Silver slips off the side. The water splashes around her, her arms flailing until I slide my arm around her, the other gripping onto the kayak.

"Hang onto me," I command. She listens, her arms gripping my life jacket.

It's easy to push the kayak so that we're blocked from the view of the others. It's even easier to lift it above our heads so that we're protected from all angles. The water's just shallow enough for me to stand, and I use that to my advantage.

Her body presses against mine, and I grip her neck, my mouth descending on hers. She moans into the kiss, her legs wrapping around my waist. I nearly groan as she grinds on me, my cock hard and ready for her.

"You evil woman," I breathe, my lips moving to her neck. I pepper kisses, speaking between breaths. "You can't talk to me like that, especially when you are so adamant about keeping us a secret." My fingers slide the zipper of her life jacket down to allow me access to her breasts.

"Did you tip us on purpose?" She gasps as I slip the fabric down and suck her nipple between my teeth.

"It's the only way to get us alone. Even for a second." I grind my length against her so that she can feel how hard I am for her. "You do this to me. Even when you were screaming at me, I was so fucking hard for you."

"Jaiden," she gasps as I pull at the jewelry decorating her nipple. Her hand covers my cock through my shorts, her palm stroking me. I groan, pressing into her touch. My lips find hers again. I'm about to slide a finger into her bottoms when I hear Wyatt yelling my name.

"Jaiden! Sterling! You okay?"

I groan, pulling away from her. Her lips are red and puffy, her eyes hungry. I want to devour her, but now's not the time.

"Fine," I snap, and Silver laughs. "I moved wrong and tipped us."

"You sure? Y'all have been down there for a while."

"Yeah, well, Sterling is a fucking weakling." I smirk at her, and she rolls her eyes at me.

"You're an ass. You're the weakling." She pokes my chest and I laugh.

I flip the kayak, meeting Wyatt's gaze almost immediately.

"She insisted on doing it herself," I shrug, and Dakota laughs.

"Yeah, there's something else I'll be doing myself later too if you don't stop talking," she mumbles and I glare at her.

"Say that again," I growl.

"Talk shit again and I will." She raises her chin, pulling herself back up onto the kayak as I steady it.

"They're fine," Dakota says with a laugh.

I lift myself into the kayak as Wyatt paddles them away. I glare at his back.

"Cock block," I mutter.

Sterling snorts before matching my paddles. I suffer through the next hour of our adventure. Every time Sterling breathes, or her husky laughter reaches my ears, I'm reminded of my half-mast boner hidden in my shorts.

By the time we reach the loading area, I can feel my temper flaring. I'm wound so tight and I feel like every *fucking* moment is a tease.

Sterling climbs from the kayak at the same moment I do. I don't waste a moment, lifting it above my head and walking it to the rental station.

"What is your problem?" Sterling pants, her legs working hard to keep up with me.

"Get in the car," I growl.

She glares at me before following directions, stomping toward the car while I close out the rental tab.

"We're going to lunch, y'all coming with?" Damian pauses, his arm resting on the wall of the rental building.

"Naw, I've got something I need to take care of," I say, keeping my voice even.

"Best take care of it then." He winks before sauntering toward his car.

I practically run toward the car, pulling out of the parking lot and speeding back to the house.

Thank fucking fuck for an empty house. I don't think I could handle another moment of having to hide my intentions. This woman is driving me mad. In the past, I wanted her—I wanted her so bad—but it was different. Now it's a feral need. After almost a year, I can't seem to get enough. She invades every corner of my mind, and my body can't seem to deny her any longer. I *need* her like I need air, and I want her to understand. I *need* her to understand how badly I want her, not just for her body, but for the fact that she's *mine.*

She's *my* Sterling, the woman who's wrecked me for everyone else. This whole time I thought that I was ruining her, that I was changing the way that she viewed sex. I was so naive to think it was me doing the ruining.

I walk on autopilot into the house and right into her bedroom. I'm barely through the door before I hear it slam behind me. I turn around, jolted from my thoughts.

Sterling prowls toward me. She's in her bikini, the evidence of her hardened nipples peeking through.

It's not often that I can't breathe. I'm *always* in control, and yet here I am, staring after the magnificent woman in front of me, my breath caught in my throat. Her hand comes to my chest, and I'm pushed backward by the force.

"You're so tense," she rasps.

I follow her lead, walking backwards until I'm standing in the bathroom. She walks past me, turning the knob for the shower before returning to me.

Water pounds on the floor, the steam filling the room. She pulls my shorts from my body and I kick them off, my eyes locked with hers the whole time.

I reach for her as she strips, but she shakes her head and I nearly growl.

"Patience," she says. "Let me take care of you."

I'm shoved under the stream of water, the heat scalding my skin for only a moment until I adjust.

She lathers soap onto a cloth before running it across my skin. I want to touch her, to take back control, but I'm following her lead. Everything inside me screams nonsense about giving up control, but I can't seem to give it any attention right now. My heart is pounding too hard as she runs the cloth down my chest. She continues in slow, torturous motions, her hands everywhere but the place I want them.

After what feels like hours, her hands come to my cock and I hiss, my head falling back. My abs clench as she works my shaft with the cloth. Her hand moves down, tightening around my balls and leaving too soon. Right when I anticipate more, she steps away, the water washing away the soap.

When I open my eyes, she's on her knees before me, and it's the most incredible thing I've ever seen. Her resolve hits her face a moment before her hands react.

She takes my hardened length in her hands, her tongue running up the bottom of my shaft. I groan, bucking into her touch.

I suck in a sharp breath as her tongue swirls across the tip. Before I can catch my breath, she's taking me into her mouth, inches at a time.

My body tenses with the sensation. Her mouth feels so *fucking* good. As if that thought kicks me into gear, I move my hands to her hair right as her hands grip the backs of my thighs.

Her cheeks hollow out as she swallows me. I moan when her teeth scrape against me.

"So fucking beautiful," I rasp, my body pumping into her throat.

She gags before taking me deeper. I can't fucking breathe. "You take me so well, Silver," I praise, her pace increasing with my movements. My breathing stutters when her hand comes to my balls.

"Fuck," I choke out, and I look down to see her smirk around my cock. I think it's the best thing I've ever seen.

Her hand leaves my thigh to reach between her legs. I see her fingers swirling her clit and I nearly groan.

"You're such a good girl," I say, seeing her pace increase. "That's it, baby, make us come."

She whimpers, her mouth stilling slightly, but it's quickly remedied when I pump into her, my hands gripping tightly to her hair.

She moans around me and I nearly lose it.

"Spread your legs for me. I want to see you." I'm going to come so hard just from watching her. I've never been more turned on in my life. My body feels hot, my muscles tightening as she gags around me.

She slides a finger through her pussy, and the moan that comes out of her mouth is fucking addicting. She increased her pace a second later, and I watch her bring herself to an orgasm. She gasps around me, her chest rising and her legs shaking after release. I want to wait, to bury myself inside of her, but I have no control over what happens next.

"I'm gonna—fuck," my voice sputters as she chokes, my body tensing with my orgasm. I see stars at the edges of my vision, my breath stopping all together. I have to grip the wall to keep from falling over.

Through it all, I can't take my eyes off her. Drops of cum spill from her mouth, and she brings her hand to her mouth to catch it. I stare at her in complete awe, her mouth sliding from my cock with a pop. Like a woman finishing a feast, she licks her fingers, looking up at me with utter satisfaction.

"You're going to kill me."

"Good."

TWENTY-FOUR

STERLING

THE STAFF CHEER as a bottle of champagne is popped and poured for our little group. Dakota's mom and sister-in-law are here for this momentous moment.

"Welcome, future Mrs. Lane! We're so excited to have you here." The staff hold out the champagne flutes, cheering again before we're guided to small couches in a private room.

"Thank you for having me," she says. I know she's feeling shy by the way she's holding her hands in front of her, but the glow on her face speaks for how she's also excited for this.

I can't believe I'm getting to watch my best friend try on wedding dresses. I'm not a crier, but I made no promises that I wouldn't cry for this.

"My name is Carly and I'll be your stylist today! Mom and bridesmaids will stay here; make yourselves comfortable. I'm going to take our bride to the back now and she can try on as many as she wants until we find the one." She looks at Dakota, waiting for a nod. When Dakota smiles at her response, Carly leads her to a dressing room slightly out of view.

"She's gonna be beautiful," Lani says.

"Mama Everly, I'm waiting for tears. Who do you think is going to cry first?"

Dakota's mom has also been my mom for as long as I can remember. She basically adopted me, and I've never been happier about something in my life.

"Oh, me, of course! Then maybe Casey next." She reaches over to grab Casey's hand, giving it a squeeze.

"How are you feeling, Sterling?" Lani lays her head on my shoulder and I sigh.

"Like a ball of nerves."

Dakota and I weren't the little girls planning our weddings, but there's always been this element of splendor around them. Maybe one day I'll be trying on wedding dresses, or dreaming about the future.

"Okay, is everyone ready?" Carly turns the corner, following behind Dakota.

Everyone gasps when we catch a glimpse of her. She's stunning, the curves of her body hugged tightly by the simple satin gown.

"This was one of the styles you sent me. It's got a detachable train with a fishtail form." She guides Dakota onto the platform and fluffs out the train in front of the mirror.

Dakota runs her hands down her sides, her eyes examining her form. It's beautiful. It has a corset top that accentuates her waist, the train flowing out from her hips. I'm in awe of her.

"Wow," Everly says, her hands on her mouth as she watches her daughter. "You look beautiful, baby."

"Thanks, Ma." She twists to the side. "I like it. It's kind of predictable though. It's very me and I do love that, but now that I see it...I think I want something different, more fairytale."

"And that's why we try them on. Sometimes you love it on the screen but end up wanting something different." Carly helps Dakota from the platform and leads her back to the changing room.

We see a few more dresses before I think we're headed in the fairytale direction. She tries on this long A-line dress with a slit up the side. The sheer corset top matches the first one she tried on. It's gorgeous, but still not what I picture to be the fairytale vision she has.

As she walks toward us, the beaded train scrapes on the floor, leading me to believe it's heavy. I know immediately that it isn't the dress for her and she confirms it a moment later with a shake of her head.

She tries on a variety of other wedding dresses, all similar in nature to the first several dresses. As she tries them on, Carly points out certain details like floral, lace, detachable trains and plunging necklines. But these aren't the dresses for Dakota. I don't know if she's losing hope or not, but as she disappears behind the curtain again, something feels different.

Dakota walks toward the platform once more, her long train dragging behind her. The dress she's wearing is very simple lace with floral appliqué. The plunging neckline is stunning, and guaranteed to make Wyatt's eyes fall out of his head. It screams modern-fairy-tale-princess, and it's absolutely perfect. I watch her as she turns, the open back of the dress catching my eye immediately. When I look up into the mirror, I lock eyes with Dakota and that's when I *know*.

The tears fall before I can stop them. I'm reaching for a tissue and sobbing like a *fucking* baby as I watch my best friend cry in her wedding dress.

"You look so fucking gorgeous," I choke out.

Lani looks at me, a smile ghosting her lips as she swipes at her face.

"I think this is it," Dakota says into the mirror.

"If we're a mess now, just imagine what it's gonna be like at the wedding," Casey says, and we all choke out laughter.

"Imagine the reactions of the guys! I have no doubts that the men will cry harder than us."

"Oh, your father is going to lose his marbles when he sees you. He sobbed like a baby fresh out of the womb when I walked down the aisle." Everly claps her hands in excitement. "It'll be so great. He's such a crier, that man."

"Ma," Dakota laughs.

Everly shrugs, her face a mixture of elation and humor. "I'm only speaking the truth."

"So, I have to ask you the question that we ask every bride. Is this the one? Have you found your dress?"

I lock eyes with Dakota before she looks back at Carly. "Yes. This is the dress."

The room erupts in cheering as the other stylists come to celebrate. They take photos of Dakota in the dress with a sign that says *I found the one* and the name of their boutique. When she changes back into her street clothes, she takes more photos, and then invites all of us to join. Lani and I crowd Dakota on either side, smiling at the camera.

A few moments later, we're walking through the aisles of bridesmaid's dresses for our turn. Dakota decided on a sage green and cream color pallet. The floral arrangements will have accents of maroon, but for our dresses, we're wearing the sage green. I'm not complaining, because green looks damn good on me.

I pull out a few different styles of dresses before slipping into the room to try them on. Stripping out of my clothes, I'm left in my see-through lace bra and matching panties.

I stare at myself in the mirror for a moment before pulling out my phone. I snap a few photos, posing in a way that makes me feel sexy. I don't intend to do it, but before I can second guess myself, I send the photos to Jaiden, a wink emoji accompanying the pictures.

Trying on the dresses, I feel beautiful. Lani, Casey and I all fell in love with an A-line style dress, the neckline more modest, but flattering to all of us. I've got a healthy amount of cleavage and that's all I can ask for. It's a common trend in my wardrobe—outfits that lend to my ample breasts; they deserve to shine.

After ordering our dresses, we leave the bridal shop, giggling and full of bubbly. It isn't until we're leaving the small cafe that we found that I finally pull out my phone.

"Oh no, Dakota spotted it," Casey says as we walk, her stride stopping to turn and look at something.

I nearly run face first into her back as I look down at the several notifications on my phone.

"I'm going in," Dakota says.

I finally look up to see a massive bookstore filling half the street.

"Coming?" Lani asks from my side.

"Yeah, I'll be inside in a sec."

She smiles before disappearing through the roundabout door.

My stomach flutters as I look back down at my phone. I've got several messages from Jaiden, and the anticipation is killing me.

Jaiden: Fucking tease.

Jaiden: Sterling, the fuck? Now I have to sit at home with fucking palmala.

Jaiden: Yeah. Nope. Where are you?

Jaiden: Sterling, where the fuck are you?

I smirk at my phone, a bit of anxiety coursing through me.

Me: The bookstore on Bloor Street. How was palmala?

I shove my phone into my pocket before walking inside the store to find Dakota in the fantasy section. Instead of bothering her, I continue onto the romance section. It's not common for the kind of smut I read to be on the shelves, but it's worth it to look.

My fingers graze across the books until I find one that looks interesting. I pull it from the shelf and read the back before I flip through the pages. I do this with several more books before I feel a hand clamp across my mouth. I gasp, struggling until I feel the firm press of a chest against my back.

"Shh," he says into my ear. "No talking in the library." He releases my mouth before I turn around to look at him. I'm a taller woman, but even so, there's a certain amount of craning I have to do to look him fully in the eye.

"We're in a *bookstore*, dumbass," I say, my voice barely a whisper. "How did you get here so fast?"

"We were having our tuxedos fitted downtown, so I came here

instead of heading back with the guys." He runs a hand through his curls before looking around. When his eyes return to me, I see a hint of heat behind them. He leans his face towards me, and when I rise up on my toes to meet his lips, I expect him to ravish me, only his lips never meet mine. He hovers above me, the ghost of his kiss on my lips.

"I thought you'd be more concerned that we're in public," he says, his lips so close to mine that I can feel the heat of his breath tickle my chin. I want to close the gap, but I won't give him the satisfaction.

"No one's around," I breathe.

"There could be. How would you know? You haven't looked." His hand comes to my face, his fingers weaving their way through my hair. I love the feel of it, and I nearly moan.

"Shut up," I say, losing my patience and pressing my lips into his.

He smirks into the kiss and I nip at his lips in reprimand.

"You're an evil woman," he says, pulling away to look at me. "Sending those photos and working me up. Is that what you wanted?"

"It's entertaining to tease you. It's even more entertaining to sneak around, and to have you to myself." I press my lips gently to his again. It's more intimate than the harsh, rushed kisses that I'm used to getting. They're sweet and tender and *new.*

His long lashes flutter before he looks at me again. "I should go before we're caught."

"Didn't y'all take one car?" I ask, my eyebrows pressing together.

Jaiden smirks, his eyes lighting up with mischief. "*They* did." Instead of elaborating, he extends his hand to me. When I take it, I feel hesitant, but decide to bury those feelings.

He leads me through the shelves and to the front door.

I follow him until he stops in front of a motorcycle. I blink several times, looking it over.

"You've gotta be joking. You ride?"

"Surprised?"

I bite my lip, looking up at him. It's kinda hot, if I'm being honest, but I'm not ready to admit that to him yet. I still don't know *what* we are. How would admitting that I find the idea of him being a bad boy *very* attractive impact the already thin line we're riding?

"Maybe," I say.

"Come with me," he says, his brow raised in challenge.

My heart pounds in my chest as I look at him. This feels like a special moment. He's trusting me with a piece of himself. If I agree, it represents a certain level of trust. Do I trust him?

I breathe, looking at the bike. It should be an easy decision, and maybe it is, but my heart is flashing warning signs. *Fuck being careful.*

"Let me tell Dakota where I'm going," I say finally.

He nods, and I run back through the doors.

When I find Dakota, she's standing with Lani and Casey.

"Hey," I say, joining their circle.

"Where have you been?" Lani raises an eyebrow. She says it with a hint of amusement.

"The guys were down the street, and I stopped to talk with Jaiden," I say, the lie slipping out easily. "Do y'all mind if I go with him for a bit?"

Dakota smirks at me, and if I know anything at all about my best friend, it's that she's enjoying this.

"Not at all. Enjoy your *ride,*" she says with a wink.

"Oh, shut up," I say, laughing. "I deserved that one, though."

"Yeah, you did. Practice safe sex!" she adds and I glare.

"No need to," I lie. "We're just friends."

"*Right*. Now, shoo. Your hot hockey player is waiting." She kisses my cheek, and I smile.

"Love you," I say to the three of them before turning away.

When I walk back into the warm summer air, Jaiden is texting on his phone, an extra helmet resting on the seat.

He spots me, his hand patting the seat before giving me his hand to help me onto the bike. I hesitate only a moment before swinging my leg across the bike and scooting back onto the seat. His long leg swings over after me, his arm reaching back to steady me before he situates himself.

"Hang onto me," he commands as he slips on his helmet.

I follow suit, my short hair pressing against my face.

"If you need something, tap me three times, okay?" He looks back, the shield lifted so I can see the smirk on his face. It's cocky, and I want to kiss him for it.

I nod, snapping down the shield as the bike roars to life. Before I know it, we're pulling away from the curb, and I tighten my grip around his waist.

My heart pounds as I lean into him. I don't want to admit that I'm slightly terrified, but it's fine. I trust him.

My eyes go wide and I'm thankful he can't see it. *I trust him? Since fucking when?* The longer I think about it, the longer I realize that I really do trust him, and I don't know if I hate or love myself for it.

We rush forward, the warm wind whipping across my body. I'm thankful I'm wearing jeans and boots today. It's so convenient.

The bike turns as the road curves. I squeeze him tighter, and when we're back on the straight road, I feel his fingers intertwined with mine on his waist. His thumb brushes across the back of my hand and I shiver. This feels incredibly intimate, and I'm enjoying it more than I thought it would.

I lift my head to watch the buildings as we pass. I'm so familiar with this place, yet I wish I'd gotten the chance to see more of it. Yeah, I grew up spending time near the city, but it's not the same as just being able to breathe and enjoy the scenery.

Sitting up straighter, I lean back as the bike slows to a stop. Jaiden's feet come down to stabilize the bike and just as I'm relaxing, his hand comes to my thigh, massaging me in such a tender way that it brings a blush to my cheeks. Is this what it would be like to be in a relationship with Jaiden Thomas?

"Where are we going?" I ask, getting close to his ear.

"You'll see," he says, lifting his leg and shooting through the intersection. The buildings pass by in a blur of colors. I grip tightly to Jaiden as we speed forward, the bike leaning with a turn. A few moments later, Jaiden pulls the bike into a parking lot.

I've been here before, a small winery and cafe. It's one of the spots Dakota and I first came to when we were old enough to drink. It's nice being back in my old stomping ground.

Jaiden dismounts from the bike, his hand extended to me as I climb off after him.

"We got to play your game, now we're playing mine," he says, a mischievous grin on his face. "Go on in. I'll meet you there in a second."

"What?" I ask, my eyebrows drawing together.

He *tsks*, his hand running across my back. "Play along and maybe you'll get a reward."

I shiver at the thought. We've been dancing around each other for a couple weeks now. The sexual tension is insane, and a part of me wants to just bang it out with him, but the moment that happens, I know that there is no going back. Maybe that's why we've done everything *but* have the kind of sex we used to have.

I shake my head, turning to walk into the winery. The cool air rushes down, my hair flying in every direction. I walk right to the bar, looking over the different wines they have on their lineup today.

This place is special to me. It's a small, family-owned cafe with a winery attached. The parents of a friend in high school ran this place. It's been passed down for generations. Her parents grow their own fresh berries and through each season, a pie with each fruit is made. My personal favorite is the grape pie—it's fucking fantastic—and I hope they have some today.

"Can I help you?" A shaggy haired man stands in front of me, a towel slung over his shoulder. I eye him, appreciating the way his short-sleeved shirt hugs his arms. When his eyes gleam as he looks at me, I nearly snort.

"What do you recommend?" I ask, looking back down at the list.

He looks me over, a contemplative look crossing his face before he turns to the wall. "You strike me as someone elegant, yet fun and bold. Maybe not bold enough for a red, more like a chardonnay girl. Something with strong berry notes and rich, deep flavors."

He looks over his shoulder at me with a brow raised as he grabs two bottles off the shelves.

I smile, curious to see which one he chooses. After what feels like minutes, he sets a bottle before me. "I think the *Niagara Estates* Chardonnay." He puts the other bottle back then opens the chosen bottle in front of me.

I watch as he pours a glass, then hands it to me. I swirl it, sniffing before bringing the glass to my lips. The moment it hits my tongue, I know he chose well. It's incredible, just sweet enough that it's not too bitter or dry, and complex enough to drive my tastebuds wild.

"Wow. You *are* good," I say, laughing.

"It's my job," he says. "The grape pie goes well with that wine."

"You don't say." I laugh, shaking my head at him. "Still as charming as ever."

"Glad to know the charm still works." He smiles wide, his dimples peeking through.

"You're trouble, Jake." I smile, sipping my wine.

"How long are you back in town? Jamie's not here today, but I know my Ma would be excited to know trouble walked back into our little establishment." Jake and Jamie are twins, their grandparents the current owners of the place. We used to get in so much trouble as kids, but it's all in the past now. The troublemaker and reckless girl I once was is long gone.

I sip on my wine when the door to the cafe opens. I look over my shoulder to see Jaiden walk through the doors, a small bag in his left hand. I look away, unsure of how to play his game.

He sidles up to the bar, his gaze directly on Jake. "I'll have whatever she's drinking," he says, nodding towards me.

"You got it." Jake pours a glass, sliding it to Jaiden.

"Come here often?" Jaiden says to me, his eyes full of heat.

Jake laughs. "Does that line still work?"

"Shush. If this kind man wants to flirt, let him flirt," I say to Jake before turning my gaze back to Jaiden. "I used to," I say, my brows raising.

"Are you sure you wanna flirt with this one? She's trouble." Jake nudges me, his laugh softening as he walks across the bar to greet another guest.

"Can I buy you dinner?" he asks.

"Depends on what we're having."

"Whatever the lady wants. I'm Jaiden, by the way." He extends a hand to me.

I snort, taking his hand and shaking it. "Sterling," I say, "but people I like call me Silver."

"Silver," he says, his voice almost like a purr. It sends a pulse right to my core. He nods his head toward the cafe and I follow behind him.

We walk through the tables, taking a seat toward the back of the room.

"I thought it would be nice to start over," Jaiden says. "In another reality, we meet something like this. I see a beautiful woman in a bar, or a restaurant, and I have enough balls to approach her. This time, I can't fuck it all up." He reaches for my hand and brings it to his lips.

"I like it." My throat tenses at the gesture. I'm not relationship material. I've always been wild, someone who doesn't tie down easily. Even with Zahraa, it wasn't something I'd done before. My fear started in high school when the kind of attention I was getting became increasingly negative. I needed attention, *craved it*, but I only got it from the wrong guys. It's hard to admit that I liked it too.

I feel unworthy of his attention. And maybe that's why I've been slow to accept that he's actually trying to fix this—us.

"Sterling," someone says, and I look up, my heart stopping in my chest.

Jaiden tenses across from me as if he can see my defensive

posture.

"Sterling, honey, what are you doing here? Oh, God, your hair! That's new." She shakes her head, a barely hidden look of disgust crossing her face before she continues. "Aren't you supposed to be at the lake house?"

"Uh—" I say, blinking at her several times.

Jaiden saves me, speaking up so that I don't have to. "Hi. I'm Jaiden, and you are?"

"Oh," she blinks as if she's just seeing him. "I'm Narissa. Sterling's...mother."

Yeah, right. She's just the woman who birthed me. Mothers care, and raise their children. I was raised by my nannies because she was too busy being unbothered to care.

"Nice to meet you, Narissa," he says, shaking her hand lightly.

"Pleasure," she says. I'm waiting for some remark about how handsome Jaiden is, and how he's out of my league.

"You're together?" she asks, her nose rising higher into the sky.

"Yes, Mother."

"Hmm."

"What are you doing here, Narissa?"

"Now, now, dear. Is that any way to speak to your mother?"

I shake my head with a sigh. "We're in town for Dakota's bridal appointment."

"Hmm," she says. "I forgot that *friend* of yours is getting married. To a savage hockey player, no less. How unsophisticated." She huffs, brushing off something invisible from her wrinkle-free dress.

Jaiden eyes me curiously and I breathe, hoping he stays silent.

"Mother," I groan. "You don't even know him. He's great."

"He's basically an animal," she hums, her voice sickly sweet. Her hand comes to my hair before she scowls. "Your hair is really *something,* isn't it? It's quite...bold."

"I like it," I defend, my body tensing. I can feel the emotions rising to my throat. I don't want Jaiden to see this, to see the way my mother treats me.

"Well, if you insist. It is quite ugly, though." She *tsks*, pasting a fake smile on her face. "You've gained some weight, too."

"I'm healthy," I snap, and she only hums in response. I don't look at Jaiden, in fear of what I will see on his face.

"Well, since I've so conveniently ran into you here, you'll have to send Diana our regards. Your father and I won't be able to make it to the wedding. We're simply too busy."

"Dakota," I correct.

"Right. That's what I said. Anyway, maybe skip on the pie today so you can fit into your dress, sweetheart." She smiles again and I can feel my face burning red.

"Yeah, that's enough of that," Jaiden says, his voice angry. "Your daughter is perfect in every way and you've insulted her appearance three times now."

"Oh, I'm just helping her. She's always struggled a little with her weight."

"Get up," Jaiden commands, reaching his hand toward me. I breathe heavily, my heart pounding.

"What?" I ask, a note of panic in my voice. He turns to my mother, his hand gripping mine tightly.

"Us *animals* are very protective of our women. You cannot speak to her like that. Sterling is beautiful and she'll fit into her dress just fine, thank you. She's got a body I can worship everyday for the rest of my goddamn life. As for the wedding, I wouldn't usually speak for Dakota and Wyatt, but I will make an exception. I'm so fucking glad you're not coming to the wedding because we don't need someone like you there. I'm sure you'd have a horrible time anyways. It'll be a zoo. Absolute madness. Men crawling around on all fours. Totally not your speed, I can tell."

Narissa gasps, a look of outrage filling her face. It gives me joy. "It was all with good intentions." She blinks.

"Yeah, whatever." Jaiden grabs my hand, tossing a bill onto the table before looking at Narissa again. "One day I might marry your daughter, and I really hope you're not there."

We don't wait a second to hear her response. Instead, we run out of the cafe like our tails are on fire.

I want to be upset, to be angry, but the look on my mother's face brought me too much joy. I've lived with her insults for years, never meeting up to her expectations or ideas of perfection. It felt good to see her speechless for once.

It's dark when we get outside, the dim street lights illuminating the street.

I walk behind Jaiden, his hand gripping mine tightly before he pulls me toward him. My body presses into his, my butt now against the seat of the bike. His mouth meets mine in a rushed kiss. I don't need him to say anything. I don't even need to talk about it, and it's as if he knows that.

I kiss him back, nipping at his lip lightly, eliciting a groan from deep in his throat. He deepens the kiss again, his hand squeezing my ass.

"Fuck. This ass. It's the best ass in the whole world."

I laugh into his mouth, shaking my head slightly.

"I'm not good at the whole feelings thing yet, but if you want to talk about it, we can."

"Thanks," I say. "I've been over it for a long time. That woman isn't my mother and I don't expect her to be. Her words can't hurt me anymore." I crane my neck to meet his lips again. "Plus, it was really fucking sexy to hear you tell her off like that."

"I'll do it again if you want me to." He nips at my ear, then stands to his full height.

"Maybe later."

There's so much more I want to say, but I don't have the guts to talk about it just yet. I'm not ready to talk about the fact that Jaiden *fucking* Thomas just casually dropped the prospect of marriage in front of my mother. And I'm not ready to talk about how that makes my heart beat faster, and my mind run through scenarios of a future with him.

Maybe later, but not now. I'll worry about those feelings later.

TWENTY-FIVE

JAIDEN

"OKAY, PEOPLE," Sterling says over the mass of voices in the living room. It takes a moment to settle down, but when it finally does, she shifts on the couch, a mischievous smile tugging at the corner of her lips.

"I apologize for the early start. Vacation is the time to sleep in and whatnot, but I have big plans for today. Lily and Hunter have been kidnapped by the grandparents so we're child free for the day, which means"—she drums against her legs to build anticipation—"bachelor and bachelorette parties!"

Lani cheers, shaking her hands around. It's quite entertaining to see them so excited. Everyone but Dakota and Wyatt are in on our plans, and I've gotta say, it's great.

"Oh no," Dakota says, her eyes going wide. "Should I be scared?" She looks at Sterling and I laugh.

"You should be asking me that," I say, rubbing my hands together.

Dallas stands from the couch and pats Dakota on the back. "You'll be fine."

"I'm so confused," she says.

"Great. That's the point." Sterling grins and I'm suddenly sad that I won't be around her today. She looks stunning in her denim shorts, cropped tank, and a flannel wrapped around her waist. The top half of her hair is pulled up into matching space buns at the top of her head and I think it's adorable. I want to say so, but for some reason, I don't know where the line is drawn. When we're alone, I can talk to her the way I want. But when we're around our friends, I suddenly revert into this awkward, unsure man. *The fuck is wrong with me?*

"Here's what's happening. Dakota; you're being kidnapped by the men today. They have planned your activities for the day. Wyatt, you're coming with the ladies, and at the end of the day we'll meet back here for the night time activities. Got it?"

"This will be fun." Wyatt pulls Dakota under his arm, kissing the top of her head. "Go get ready, love." He kisses her again before releasing her.

My stomach clenches as I watch them. They have the freedom to express their feelings. If I hadn't been such an idiot in the past, maybe I'd be in the same position.

I look over to see Sterling watching me. She smiles knowingly before her attention moves to Dallas. He sits beside her, his wife on his opposite side. They talk amongst themselves as we wait for Dakota to return.

Familiar green envy runs through my veins as I watch the way Sterling converses so easily with everyone else. I have so many regrets when it comes to us, and it makes me want to scream and yell. I'm fucking *trying* to get her to trust me and yet when I give her an inch, it feels like she retreats a mile back. We're back in the friends with benefits territory and it's where I need to be content for now. But I'm not. I want more.

"I'm ready," Dakota says, returning to the room. She wraps her arms around Wyatt before leaning up so far on her toes that she's still not close enough to his face without him craning to meet her. They kiss, quietly exchanging words before Sterling makes noises of protests, pulling Wyatt away.

"Enough, love birds! You'll see each other tonight." Sterling winks, blowing me a kiss before she shoves Wyatt out of the door, the rest of the women following closely behind. "Bye, bitches," she yells over her shoulder.

Dakota meets my gaze, her eyebrow raising.

"I don't fucking know," I say with a laugh.

"I've known her my whole life and I still can't figure her out, so...same." She laughs, walking to the door.

Dallas slips an arm over her shoulder as we walk toward the car. "So, are we just not going to talk about the fact that you set up a whole fake dating scenario to get Jaiden and Sterling back together?" He says it loud enough for all of us to hear and I nearly choke on air.

I cough into my arm, and Roman claps me on the back.

"That was fun," Damian says, slipping into the back seat of my car. I shake my head before climbing into the car myself.

"It fucking worked, didn't it?" Dakota punches Dallas's arm. I see her grab the handle before she steps into the car, sliding into the front seat. "It's quite humorous to see the three of you piled in the back of the car." She kicks her Chucks up onto the dashboard for a moment, then looks over at me expectantly through her full lashes.

"You can't just bat those things at me and expect me to spill the beans. You have to wait." I chuckle, pulling the car down the long driveway and out onto the main road. "You should buckle up, though. We've got a ways to go."

Dakota huffs. I know she hates surprises, but that makes this a hundred times more fun.

"You're like Lily when it comes to surprises," Roman says, his voice laced with humor. "She hates them and has absolutely zero patience."

"I've got FOMO, but only when it comes to my friends. I am perfectly fine missing out in other ways. I just like feeling included." She sets her hands in her lap, getting comfortable as we pull onto the freeway.

The conversation flows steady, but I remain mostly focused on the road until Dakota opens the glovebox.

"You fucking didn't," she says, holding up a rubber duck.

I look over at her, smiling before looking back at the road. "Sterling said she's always wanted to do that, so I'm keeping them in my car now."

The car is silent for a moment and I look in the rear view mirror to see Damian looking at me.

"You got it fucking bad, dude." Dallas snorts, the rest of the car laughing.

"Yeah, yeah. Not like it fucking matters."

"What does that even mean?" Damian asks.

"It means she's determined to keep me at arms length for the foreseeable future." I drum the steering wheel, feeling the tension in the car rise.

"Well—" Dakota pauses, looking down at her hands. "That's nothing a little scheming can't fix."

"Oh, no. Absolutely not! No more scheming from any of you." I look over at Dakota, my eyes boring into her, and she holds her hands up.

"Fine, fine."

Their voices lull into the background. I zone in and out, joining in on their conversation until we finally pull off the freeway and into the security station. The guard directs us into the parking structure before we're parking in a spot near the top.

As everyone files out of the car, Dakota looks over the edge and down into the stadium. "Baseball? We're going to a baseball game?"

"Did you know that if hockey didn't pan out for Wyatt, he wanted to be a baseball player? Can you imagine it?"

Dakota laughs, shaking her head. "It's so much like him to believe he could just fall back on baseball."

"Today is the embarrass Wyatt tour. You gotta know what you're getting yourself into." Roman winks, patting his hand on Dakota's head. He's the tallest of us all and beside her, he looks like a goliath. It's not as if she isn't small, but something about seeing Roman pat her head like a child makes me laugh.

They all look over at me and I shake my head. "I'm sorry, it's just that Dakota looks like a child next to you, and it feels like I'm seeing it for the first time."

Dakota scowls, her arms crossing. "I thought it was embarrass Wyatt day."

"Oh, it is. Just you wait."

When we enter the stadium, we go through the security checkpoint into the VIP section until we walk into the box.

Taking our seats, we look out at the field, the players warming up for the game.

"Since we know you love games, we've made today into something of a game," Damian says, his legs kicked up against the railing. "Every time our team makes a homerun, you get to pick one of us to share an embarrassing story, either about Wyatt or ourselves."

Dakota claps. "I like this game. It's a win-win for me. Best bachelorette ever."

"Dakota knows all of my embarrassing stories," Dallas says, crossing his arms across his chest like he's safe.

"Oh, but we don't know everything about you. It's bonding time, bud." I clap him on the back and he scowls. "You can thank Sterling," I add with a wink.

"Sterling's the crazy sister I never asked for." He says it with a huff and Dakota laughs, her eyes watering.

"You love us. Don't lie."

"Yeah. I do. But she's still a terror, and the two of you together are even worse. Thank God Lani is a sweet baby angel."

Dakota laughs again. "Sweet to you," she says.

We eat, chatting while we wait for the game to start. When it finally does, the secrets start flowing. I don't think I've ever laughed this hard in my entire life. The whole time is spent roasting each other, really.

What started as a way to share stories from our college days, quickly turned into a roast of the best sort.

"Do you remember that time we all had a panic attack over Lily's supposed *feelings*?"

Roman throws his head back, laughing. "Holy shit, yes." He

turns to the group, shaking his head. "When Lily was old enough, I started taking her to daycare and the teacher told me that they were going to start introducing the boys and the girls classes. So, before that could happen, I sat down with our scarily intelligent four-year-old and talked about boys and feelings."

I laugh, my stomach clenching so hard as I try to breathe. I wheeze before speaking. "I believe the conversation went a little like this: Baby, I want to talk to you about the boys, and Lily asks something like 'what about the boys?' and Roman says that one day she'll have feelings for the boys and she deadass"—I pause for dramatic effect, looking at them closely—"dead-fucking-ass said, *I already have feelings for the boys, Daddy.* And Roman has this look of full-blown panic." I wheeze, unable to catch my breath because I'm laughing so hard.

Dakota shakes with laughter. We're not even paying attention to the game anymore and it's totally worth it.

Roman continues the story. "I asked her afterwards what kind of feelings she was having and after a moment or two of thinking, she looked at us and said that the boys made her angry. I've never been so relieved."

"Oh my gosh, I'm terrified to have children," Dakota says, her cheeks pink from laughing.

"I can guarantee you that Wyatt will be the best dad. He's made for that shit."

Roman's an incredible father, but something about the way that Wyatt is with Lily is different. He had the instincts right at the beginning that neither Roman nor I had at all. It got easier with time, but most of the time he just *got* it.

The crowd cheers as we miss yet another homerun. It's nuts in the stadium, but here, I feel like it's finally more normal. I've bonded with Dakota before, but this is different. I saw her at her worst last year, aided her through a panic attack, and I wish I could have done more. But being here for this moment, and to support my brother and best friend, it's different. There were pieces of me that didn't believe that I'd make it here. Months ago, my life was fucked. Now, here we are, laughing our asses off during the most ridiculous bachelorette party ever.

We barely register our home team winning before we're fighting the crowd to make it back to the car. We've got to make it back to the lake house for dinner and it's an hour and a half drive home.

It's damn near silent the whole drive home. Dakota's in the passenger seat, her face pressed against the window as she sleeps. The rest of the car is either passed out or lost in silence. It isn't until I look up into the rear-view mirror that I lock eyes with Damian. He nods, his brow raised. The unspoken question passes between us.

"We're good," I say. "I just hope I get the girl in the end."

TWENTY-SIX

STERLING

LANI, Casey and I are driving Wyatt nuts by the time his Bronco pulls into the parking lot of the thrift superstore. We've been singing to the songs Casey chooses, filling in the lyrics when she stops at a random point in the song.

I know Wyatt isn't truly bothered because he's joined in several times. It's one of the things I love most about Wyatt: he's just plain fun. It's easy to have fun with him because even though I know our screeching singing voices were terrible, he was still eager to jump in at certain points. He's not afraid to make a fool of himself. That is *exactly* why we chose this specific activity for his bachelorette party. Is it a bachelorette or a bachelor party? I haven't decided yet. Either way, I'm going to have so much fucking fun.

"Why the thrift store?" Wyatt steps out of the car, closing the door behind him.

"The girls already know what's happening, so I suppose I'll explain it to you now." I waggle my eyebrows at him and he laughs.

"I'm ready for whatever shit you have up your sleeve."

"Are you sure?" I challenge.

"Absolutely. Bring it on." He crosses his arms over his chest, widening his stance as he waits.

"Okay, everyone has fifteen minutes to find a new outfit in the thrift store. It can be any style you want, but at the end of the fifteen minutes, we'll pay and run to the fitting rooms to put them on. That's all I'll say because I don't want to ruin the rest of the surprise."

"The timer starts the moment we walk through the door." Casey winks at me from the side. "Better kill it, bro. That's weird... You're going to be my brother-in-law soon."

Wyatt laughs. "Why is that weird?"

"I've never had brothers before, and I'm basically gaining four of them with you."

"Sounds like a pretty solid deal to me," he says, a cocky grin overtaking his face.

We walk toward the front doors, and I pull out my phone and open the clock app. After I set my timer, I look to either side of me, nodding once before rushing through the doors and starting the timer.

Fifteen minutes rush by too quickly. It was so easy to find a top that fit, but I struggled with bottoms until I found this pair of neon green biker shorts. They were perfect, and I couldn't say no, so I formed my whole outfit around them.

I'm hiding my outfit while I wait in line to pay. The others are being secretive as well. After we pay, I rush into the dressing room, slipping into my eighties-inspired outfit.

When I step out of the room, I turn to look in the mirror, laughing maniacally. I look ridiculous and I love it. It matches my little space buns perfectly.

My high-waisted, neon green biker shorts are paired with a black and green sports bra. I threw on a loose cropped tee over it, my wind breaker, high socks and sneakers completing the outfit. I love it so much.

When I turn around, Lani walks out of her room, her outfit nearly bringing me to my knees. She's in a green and purple sequined romper. Lani is by far the most grunge of our group, often sporting band tees and plaid pants. It's the complete opposite to her ray of sunshine personality, but for some reason, it suits her.

This, however, is the complete opposite of her style and I'm wheezing with laughter. She looks like a disco ball and I can't breathe.

Lani points at me, laughing. "You're so bright, what the hell?"

"*I'm* bright? Look at Casey!" I point to where Casey is walking from her room. She's wearing neon pink wind joggers, a black belt and a black tank crop top. She looks nothing at all like herself and I love her for it. So far, we all have gone for something out of our comfort zones.

I knock on the door Wyatt is in. "You good in there?"

"Perfect," he says, his voice breaking with laughter. The lock clicks and when I see him, I can only stare. He looks between the three of us, waiting for a reaction.

I break first, bending over with laughter. I wheeze, pointing at him, and he laughs too, striking a pose.

"You like?" He flexes, the material tightening around his arms.

He's decked out in a one-piece romper, which isn't even the best part. It's got bright pink flamingos and blue umbrellas all over it.

I try to breathe through the laughter, but it's a losing battle. It's so funny to see this giant man wearing something as ridiculous as a flamingo romper.

Lani and Casey wheeze, shaking their heads.

"You win," Lani snorts. "That"—she points to his outfit—"is epic."

"Okay. What's next in our adventure?" Wyatt shoves his hands into the pockets of the romper and I snort again.

"It's really hard to take you seriously like that." I fight a smile as we walk through the thrift store, eliciting many strange looks from the shoppers around us. "We're not far from our next destination."

Wyatt starts the car and we climb in. I plug the address into his GPS and we're peeling out onto the main road toward the roller-skating rink. When we pull into the parking lot, it's nearly empty.

"I thought about having us play roller derby, but honestly, I'm a little afraid of being plowed down by Wyatt. So, roller skating it is."

"Don't forget the arcade," Casey chimes in.

"Yes, and the arcade, because we all want to lose to Wyatt at every game."

He laughs, and it's a glorious sound. I thought this day would be fun to do something ridiculous. I'll admit that it's more for me than anyone. Seeing him dress up in something silly and skate around is absolutely hilarious, and I couldn't help myself. But as we lace up our skates, waiting to get into the rink, I can tell he's enjoying himself.

"This is not at all how I pictured my bachelor party, but I'll admit, it's probably better."

"Well, I'm glad you're enjoying yourself." I knock him with my elbow, smiling.

"I never got one of those *hurt her and you die* talks from you. Is it the time for that yet?" He smirks and I narrow my eyes at him.

"All it takes is one look, Lane, one fucking look, and I'll end you." I muster the meanest face I can before smiling sweetly. "But I know you won't hurt her, so I needn't worry."

"I'll protect her with my life."

I don't need to tell him that I know he will, because I've seen it. I've seen him protect her and I've seen him go above and beyond to ensure her safety and happiness. It's another thing I love about Wyatt; I can trust that my best friend is safe with him. For many years, I was her protector, and now she's got Wyatt too.

The music starts playing and the few people in the building start skating circles in the rink. Lani grips my hand as we walk toward the entrance and mix into the crowd.

"I suck at walking, let alone skating." Lani's voice is loud in my ear as she yells over the music.

"Oh, that won't do." I grin, looking around for Wyatt. When I lock eyes with him, he cuts through the crowd to catch up to us.

"Ladies," he says, flipping around to skate backwards and face us.

Lani laughs right as Casey catches up, looping her arm through my free one.

"Lani can't skate and we need you to teach her." I waggle my eyebrows, hoping that Wyatt will accept the challenge.

"Of course. You know, I wanted to teach the littles to skate once. I still think about doing that some days." He continues skating backwards, making it look effortless. He reaches his arms out to Lani and she releases her death grip on my hand.

"I won't let you fall," he promises. When he grabs her hands, he skates backwards, letting her adjust on her feet. "Okay, so, I'm going to show you what to do with your feet first. Look down at my feet and I'll keep holding you up. I'll just be bringing you with me as I skate. Okay?"

Lani nods, and I can't help but smile. It warms my heart that he's taking the time to teach her. Casey and I skate, watching Lani's progress.

By the time we're ready to leave the rink, Lani is skating circles around the three of us. I don't know how he did it, but her confidence on her feet is different. If Damian ever pulls his head out his ass, he'll be able to take my sweet angel baby skating. I smirk to myself at the thought.

The sun is disappearing in the sky when we pull into the driveway of the house. Wyatt immediately walks to the grill with the burgers when I hear voices inside the house.

Lani and I look over our shoulder to see Dakota walking through the front door behind Damian. They're arguing about something and I laugh, looking back out at the water.

The sunset is in full bloom, the sky lit up with purple and pink. It's incredible, and I don't want to turn away, but when I do, I catch sight of Dakota standing with Jaiden. They're talking so easily, her arms moving as she speaks. He tosses his head back as he laughs and my stomach twists.

I swallow as I watch him. His dark brown curls are piled neatly on the top of his head, and his tanned skin looks golden in the light. My eyes hyper-focus on his hands, the rings decorating his fingers drawing my attention like usual. My core clenches as I think about the things his hands have done to me. As I watch him, admiring his perfectly put together attire and appearance, I want to do *more* with him. I want to see what life with him would be like outside of our little bubble of vacation. Everything here is safe, but out there in the real world, there are more things to fear than I can count.

I shamelessly watch him until he finally looks up, meeting my eyes. I should look away, but I don't. I hope that, for once, he can see the desire in my eyes, even if I'm too scared to say it out loud.

"Burgers are ready," Wyatt yells from the grill, his hands gripping the tray of cooked patties.

I jump to my feet, flicking on the porch light and opening the bag for the hamburger buns. It's all I can do to keep myself busy for even a moment.

"Hey."

My body reacts immediately to the sound of his voice, a delicious tingle running down my spine. His voice is deep and husky, full of seduction, even when it's not meant to be. I can't get enough of the sound of it, and I don't think I ever will.

"Hey," I say, trying to keep my voice calm. I don't think it's working though. He looks at me, his eyes soft, and for a second I think he might kiss me. Is it bad that I want him to? I want him to kiss me right here in front of all our friends. At the last second he looks up, his eyes going wide.

"What *the fuck* is Wyatt wearing?" His voice is loud, Dakota looking over at us to see what's happening.

She walks through the back doors, her eyes searching for her fiancé. The moment she sees him, her body bends as she laughs.

"Holy shit," she breaths. "I think that's the sexiest thing I've ever seen." She laughs, clapping her hands and I stare at her, my mouth gaping.

"Hear that ladies? My woman digs the flamingos. Come here and get a piece of this." He runs his hand down his body and she walks to him, laughing. He grabs her butt, pulling her to him as she leans up to kiss him.

There are several groans and laughter from around us. They're so in love and it's disgustingly cute.

"Don't be gross," I call. "I want to have an appetite when I eat, thank you."

Wyatt flips me off and Jaiden laughs. "This was clearly a much needed bonding experience for all of us," he says.

"Very. Lani learned how to skate today. It was very eventful." I look over my shoulder at where Lani and Damian are talking. "Okay, I am starving, so it's time to eat."

We grab our food, gathering around the fire pit for dinner. It's chilly enough in early August to cool off in the evening, so the fire is a welcome warmth to my legs.

With full bellies, we continue sitting around the fire until I break the silence. "The night is not over, friends. I've got a few more games in store for us." I raise a brow, my smile slightly devious. "With no kiddos, I thought it would be fun to play some drinking games."

"You just want an excuse to take shots," Lani says, and I laugh.

"True, my friend. True." I pull the bottle from the cooler, while Damian lines up glasses for the shots. I pour a round, everyone taking a shot just to start off the night.

As we continue on, I feel the booze flowing through my body, my limbs loose and relaxed. We've been playing games for hours, my stomach hurting from laughing. Truth or dare was on the table for a minute until Damian suggested spin the bottle. So here we are, a group of grown ass adults, sitting around an empty beer bottle.

"Who goes first?" Dakota asks, her eyes dropping a bit.

I've reached my limit, and I have to tap out, so I pop open a bottle of water, sipping on it while I wait.

"Well, if no one is going to volunteer, I'll go first." Roman surprises us all by reaching for the bottle and spinning it.

"My wife is off limits," Dallas says, holding his arm up weakly. "Except to me." He grins, wiggling his eyebrows.

"Oh, shut up," Casey says. "You wanted to play this too."

We laugh, the bottle slowing to a stop in front of Dallas. Roman and Dallas lock eyes, and for a moment I think they contemplate what to do next. We're all waiting to see how this game is going to go. When Dallas stands, I laugh, watching him plant a sloppy kiss on Roman's cheek.

Dakota snorts, slapping her leg at the stunned expression Roman wears. "Never did I ever think I'd be playing spin the bottle with my brother present."

"Gross," I say, and he points at me in agreement.

Dallas spins the bottle, and it stops on Casey. He wastes no time prowling toward his wife. She giggles when he kisses her face all over then lands one on her mouth. It's adorable, and so very Dallas.

"Okay, next!" I shout. It goes on like this for a while until it's finally getting interesting.

Lani spins the bottle, and it quickly lands on me. I smirk at her, raising both my hands to urge her toward me.

"Hit me, babes," I say, a little too enthusiastically. She laughs as she plants a soft kiss on my lips before walking back to her seat.

As I spin the bottle, I cross my fingers, hoping for someone good. I'm disappointed when it lands on Wyatt. Dakota laughs, and I glare at her.

Well, I better make this good then. I make a show of walking to Wyatt, walking around his chair and running my finger over his shoulders. He laughs when I flick his ear. I fall into his lap, wrapping my arms around his neck, and planting a kiss on his cheek, but before he can get any words out, I boop his nose.

"You're so not my type," I say. "Sorry, Wyatt."

Dakota laughs, her back nearly hitting the ground when she rolls with laughter.

"Totally fine," he says with a chuckle.

I stand from his lap, locking eyes with Jaiden. The only way I can describe his expression is hungry and maybe a bit jealous. I wish I knew what was going on in his head.

Several turns go by before I'm fully paying attention again. I watch as Damian smacks a longing kiss on Lani's lips. His hands grip her face lightly and I see the way she presses into him. We all cheer them on and when they pull apart, there's a moment where they just stare at each other, oblivious to the attention around them.

Lani sits back down, her cheeks pink as she brings her fingers to her lips. When Jaiden takes a turn, his bottle lands on Wyatt and I can't help the sputter of laughter that spills from my lips.

"Spin again," Wyatt says. Jaiden just stares at him, his lips pouting. "No fucking way. Don't look at me like that." He chuckles, despite the fact that he's trying to keep his face straight.

"You mean you don't want to kiss me?" He looks at Roman, his brows furrowed. "Do you hear this, Rome? Wyatt doesn't love me."

Roman looks at Wyatt, his head shaking. "Shame. Is the bromance dead?"

Wyatt rolls his eyes aggressively as Dakota shakes at his side. She's laughing so hard and it's only increased when Jaiden moves, prowling toward Wyatt on hands and knees. He purrs and Wyatt backs away.

"Get the fuck away from me," he laughs and Jaiden gets closer.

"Kiss me, Wyatt. You know you want to."

I can't tell if he's really fucking drunk or if this is just a regular occurrence. Either way, I'm living for the vibes. It's hilarious and I can't breathe as I watch them.

Finally, Wyatt gives in. Jaiden smacks a kiss on his lips and Wyatt groans, wiping his lips immediately and scowling.

"Yep, that's gross."

"I've always wanted to do that," Jaiden says with a wink.

We're all laughing. "Okay, I gotta tap out. It's been fun, but I'm done." Wyatt stands, stretching out his legs.

"Wait," Jaiden pouts, stomping his leg a bit. "I haven't kissed Sterling yet. I want my turn."

"Dude, you're drunk. Go to bed," Roman says, patting him on the back.

"I just really want to kiss Sterling, though," he says again, and I can feel my cheeks heat.

Damian looks at me, his eyes wide as he laughs.

"Well then, big boy, come here and kiss me so we can get you to bed." I tap my cheek lightly and I can see the way his eyes darken.

I've never been afraid of Jaiden, but right now, my heart fears for what would happen if he kisses me, right here and now, with all of our friends present. He's drunk, and it won't mean the same to him, but to me... My heart's already involved more than I wanted it to be. Learning to trust him was a silly excuse to make him wait. The truth is, I trusted him the moment he accepted me for me. I trusted him the moment I told him about my sexuality, and there's nothing I can say to convince myself otherwise.

Jaiden walks toward me, and it's full of purpose and intention. I pause, hoping our friends will clear out, but my heart stutters when I realize they're all still watching.

His hand comes to the back of my head the minute he makes contact. I barely breathe before his lips meet mine, the warmth from his skin sending fireworks throughout my body. He tastes like sugar with a hint of alcohol, and when his tongue runs across my lips, I don't hesitate to let him in.

I hate the way my body melts into him, his fingers twisting into my hair and making me completely pliable to his will. I release a small moan before I realize what I've done. We pull apart abruptly, my hand coming to my mouth to block my expressions.

Jaiden looks at me, his hand running through his hair as he stumbles back a bit. "Fuck. I think I'm in love," he says. He blinks, his chest rising and falling, and I gape at him.

"Are you serious?" I say, my tone clipped.

"Did I say that out loud?" he asks, his head shaking. "Wait. Yes. I'm serious. I'm definitely in love."

"O-kay that's enough from you," I say, my face burning. I can't hear this right now. He doesn't know what he's saying. "You need to go to bed now. Let's go." I grab his hand, dragging him behind me.

I open his bedroom door, dragging him with me. "You need to sleep and when you're sober, we'll talk."

"But I'm serious, Silver. I mean it." He tries to reach for me and I shake my head.

"No." I hold my hand up to him, causing him to stop his movements. "This is not how we're having this conversation. You can't play with my heart like that, Jaiden. No *fucking* way. Go to bed and find me in the morning."

I breathe deeply before rushing from his room. I couldn't risk looking at him, to see the look on his face. Even if he did mean it, it's too soon...right? *Fuck me.*

I want to scream, and maybe to run away. I go to the kitchen to grab some water and a bottle of aspirin. When I return to Jaiden's room, he's laying on the bed, his pants and shirt tossed onto the floor by the foot of the bed. His breathing is even, so I head to the night stand to leave the water and pills.

I barely survive long enough to sneak out, my back pressing against the door as I stare at the wall across from me. What does this mean for me if Jaiden Thomas does actually love me?

It changes everything. Right?

TWENTY-SEVEN

JAIDEN

I WAKE to the sounds of breakfast being made. My head pounds, but nowhere near as badly as I thought it would.

Even though I *was* technically drunk last night, I was completely present, my mind fully mine. Yes, maybe I hadn't meant to confess my one secret out loud, but I'm glad it happened nonetheless. The most sobering feeling is that I actually wanted her to know. I've wanted to tell her for a while now, but I don't think my heart was ready to assign the feelings I had for her as *love.*

I'm a fool to think it was anything but love. I love her. I love Sterling Bexley and I need to tell her again.

Sitting up, I wipe the sleep from my eyes and wander to the shower. After a very cold and sobering shower, I run some curl product through my hair and dress myself for the day. I don't know what to expect this morning, but I refuse to shy away from the consequences.

When I exit my room, Sterling's door is still closed, so I walk past and right into the kitchen. I'm surprised to see Sterling at the stove, her headphones in as she cooks bacon and eggs. I don't want to startle her, so I flick the lights until she notices.

When she turns around, she pulls out her headphones and smiles at me, the spatula in hand.

"Hey," she says, smiling. There's a bit of hesitancy in her stance, so I move toward her, testing the waters. When she relaxes, I pull her into my arms and press my face into her hair, the amber and vanilla scent filling my nose. I don't know what perfume she wears, but it's very *her.*

"How are you feeling?" I ask into her hair.

She huffs a breath and I feel the warmth of it on my chest. "I didn't sleep much because my brain wouldn't turn off," she admits.

"I'm sorry." Am I really, though? *No. I'm not.* "Is now a good time to talk?"

"Yeah." She turns to the stove, removing the eggs and bacon from the heat. After loading them onto a plate, she walks it to the table and pulls out a chair to sit.

I sit across from her, then grab a piece of bacon before biting off a piece as I watch her. She watches me too, her eyes assessing the situation.

"Ask me anything," I say.

"Did you mean it?" she shoots immediately.

"Yes," I say plainly.

"And you remember everything?"

"Everything," I confirm, holding her gaze. I'm not backing down.

"You love me." It's a statement, but it sounds like a question. "You're in love with me."

"Correct."

"How long? Why? I don't understand."

I sigh, running and hand through my hair. "Honestly? Probably before we 'broke up' the first time. But definitely since Pride. And why? Because you are the most infuriating woman I've ever met." She begins to protest and I hold up a hand to shush her. "You make me want to be a better person. After my mom passed, I didn't know if I could love again, but you proved me completely wrong. You're the only person who sees right through me and that's scary as hell, but I wouldn't have it any other way. I could say more if you want me to."

She blinks several times, just absorbing the new information. Finally, she breathes, her mouth opening and closing. "We're not even dating, and you love me. Isn't it soon for that?"

"I've known you through two seasons, I've spent more of my private life with you than anyone else. That is two fucking years of my life, Sterling. I don't have to date you to know that I'm so fucking done when it comes to you. You're it for me. There is no one else. Even when I wanted there to be someone else, it's always been you."

"Jaiden, you can't be serious. I'm—"

"You're what? This doesn't fucking mean we're going to run off and get married. I want you. I want you so bad, and I am so sick and tired of having to pretend like you're not mine, because that's exactly what you are." I raise my voice, my chest heaving.

I can't stand another moment of her pushing me away, acting like we're just friends, because we're fucking not. Nothing that I feel toward her is friendly. I want to rip her clothes off at every second. I want to make *love* to her until I can see the sun streaking through the blinds. I want to hold her hand in public like a fucking sap. Jesus Christ. I can feel my heart ripping from my chest as I stare at her, waiting for her to speak.

Her lips quiver as she looks at me, a lone tear sliding down her cheek. She's quick to swipe it away. "We're very untraditional, aren't we?" She finally looks at me again, her face softening.

"I wouldn't have it any other way. First comes love, then comes...dating?" I say it like a question. "I want to take you out on a proper date, and I want our friends to know."

She purses her lips, her full lashes hiding the depth of her expression. "I think I love you too. And I want to date you, and I also want our friends to know."

If there was a word for what I'm feeling right now, I would scream it, but I can't think hard enough to assign a specific word to the feelings. She leans forward, her arms resting in the middle of the table as she brings her face closer to mine. Leaning forward, I capture her lips, my hands coming to her neck to urge her closer.

"I didn't need you to say it back, but now that you have...*fuck.*" I nip at her lip and she smiles into my kiss.

"How are we telling the friends?" She breathes between kisses.

"Want me to go out there like *hey, we're together now*?" I kiss the corner of her mouth gently, my hand palming her hair.

"Mmm," she says, and I laugh. I continue kissing her until my lips feel numb. It's the best feeling in the world and I never want it to end.

Her hand runs down my arm until she can slide her hand into my shirt. When her cold hands press against my chest, I bite down on her lip, eliciting a whimper from her.

"If you continue making those noises, I'm going to fuck you right here on this table."

"Do it," she says through kisses. "Everyone's gone. I told them to get the fuck out."

I groan into her mouth, my arm coming to her waist. She crawls further onto the table until she sits in front of me, her legs hanging off the side and into my lap.

"Want to christen the table? It's mine now." She says, a delicious smirk toying at the corner of her mouth. Her eyes darken, the lust and desire swirling behind them.

"You own the place?"

"Signed the papers this morning. Mother dearest called it a *peace offering*."

"Fuck her," I say, sliding my hand under her shirt, my fingers pulling at the fabric of her sports bra.

"Fuck me," Sterling replies. "Here. Right now. No more games."

"Yes, ma'am." I strip her shirt in one motion, the fabric dropping to the floor beside me. She doesn't waste a second pulling off her bra, her breasts completely exposed to me. I can't help it, I pull her nipple into my mouth, my tongue flicking at the jewelry. She tosses her head back, moaning. I feel her hands come to my head, her fingers twirling through my hair.

Flicking the button on her jeans loose, I pull down the zipper to allow myself access. She spreads her legs, lifting so that I can pull down her jeans. When they reach her ankles, she kicks them off, her legs opening wider.

I stare, her body sculpted just for me. Standing, I yank down my joggers, before my hand comes to her pussy. She's soaking already, and the feel of it sends a pulse right to my cock. I fucking missed this. I missed her.

Sex with Silver has always been great, but for ages we toyed with each other. I'm done playing. My finger slides into her panties, pushing them aside before I find her clit, rubbing the sensitive bud for a moment. She tosses her head back, moaning and panting already. She squirms, and I chuckle.

"Patience, sweetheart. Just one, and then you can have me." The chair that I'd been sitting in is quickly forgotten as I push it back, the sound of it falling ricocheting off the walls. My fingers slide into her, pumping as she gasps. I lean into her, kissing her neck, my free hand sliding to her breasts.

"I'll never get enough of you," I say, kissing a trail down her body. She's my poison of choice, and I'm more than content to fuel my addiction to her.

She moans, my fingers pumping her faster, edging her closer to her climax. It's the most beautiful sight to see, her body writhing beneath mine, and the way the dark ring of blue in her eyes spread when she's close.

My thumb rubs her clit and suddenly, the breath leaves her body, her hands fisting my hair.

"Fuck," she says, her core clenching around me, the waves of her orgasm washing through her. I swallow the moan that leaves her mouth, reveling in the fact that I did that to her.

She comes down, her body shaking slightly. "Jaiden, if you don't give me your cock right now, I'm going to—"

"You're going to what?" I say, my brow raised. She stares at me, the challenge written all over her face. She watches me as I slip my fingers into my mouth and suck the taste of her off.

I don't waste a second. My free hand slides under her, bringing her closer to me so that our bodies connect. I kiss her deeply before I'm flipping her so that she's bent over the edge of the table. My hand connects with her ass and she moans, arching into the table. Red streaks her ass but she doesn't seem to mind.

"Jaiden," she pants. "*Fuck me,*" she commands, and I almost want to give in.

"Have you forgotten who's in charge here?"

There's a sense of urgency in the air. I want nothing more than to be buried inside of her right now, but if we're going to do this, we're going to do this *right.* She knows the deal, and that's what will make this more fun.

"N–no," she says, her upper body lifting to look at me. Her eyes widen in surprise when I sink to my knees, spreading her legs apart. She barely gets a moment to breathe before I flip her over, my face connecting with her pussy.

The long moan that leaves her mouth is one of the sexiest sounds I've ever heard. My cock is sorely neglected right now, but it'll be worth it.

"You said—"

"I said what?" I lick my lips, the taste of her making my cock throb in my boxers. If anyone were to see us right now, they'd get an eye full. My feast is splayed out on the table just for me, my joggers piled around my ankles as I kneel before her.

I look at her through my lashes. When she doesn't speak, I run my tongue through her and she hisses, bucking into my face as her head falls back.

"Tell me." I nip at her clit, eliciting a breathy moan from Sterling.

After several moments, she looks up at me, her eyes pleading. "You said just one and then I could have you. I want *you.*"

"You'll have me," I promise. "Be patient."

She growls. "I am *not* patient."

"You'll learn." With my tongue, I bring her to the brink of another orgasm, and at that point, I stop, looking up at her. "Who's in charge here, Sterling?" I look at her, feeling the waves of frustration roll off her. Her face is scrunched, her body shaking with need.

Her jaw clenches before she speaks. "You."

"Do you want me?"

She nods her head, a tear sliding down her cheek. "Always," she breathes, and it nearly breaks me. "So badly."

"Then you'll have me."

Flipping her over, I free my cock from my boxers, lining myself up with her entrance. In one swift motion, I thrust into her, my hand gripping tightly to her hips as I push into her. I damn near see stars, my jaw tensing as I feel her adjust to me. She squeezes me and I groan, not moving.

"Fuck. Don't do that." I smack her ass again and she hisses, her back arching as she presses into me. My fingers weave into her hair and I yank her head to me, capturing her lips. When she clenches around me again, I groan. "Fucking hell, Sterling. Give me a damn minute."

"Why?" she laughs.

"Because it's been so damn long since I've been inside your pussy and I'd forgotten how fucking good it feels. Unless you want me to come in two seconds, I suggest you stop."

She clenches around me again, not following directions, and I smack her ass. She moans, and I shake my head.

I breathe, pulling out slightly, then pressing back into her with increasing need. She's so damn tight, and it feels like heaven. "God, I love you." My hand grips her hip, *hard,* and I thrust into her again and again. She gasps, her pussy clenching around me as our bodies meet. I don't think I could ever be more turned on by her than I am right now.

It's been ten months, and I'd forgotten how fucking addicting she is. I want to breathe her in, swallow every moan. Something primal in me awakens, screaming to see her, to watch as each moan escapes her perfect lips. So when I flip her to face me, I watch every face she makes, enjoying what *I* do to her.

My thrusts grow more frantic, her movements matching mine. I see her move her hand to tweak her nipple and I groan as I watch. I love a woman that knows what she wants and isn't afraid to take it.

My hand comes to her clit, massaging as I feel her tighten around me. A moment later, her cries of pleasure fill my ears, her pussy clenching around me in the most delicious way. I groan, rubbing her clit through her orgasm. She pants, her body relaxing, and it's then that I slam into her once more, my body tensing before I come, stars blurring the edges of my vision.

I heave in breaths, my hand still holding onto her hip like my life depends on it. It's when she looks back at me with a satisfied smirk that I slump forward, pulling her hair until her lips meet mine.

"Let's not tell our friends we fucked on the table," I whisper.

She laughs. "Yeah, maybe not. But we should get out of here. They're coming back soon."

I grab our clothes from the floor, ushering her to the room so we can shower away the evidence of our activities. When her body presses against mine under the warm stream of water, I can't help but allow my hands to roam. She does the same, my cock hardening again at the feel of her.

She takes me into her hand, stroking me, and when I lift her, she doesn't protest when I thrust into her once more. After several moments, we're panting against the shower wall, my cum dripping down her leg.

We barely make it out of the shower and into the main room before our friends come barreling through the front door.

I take a bite of the eggs, chewing as I listen to their conversation.

"I have a whole Pinterest board. It'll be easy, I swear." Dakota pokes at Wyatt's arm, a grin spreading across her face.

"Easy for you. You ooze creativity, and I draw stick figures." He laughs, his fingers intertwined with hers.

"Hey, I still draw stick figures, too. I promise, we can make it ourselves." There's some grumbling as the guys follow behind them. "Oh, shush. When all of you eventually get married, I'll go above and beyond for you too, so don't complain."

"Married? Me?" It's Damian that speaks and I choke on my eggs when I try not to laugh.

I cough, Sterling tapping my back as the group enters the kitchen.

"Hey, guys!" she says brightly.

"Hey," Dakota says. She walks to her friend and pulls her into her arms. "I missed your face. Never kick me out again, okay?" She winks.

I cough again and Roman eyes me suspiciously. I stare at my friends for a moment, the silence deafening. Finally, I grab Sterling's hand, linking our fingers. "We're dating now. End of."

"Fucking *finally*. I thought I was going to have to deal with the two of you eye-fucking each other from across the room for an eternity." Damian rolls his eyes, but it's full of humor.

Sterling bends over laughing. "Oh, that'll continue. Have you *seen* Jaiden?" She gasps, shaking her head. "Wait. I have something to give you." She drops my hand, running down the hall and returning a moment later. She's holding her arms behind her back before she extends a beaded bracelet to me. "I made it this morning."

I take the bracelet from her, examining it. Instead of that stupid clown and shrimp bracelet, this one reads *Property of Sterling* with a camera charm on the side.

"Damn straight," I say, grabbing her ass and pulling her toward me. She drops her face to mine as I kiss her, oblivious to the stares of our friends.

Dakota snaps her fingers, and when I open my eyes, she's smiling wide.

"Great. Now, we've got work to do. It's wedding crunch time. Chop, chop everyone."

TWENTY-EIGHT

STERLING

"OVER IS THE ONLY RIGHT ANSWER," I argue, tossing a pack of screws onto the lumber cart.

"You could've carried those, you know, and I firmly disagree. It's under, you psychopath." Jaiden pushes the lumber cart down the aisle of the hardware store. I stop to glare back at him, but instead I catch Roman's eyes. He laughs, shaking his head, and I point at him.

"What do *you* think, Roman? Under or over?" I prop a hand on my hip, as I look at him. Jaiden stops the cart abruptly to avoid hitting my legs.

"Nope. Don't bring me into this."

"Thank fuck we're not living together because I'll keep my toilet paper under, thank you very much."

"Who says we're not going to live together?" I tease, turning back to continue down the aisle.

"Me. You'll drive me nuts, you psycho. Next, you'll say you like pineapple on pizza." Jaiden huffs and I laugh.

"I do like pineapple on pizza. You forget—I'm mixed. My Hawaiian blood loves pineapple. I can't believe I'm dating you. How are we going to last?" It's a joke, and I make sure my tone is lighthearted.

"That's the fun," Roman interjects. "Y'all may have spent a lot of time together in the past, but just wait until you experience domestic bliss. I just hope the two of you don't burn down any buildings with your fighting."

"No burning from me," I say, a sweet smile spreading across my face. "Now, let's get the hell out of here. It's time to build Dakota her perfect arch."

Jaiden grumbles something and I glare at him. This is my best friend's wedding, and I'll do anything to make it the most magical day possible for her.

"It's hot as Satan's balls outside."

"You'll be fine, big man. We got this." I punch his arm lightly and Roman laughs at us.

I'm enjoying this new-found freedom. Jaiden and I are getting along reasonably well. Although, I think there will always be bits of us that disagree on things. I've gotten so used to the fighting that this new teasing side of our arguments comes naturally.

"Speaking of domestic bliss, ever since we locked y'all into the pantry, I think it's haunted or something." Roman scratches his head, an almost ghostly look crossing his face.

I laugh, looking over at Jaiden with wide eyes. "Wait. You think your pantry is cursed. Why?"

"Things have been disappearing. I've been shopping so many times and I swear, every time I seem to buy more of the same things that should've lasted two people, one of which is a child, several weeks." Roman runs a hand across his face, staring.

Jaiden and I exchange a look, the amusement toying at the corners of his mouth. "Oh. Well maybe your mom should sage the place. That should keep the ghosts away. Cleanse the environment." He snorts, looking over at me. His eyes are mischievous and full of humor. He knows the reason for this supposed haunting in the pantry.

"Yeah...Yeah. Maybe I'll try that," he says absentmindedly. He walks away and I look up at Jaiden, hoping for an explanation.

He just chuckles, shaking his head. "The guys and I have been stealing shit from his pantry every time he goes shopping. It started with minuscule things to fuck with him, but I'd completely forgotten it was still going."

"We're going to give that man an ulcer."

"Probably," Jaiden agrees with a laugh.

We check out at the front, being quick about leaving the store and loading up into the car. When we pull up to the house, it takes barely a minute before the sweat falls down my back. It's unusually hot and although I normally love the heat, it's not lending to proper arch-building activities. We've got less than two weeks to finish everything for their wedding, and mama isn't messing around.

Rushing inside the air-conditioned house, I make it to my room where I'm quick to change into my bikini. Grabbing a loose shirt from my closet, I shove it over my head as I walk through the house and out the back door. If all else fails, I'll run to the water to cool off.

Damian wipes sweat off his forehead as he brings the saw down onto the wood, cutting it to size. He's shirtless and I notice the way Lani stares at him every so often.

I sit beside her before Jaiden gently places a cut of wood in front of us. He winks at me.

"My evenings don't normally start out with an erection...but my morning wood." He snorts when I point my finger at him, my laughter barely contained. Lani giggles beside me.

"I'll do you one better. What do you call a tree that only grows at sunrise?" I raise my brow and Jaiden's cheeks rise as he smiles.

"Morning wood?" he asks, and Lani and I both laugh.

"Correct. Now take your dirty jokes elsewhere so we can stain this." I slap his butt lightly with the clean towel before dipping it into the stain.

In the distance, I hear Lily giggling with Wyatt over something. I look in their direction to see Wyatt sitting on the ground in front of her. He's teaching her one of those hand games we used to play when you waited in a long line or when you were at school with your friends. He turns his hands around and she mimics him until they've got the pattern down. It's so cute. I can easily see Wyatt being a father.

I've never seen myself as someone who'd have the life that many women dream of. I've never wanted the white picket fence, or the fairytale wedding. I don't think I'll ever see myself getting married, and maybe that's why Jaiden's words from weeks ago scared me so much.

There's still so much we have to work out in our relationship, but for now, I can be happy.

I rub the stain into the board, seeing the way it darkens into the ebony color.

After an hour of staining planks of wood, I'm sweaty and hot. The guys groan, and I look over to see Jaiden uncapping his water bottle and taking a long swig. His throat bobs as he swallows, and I get the sudden urge to run my tongue up and down his neck. I look away before he can catch me staring.

It's so fucking hot that I can feel sweat dripping between my breasts. It's fucking nasty, and I have half a thought to run into the water, but I've got a job to do.

Pulling off my shirt, I toss it aside, my bikini top allowing for the cool air to hit my skin. I grab the rag, wiping the stain across the last bits of the wooden arch. While Lani and I stain, Jaiden and Roman have been putting the stained pieces together. Damian has, surprisingly, a propensity for floral arrangements. So, he and Wyatt are helping Dakota twist the fake vines around the arch.

Lani stops staining the little blocks of wood to swipe at her forehead.

"I'm going to die of heat exhaustion," she says, falling into the seat beside the wood planks.

"There's something we can do to fix that," Damian says with a smirk.

Everyone looks up at him, waiting for his next move. I write him off until I hear Lani shriek beside me, Damian tossing her over his shoulder and running toward the water. She screams, laughing when he runs them both into the water.

I shake my head, dipping my rag back into the stain and swiping it across the plank. It's going to be a beautiful arch when we're done with it, but right now, I really want to chuck it into the garbage.

I'm staining, my focus solely on the plank, when cool water drips on my back. I immediately sit up straighter when I feel arms reach around me, lifting me into the air. I breathe deeply, smelling lime and cedar and sweat. Despite the fact he's been outside all afternoon, he still smells good, and still looks insanely fuckable.

"No!" I shriek. "No! Absolutely not." The words don't match the way my core tightens at how his hands grip my waist and legs as he runs.

"Absolutely, yes," he says, running us toward the water. I barely have a moment to look up before I see the amused faces of our friends.

Seconds later, I'm being thrown into the cool water of the lake. Lani splashes me, her laughs bringing me joy.

I smile at her, my hair sticking to the side of my face. When I swipe it away, Jaiden's hands come to the back of my neck, holding tightly before he brings his dripping face to mine. I deepen the kiss, leaning up to grip the back of his head.

He pulls away a minute later, his forehead pressing into mine. "So glad I get to do that now." He pecks my nose before pulling away, splashing water at me. I feel love drunk, my body high on Jaiden Thomas.

Lani splashes water again, her aim at Damian, but it hits Jaiden and I.

They continue splashing around and I dunk myself under the water once more before walking back toward the house. Jaiden follows me and suddenly I feel the sting of a slap, a moment before his hand grips tightly to ass. My eyes go wide as he smirks at me, but it drops the moment Roman yells from across the way.

"Jaiden!" he yells, his eyes angry. "Children! There are children present. You can't go slapping your girlfriend's behind like that in front of her. She copies!" Roman slaps a hand over his face before his hands rub his temples. Jaiden looks like a kid being scolded by his father and I can't help but bend over laughing.

He raises a hand, his face slightly red. "Sorry, Rome." He gives him a tight smile before ushering me toward the house.

I giggle into my hand, shaking my head the closer to the house we get. When Jaiden looks over at me, his face breaks, a laugh sputtering out of him. We topple through the back doors, laughing uncontrollably, and it's the most fun I've had in a while.

ROMAN RETURNS TO THE TABLE, SLIDING INTO THE SEAT across from Damian. I stand at the counter, sipping my drink as I listen to their conversations.

"I'll tell ya, that girl is going to give me a heart attack. Never in my life did I think I was going to father a daughter without her mother here."

"Good thing you've got us then, right?" I wink, holding up my drink.

"Definitely. There will be a day I need to explain periods and I think I might die inside when that day comes." He shakes his head, his eyes wide. "Thankfully, I can still enjoy early bedtimes and the lack of boyfriends for now."

Wyatt laughs, his fingers intertwined with Dakota's. He raises their joined hands to his lips, kissing the back of her hand. She smiles at him, a gleam shining in her eyes.

The music hums through the speakers and when a country song comes on, Roman stands, offering his hand to Lani. "Care to dance?"

I've learned over time that Roman has a natural talent for dancing. He's got this southern charm, his roots shining through in everything he does. It's evident in the way he damn near charms the pants off of the ladies. It's unfortunate that he's not looking to date—he'd make an amazing partner for someone.

Lani places her hand in his, and he swings them toward the living room. He twirls her around, Lani following his lead almost effortlessly. I walk toward Jaiden, my hands coming to his shoulders. I stay there for a moment until I move to sit in the chair next to him, but I'm quickly pulled backward until I'm sitting on his lap. I yelp quietly, laughing when he snuggles his scruffy face into my neck.

"You smell like fuckin' heaven." His voice is quiet and sensual as he speaks. Goosebumps spread down my spine at the warmth of his breath on me. I feel like I'm always craving him, my body ready to come apart under his touch.

Our friends are intently watching the performance Roman and Lani are putting on, and when the next song starts, he begins teaching her how to line dance.

I wiggle, trying to get comfortable on Jaiden's lap, and he stiffens slightly.

"Don't tease," he breathes, his hand sliding up my bare thigh. After our adventure in the water, I dressed in one of his t-shirts, enjoying the way that it hangs loosely on my body like a dress.

"I'm not," I whisper, keeping my eyes trained on our friends.

"You are," he says.

My breath stops when his fingers trail higher on my thigh. I want to clench my thighs to stop him, but he nips my ear lightly and I forget what I'm thinking.

"You in that damn shirt, sitting across my lap, is a tease. Everything about you is a tease for me. I haven't stopped thinking about how fucking sexy you looked today, and then you do this to me." His nips my ear again. "How about I tease you?" His voice is so low, meant only for me.

I'm about to ask him what he means when he adjusts me on his lap so that the table is hiding us from view. His hand slides under my shirt, his fingers grazing my clit over my panties. I gasp, immediately slamming my mouth shut.

"Quiet," he purrs into my ear. "And maybe you'll get a reward."

I tense as he continues to swirl his thumb over my clit. My eyes dart across the room, ensuring no one is watching us, but everyone's attention remains on Lani and Roman.

I grip his leg to keep from moving or making noise. I can feel the moisture gathering in my panties, and when he *finally* slides his finger under the thin fabric, he hisses under his breath.

"You're so wet. I think you like my fingers on your pussy in front of our friends." His thumb presses against my clit right as one finger enters me.

I bite my lip to keep from moaning, but it doesn't stop the way my body pulses with arousal.

"Keep your eyes on our friends, baby. You don't want them to think you're getting fucked, right here at our table."

I shiver, my breathing increasing as he pumps in and out of me. My face flushes, and I spread my legs wider for him. My grip tightens on his legs as my body coils tighter.

Roman spins Lani, and she laughs when he lifts her into the air effortlessly.

Jaiden kisses my neck, his stubble sending my senses into overdrive. I feel my heart pounding in my chest, and when I lean back farther into Jaiden, his body is warm against mine.

His fingers pump into me, curving in the way that should be making me scream right now. Instead, I'm clenching my jaw shut, my body shaking as I near the edge. His free hand runs across my arm, soothing the tension. It's full of unspoken declarations of love and admiration. I've never had a man worship me in the way that Jaiden does. It's an experience that I never thought I'd have, and as I sit here, his fingers doing incredible things to my body, I can't help but feel in awe of him.

I swallow back a whimper as my body coils so tightly, a rush of arousal and pleasure running through me. With a final swirl of his thumb, I'm falling over the edge, my head turning to bite into his shoulder to keep from screaming. His movements don't cease, his thumb continuing to move as I ride out my orgasm.

"Good girl," he says into my ear. "You're such a good girl, being quiet. Look how perfect you are." He kisses my head, and I nearly cry into his shoulder. I come down, my body shaking with the after effects of my orgasm.

Breathing deeply, I try to compose myself enough to look back at our friends.

"Are you okay, Silver?" Dakota sounds concerned, and I still, Jaiden's fingers still inside of me, his other hand grasping my arm. I don't think I can speak properly so I nod into Jaiden's shoulder.

"All good," he says. "Just having a moment." He kisses my head and I laugh, turning my head to look at Dakota.

"I'm fine. Just...emotional." My eyes flick to Jaiden and he smirks. *Fucker.*

Dakota seems satisfied by that answer, her hand gripping Wyatt's before she turns back to our friends.

"We're just fine," Jaiden says, his fingers pulling from me a moment before he brings them to his mouth and sucks them clean.

TWENTY-NINE

JAIDEN

I HUFF A BREATH, holding my dumbbells tight at my sides. Today we're doing mixed mobility training for our off-season program. These Russian step-ups are killing me, but I know I need to improve my hip mobility and balance.

Wyatt is at my side, running through the one-arm cable press. We're on our last set, and I can't wait to run it off before we hit the showers and head back to the house.

I stick my tongue out at Damian as he does the barbell Romanian deadlifts. He shakes his head at me, his face full of concentration.

"This time of year reminds me how much I need to stay in shape. Too much pizza," he huffs, dropping the barbell to the floor.

"Don't be pussies," Roman says from the pull-up bar. He makes it look so damn easy, and I want to punch him for it.

I count internally, my leg shaking as I finish my last rep.

"What's last?" Wyatt asks, standing straight. He wipes his face with a towel, before looking over at Roman.

"Prowler sprints," he says, dropping from the bar. He pulls out the prowler and we take turns sprinting for the last twenty minutes.

I'm sweaty and gross by the end of training, but I couldn't be happier about it. I've been running and working out at the house, but it's nothing like getting back into the gym.

Off-season training is so important. Our bodies become attuned to the stance we hold on the ice, and mobility is one of the focuses of off-season training. I won't be surprised if Roman runs us through barre training next. Even with the wedding planning in full swing, we've still made time for this. It's a sense of normalcy that I'd been missing for a while now.

Nothing about this summer has been normal. I'm going to head home with a girlfriend... *Fuck. That isn't something I thought I'd ever say.* Not only that, but there are things we've yet to discuss. Living situations, logistics of the new relationship status with our team, and the fact that this may be the closest to a wedding I ever get. I've never seen myself as the marriage type. Maybe Sterling makes me question that? It was a slip up with her mother, a moment of passion. And yet, my mind can't stop reeling over the fact that she may want to get married one day, and I don't know if I could give that to her.

I run a hand through my stubble as the car pulls up the driveway.

"Dude, you look like you're about to bust a nut from thinking so hard." Damian claps me on the back before sliding out the passenger side door.

I shake my head, my eyes rolling. "Yeah, yeah. Thanks for that."

"How's the honeymoon phase treating you?" Damian opens the trunk before he reaches in and pulls his duffle bag out. I follow suit, slamming the trunk closed.

"It's great. I'm just waiting for the other shoe to drop when we have to deal with the repercussions with the team."

"You'll be fine. Coach has always had an inkling about the two of you."

"Can confirm," Roman tosses over his shoulder from ahead of us.

"Are we just stupid?" I ask, not really meaning it. It seems like everyone around us knows more about us than we do. I follow him through the front door, and walk down the hall toward our rooms.

"Yes," Dakota and Lani yell from somewhere inside the house. I look at Damian and he shakes his head.

"You're an idiot. Y'all thought you were better at hiding it than you actually were. We've all known you've been in love with her for ages."

"And what about you? You've been simping over Lani, but I doubt you'll ever do anything about that. Mr. *I-don't-want-to-be-tied-down*." I lower my voice and he glares.

"My life is simpler that way. I like simple."

"Right," I say nodding. "And fake dating Sterling was simple. I call bullshit."

"It fucking worked," he huffs. He's right. Everyone is right. It did work, and I'm tired of hearing it. I'm tired of feeling like I was an idiot for so long.

I roll my eyes, waving him off before I disappear into my room.

Sterling's laid across the bed, her laptop resting in her lap. When her eyes flick up at me, they're hungry, and I immediately slam the door behind me.

"Do you remember when we went to the bar and you danced on stage with the drag queens?" She sets her laptop aside, her legs coming to a crisscross position.

"Yeah." I walk toward her, lowering to the edge of the bed.

"I've had this fantasy of you singing for me while you strip and dance." She smirks, her eyes a deep indigo color now. It's full of teasing and arousal and I don't know which I like more.

"You want a repeat of the club, except just for you?"

"Oh, definitely. I'd love a performance from *the* Jaiden Thomas." She winks at me and I can't say no to her.

"You pick the music," I say, turning my back to her. She laughs with glee. I hear her swipe her phone off the table before she hums.

"Ready?" Her voice drips with amusement and I decide to put on a real show for her.

"Sit on the edge of the bed, sweetheart." I look over my shoulder at her with over exaggerated seduction. She cackles, crawling to the edge and letting her legs dangle over the edge.

I turn back to the door, and the moment the music starts to play, I put on my game face.

Vegas by *Doja Cat* blasts through her phone, my legs bending as I sway my hips, my arms crossing over my chest and then slowly dropping to my sides. When I turn toward her, she's smiling so wide, but I don't let my character break.

I lip-sync to the music, the words coming easily to me as I prowl toward her. When I reach her legs, my hands slap down at her sides, my face moving close to her. She startles, laughing when I seductively lower the floor at her feet.

Looking up at her, I run my hand down my chest before it slips under my shirt, slowly removing it.

Silver's face twists as she tries to keep the smile at bay. I lick my lips, twirling the shirt above my head. Rising to my feet, I bring the shirt around her, pulling her toward me and grinding on her softly. She snorts, and I bring my lips to her ear. She gasps when I suck the lobe into my mouth and then push her away, dropping the shirt.

She falls back onto the bed, laughing uncontrollably, and I break finally, a smile curling at the corner of my lips.

I lower myself to her again, grinding before I sit up, twirling the strings of my joggers. She slides her hands into the waistband and I feel myself growing hard at her nearness.

The song comes to a slow, and I slide my joggers down my hips just a smidge, and Sterling's eyes darken again. Her tongue slides across her lip, and I continue pushing my joggers until my cock slides free, slapping against my abs.

"I lied. Weeks ago when I gave Damian the BDE bracelet. This" —she grips my cock firmly between her fingers, and I groan—"is the best dick I've ever had. And baby, you've definitely got big dick energy."

"Damn right," I say, moving my arms to her and lifting her to me. She automatically wraps her arms around my shoulders, her eyes searching mine a moment before our lips crash together.

I hunger for her, every fiber of my being starving for her touch. She's the perfect addiction, every bit of her sinfully delicious.

"I waited too long for you to pull your head out of your ass to wait any longer for you to fuck me in your bed."

"How vanilla of you," I say, winking. "Who fucks in bed? People still do that?"

"Shut up," she says, kissing me, and I laugh into her mouth.

She lifts her shirt, breaking our kiss to pull it over her head. When she returns to my mouth, my hands roam across her bare back. I trace the lines of her tattoos, knowing exactly where they are without looking for them.

Her bare breasts press against my chest and I marvel at the feel of her piercings on my skin. We lay back, my hand sliding between her thighs. She spreads her legs for me, allowing me better access. I never want these moments with her to end.

I kiss my way down her body, sucking her pebbled nipples into my mouth. She moans, arching her body. I could watch her forever, enjoying the way she reacts to every touch. She bites her lip when I circle her clit with my thumb before pressing a finger inside of her.

She moans a breathy sound and I feel my cock pulse. The tip is weeping and I ache to be inside of her. When she clenches around my finger, I groan.

"I fucking love you," I say, removing my finger to stroke my cock a few times. I line myself up with her entrance and thrust inside of her, not caring to go slow. The gasp she releases sends a shiver down my spine. She feels incredible, just like she always has.

I could lose myself to her, staying like this until the end of time.

Her legs come to wrap around my waist, urging me deeper. I chuckle, loving the way that she takes control.

I tweak her nipple between my fingers right as I thrust again, deeper this time. We both moan, her hair falling across her face.

"I want to be on top," she gasps. "Let me ride you. *Please.*" She pants it as I thrust into her again.

I stare down at her, looking between her eyes. I nod, thrusting again before I flip us over so that she straddles me. She looks at me, a beat of shock gracing her face before it disappears. What she doesn't understand is that I would do anything she asked of me, including giving up my control. Silver will be my undoing.

When her hand comes to my chest, I know I'm a goner. She swirls her hips, and I groan, unable to stop the way my hands grip her thighs like my life depends on it.

"You're going to leave bruises," she says, rising up, and slamming back down onto me. Her head falls back, eyes fluttering closed. She's exquisite.

"That's the point. I want *everyone* to know that you're *mine*." My breath escapes me as I feel her move above me. I know she's close, and that fact alone brings me closer to the edge.

She plants both hands firmly on my chest as she rises up and slams down multiple times. Her movements grow more frantic, her chest heaving.

Releasing her thigh, I move my thumb to her clit, rubbing it in the way that's sure to send her screaming.

She whimpers and when I pull her to me, my teeth nip at her bottom lip. I meet her, thrust for thrust, my thumb working her clit. With one last thrust, I feel her come undone. Her chest heaves and I swallow her screams of pleasure. I don't even realize when I come, my orgasm hitting me so abruptly that I moan into her, loving the feel of her around me.

Her head drops into the crook of my shoulder as we come down.

"Fuck. You're incredible," I say, kissing her cheek.

Silver laughs, and it's a raspy sound that causes my cock to twitch inside of her.

"Again?" she asks with a laugh.

"You underestimate my stamina when it comes to you."

"I'll never underestimate you again." She kisses me deeply, taking her time to explore. It's tender and loving, and it shocks my heart into action once more. I feel like for the first time in a long time, I'm truly living. Like my heart is alive for the first time in years. It's scary as fuck, but for some reason, I don't mind being scared.

THIRTY

STERLING

"YOU CAN MOVE those to the back. There's a path along the side of the house. I'll have the big guns move them to their proper spots later." I point to the left of me, the delivery men nodding before they disappear with the farm style tables.

Dakota's family is due to come today for the final bits of wedding prep. The wedding is in just a few days, and we still have so much left to do.

I can tell that Dakota is getting nervous. There's a crease at the top of her forehead that never quite eases, the stress in her eyes evident. I know that Wyatt is trying to calm her, but it's not helping much. This is a huge event for her.

Wyatt said that the team is arriving tomorrow to help with the heavy lifting. I've never been so thankful for a whole team of burly men.

I watch as the men move the tables to the back of the house. Jaiden runs back, grabbing a table with one of the delivery men, and disappearing once more.

My stomach clenches with anxiety. I want this to be absolutely perfect for her. There's nothing I wouldn't do for my best friend. She's really the only family I've ever had, and that adds to the pressure.

"That's the last of them," Charlie says, handing me a clipboard and a pen.

I sign off, handing it back to him and giving him a tight smile. "Thank you. I really appreciate it."

He nods. "Of course. Jake spoke highly of you, so I'm happy to help."

I smile again, the tension in my body relaxing a bit. "Jake's the best. He's bartending for us."

He laughs. "I've heard. Almost non-stop every time I go home. I guess everyone knows about Dakota marrying some famous hockey player."

"Home? You live with Jake?" I smile, leaning against the railing to the house.

"Yeah. We're together," he says with a smile. "I go home to his dumb face every day."

I laugh, shaking my head. "That's incredible. I'm happy for you both." My hands move to my pockets right when Jaiden rounds the corner. He spots me, and I see the way his eyes dart possessively between us.

"Speaking of dumb faces, this is my boyfriend. Jaiden, meet Jake's boyfriend Charlie."

Jaiden walks over, his spine snapping straight as he stands tall next to me. I want to scoff at the possessive nature of it, but I signed up for this when I agreed to date him. Nudging him lightly, I laugh when he finally extends his hand to Charlie, a tight smile on his face.

"Don't mind him. He's a big, burly, jealous hockey player who is threatened by every man who talks to me."

Jaiden stutters. "That's not true. It's hot people, okay, and Charlie here is attractive."

Charlie laughs, his cheeks reddening. "Thanks, but I'm taken." He pats Jaiden's shoulder and I laugh at their interaction. "Anyways. I must be going. Thank you for all your help." He directs that last statement at Jaiden before turning away.

Jaiden wraps his arm around me, his lips coming to my cheek. "Sorry. Still not used to the fact that I don't need to be jealous."

"It's okay, babe. You'll get there." I pat him on the chest before walking back into the house.

What feels like mere moments later, a car pulls up the driveway, Dakota's parents exiting the vehicle.

I open the front door, walking toward them. "Mama Everly, Papa Gray!" I say with a goofy smile on my face.

Everly smiles, pulling me into her arms. "Hey, babygirl. How's my kiddos doing?" She kisses my head before pulling Jaiden into her arms.

"We're staying out of trouble. Your daughter is an anxious mess, though. Don't tell her I told you."

I step away from her, hugging Gray before walking into the house after them.

"Where's my future son-in-law?" Gray says loudly into the house. "I never got to scare the shit out of him."

Wyatt peaks his head out of the kitchen. "You certainly did, sir. I was quite terrified that first time."

"Dad!" Dakota yells. "Please don't." She steps into view, her hair freshly trimmed and highlighted.

"It wouldn't be a wedding without the crazy dad, now would it, darling?" He smiles, walking to his daughter and pulling her tightly into his arms.

"Okay, enough affection. We got work to do," I say, clapping my hands. "Chop, chop."

Everly points at me, her nose wrinkled. "You're speaking my language."

I gather everyone around the table, divvying up the jobs into small groups. The women are working on decorations, while the guys hang the lights and move the heavy things around. When I look over, I see Jaiden and Damian walking with the arch. They set it down at the far corner, the sun shining through it in the most beautiful way. I pull out my camera quickly, shooting a few pictures. Zooming my lens, I watch Jaiden's face. He smiles as he talks with Damian and I can't help but photograph them. He looks so happy —happier than he's been in a while.

When I turn my camera, I see Wyatt dancing with Dakota by the fire pit. They've taken a moment to themselves. I don't usually believe in fate or soulmates, but something about them is so perfect and makes me reconsider my stance on it. They're meant to be, understanding each other in a way that normal couples can't. I swear they speak their own language. I watch them through the lens of my camera for a few moments before I return the camera to my bag.

Sometimes I regret living life through the lens of a camera. It's times like this that I remember to live in the moment, and to enjoy the small things.

"I don't know how you do it." Lani stands beside me, her head leaning on my arm.

"Do what?"

"See the beauty in everything."

"Babes, you do see the beauty in everything. I mean, look at the art you create! It's incredible." Wrapping my arm around her shoulder, I pull her close to me.

"I forget. My life's been a little messy lately. I'm scared that when I go home, it's all going to go to shit."

"We're not going to let that happen. I gotta protect my ray of sunshine." I pause, looking out onto the water. "Can I tell you something?"

"Always," she says, turning her head to me.

I sigh, avoiding her gaze for a moment. "I'm scared to leave this bubble of bliss. I'm scared that when we go home, that reality will hit and something will happen with Jaiden and I. I'm still worried that he'll freak out and run away again. So truly, I don't blame you for being afraid."

"We're all afraid of something," she says. "We'll get through it together."

"We're survivors." I hold two fingers up to her, and she places the pads of her fingers on mine.

We watch the sunlight slowly disappear in the sky, our day almost complete. We're all tired, so as a much needed break, we sit around the fire pit, the guys pulling fancy cigars from a case and smoking them.

It's a serene moment, something that will go in the memory bank for life. Especially when the music shifts and Lani and Dakota get up to dance around the fire. Wyatt joins them and I decide to sit back with the others.

Looking over, I catch Damian watching Lani with something like confusion on his face. We all know that he's sworn off dating, spewing bullshit about being destined to live the playboy life forever. But as I watch him watch her, I know that's not the case. He may not admit it to himself now, but that man is taken with Lani, and it's only a matter of time before he realizes it too.

I quickly get to my feet, walking over to Jaiden and plopping myself in his lap. He doesn't seem to mind until I swipe the cigar from him and bring it to my lips before blowing a cloud of smoke in his face. He glares at me, but it's lacking any weight. Instead, his gaze is full of heat that shoots right to my pussy.

"Sorry," I say with a shrug and he leans into me, his fingers weaving through my hair as his lips brush my ear.

"How sorry?" His voice is barely a whisper but the growly tone to it makes me shiver.

"Very," I say, my voice weak.

"I expect you to show me how sorry later." He nips at my ear then leans back, swiping back his cigar and taking a long pull from it.

Damian's still watching Lani when I lean toward him.

"There's something I've been meaning to talk to you about," I say, keeping my voice steady.

"Huh?" Damian's eyes slowly slide to mine as though he doesn't want to look away from her for a moment.

"You like her," I say plainly.

"I—what?"

"You like Lani," I repeat.

"I don't."

Oh. Okay, we're in denial then. Great.

"You do." I sigh, shifting in Jaiden's lap and I feel him grip my hip, tightening his fingers. If I weren't about to threaten Damian, I'd be trying to find a way to sneak away with Jaiden because holy fuck is he hard. I can feel it pressing against me and it's making it hard to think. I clear my throat, focusing.

"Look, I love you, Dame, and I think I know you well enough to know when you're lying. You like her, whether you're ready to admit it or not. But let me make something painfully clear." I look at him, holding his gaze. "If you hurt her, I'll kill you. She is not in the headspace to be played with. She's been neglected by someone who was supposed to love her and if you can't be the something better that you preached to me about, then let her go."

He blinks several times, his chest rising and falling with his breaths. When he nods, it's full of resolve, and I hope that whatever he's decided is for the best.

"Help!" Someone yells from the distance and my head snaps to the right. My heart pounds and I jump to my feet. "Help! Wyatt! Dakota! Anyone!"

I run to Everly's side, seeing Gray on the ground beside her. He's gripping his arm that doesn't look quite right.

"Wyatt!" I scream, and hear the sounds of running. "What happened?"

"He fell. He was on the ladder putting the lights up around the house and I looked away for a second, and he fell." Her voice is frantic. "He's definitely got the wind knocked out of him, but from what I can tell, he fell on his arm."

I look up at the ladder and panic. It's a solid ten to fifteen feet at least, depending on how high he went up. A fall like that could have killed him if he landed wrong. I try to think rationally, slowing my breathing. Gray is just as much my father as he is Dakota's and everything in me wants to cry, but I need to be strong.

Wyatt and Jaiden appear at my side a moment later, Dakota running up after him.

"Daddy! Are you okay?"

"I think my arm is broken and maybe something else," he pants, his voice full of pain. "Maybe my collarbone? It hurts to breathe." He shakes his head and I shake my head at him.

"Don't move, Papa Gray. We don't know what's wrong yet, and I don't want you to hurt yourself further."

He nods slowly, taking shallow breaths. I open and close my fist several times, needing to do *something*.

"Call 911!" Wyatt yells, and Jaiden yanks out his phone. I hear him speaking quickly and I drop to Dakota's side.

"He's gonna be okay," I say.

"Can you move, Gray?" Roman stands beside him. "Wiggle your toes, move your fingers, things like that?"

Gray pants, looking up to wiggle his toes. "Yep," he says, his face contorting with pain.

"That's good," Roman says. He looks between Dakota and I. "Gray's older, but he's strong. That fall could have been bad, but from what I can see, he's okay."

Dakota looks at me, gripping my hand and squeezing. "He'll be okay." She shakes her head and I can see tears forming in her eyes.

"Can you tell me about what you're most excited about with the wedding?" Roman speaks to Gray and I'm thankful for it.

"Uh–I'm excited to walk my first daughter down the aisle." The sentiment hits me square in the chest. I know that he's considered me a daughter, but hearing him say that feels different.

Roman nods, urging him to continue, and I smile, knowing what he's doing.

I turn to face Dakota. I can see the panic written all over her face. "It's gonna be okay, Koda." I squeeze her hand again for reassurance.

The sirens sound, and I hear voices before the emergency staff rush to where we are. Everly speaks to them, the staff moving us away from Gray so that they can triage him.

We step aside, before Dakota crouches to the ground, her breathing rushed and panicked.

"My wedding is in three days," she says, tears falling down her face. "I can't do it without him."

"He's gonna be okay. I promise you. He'll be okay."

"We still have so much to do," she says, her voice breaking. "We don't even know how bad it is. This is my dad. I—" her voice breaks as she cries. I look up and see Jaiden watching us.

He kneels beside me, his hands coming to Dakota's shoulders. "Look at me."

Dakota wipes her eyes, looking up at him. "Don't worry about anything. It's going to be okay. We'll figure it out. Go be with your dad. If we need to cancel, we will cancel, but until then, I'll handle everything." He holds her in his arms. He speaks to her, soothing her, and she nods into his shoulder.

"Can you come with us?" Dakota looks at me, stray tears still falling down her cheeks.

I breathe deeply, nodding my head.

Wyatt is talking with the EMT's when he looks over and sees Dakota. I see the question in his eyes and I nod. He nods his silent thanks before turning back to the crew.

Once Gray is loaded up on the gurney, they roll him away. Everly follows Dakota and Wyatt around the house until they disappear.

I take a moment, looking up at Jaiden, my eyes watering. He pulls me into his arms, and I release a sob into his chest..

"He's gotta be okay," I say. "I need him too. I need him as much as Dallas and Dakota do. He's my dad too." I cry the words, letting myself panic for the first time.

"Dallas," I gasp. "We need to tell Dallas."

"Wyatt texted him. He's on the way now." Jaiden's breath caresses my cheek, and I relax into him. "I know the fear of losing a parent, and I want you to know that you're not alone. It'll be okay."

I nod into his chest.

"You need to go. I'll be here when you get back, okay?"

"Okay," I breathe, hugging him tightly before releasing him.

He kisses me goodbye before I rush from the house and to the hospital to be with my family.

My neck is sore when I wake up to the sounds of rushing footsteps. We've been here for a while and because I'm not blood family, I can't go back and see him until he's been cleared for visitors. Wyatt's seated beside me to keep me company and I see him shift as I stretch.

"They brought in the orthopedic doctor to look at his x-rays. Dakota thinks maybe another hour before he's cleared."

I hum, sitting up straighter in the waiting room chair. "Do you think they're keeping him longer because of his age?"

Wyatt nods. "They were worried about broken ribs because of the way he fell, but it looks like he got off lucky. Gray's a fighter."

"That he is," I confirm. Pulling out my phone, I look at the screen, seeing that it's nearly two in the morning. We've been here for six hours. The hospital itself has been busy, but I didn't expect to be here this long. I'm tired and emotionally exhausted. Not to mention that I feel incredibly lonely without Jaiden being by my side.

Dakota has Wyatt, Dallas has Casey, and I have no one. A text message isn't the same as Jaiden being here, and for the first time, I really want him here. I don't want to be strong.

Sandals click and I look up to see Dakota and Mama Everly walking toward me.

"He's fine. He's cracking jokes with the hospital staff and loopy on pain meds. They're going to keep him until they can get someone to get his arm in a cast, but it looks good."

I sigh a breath of relief. "That's good. Very good."

Dakota sits next to me. "It's been a long day—do you want to head home? Wyatt and I are going to stay in a hotel room down the street to be closer to the hospital."

"Are you sure?" I twiddle my thumbs over my phone, trying to keep myself busy.

She looks at me, her brow raised. "Babe, I know you enough to see what's going through your head. Go home, be with Jai. You need it."

She's right. I really, really do. I guess that's what family is for, to know the depths of you even when you can't figure it out yourself.

"Thanks, love." I lean into her, wrapping my arm around her shoulder and resting my head against hers. We stay like that for a minute and it's probably the most peaceful I've felt for hours. I don't think I've ever told Dakota how truly thankful I am for her friendship. She's put up with my bullshit for the majority of our lives and never once has she made me feel like a burden like my parents used to do. Words aren't enough to express my love for my best friend, and I don't think I'll ever be able to convey it, but starting now, I'll never take her for granted.

"I love you," I say through a wave of emotion.

"I love you, too," she says, lacing our fingers together and squeezing. "Go home. Be with your man." She kisses my cheek and releases me, shooting a teasing wink my way before walking back down the hall.

It takes me only a few minutes to gather the strength to stand and leave the hospital. By the time I get home, the house is dark, but it's not dark enough to hide the fully decorated home and yard.

I'm shocked to my core, even more so when warm hands wrap around my middle pulling me back against a solid chest.

"Surprise."

THIRTY-ONE

JAIDEN

EVEN IN THE DARKNESS, Silver's shocked face is prominent. I expected her to be surprised, maybe even a little angry that I took away the joy of planning and setting up her friend's wedding. But there's only awe on her face now. Her mascara is slightly smudged, probably from crying earlier, but even so, she's incredibly beautiful. She's a sight to behold.

If I thought I couldn't love her any more than I already do, I'd be proving myself wrong at this moment. My heart is enamored with her and there's nothing I wouldn't do to see that exact look on her face again.

I walk toward her silently before wrapping my arms around her middle. As she collides with my chest, I hear a shocked gasp leave her before she relaxes into my grip.

"You're home early," I say into her hair.

"I missed my person." She turns to face me, wrapping her arms around my back, her gaze locked on mine.

I lean down, kissing her forehead then pressing a firm kiss on her lips. Kissing Sterling is like heaven on earth. None of my dreams could ever compare to the real thing. I hate myself for taking so long to get here, but I'll make it up to her at every possible moment. I know we'll fight because it's just who we are, but she's not getting rid of me. *She's mine.*

"I can't believe you did all of this." She pulls away from me to walk through the house that's cleaned and decorated. I follow her as she watches to see every bit of space I put together, not without help. Her footsteps sound through the quiet house until she walks to the back door and pulls it open to reveal the completely finished ceremony and reception spaces. "Is there anything left for me to do?"

"I'm sure you'll find something," I say with a teasing tone. She looks over her shoulder at me and I already know she's thinking of something.

"You're right." She rolls her eyes, but smiles. "I don't know how to thank you for this."

"I can think of a couple ways." My voice is rough as I say it. I'm already half hard just looking at her. There's never a moment that I don't find her sexy as hell.

"Oh?" She raises a brow, turning to press a hand to my chest. "Care to show me?"

I nod. "Do you trust me?"

She swallows, her eyes darkening as she looks at me. "Yes."

It's all the encouragement I need before I scoop her into my arms and walk her to my room. She giggles quietly as I squeeze her ass in my palm. Her laugh is one of my all time favorite sounds, but as she moans while I slide her panties aside, slipping a finger into her pussy, I'm reminded of my most favorite sound.

I kick the door to my room closed, then toss her on the bed. She watches me walk to the dresser to pull out a handful of ties from my drawer.

"I'd ask why you brought that many ties to a beach vacation, but I'm starting to think I don't care."

"You never know when you'll need to dress up," I say, walking toward the bed. "Scootch." I nod my head toward the headboard, and she scrambles to the top of the bed, tossing off her shirt a second later.

Laughing, I crawl to her, not needing to instruct her to put her wrists together; she just *knows.*

After her wrists are firmly secured to the headboard, I lean to kiss her, nipping at her bottom lip and kissing a trail up and down her body.

She squirms, her pupils blown as she looks at me. "Trust me," I say as I lift her head and loop the second tie around her eyes.

Sitting up, I look at my beautiful woman. "Where should I start?"

She laughs, her stomach moving as she breathes. "Anywhere. Just *please*, touch me."

"I do love it when you beg, baby." I unclasp her strapless bra before pulling her hardened nipples into my mouth. She arches up into me, moaning as I give her breasts some much needed attention.

"More," she gasps, moaning at every touch. It's easy to get a reaction out of her. I'd love to take a course on her body, learning every way to make her moan and scream with pleasure. Thank God I don't need a course though. She tells me with every reaction to my touch.

She mewls when I nip at the piercings again, before licking from her collarbone to her chin.

"Jaiden," she groans. "*Please.*"

"Be patient," I growl, capturing her lips in a bruising kiss. Pulling my shirt off, I run the fabric down her body, knowing that her senses are heightened right now. It's when I bring my mouth to her pussy that she moans long and loud.

"Fuck," she groans, her body bucking as I slide the flat of my tongue through her folds. "Oh, God."

She cries out the longer I eat her pussy like my favorite meal. I use my thumb to circle her clit before sliding a finger inside her. She clenches around me, and a few minutes later she's coming on my fingers, quietly chanting my name. It's the most beautiful sight and I'm so goddamn hard just watching her.

My cock is weeping by the time I pull it from my boxers.

Stroking it a few times, I groan, feeling the precum coating my fingers.

Using my hand, I lift her ass into the air, running my aching cock through the folds of her pussy. She moans as I tease both of us, until I can't take another moment of it.

In one swift motion, I push into her, feeling her stretch around me.

"Fuck," I curse, moving more frantically when she squeezes around me. "Fuck, fuck, *fuck*. You feel fucking incredible."

"Harder," she commands, and I chuckle in response. I won't fight her this time, because fuck if I don't want to lose myself to her right this moment. I'd give her anything she'd ask of me. "I want to touch you," she pleads.

Reaching behind her head, I free her arms, feeling her nails immediately come to my back. The pain of her digging her nails into my skin sends pleasure through me.

I pound into her, thrusting harder and feeling my brain cloud with pleasure. My abs clench and the sounds of our moans encourage me on.

"I fucking love you," I say a moment before she shatters around me, pulling me right off the cliff with her. I'm panting, my body collapsing beside hers. I pull off the blindfold, kissing her deeply and lazily.

"I love you, too," she says when she catches her breath. "So fucking much."

I can't tell if it's the come down, or if a beat of hesitation crosses her face, so I brush pieces of hair from her face, looking into her eyes as though I could decipher her thoughts.

"What's going on in that head of yours?"

She sighs, looking away, but I turn her gaze back to me. "What happens when we go home? Is this just a perfect little vacation bubble we're living in? I could lose my job, Jaiden."

"You won't," I say matter-of-factly.

She huffs, rolling her eyes. "That didn't answer my question."

I lean in, kissing her eyelids softly. "What happens," I say, kissing her cheeks now, "is that we'll go about life like we are now. We'll travel together, we'll fuck until we can't see straight, and we'll sit through family dinners, fighting occasionally just to keep our friends on their toes."

She laughs, shaking her head. "Jai, that's not what I mean, but I'm glad you've got it all planned out."

"I do, enough so that I'm confident that you won't lose your job."

She stares at me, her expression telling me that she's not at all convinced.

"Ask me how I know."

"How do you know?" She squints, her beautiful eyes growing irritated and I have no shame that it turns me on.

"Because I already talked to HR and my publicist. When we go home, we'll be signing paperwork to make it official."

"So, I'm not going to lose my job?"

I shake my head, and I see the relief immediately cross her face. Then she leans into me and punches my arm with zero conviction.

"Ouch," I say mockingly.

"Don't do things behind my back."

I hold up my hand like I'm giving her my scouts honor. "I promise that after today, I won't do things behind your back. I make no promises for surprises though. I won't give that up."

"Ugh, fine." She purses her lips before her eyes linger on my lips.

I bring my hand to the back of her head and kiss her deeply. It's easy to be with her like this, to kiss her silly. As we fall asleep, our bodies tangled, I enjoy the peace and the comfort that comes with being Sterling Bexley's boyfriend. I think I've finally made it to where I want to be, and it's right here with her.

Sterling sits up in a panic the next morning. She scrolls through her phone, seeing something concerning before looking over at me.

"Jai," Sterling says, her voice stressed. "Everly was supposed to pick up the dresses." She throws off the blankets, moving to get out of bed.

"Baby," I say, stopping her with my hand. She stills, finally turning her face to look at me. After taking a few breaths, I see some of the tension dissipate. "I'll take care of it. Don't worry about anything. Take care of what you need to here, and I'll go get the dresses."

Sterling nods, not fighting me on it. She leans into my chest, pressing her face into me, and I hold her tightly. "I know you want this wedding to be perfect for Dakota, but you're going to run yourself ragged worrying. Let me help you. The setup is done, and I have no doubts in my mind that you have a mental checklist of last-minute things."

She laughs into my shirt, and I run my hand through her short hair.

"I love you," she breathes, and I kiss her head.

"I love you, too."

I leave her to her mental list, showering quickly before pulling on jeans and a shirt, and rushing from the house.

I connect my phone to the speaker of my car as I drive down the main road. It takes less than two rings for Everly to answer my call.

"Mama Everly," she says, her voice calming. My heart clenches a bit at the reminder that I won't get a greeting like that from my mother ever again.

"Hey. I'm on my way to pick up the dresses. Could you tell me what I need to do? I didn't want to bother Sterling with it."

I hear quiet laughter through the speakers, and a blush of embarrassment creeps its way up my neck.

"You're a good man, Jaiden Thomas," she says, her voice soft and sweet. "Okay, all you need to do is go into the bridal shop and tell them you're picking up an order for Dakota Lane. I've already paid for everything. They'll need your signature to confirm that you've picked it up. Normally they would want her to try it on to make sure it fits, but I've already told them the situation."

"Sterling mentioned dresses—plural. How many dresses am I picking up? I want to be sure." I merge onto the freeway, just barely starting my hour-long journey into the big city.

"Five. One for all of the bridesmaids, one for me, and of course, Dakota's wedding dress. Be extra careful with the wedding dress. It's precious cargo." Her voice gets quiet as she says the next bit and I smile at her tone. "There are ears everywhere and this next bit is a surprise. Dakota had a baby blanket and I had them sew a piece of it into the train so her blankie will be with her on her wedding day." She chuckles, and I can hear the smile.

"Is that her something old?" I'm not so dumb that I don't know some wedding traditions.

"Smart man," she says. There's muffled voices on the other end of the call and I just listen for a moment. "My husband is making a scene in our hotel room asking for me," she says with a laugh. "If you have any questions, feel free to call me. Alright?"

"Alright," I say. "Thank you, Mrs. Easton."

"Oh, call me Mama Everly."

I laugh, shaking my head as I continue on the freeway. I pass several cars, trying not to speed but who am I kidding? "Okay. Mama Everly it is. Thank you." I end the call, letting the music filter through the speakers.

There's a feeling prickling in my chest and for the first time in a long time, I let myself feel it. As the cars continue past me, I feel the tightening in my throat. It's been a long time since I've had a motherly figure in my life that wasn't Roman's mom. She's great, don't get me wrong, but she's not interested in being a mother to a bunch of hockey players. She's always been more of a free spirit, someone who wants to live their own life. Plus, Roman's never been interested in pursuing a relationship with her, even though she's worked hard to be somewhat of a grandma to Lily. This is new to me, and I'm not sure what I'm feeling, but suddenly I'm thankful that I'm once again less lonely in this world. I sit in the feelings, smiling softly as I let the music rush through the car.

An hour later, I pull up to the front of the bridal shop. When I walk inside, several heads turn in my direction, a couple of the attendants walking toward me.

"How can we help you?"

"I'm here to pick up dresses for Dakota Lane." I walk slowly, stopping when I approach the front desk. Once my arms are rested on the top, I lean in, trying to appear relaxed.

"Ah," she says. "You must be the groom." She turns and I stumble over my words, and my face must have shown my reaction because one of the other attendants lets out a snort.

"Not the groom, I'm assuming by that reaction," she says with a laugh.

I nod. "Best friend," I confirm.

She smiles, batting her lashes as she approaches the counter. "So, that must mean you're a hockey player, too."

"I am," I confirm, trying to keep my tone curt. It doesn't phase her.

"Hmm," she says, setting her head into her hand as she leans toward me. "I like hockey players. I heard they're not afraid to throw a woman around every once in a while." She winks and I don't let any reactions seep through.

"They do. My girlfriend would know," I say, reveling in the way she recoils slightly.

"How fortunate for her." Her jaw clenches slightly before she plasters on a forced smile. "Well, if you ever tire of her, you know where to find me." An easy smile crosses her face now. I nearly roll my eyes, but I'm saved by a woman holding several garment bags. She smiles as she approaches me, laying the dresses on the counter between us.

"The top dress is the bride's, the second is the mother-of-the-bride's dress and the others are the bridesmaids dresses. I won't show you because I'm on strict instructions from Mama Everly, but I saw to it that everything was correct myself, so if there are any issues"—she looks around her before grabbing a business card from a drawer—"this is my contact information and I'll come out personally to fix it."

I thank her before grabbing the dresses and leaving the shop. It's a quick ride back, my only thought that I can't wait to tell Sterling everything that happened. I nearly freeze at the ease of that thought. I've wanted Sterling for so long and to have her in my grasp feels incredible.

She's rushing through the kitchen when I walk through the doors. She spots me immediately, her eyes smiling before it reaches her mouth. I nod my head in the direction of the stairs and she follows until we're walking into her room. I lay the garment bags on the bed before turning to her.

"How was it?" she asks, stepping into my arms and breathing me in.

"Perfect, except that one of the attendants made a pass at me." I tuck my chin into her hair, the pale silver color growing out and her natural brown color peeking at the roots. The silver has grown on me. It suits her in more ways than one.

"So, what you're saying is that I need to drive my ass down there and stake my claim?" She grumbles it into my chest and I laugh.

"No. I made it perfectly clear I wasn't available, but suddenly I'm in the mood for copious amounts of attention from my girlfriend."

She pulls out of my arms before pushing me until I fall back onto the bed.

"I'm always willing to give attention," she breathes, coming to straddle me. I grip her hips, reveling in the way she looks from this angle. Her hand comes to my hair, her fingers tangling between the curls. When she tugs lightly, I buck up into her, sending her forward. I capture her lips, groaning into her mouth as she discreetly rubs against my growing erection.

Breaking our kiss, I bring my lips to her throat. "Clearly, I needed the reminder that I'm taken." I kiss up the side of her neck, nipping at her ear as I slide my hand into her shirt, twisting that jeweled nipple between my fingers. She whimpers.

"You're very taken," she says. "Very, *very* taken." Her hand grips my cock through my pants and rubs. My eyes nearly roll back into my head. I'm not starved for attention, nor am I starved for touch, but any time I'm with Sterling, I can't get enough.

I bring my mouth to her nipple, my tongue toying with her jewelry, when a knock sounds on the door. I glare at it, not wanting to stop, but I know it's likely we'll have to.

"What?" I clip.

"Lily has requested your presence on the dance floor," Roman says through the door. I can hear in his voice that he's irritated and I nearly laugh. Instead, I roll my eyes, removing my hands from Sterling's waist and righting her shirt.

"We'll be right there," I say, my voice softer this time.

"Later," Sterling says, the promise in her voice being the only reason I can safely leave this room.

I bring my lips to hers once more. "Later indeed. My lady requires ravishing."

THIRTY-TWO

STERLING

I STIR from sleep when the front door shuts quietly. Jaiden's chest rises and falls, his breathing remaining even beneath me. I don't remember when it happened, but once the other guys on the team showed up, we danced and played games until my feet hurt. Eventually we ended up camped out in the living room, our conversation slowing as people made their way from the house or falling asleep on the floor. Jaiden's massive body is wrapped around mine still, and when I crack open my eyes, I see Wyatt and Dakota creeping through the front door.

"Hey," I whisper, and Dakota creeps around the sleeping hockey player on the floor.

"Hey. Why are you on the couch?" She kneels to the floor.

"I honestly don't know. I guess we just passed out." I feel Jaiden's arm tighten around me when I try to move and Dakota chuckles quietly.

"He's protective in his sleep too, apparently," she laughs. "Dad's okay. They're staying in their hotel room to rest, but they'll be here Saturday morning. I asked if he wanted us to push the wedding, but he's insistent that the day goes on."

"Sounds like something he'd say." I shift so that I can sit up to look at her. "I've got one last thing I need to work on, but everything is set so you and Wyatt and relax all day tomorrow."

Her green eyes grow misty and I point at her. "Don't start that with me or I'll start crying too. I love you and I'd do anything for you."

"Thank you. I don't deserve you."

"You do. More than you know." I nod my head to where Wyatt is pretending not to snoop. "Go get some rest. I'll talk to you in the morning."

Dakota nods, smiling before standing and walking to her room.

I nuzzle my head back into Jaiden's chest when I feel him smile against my head.

"You're a good friend," he says, his breath warm against my ear.

"Dakota's my soulmate. Her family is my family, and I know she'd do the same for me if I wanted it."

"Do you want it?" he breathes, and I can feel his heart beating harder in his chest.

"I'm content just being with you, Jaiden. I don't need to get married in the future. Once I'm committed to you, I'm committed."

"I'm okay with that. I'll be honest, marriage scares me." He moves his hand to run through my hair and I relax further into his embrace.

"Me too. I never had a good example of what a marriage should look like. I'm excited for Dakota. This is the way her life is supposed to go. She's always wanted marriage and kids, but that's never been my dream. I made that decision for myself ages ago when I got my tubes tied. I'm content being an auntie for the rest of my life." I panic as I say it, not willing to meet his face in fear of what I'll see.

His arms squeeze around me, and I release a sigh of relief. "Sterling, you don't have to be afraid to talk to me about this. I suspected as much, even though you've never said it outright. I'm content with what we have now. If you want kids in the future, we can always adopt, but I need you to know it'll always be your choice. I choose you, and that's enough for me. You're perfect, you know that?" He kisses my head.

I smile, taking a breath. "I do, but please, continue feeding my ego." I reach behind me to hold his face. "Now, go back to sleep. My final project requires me to be in tip-top shape."

"What? I didn't hear you. I'm asleep." He snores loudly and I laugh. I don't remember when it became so comfortable to be like this with Jaiden. Even before, we were hiding any feelings between us. Our friends saw a friendship, but there was always more.

It's the *more* that scares me the most sometimes. Now that I've admitted to myself and to Jaiden that I love him, I find myself struggling to believe that he actually loves me back. After years of telling myself that I didn't deserve to be loved, I'd started to believe it. Especially when my parents treated me more like an obligation than someone worthy of their attention.

It's a surreal feeling to be loved by Jaiden, to know that he's mine and that I'm his. I'll battle my fears and doubts because I want to finally believe that I'm deserving of the love I read about in books.

When I close my eyes, I allow myself to ignore the fears and to dream of what a future with Jaiden could look like. It's the feeling of Jaiden's heartbeat against my back that finally lulls me into sleep, fearless and free.

My legs cross as I lean against the headboard. My laptop is resting in my lap, my index finger tapping the arrows to scroll through the myriad of photos I've collected over the past several months.

I stop on a photo of Wyatt's hand pressed against the glass, Dakota smiling at him with a gleam in her eyes. One of my favorite things to photograph outside of hockey is moments like these. I'd love to be able to look back at my photos and see the people I love at their happiest. Dakota and Wyatt were happy here, their love palpable even through a still photo.

Dragging another photo to the video, I play the clip over to make sure the photo fades when I want it to. I do that several more times before I'm satisfied. Moving onto the next portion, I look up when the door clicks shut.

Jaiden stands on the opposite side of the room, his eyes full of mischief.

"Nope. Don't give me that look. I'm working, sir." I wave my hand at him and he chuckles.

"What if I told you that you could still work?" His voice is deep, no doubt from all the yelling I heard. I don't know what shenanigans they were getting into, but we're *supposed* to be resting and it didn't at all sound like rest.

"I would be intrigued," I admit, raising a brow.

"Take off your pants," he commands, licking his lips. He walks toward me, his curls wild atop his head. His skin is darker than usual and I feel a flutter deep in my belly the closer he gets.

"Would you ever let Dakota tattoo you?" I ask, distracting myself.

"Already planning on it. She's a busy woman." He raises a brow and I do as I'm told, setting my laptop aside to slide my shorts from my body.

"Now, work," he says with a mischievous grin. "And don't stop, or there will be consequences."

I swallow, my core clenching at the command. I don't know what wicked thing he has planned for me, but I know it's something delicious.

Sliding my laptop back into my lap, I scroll through my folder of photos, picking out the ones for the next section of the video.

When I'm well and focused, I jolt, feeling Jaiden slide my thong aside. His finger grazes my clit and I hiss.

"What did I say?" His finger stills and I look back at my screen, breathing deeply. "Good."

He moves again, my body clenching as slides his fingers through me. It's hard to focus, but I force my eyes forward.

I place several more photos, working quickly. It's when Jaiden moves his face to my core that I feel the pleasure coiling tightly.

I whimper as he strokes my clit with his tongue, his finger slipping inside of me.

My body shakes as the pleasure builds more and more. I'm finding it harder and harder to focus, his magical tongue working me to my downfall.

I breathe deeply, moving photos and video clips at an alarming pace. Blocking out his torture is hard, but keeping my hands from shaking and my breathing even is harder. I arrange them quickly, my video nearly done. All I need is music and a closing image from their engagement shoot.

Sweat beads on my forehead, my hand stilling on my mousepad.

"Fuck," I whimper, as his hands wrap under my legs, pressing my clit to his face. He looks up at me, smirking before nipping lightly and sending me falling over the edge.

"Jai," I scream, my legs shaking and tightening around him.

His strong arms pin me in place as I ride out my orgasm. I barely get a moment to breathe before he pushes my laptop aside and flips me over.

"You're so fucking beautiful," he says. "Get on your knees for me, baby."

I nod, eager for more. Eager for *him.*

I position myself on hands and knees, his hands gripping my ass.

"I brought an old friend," he says, slipping something from his pocket. "Remember this?"

Looking over my shoulder, I see him holding a purple butt plug between his hands.

"You kept it?" I laugh, remembering the day we bought the plug together.

"Of course. I do love to torture myself." He holds a small bottle of lube, clicking open the top. I lick my lips as I watch him pour some on his fingers.

"Why the hell did you pack it for this trip?" It's the same with those damn ties. Did he know we'd be using it?

"I may be an idiot, Silver, but I came on this trip hoping that I'd have use for it. It took me a while to pull my head out of my ass, but I knew deep down that I wanted you. Now relax, baby."

"I think that's the most romantic thing you've ever said to me," I joke.

I look back at the wall, expecting the cool feel of lube, but instead I'm met with a harsh sting.

"That handprint should last a few days," he says, proud of himself. "You're mine, Silver. Don't forget it."

"I always did love when you marked me," I say, pressing back into him, right as his thumb caresses my ass, the cool feeling of the lube on his thumb sending a chill of anticipation through me. I feel the slide of the plug a moment later, and I hiss before relaxing into it.

"Ready?" he asks as he slides down his shorts, his cock slapping against his waist. I watch him stroke himself, my core clenching in response. I nod eagerly, ready for the feeling of fullness that I've grown accustomed to.

I whimper as he enters me, slow and deep, his thrusts almost painful as I ache for him to claim more of me. I want all of him. I want him to destroy me, from the inside out. I tell him so with my moans, my body pressing into him.

I look back at him. There's a vulnerability in his face as he looks down at me, his face focused as he controls each movement. This isn't just sex—it's something deeper, more meaningful. I know how we got here; I just don't remember when he started looking at me like that. Like he doesn't care about my crazy, or that I continuously told him that I hated him.

I'm taken by surprise when the vibrating starts. I'm overwhelmed with sensations, his cock slamming into me as the plug vibrates. I feel full; the feeling of him inside of me alongside the plug is a delicious sort of torture.

He moans, his hands gripping my hips with force. Our moans

reverberate through the room, and I couldn't care less about who would hear us. This is *my* fucking house.

"Fuck," he pants. "Sterling, you feel so fucking good." His compliments send a coiling feeling in my stomach.

"I love you," I cry, my eyes watering as the feelings overwhelm me. *More. More. More.* I hear myself beg him to give me everything, his body slamming against mine.

When his fingers graze my clit, I lose control, my body tightening around him as I come with a scream.

"That's it, baby. Come for me."

I clench around him, feeling the way his body seizes with his own orgasm. He fills me so fully, so perfectly. It's something I've always wanted, but never got. Not until *him.* Jaiden is mine in every way. I never want this to end.

He slumps, the vibrating continuing inside of me. I shiver when he clicks the remote, putting me out of my misery. He pulls from me, laying at my side.

We lay in a post sex heap; all sweaty limbs and satisfied expressions. When his hand comes to my face, his fingers brush through my hair, his eyes alight with adoration.

"I want to do everything with you," he says. "I want to try every position, to fuck you until I'm dehydrated and shaking. I want to experience life with you, and to actually enjoy the traveling we do with the team. I want it all."

"I want that, too." I run my fingers over his brow before placing a kiss onto his lips. "Let me clean up, but then do you want to watch the video with me? Help me pick music?"

"I'd do anything you ask me to do. I'm putty in your hands." He kisses my forehead.

"Good. Take this plug out so I can walk again."

"Yes, ma'am."

THIRTY-THREE

JAIDEN

THE ALCOHOL I've been milking for the last half hour has done nothing for my damn nerves. I run my thumb down the glass to keep my hands busy while I wait. Suddenly my tie feels too tight around my neck. For someone who owns every color of suit for game days, I'm used to the feel of a tie around my neck, but something about today feels different. The pressure is on, and I'm sweating in places I shouldn't be sweating.

"You okay, man?" Dallas claps me on the back, drawing me from my thoughts. I look over at him, his matching greige linen suit accented with his boutonniere.

"Yeah. I'm nervous, though." I take another sip from my glass, savoring the burn as it slides down my throat.

"I get it. Your best friend is getting married. It's a big day."

"Yeah," I mumble. *It is.*

"Okay. Everyone in position." Everly claps her hands as Sterling follows behind her. My eyes lock with hers, my heart stopping in my chest. She's the most beautiful woman I've ever laid eyes on.

"Yeah. Keep the bedroom eyes in the bedroom, love birds." Dawson chuckles, standing beside me with his back facing toward the water. We're on the deck, waiting for a first look. Apparently, Dakota wanted to reveal herself to us before the wedding.

Sterling holds her camera tightly, waiting to snap photos of the moment. "Okay, ladies," she says with a teasing tone. "Dakota is going to walk in and when I tell you to, you'll turn around. Got it?"

"Yes, milady," Dawson yells with a thumbs up. Roman shoots him a look and I laugh. I lean forward, setting my drink down on the ledge.

"This is going to be fun," Damian mumbles from my left. "A bunch of rowdy hockey players. What could go wrong?"

"Nothing. Nothing will go wrong. I'll ruin each of you if you mess up all of Sterling's hard work. Got it?"

"We'll be on our best behavior." Luca salutes, and I see Sterling shake her head before I turn away from her.

I hear talking, and my FOMO screams at me to turn around, but I keep my eyes trained on the water. There's shuffling, and Everly says something in a hushed voice before I hear the click of the camera.

"Okay. On the count of three. One..."

My heart pounds so quickly.

"Two..."

Why am I so nervous?

"Three..." I turn, catching sight of Dakota. There's a multitude of reactions happening around me.

Damian yells, "Damn, girl! You're hella fine!" and the guys laugh at his outburst. I see Roman shaking his head, a wide smile overtaking his face.

Dallas looks at his sister, walking toward her and pulling her into a tight hug. "You clean up nice, sis. Who knew?"

Dakota laughs, flicking him.

And then there's me. I don't move, my breath leaving my body. Dakota and I haven't been the closest after my fuck up with Sterling. But in the last few weeks, I've realized how incredible of a friend she is. So maybe that's why my eyes grow watery as I look at her.

"Fuck me," I say, my voice shaking. I ignore the click of the camera around me, Sterling moving around us.

"Who knew Jaiden would be the crier?" Damian says, smiling.

"Don't start that, Jai," she says, her voice breaking. "You'll make me cry."

"You look stunning," I say, stepping toward her and taking her hand in mine. Spinning her, I get a good look. "You're gonna make my best friend real happy. Not like you weren't already a part of the family, but damn, I'm excited to welcome you into our family."

"Thanks, Jai," she says, pulling me into her arms.

"Lily! You can come out now." Sterling clicks her camera right as Lily runs in, dressed in a tulle dress in a color that matches Sterling's.

"Daddy!" she says, spinning around in a circle. "I get to be the flower girl, and Auntie Dakota said I could wear a crown."

"Of course you do, baby."

"Are you crying, Uncle Jai?" Lily walks to my leg, hugging me. "Don't be sad."

I laugh, wiping the stray tears away. "I'm okay, princess. Your aunt Dakota looks so pretty and I'm a weenie."

"A weenie," she repeats, laughing.

"I hate to break up the love fest, y'all, but we're on a schedule. Go take your places for the ceremony." Sterling claps her hands to get everyone's attention.

Everyone files out and I stay behind, slipping an arm around her waist.

"You're the most beautiful girl in the room. Remember that." I kiss her cheek, knowing she'll murder me for ruining her lipstick.

"I would love to peel you out of that suit right now, but I can wait until tonight." She winks at me, blowing me a kiss before running off after Dakota and Everly.

Time moves quickly after that.

The moment the music starts, we walk down the aisle on cue. When it shifts to an instrumental song that sounds a lot like something right out of *Pride and Prejudice*, the crowd stands. I look across at Wyatt, seeing him twitch nervously. Sterling smiles behind him, and I wink at her before I turn my eyes to the aisle.

Dakota rounds the corner, her blond hair braided down the side of her shoulder. Her arm is looped through Gray's good arm, his cheeks red beneath his beard.

The closer they get, the more I notice Wyatt swiping at his eyes.

It's when Gray hands her off that I realize that I've known what love was this whole time. I love Wyatt, and Roman. I love Lily, and I love Dakota. These people are my family, and this whole time, I've had love at the tips of my fingers. Dakota loved me even when I was a miserable bastard.

I don't deserve my friends, but here I am, having the biggest revelation of my life.

Emotion swells in my throat as they say their vows, a series of *I do's* exchanged as they place the rings on each other's fingers.

The crowd goes wild when Wyatt dips Dakota, their lips meeting in a passionate kiss. I clap, my thoughts coming back to the present.

"Please welcome, Mr. and Mrs. Wyatt Lane." The officiant follows behind Wyatt and Dakota, the rest of us following suit.

"May I step in?" I lay a hand on Wyatt's shoulder. He grins, kissing his wife on the cheek. "Congratulations, bro." He pulls me into a hug, his arm slapping my back.

"Thank you for helping this come to life." Emotion fills his words and I nod at him before he steps away.

Taking Dakota's hand in mine, I lead her deeper onto the dance floor.

"I realized something today." I spin her, then pull her back into my arms.

"And what's that?" Her voice has this sultry sound to it from the overuse of her voice.

"Please don't think I'm weird," I cringe, suddenly feeling my confidence shrinking.

She laughs, her hand squeezing mine. "I'll never judge you, Jaiden. I've got nothing to judge."

"I realized that I love you," I say it quickly. "As a friend of course, but I'd been telling myself I didn't know what love was when I'd had access to it all along."

We stop dancing, the people still moving around us.

"Oh, Jai," she says, her eyes looking rather misty. "I love you, too. I would've told you that one brother was enough when we first met, but I feel differently now. I gained another set of protective brothers when I met Wyatt. I'm thankful for you, and for everything you did for Wyatt and me this weekend." She hugs me, her head resting on my chest for a moment. "This vacation has done you a lot of good, Jaiden Thomas."

I choke on a laugh. "Yeah. You have this streak of good ideas. Thank you for kicking my ass enough that I finally made the right moves."

"That's all you, babe. You just needed the push." She smiles at me, her eyes shining. I spin her once more before Wyatt returns to reclaim his wife. And I don't complain when they pull me into a hug before I disappear to find my girlfriend.

THIRTY-FOUR

STERLING

MY FEET HURT MORE than they ever have, but it's worth it. I've been switching dance partners for the last hour. By the time Jaiden finds me, he's got this goofy grin on his face, and I'm eager to smudge my lipstick.

"Hey, babe," I say, shoving my face into his chest and breathing in his signature scent.

"Hey," he breathes. "You did an incredible job with this wedding." He runs a hand down my bare back and I shiver.

"I had lots of help." I start to say more when Gray wanders over.

"Looks like I've got another man to scare now," he says, his brow raised at us. "That's my second daughter, you know, Jai."

"Yes, sir. I do."

"Well, good. You treat her right, or you'll have me to answer to." He shoots finger guns at us before he walks away.

I laugh, shaking my head. "He's definitely high on pain meds."

"Even so, he's still terrifying." Jaiden laughs, his fingers trailing up my spine.

I hear shrieking, and look over to see Wyatt spinning Lily around on the dance floor. When they finally stop, he kisses her head and turns toward Coach who's talking with Roman.

What happens next sends me falling over in a fit of laughter. Lily smacks Wyatt on the butt, then releases a squeal of laughter.

Roman's eyes go wide. "Lily," he says, his voice harsh. "Don't do that."

"Why? I saw Uncle Jaiden do it with Auntie Sterling!" She giggles, spinning in circles.

Roman's eyes snap in our direction. I'm already bent over laughing when Roman points.

"Fix this," he says. It sounds more like a plea, and I can't help the second wave of laughter.

Jaiden sighs deeply, shaking his head. "I'll be back."

I wheeze, nodding, and when I finally compose myself, Dakota slips beside me.

"Look," she hisses, pointing. "I think we've got trouble on the horizon."

Lani's dancing with a group of hockey players, the guys passing her around. She's laughing, her eyes full of joy. It's when I look to the right that I see the longing way Damian is gazing at her.

"He told me he wasn't interested in dating. He looks like a sad puppy."

"How long until he breaks?" she asks, waggling her eyebrows at me. "Forty bucks says they're dating in a month."

"Oh, you're on," I say, laughing. "I give him six weeks, after Lani tattoos him."

"Oh, damn. That's smart," she says. We shake as Wyatt comes to our side.

"What shenanigans are you two getting into now?"

"We're making bets on when Lani and Damian will date." Dakota blinks up at him innocently.

"Bets on the future of my friends' love lives? Scandalous."

"You love me," she says.

"I do love you, wife." He kisses her. "It's time for our big exit, love. I'm ready to whisk you away before it's back to Boston for training."

"Okay. I'll be there in a second. I want to say some goodbyes."

Dakota hugs me when Wyatt walks away. "I know you won't tell me if you're worried, but I have a feeling you are. It's going to be a transition for you two going back home. And before you huff and puff, I *know* I'm going on my honeymoon, but I'm only a call away. Help Lani get settled, then figure out your life. It's going to be okay. Jaiden is...different, and I just have a feeling it's going to be okay."

I stare at her, blinking for several moments. "It's scary how easily you read people."

"Lots of time protecting myself from people," she says with a smile. "Picked up a thing or two."

I hold her tightly in my arms. "I love you, Koda. Have the best honeymoon ever. Go be with your husband. We'll be okay."

"You better be." She pulls away and I kiss her cheek.

They exit in a flurry of sparklers, the fairy lights illuminating their backs as they slide into the vintage Aston Martin.

The chill of the air reaches me, but when a jacket slips over my shoulders, the cold is quickly forgotten to me.

"What now?" Jaiden runs his hands down my arms.

"Now we clean up, pack our things, and go home, I guess."

"Want to stay at my place for a few days?"

I look over my shoulder at him. "I'd like that, but I have a best friend I need to take care of first."

He nods, and I turn back right as the car pulls down the long driveway.

"My door will always be open to you," he says, resting his chin on my head. "We've been living in a fantasy world these past three months, but that doesn't have to end."

"I'd imagined this a million times when I first took the job with the Yellow Jackets. I never saw it going *this* way, but we're anything but predictable."

"Predictable is boring, my love."

I love control, and the carefully calculated plans that make up my life. But for once, I might agree with him.

THIRTY-FIVE

JAIDEN

"FOOD'S HERE," Sterling calls from the living room of my condo. She's been here plenty of times, but it feels different having her in my space while we're *together.*

I love it.

I love her. *This is weird.*

My bare feet pad down the hallway, my hair still wet from my shower. It was a long drive, and the only thing we wanted to do once we got back was order food and turn on a movie.

One of Sterling's favorite chick-flicks is loaded up on the tv, the front door closing shut as she steps inside. She holds out the take-out bag to me with a smile.

"It smells so fucking good." She breathes deeply, her eyes closing in pleasure.

I grab plates from the kitchen then walk to the living room, setting them down on the coffee table.

"Have you had these before?" she asks, pulling a seaweed wrapped thing from one of the containers.

"Maybe once? It's been a long time." I grab one, setting it on my plate, then dishing some of the pork and mac salad.

"It's Kalua pork and spam musubi. For our high school graduation, Papa Gray slow-cooked a whole pig for us. It was like a traditional luau." She shoves the musubi into her mouth, moaning over the bite.

I watch her, my cock twitching as I listen to the sounds she makes. *Fuck.*

Turning back to my food, I take a bite of the musubi. It's like an explosion of salty flavor in my mouth. There's a sweet sauce on the rice and I savor all the flavors.

"Damn. That's good." I take another bite, and she nods at me, smiling. Clicking the remote to start the movie, we sit back, watching as we eat. Eventually the movie is approaching the end and Sterling is resting against my arm.

Her hands roam across my body, her fingers leaving goosebumps in their wake. *Such a fucking tease.*

I can hardly focus on the movie when her hands slide to my thigh, rubbing up and down the length of it.

"Let's do something else," I say abruptly. My body is alive with arousal.

"Like what?" she says a little sleepily.

"Strip poker."

"You just want to get me naked," she says, looking up at me through her thick lashes.

"I do." It's true. I won't lie about that.

"Fine," she says. "But you're going to lose." She stands, grabbing the poker set from the drawer of the TV stand.

"So confident, love."

I watch her shuffle the cards, then deal them.

We play a few rounds to get the hang of the game before the stakes rise. We start taking bets, and when Sterling raises the stakes, I smirk at her, sliding the cards between my two fingers.

"It looks like you'll be stripping first, babe." She lays down a flush, her brow raised.

I keep my face straight, my eyes not giving me away.

"I get to pick the piece of clothing," I say, laying down four of a kind. "Shorts. Off. Now."

She huffs a breath. "Fucking hell. How do you do that?"

She strips, looking slightly uncomfortable. I take note of her body language, observing her as we continue on.

By the end of three rounds, I'm missing my shirt and Sterling is left in her bra and thong.

She's covering herself slightly when we start the next round, and when she reaches for a blanket, I finally lose it.

"Stop that," I command.

"What?" she asks, blinking at me.

"Stop covering yourself like that. You're beautiful." I lay my cards down on the table.

"I feel exposed and really not cute in this position."

"Why?"

Her eyes lock on mine, her cheeks reddening. "I don't know. My mom always told me I needed to sit up straight, or work out more so that I don't have belly rolls. She'd point out every imperfection she could find, and I just feel a little self conscious." Her voice is small and weak as she sits before me.

"Silver," I say seriously. "You are the most exquisite woman I've ever laid eyes on, and I wish you could see yourself the way I see you." As soon as the words are out of my mouth, I get an idea. "Stand up. Where's your camera?"

I walk to where our suitcases are laid haphazardly by the door. I see her camera bag immediately.

"Jai! I look gross. Not now."

"Yes, now, Sterling. Let me show you how beautiful you are." I unclip the camera bag, pulling out her gear gently before I reach the smaller of her two cameras.

"Do you even know how to use that?" she says, her voice weak.

"I do. I watch you enough to know some things."

I fumble with the camera for a bit before I turn it on. Bringing the camera to my face, I look at her through the lens. She's frowning, her cheeks red, and her arms wrapped protectively around herself. She's seated on her knees, a blanket gathered around her legs. Even as she tries to hide herself, she's stunning.

"Talk to me. Tell me about some of your favorite memories." I keep the camera close to my face.

"Uhm—one time Dakota and I found a stray dog and brought it home with us. We named her Bella because at that point, we were reading all the *Twilight* books and it became an addiction." She relaxes a bit, her plump lips turning up into a smile as she thinks.

I snap photos, catching the moments where she's relaxed, the slightest bit of confidence returning to her.

"What else?"

"Dakota and I went to summer camp one year and they had a bunch of goats. Apparently we pissed off a buck while we were there and we were chased around until we ran to this massive tree in the middle of the camp and climbed it as high as we could. The tree was the only way to escape its rage and I've never been more thankful for a tree." She laughs, her eyes squinting as she smiles. "I don't think we were stuck there very long, but it felt like hours. The animal wranglers had to come and rescue us."

"How old were you?" I continue watching her through the lens, snapping photos of her.

"Uh—Maybe thirteen? It was shortly after my birthday."

She continues on for a few more moments, telling me stories of the shenanigans they'd get into as kids. I savor every moment until finally, I pull the camera away from my face.

She looks at me as I walk toward her. It doesn't take long to pull up the gallery of photos. Sitting beside her, I scroll through them.

She's beautiful, just like I said. It's raw and candid, her face lit up as she talks and laughs. Her body is incredible and I hope that she can finally get a glimpse of the way she looks through my eyes.

I'm lost in the photos when I hear a sniffle at my side.

I look over at her, my heart beating. "What's wrong?" I drop the camera into my lap before I wrap my arms around her.

"I can't believe you did that," she says as she swipes at her face. "They're beautiful."

"You're beautiful," I counter. "That's all you."

She takes the camera from my lap, scrolling through the photos.

Her face changes the further she gets. After several minutes, she looks at me, her blue-green eyes watery. "Thank you. I'm on a journey of loving my body the way it deserves to be loved, and I can't tell you how much this means to me. Even if I hated it in the beginning."

"I love you, Sterling Bexley. You, and all of our friends, have taught me what it feels like to love again. It's only fair that I support you through your journey too." *Fuck me. I'm becoming a sap.*

"I think it's time you get naked, Jaiden Thomas. My tongue has an appointment."

"Anything for you." And it feels like the truth, finally. I'd walk through fire for her.

I'm never letting her go.

THIRTY-SIX

JAIDEN

VACATION IS FINALLY OVER.

We picked Wyatt and Dakota up from the airport last night, and I was up at the buttcrack of dawn for training this morning. It's only pre pre-season, but it's time we get our heads where they need to be.

Wyatt runs across the ice, Damian staying close beside him. We've been running drills for an hour and I'd forgotten how much I love being on the ice. The break was great, but it's time for us to start training again.

Roman passes the puck, running drills with me for the remainder of our time on the ice.

I run through quick hands in tight and a three-sixty with the puck before I see Sterling walk through the doors of the rink with one of our assistant coaches.

We're due to have pre-season photos taken and it's not uncommon for her to make an appearance inside the rink for these things. It just doesn't help my focus because she looks damn sexy.

She stops, turning toward him as they speak. He shoves a hand into his pocket and I watch them closely, trying to read his body language.

"Jai, I want to run a figure eight. Pay attention." Roman drops two pucks to the ice, grabbing another two and waiting for me to get into position.

We run the figure eight, swapping pucks at the last minute to take a shot.

Roman does a couple crossovers then stops by my side. "Again?"

"Let's do it."

Running the drill a few more times, I feel confident moving on, but it's when I hear Noah's slimy voice that I stop.

"How was your vacation, gorgeous? You're looking tan."

"Oh, hell no," I say, skating to the glass and slamming my fist against it.

Sterling jumps, looking over at me before she glares.

"Noah, you slimy fuck, stay the fuck away from my girlfriend. This is your last warning. You work together, that's it."

"Jesus fucking Christ, Jaiden. I'm just talking."

"No, you're not. You flirt with everything that breathes. She's taken. Move the fuck along or next time it won't be the glass I slam my fist into."

He has the wits to look scared before he nods, taking a step back from Sterling. She shakes her head, rolling her eyes before I see the ghost of a smirk cross her mouth.

I skate to an opening in the rink, nodding my head for her to follow. She sighs before walking, her heels clicking on the floor.

She looks so fucking sexy, so when she reaches me, I remove my glove, tangling my hand into her hair before I crush my lips into hers. She tastes of candy. Probably from the sweets she keeps in the drawer of her desk. She doesn't know that when I visit the offices, I stop by her desk to steal a piece, even though I know I shouldn't.

She moans into my mouth and I smile through my victory. When she realizes that I'm smiling, I hear the distinct sounds of her curse.

"You fucker. You're lucky I love you."

We pull apart, my smirk barely contained. "You can punish me later," I say with a wink. I rush back onto center ice before Coach dismisses us for the day.

Excitement rushes through me as I reflect on these last few weeks. Hockey is my life. It's always been just hockey and my small family. It's not so small of a family now, and I have no gripes with that.

I'm entering this season feeling fucking powerful.

The first two games of the season fly by in the blink of an eye. It's always a whirlwind after the break. Everything is happening so fast, and before I realize it, we're back on the road.

"Pack your bags, ladies. We're off to Florida. Meet here in the morning, and be sure to get lots of sleep." Coach dismisses us before we file from the locker room.

My feet are killing me and it only gets worse as I walk through the doors to my car. Sterling is already waiting by the car when I damn near waddle to the driver's side.

"Are you okay?"

"Yeah," I groan. "My feet are killing me."

"I'm already packed for tomorrow. I prepared," she winks. "I can come over and make us dinner, rub your feet...We can watch a movie?"

I snort. This is new territory for us and I'm loving learning with her. "If you want to come over, all you have to do is say so." I lean across the center console to kiss her. She smiles into my mouth.

"I hate you," she laughs. "I want to come over, you brat."

"Now, was that so hard?" I have half a thought to praise her, but instead I pull the car from the parking lot and make the drive home.

"No," she mumbles, her head turning to look out the window. We drive home in comfortable silence, jumping out of the car and shuffling into the condo several moments later.

It's one of the things I enjoy most about this new relationship with Sterling. Silence doesn't need to be filled with useless conversation. I can enjoy just being in her presence without the need to find something to talk about. Like on the days I'm exhausted, my brain fried from practice, I can just sit and be.

I walk up behind Sterling as she stands at the stove. The food smells incredible and I tell her so. When my arms run down her sides, she leans back into me, relaxing her weight into my chest.

"Who knew life could be this good?" I say into her hair. "All last year, I could've had this."

She looks up at me. "I think we needed the summer to figure our shit out. I'm just happy we have this now."

She's right. I needed to pull my head out of my ass long enough to get my shit together. I don't know what would have happened if we tried to force this sooner than it was meant to be.

After serving food, we sit down on the couch, flipping through the different movie options. I let Sterling choose, shoving food into mouth.

When my phone pings at my side, I put my food down, slipping it from my pocket.

My heart stops, my jaw clenching when I see the text on the screen.

Richard: Son, it's your father. I'm in town this week and I'd love to see you.

I clench my teeth trying to keep my breathing even.

Me: What do you want?

Three dots bounce, over and over, and each minute I stare, the more my anger and nerves get to me.

Richard: Why would you think I need something? Why can't I just see my son?

Me: You've only ever reached out when you needed something. So I'll ask again. What do you want?

Richard: Fine. I was evicted and I need help. I was hoping you could lend me some money.

I shake my head, trying to swallow, but my throat has gotten so dry that it's like swallowing sandpaper.

Right when my life has finally changed, he decides to reach out again. This is the last thing I need. I sigh, grabbing my food and taking another bite. When I look up, Sterling is watching me.

"Is everything alright?" She slips her fork into her mouth, biting on it as she waits.

"Fine," I say a little too quickly.

I don't have the energy to talk about this right now. My father is not someone I'm proud of. I made the mistake of *helping* him last year. I thought it would bring my father back, but all he wanted was to use me, just like all the times before.

"Okay," she says, her eyes downcast.

I'm pissed after that interaction and I don't know what to say to him. My mind spirals as we watch the movie, every shitty scenario running through my head. By the time we make it to bed, I lay awake, Sterling turning away from me the whole night.

I want to talk to her about this, but I don't know how. So instead I lay there in silence, hearing the tick of the clock until my alarm warns me of our impending flight.

THIRTY-SEVEN

STERLING

I WATCH Jaiden sleep on the plane, his breathing even and calm. I know we both didn't sleep last night and I can't help but feel a pit in my stomach grow.

I don't know what's wrong with my head, but I can't get it together. It felt like he was pulling away from me last night. He'd gone rigid, his face a mask of emotionless calm.

After laying in the same spot all night, I still couldn't sleep. I stared at the wall, my mind sending me to that dark place I'd once been.

The last time he ghosted me, I hadn't seen it coming. When I look back, I notice the way he'd done something similar to last night. I don't know what he saw on his phone, but it's causing him to retreat and I hate it.

He's going to leave you.

No.

You're going to get hurt. You knew that.

No. I trust him.

Do you?

I fight back the intrusive thoughts, trying to keep myself from the spiral of emotions I know I'm feeling.

"You okay?" A hand taps my arm and I swipe at my eyes before I look through the crack in the seats to see Damian looking at me.

"Fine," I say quietly. "Just tired. I didn't sleep."

His liquid gold eyes study me, and I feel slightly naked under his gaze. I know he can see the lie, but instead of calling me on it, he nods, leaning back into the seat.

"Promise you'll talk to me if it continues to bother you?" he says, his eyes closed as he relaxes into the seat.

"Yeah," I say. "Promise." There's no conviction in it, and when I see Wyatt watching me, I muster the best smile I can.

I think over Damian's question again as he relaxes in his seat. Am I fine? I'd be lying to myself if I said I was. I'm experiencing a whirlwind of emotions, most of them rooted in fear.

I suddenly feel undeserving of a happy ending. I'm not proper enough, not pretty enough, not someone a man wants to keep forever. These thoughts are rooted in the ideology my *perfect* mother raised me with. If she had any say over my future, I would've been unhappy like her, working in an office somewhere and making rich people richer. Creativity isn't a word in her vocabulary.

Why do I feel like this? Why is it so hard for me to believe that Jaiden is here for good? Maybe it's because the moment he shut down last night, I shut down too. I felt the pull, the way my insecurities crept in. I put on a mask of confidence, but I'm not the girl that plows through life with ease. Only one person truly knows the fears I have, and even she doesn't know the full extent of it.

By the time the plane lands, I am thoroughly shaken up, my head swimming with black threads of fearful thoughts. Even to the point that when Jaiden leans in for a kiss, it takes everything in me not to shy away from his touch. *He still wants me. I'm still his.*

I run through the weekend on autopilot, barely remembering to do my job. When we return home, Jaiden pulls me into his arms, his nose pressing into my hair.

"What's up with you lately?" His breath feels hot against my head and I relax for the first time in days.

"I can't get out of my head," I admit, laughing it off as though it's nothing.

"Want to talk about it?" His arms run down my back, his palm sliding to my ass, giving it a firm squeeze. I laugh, shoving him slightly.

"Jai," I shriek. "Your coach could pop out at any minute."

"Yeah, and? We're all adults here." He removes his hand, bringing it to my chin and raising my face to meet his. When his lips descend on mine, I'm lost in his kiss. Every fear is erased within seconds, my body melting into his.

"Come over," he says as he pulls away. He rests his forehead on mine, his long lashes shielding his gorgeous gray eyes.

"I can't," I say. "I have to help Dakota tomorrow at the shop. I need to actually get some sleep tonight."

He pouts, jutting out his lower lip, and I shake my head.

"Then promise to call me when you get home. I want to know you're safe." He pulls away, his hand running through my hair.

"Promise. I'll see you this weekend," I say. That seems to satisfy him, because he finally releases me, kissing me once more before slapping my ass lightly as I turn away.

It takes me minutes to drive home. I've only been here a handful of times since the beginning of the season. Most often I stay at Jai's, and when he comes here, we're decked out in hoodies and hats to hide our identities due to the more central location of my apartment. He's got more security, so it's become an unspoken agreement that we spend more time there.

The media hasn't been a huge issue yet, but I'm waiting for the day it becomes a big deal that one of Boston's playboys is off the market.

I hit the call button on Jaiden's name, the line ringing only once before he answers.

"Babe," he says, his voice immediately comforting me.

"Hey," I breathe, holding the phone against my ear with my shoulder as I turn the key in my lock.

"I want to take you out on a proper date. Things couples do. We skipped the courting part and I think we need to do it right." There's ruffling in the background of the call. It sounds like he's cooking dinner, the popping of something in a pan.

"I'm not opposed to being courted by Jaiden Thomas." I set my things down by the door, kicking it shut before I turn to lock it.

"Great. It's a date then." He clicks off the stove, and I hear the sounds of food being plated.

"It's a date," I repeat. It's when I'm pouring water into my cup noodle that I hear him drop something before shuffling.

"Great. This weekend then." He starts to say more, then suddenly stops, his voice pausing.

"Babe?" I ask, popping my noodles into the microwave.

He's silent for several moments, the muffled sounds of voices.

"I gotta go. I'll talk to you later," he says in a rush. "Love you," he bites out, ending the call before I can respond.

My heart beats at a frantic pace. Every panicked thought from earlier comes flooding in.

What the fuck am I going to do?

TWO DAYS. TWO FUCKING DAYS AND IT'S BEEN RADIO silence from Jaiden. I've texted him a handful of times, but I've got nothing back.

I feel like puking. Wyatt's assured me that it's fine... *It's NOT fine.*

I'm not fine.

Every fiber in my being is reminding me of the moment this happened last time. Two days. Two days will turn into four days, and four days will turn into two weeks, two months... How long do I have to wait for him to communicate with me? Aren't we a team now? Isn't that what we're supposed to be?

"Stop making that face," Lani says from across the studio. She swipes her towel across the skin of the client she's working on before looking up at me with her brow raised.

"What face? I'm not making any faces." I slouch into my chair, turning my phone face-down on the desk.

"Yes, you are. I'll call Dakota—don't make me do it."

The buzz of the tattoo gun drowns out my thoughts, and I sigh, trying to avoid staring at my phone and waiting like a hopeless puppy.

"Call Dakota for what?" The woman herself walks through the doors of the studio, Wyatt following behind her. Both of them are gloriously tan from their honeymoon and it looks damn good on them.

"No reason—" I say, but Lani interrupts me.

"Silver's got that *look* on her face again." Lani says it with her eyes still down on her client, and I know she can't see me glare, but I do it anyway.

"He missed practice again today," Wyatt says. "But I promise you, he's got reasons."

"Reasons everyone has to be so secretive about? Why can't I know?"

"Not my story," Wyatt says simply, his shoulders shrugging. "He needs to share this on his own."

"I fucking hate this," I grumble as Dakota sits by my side.

"What's going on in your head?"

"Lots of things I don't care to talk about." I spin in the chair, tracking the wall as I move in a circle.

"Well, I'm here when you're ready." She gives me a sad smile before standing and walking to see the piece Lani is working on.

"Is he okay?" I ask, keeping my voice low.

Wyatt watches me, his arms crossed. "He will be." And for some reason, I don't quite let the words sink in, because I don't know if *I'll* be okay after all of this.

After a week of damn near silence, I lose my patience, the self sabotage setting in.

Jaiden missed every practice this week, and everyone seems less than concerned. I've gotten nothing but a short text promising me that he'll update me when he can, but something important came up. It was followed by a simple *I love you*, and despite the fact I know in my gut he means it, I can't accept it. So now, here I am, pacing across my kitchen with an unsent text on the screen of my phone.

I pace, and pace, and pace, until my feet hurt. After another fifteen minutes and a raging stomach ache, I finally hit send.

Me: This isn't working out. I think we should break up. Enjoy your life, Jaiden.

It may be the most immature thing I've ever done, breaking up with someone over a text, but I can't live with it any longer. I can't keep waiting for Jaiden to dump me, to leave me a sobbing mess on the floor. So instead, I'm taking my power back, breaking my own heart and sabotaging any future I may have with him. All because I'm scared.

THIRTY-EIGHT

JAIDEN

"WHAT ARE YOU DOING HERE?" I ask, my voice harsh. I stare down at the man who calls himself my father. His hair is messy and he looks like he's been living in a garbage can. His normally pale skin is tanned from sun exposure, and gray from dirt and grime.

"I've got nowhere else to go." He looks sad, his face both sunken in and slightly swollen. He's more frail than the last time I saw him. I suppose that's what addiction does to a body.

I don't want to hate the man in front of me, but hot rage rushes through me. He wasn't here when my mom passed away. He couldn't sober up enough to be present for that, but he can come here now, asking for what? A place to stay... Money for more substances?

Everything in me screams to turn him away, to send him packing to wherever he came from, but as I take a breath, I feel something I didn't expect to. *Pity.*

"Okay," I say, opening the door wider.

He smells of garbage as he walks by me, and I hold my breath.

"I have rules. You can stay for the night," I say, my voice firm. "You shower and you stay out of my liquor cabinet. I'll know if you touch a thing. Tomorrow, I'm driving you back to Jersey."

"I don't have anywhere to go in Jersey."

"Don't worry, I'll figure it out." I hold up a finger to him, signaling him to wait here. Walking into my room, I pull a pair of basketball shorts and a t-shirt from my drawers. They'll be slightly big on him, but it's better than nothing.

"Here," I say, walking back out to the living room. He's standing looking at the photo of Sterling and I that I put up a few days ago.

"Your girlfriend?"

"Yep. She's a photographer." I don't know why I share it, or why I'm willing to share any details of my personal life, but I do it anyway.

"Thanks." He takes the clothes and retreats in the direction I point him. I hear the shower running, the spare door to the spare bedroom closing.

I fall backwards into the couch, my fingers tracing circles on my temples.

"The fuck am I supposed to do?" I mumble to the empty room.

I lay in bed that night wide awake until the sun blares through my curtains. When I hear the opening and closing of cabinet doors, the worst thoughts run through my mind.

He's stealing my shit. He's looking for my booze stash. He's going to leave me again after he's gotten his fix, just like he always does.

I hadn't expected to see him cooking breakfast, the smell of bacon wafting through the condo.

"Uh—" I say, unable to keep my mouth shut.

"Oh. Morning," he says, a spatula in hand. "I don't know where everything is, so I hope this is okay."

"Yeah," I mumble, shuffling toward the island to rip a piece of bacon off the plate.

It's silent for a while, the only sounds coming from the popping of the bacon. I don't know what to say to the man who contributed to my existence, but didn't care enough to stick around.

"What happened this time?" I ask, pushing my eggs around on my plate.

He stops, turning toward me. He looks older, a smattering of white hair decorating his beard and unruly hair. His eyes are sunken in slightly, and I see glimpses of myself in the signature gray Thomas eyes.

"My boss caught me drinking on the job and fired me. I was evicted a few days later."

I don't respond, not trusting myself to say something kind. Instead, I resort to shoving food into my mouth.

"We'll leave in an hour. I need to pack clothes and let my coach know I'll be out of town."

"Right. You're a hotshot now. Always knew my genes would come in handy one day." He says it with pride and I have the urge to disagree, but I don't. I pity the man before me. I've held so much hatred and disgust toward him, and now that I see this small man, I only feel sadness.

I walk away without another word, packing quickly for my journey.

It's a brutal five hour drive. I didn't have much to say, and it seems my father only wanted to discuss my fortunate circumstances. I *worked* so fucking hard for my place on my team. I worked, and I trained, and I committed my life to hockey. It's got nothing to do with fortunate circumstances. I trained to stand out within the pool of hockey players. And here I fucking am.

"I booked us a hotel for the night so that I can figure out what to do from here."

Richard jumps out of my car, stretching his legs, before we walk into the hotel lobby. After checking in, I drop my bags off in the room, locking the door again.

"You need clothes," I say plainly.

"I have some. My buddy had some of my stuff."

"Yeah, no. I don't trust your friends." I cross the street toward the outlet mall without waiting for him. When he finally catches up, he's out of breath and sweating.

We pick out clothes, enough for a couple weeks, before I hand over my card to the cashier. She takes it gladly, singing about it being the biggest purchase she's seen in a while.

Her hair is cropped short to her head, and I'm reminded of Sterling.

"Fuck," I say. "Give me a minute." I step away from the register while she bags the clothing.

I type out a quick text, hoping it will satisfy her until I can explain more. I don't trust the details of our life together with Richard.

"What are you going to do with me?" Richard appears at my side, a couple bags in his hands. I grab the rest, walking out the door behind him.

"I'm still figuring it out," I say between clenched teeth.

"I can find a job," he says.

"Why didn't you do that before you came to find me?" It comes out more snippy than I intended it to, and I sigh, running my hand across my scruff.

"I—I needed a drink," he says, shaking his head. *Right.*

It's that sentence that solidifies my decision. It's why I leave him in the room to eat his dinner alone, and it's why I spend the next several days arranging the details of his new home.

"I can't stay here," he says, his voice panicked.

I don't need to see the look on his face to know that he's freaking the hell out. I pull the car up to the front of the rehab center I contacted a few days ago. We're in Jersey so that he's not too close to me but not too far either. I need him to make the *choice* to change. For real this time. So that's why we're here, and not pulling up to some new cushy apartment for him to lose all over again.

"You need help, Richard. I can't give you money and leave you here. I would be doing you a disservice."

"No, you wouldn't."

"Yes, I would. Who knows what you'll spend the money on?

Last time you came to me, I made that mistake. I set you up, got you a job, and you fucked it up."

He winces, and I sigh again before jumping out of the car, urging him to follow.

"Look"—I gesture toward the rehab center—"You need this. I can't be the person you run to every time your life implodes. I've been so angry, and sometimes I still am, Richard. I forgive you for the shit you put me through, and for only coming to me once you needed something, but I won't forgive you if you continue destroying your life like this. I'm offering you a solution and I need you to take it. If not for me, then for yourself, or *fuck,* for mom. If you loved her at all, do it for her."

I grip the bags of his clothing, trying to keep my hands busy. He stares for several moments, his face experiencing a range of emotions, before he lands on defeat.

"I did love your mom," he says, his voice gruff. "I did love you, too. I chose my lifestyle over the two of you but from what I can tell, she did a good job with you."

"She did."

"You'll come visit me?"

"Maybe," I say honestly. "I don't trust you, but if you get well, I'll consider letting you into my life."

"Fair." He nods several times before turning to the doors of the rehab center.

"Yeah."

I follow him in, dropping his clothes off into his room before signing the paperwork with the office. I lean against the wall, waiting for the women to finalize everything when my phone vibrates. It's been a week since I've been home and I've kept my contact with Sterling short, so when I see her name on the screen, I feel a sense of peace. That is, until I read the words on the screen.

"You've gotta be fucking kidding me," I say under my breath, red hot rage rushing coursing through my veins. I didn't wait for them to finish, just signed on the dotted line, before I rushed through the doors and right to my car.

THIRTY-NINE

STERLING

"WHAT DID YOU DO?" Dakota slams my door, her eyes searching mine. "Why did I get a frantic call from Jaiden asking where the fuck you were?"

"He called you?"

"Yes. About a million times."

Right on cue, another call rings through, Jaiden's name flashing on my screen. I flip the phone over, pressing a button to silence it.

"Nothing," I say, finally. " I didn't do anything. Just self sabotaged like I usually do."

"Silver," she huffs. "What is going on?" She pulls out the barstool, slipping into it.

"He ghosted me for a couple days and I freaked the fuck out. Days ago, he got this look while we were eating dinner and my brain just assumed the worst."

"Girl," she sighs.

"I *know.*" I finally break, the tears falling. "Why am I like this?" I sit in the chair beside her, my hands shielding my face from her.

"I know why. Because your parents are neglectful, rich assholes who had a child because it was some sort of weird social standard for them. They practically pay you off to pretend like you don't exist to them. Growing up you acted out for attention and when you learned it wasn't going to work, you just continued because it was what you were used to. How am I doing so far?"

I lick my lips, then open my mouth in a terrified smile.

"I thought so. You started sleeping around under the ruse of not wanting to make commitments, but in actuality, I don't think you ever really believed in love for yourself because again, your parents suck. So, when you met Jaiden and started feeling"—she jazzes her hands out like their shooting sparkles from her fingertips—"*things* for him, you freaked out, but wanted to continue. As much as we all want to blame Jaiden for being an idiot, I think that a part of you was glad that things didn't work out because then you didn't have to deal with it." Dakota eyes me, searching for any reaction.

My heart pounds. I feel like I'm being ripped right open, the raw bits of myself being exposed.

"I think that ultimately you don't feel worthy of love, but let me tell you something, Silver. *You* are the most worthy person I know. You love so deeply and you deserve that back. When I was broken and crying on the floor for days at a time, you helped me pick up the pieces one by one. I love you *so* much, Silv. I love you more than words can say and all I want is for you to be happy. So, get off your ass and fix it. Talk to him, at the very least, and hear what he has to say, because I guarantee that you'll take back that fucking *break up text* you sent when you hear it."

I blink at her several times, opening and closing my mouth because words won't come. I stare at her in disbelief for several moments. All of it is true. My parents are assholes, and I've never felt deserving of love.

Every bit of my pleasure-fest with men had been a way to act out at first, a way to become the complete opposite of who my parents wanted me to be, but in turn, I lost pieces of myself in the process. I lost the value I held in myself because I didn't think I was deserving of something better.

"I kinda hate you right now, but I also love you more than I can ever express, so it counteracts the hate."

"That's fine," she says with a shocked laugh. "You came all the way to Canada to pull me off my ass last spring, so it's about time I returned the favor."

"Yeah, yeah. I thought I was supposed to be the bold friend. I'm scared I'm rubbing off too much on you and Lani."

"Hazard of spending too much time together. We're corrupting our ray of sunshine."

I laugh, leaning forward to rest my head on the counter. "I fucked up," I groan.

"Yeah, you did. Now, fix it." She stands, bringing her hands to my face so that I look at her. "I love you. You deserve all the love in the world. You deserve the love that Wyatt and I have, the fairytale ending, just sans wedding and babies and, ya know, all the typical fairytale ending shit." She laughs, still holding my face. "I know it's the farthest thing from what you actually want. Marriage, no marriage, babies, no babies; you deserve the ending you want and choose for yourself. Fuck your parents and their stupid ideology. You are one of the most talented people I've ever met and I fucking proud of you."

"Dakota Lane, I think you've dropped more f-bombs tonight than you ever have before."

"Yeah, well, I'm passionate about this. I'm so proud of you and you needed to hear it from someone."

"I love you," I say, keeping the tears locked away.

"I love you, too." She hugs me before slipping out of my apartment.

The second the door closes, I cry, the dam of emotions breaking free. I hadn't realized that I'd wanted someone to be proud of me, to tell me that I deserve to be happy. And now that it's been said, I cry out the feelings of hatred that I've felt toward myself.

Jaiden and I aren't perfect—far from it—but that doesn't mean we won't work, that he's going to run every time life gets hard. I panicked...assuming the worst. And if I'm being honest, I was the one who ran this time.

My phone rings again and I ignore it, not ready to face him yet. I hunker down on my couch, hearing the sounds of a building storm outside.

The cracks of thunder and lightning sound before the rain pours. When there's a pounding on my door several moments later, I almost mistake it for thunder, until I hear my name being yelled on the other side of the door.

"Sterling! Open the damn door."

My blood runs cold, my heart stopping in my chest.

I shake as I walk to the door, cracking it open to see a soaking wet Jaiden.

"Let me in," he says, and like the stubborn, bratty bitch I am, I shake my head. "Then come out here."

"Why?"

"Why?" His eyes go wide, his sopping wet hair falling into his face. "You fucking dumped me over a text, Sterling. Over a *text.* Not to mention the fact you didn't provide a reason, either. So, either get your ass out here, or let me in."

He looks like he ran here, his jacket poorly thrown over his shoulder like an afterthought. I think about it for several moments before I step outside, clicking the door shut lightly behind me.

"What?" I say, unwilling to give in just yet.

"My addict father showed up at my door a week ago, asking for help. He'd contacted me the first time things fell apart between us, but I didn't know how to handle it, how to manage the chaos that was my life and my growing feelings for you. I got him a job, set him up in Jersey with this cushy life, and he fucked it up again when he started drinking." He's dripping wet, the water falling down his face, resting on his lashes.

Water drips onto me and I feel a chill. I start to open the door when Jaiden grips my hand.

"Oh, hell no. You made your choice, now wait it out. My game now, sweetheart." Rain falls onto my head and I protest until he glares at me. I shiver, holding myself as I urge him to go on.

"He came back after his life imploded, and I didn't know how to tell you, at least not yet. I don't trust him and he doesn't deserve to know the perfection that is you, so sue me for waiting. But Jesus, Sterling, I told you I'm in this. You're fucking stuck with me."

I swallow, shifting my weight as I shiver in the cold. Hot tears slide down my face, but they're hidden by the rain.

I love him. I love him, and I'm an idiot.

"This"—he gestures between us—"is forever, or as long as you want me. But fucking Christ, if you dump me again over text, I'll have a heart attack. You drive me nuts, Sterling." He tosses his hands down at his sides in frustration. When he spins, I bite my lip to hide the smile. His frustration is sexy, but I can't say that. Not yet. "I wanted to deny my feelings, to hope they'd go away. But you came barreling into my life like a fucking freight train and you changed everything. I wanted to love again, and fuck me, I didn't know how. But I do now. I need you to trust me."

"I do," I say, my voice quiet.

"Do you?" he asks, his voice deep and husky. "Do you trust me?"

"Yes." It's the truth.

"You're not getting away that easy," he says, pulling me to him. Even in the cold, even with the visual of his breath in the rain and the cold, he's still warm. "I fucking missed you. I thought about you every day I was gone, and I was in a mad rush to come home, to tell you everything."

"So, just to clarify... You weren't going to dump me and when you shut down on the couch...it was because of your dad."

"Fuck, no. I just got you, why the hell would I dump you? My life has been better these past few weeks than they've been in years. I'm keeping you forever."

I cling to him. "Please do," I say. "I'm sorry. I love you. I got scared and I thought if I dumped you first, I wouldn't get hurt."

"I get it. Just don't do it again." He slides a hand through my soaking hair as he looks down at me, his eyes penetrating. He brings his lips down to mine and I nearly moan at the intensity of the kiss. His tongue brushes against my lips before he pulls my lip between his teeth. He bites, and when I open my eyes, his eyes are dark, his pupils blown. "I'm going to fuck you now. You're mine, Sterling Bexley."

"I'm yours," I gasp, his mouth descending onto my neck as we move backwards toward my apartment.

"*I'm yours,*" I repeat, and it's never been more accurate. He owns me, heart and soul. I may be weak at times, but he makes me want to be strong, makes me feel the love I've craved and deserve.

We're perfectly imperfect and that's all I could ask for.

Jaiden Thomas is mine, and I am his.

Who knew a year ago that we'd be here? I certainly didn't.

EPILOGUE

FOUR MONTHS LATER

MY FINGER SLIPS inside her a moment before I slide the toy in, making sure it's snug in place.

"I can't believe you're making me do this," she says, stepping away to wiggle. I watch her as she slips her thong over her feet, sliding it up her long legs. She locks eyes with me in the mirror as I slide the zipper up her back, leaving a trail of kisses along the way. There's heat in her eyes, but it's not something I'll address now, for the sake of our *game.*

As she pulls the cape over her shoulders, aligning the padding and slipping her arms through the slits, I realize how sexy and sophisticated she looks. Sexy enough that I can feel my cock growing in my slacks. But am I really surprised? At this point, Silver could breathe on me and I'd be hard. That's how fucking gone I am for her.

Thank God for formal events like this. I'll never tire of seeing my woman dressed up and emanating power.

She points at me through the mirror and I know she's going to remind me of what I already know. "We are here to work. To work. And *then* play. Just because the whole gang's here in Vegas does not mean you get to press the button on that remote every —" She freezes, stiffening as I press the button once. She releases a small whimper, then realizes what she's done. I click the remote again, stopping the vibrations, and she sighs. "Jaiden," she says through gritted teeth and I can't help the wicked smirk that breaks free.

"This is going to be fun," I say, my eyebrow raised.

"I fucking hate you," she says, slipping on her heels with ease.

I walk behind her, looking at her in the mirror. Sliding my hand up her neck, I nudge her chin back until I can bring my lips down to meet hers. She moans into my mouth as I press my erection into her back. "You get the reminder that you do this to me. It's as much torture for me as it is you."

I kiss her again before I step away, adjusting my tie again. We walk through the hotel, the lobby filled with other members of my team. We're on track for the finals again and today is a media day for a big charity event hosted by the NHL.

Lani and Dakota are standing with the other partners as they wait for the photographer, who just so happens to be my girlfriend. What she doesn't know is that she gets to be in the photos today instead of being behind the camera.

Sliding my arm down her back, I guide us until we're standing by the others. Damian waves at Lani and she wanders over to him, her sunset hair braided down her back.

I see Sterling nudge Dakota as they watch her. "I'm pissed," she whispers.

"Me too. Who knew we'd be wrong? Maybe they need a gentle nudge," Dakota says with that familiar glimmer in her eyes.

"None of that," Wyatt says, sliding his arm around his wife. "No meddling. Those days are over."

Both Sterling and Dakota pout and I lock eyes with Wyatt, shaking my head.

"These two—they're trouble. I should've listened to Jake when I had the chance." I click the remote secretly in my pocket and Sterling stiffens, crossing her legs and pressing her thighs together. I press my lips against her ear. "Relax, baby."

Her lips purse as she glares at me, her pupils dilating slightly.

When I click it off, she relaxes again, running a hand across her face to hide the flush.

"What kind of twisted game are you two playing now?" Dakota asks, her eyebrows raised.

"Just seeing how long Sterling can behave. The stakes are high."

Dakota laughs. "Sterling? Behaved? Never." She pokes her arm and I see Sterling glare. I click the remote again and I see every muscle in her body tense, before relaxing a moment later.

She walks to the bar, grabbing a champagne flute and taking a large gulp. "Liquid courage," she says to Dakota.

Lani and Damian walk toward the group. She's hanging on his arm, poking him and teasing him about something. It makes me smile to see my friends having fun and laughing together.

"Okay, I had a thought," she says when they finally reach our group. Roman follows close behind, stopping to join the circle. "Everyone has nicknames. Well, for the most part. I've been calling Damian *Dame* and *monkey*." She looks at Damian knowingly before continuing. "There's Koda for Dakota; Silver for Sterling; Rome for Roman; Jai for Jaiden; and Lani for me. But Wyatt doesn't have a nickname."

Her big doe eyes turn toward Wyatt and I think it clicks for all of us at the same time. Wyatt really doesn't have a nickname.

"We must remedy it immediately," Damian says, his brows waggling.

"I vote for Wy-Wy. *Oh, Wy-Wy*, how's it feel to know you don't wear the pants in your marriage?"

Wyatt glares, coming to run his knuckles over my head when the group starts laughing.

"I've been calling him Wy-fi since our honeymoon," Dakota says, kissing his arm.

I laugh. "Only Dakota knows the password. What a shame. I thought our kiss this summer was magical." I pucker my lips at him and a horrified expression crosses his face.

"You fucker," he says, lunging for me again and I shriek.

"Boys! Not in the lobby!" Coach yells as he enters the room, the bonus photographer following him. "I swear, I'm like a glorified babysitter," he huffs and we laugh.

"Okay, everyone, line up! Players only for this one, and then we'll move onto players and partners before we release you to the party. We are in Vegas, after all."

We line up, taking serious photos until I grab Wyatt's sides like an awkward prom photo. He initially shoos me away, until Roman and Damian join in, posing in ways that make our Coaches' eyes roll back into their heads.

After the partners take photos, we're dismissed, shuffling into the ballroom to enjoy the party.

With wine flowing, it's easy to tease Sterling from across the room. During dinner, she sits beside me, her legs crossed elegantly. I run my hands up her thighs under the table.

She talks with Noah and Damian, and suddenly I crave her attention. When she goes to take another bite of food, I click the remote, sending her body into a fit of pleasure. She tenses, the fork dropping to the floor. When it hits the table, Noah looks at her before flagging down a server for another fork. She breathes, squeezing my thigh so tightly that I run my thumb across the top of her hand.

I can see the way her body shakes, and her eyes flick to me, pleading for release.

But that's not the game.

She's close, and I can see it in the way her breathing changes and how her leg shakes ever so slightly, so I hit the button, stopping the vibrations.

She relaxes instantly, her face now flushed. She bites her lip, adjusting herself in her seat, her hand fanning herself lightly.

"Is it hot in here?" She takes a drink from her champagne flute, fanning herself again.

"Are you okay?" Noah asks, his eyes concerned.

"Fine," she bites out. "I think it's the alcohol getting to me."

I lean in, kissing her neck. "You're doing so good," I praise.

She immediately reacts, her body leaning into me at the praise.

We continue the night like this, her body reaching the edge, but never falling over. And finally, when she's across the room and talking with a group of players, I hit the button on the remote and she freezes. I see her drop her purse and crouch to the floor.

"Sterling, you good?" Dakota looks at her and she nods. She mumbles something and they look at me. A second later, Dakota is walking in my direction.

"She asked for you. Maybe a lady emergency?"

I snort, nodding. "I got this."

Walking slowly, I crouch beside her until her hand wraps in my tie, her eyes feral.

Her voice is low when she speaks. "If you don't take me into that bathroom right now and fuck the life out of me, I'm going to scream right here and it won't be pretty."

I smirk, my brows raised. "Yes, ma'am," I purr, helping her to her feet.

We walk slowly to the family bathroom out of sight. I see Lani dancing with Damian, her cheeks pink from alcohol consumption. He's got his arms wrapped around her and the funny stares they're getting don't seem to phase them.

They're the strangest pair ever. We're all just waiting for them to date, but so far, it's yet to happen.

Sterling pulls me into the bathroom and slams the door shut a moment before she presses me against it.

"You have tortured me all night," she says, her hand coming to the back of my neck. I smirk, enjoying the power radiating off her right now. She's the only woman I'd give up control for.

She moves her hands through my hair until she's sliding down my body, her hands fumbling with my belt.

When she unbuttons my pants, she's slow to pull down the zipper, and even slower to free my cock from my slacks.

I groan when she fists me, the bead of precum sparkling on her thumb. She pulls me into her mouth, her tongue sliding across the head of my cock. A guttural groan leaves me. She's beautiful, especially when she's knelt between my legs. I buck into her mouth and she gags, taking me deeper. It's only a moment later that she releases me with a pop and quickly stands to her feet.

I'm guided to the small loveseat in the luxurious bathroom. She presses me into the seat as she hikes her dress up over her hips.

"Take it out," she commands, and I do as she says. Sliding a finger inside her, I pull the small toy from her.

She's soaking, and that bit of knowledge shoots right to my cock. I hold her hips and she mounts me, lining herself up before she comes down, taking me inside of her torturously slow.

She tosses her head back, a moan leaving her as she rides me in a perfect rhythm.

"Fuck," I groan. "Is there anything you won't try?"

She pants, her hands now planted firmly on my chest. "You'll never pee on me. Hard limit." She smirks, rising up to slam back down.

I can't form words, my mind going blank as she clenches around me. Her moans grow louder the closer she gets. It's shameless, and sexy as fuck.

Sliding my hand into her dress, I tweak her nipples and that's what sends her over the edge. When she comes, it's a beautiful display of feminine power. I watch her with awe, loving the way she took control. I pull her mouth to mine, swallowing her moans, and when she comes down, I slam into her, coming apart a moment later.

"You were made for me," I say into her hair. "I'm never letting you go."

"You better not," she says. She kisses me slowly, pulling my lip into her teeth and biting softly. We stay like that for several moments until we stand to clean up.

"Think people will know?"

"Let them. Everyone should know you're mine."

"You're a possessive brute." She flicks my arm then kisses it.

"You love me," I say, intertwining our fingers together before we exit the bathroom.

"Always."

The party is still going when we step outside the bathroom, the team knocking back drinks and celebrating another milestone for the Yellow Jacket's. At the end of the night, we're all in an alcohol induced haze, rushing off to bed to sleep it off for the trip home.

I WAKE WITH STERLING'S ARMS WRAPPED AROUND ME. I kiss her until we make our way to the bathroom, making love until we're pruny and forced to meet everyone for breakfast downstairs.

Sterling talks with Dakota as we load up our plates from the breakfast buffet. I plop strawberries onto Sterling's plate when she isn't looking. I didn't have room on mine, and so I'll steal them from her later.

We pull out chairs, waiting for the others to join.

"How's your dad doing, Jai?" Roman takes a bite of bacon, chewing as he waits.

"He's good. Getting out of rehab in a few weeks. I guess we'll see then, for sure." Sterling rubs my leg and I'm calmed by her silent reassurance.

"That's good," Roman replies, his phone ringing on the table.

"Where's Lani and Damian?" Dakota asks, looking around the room. There's an excited gleam in her eye that I see in Sterling too.

A second later, Lani and Damian walk into the ballroom, their hands interlocked.

"Oh, shit," Wyatt mutters, his brows raised.

Sterling and Dakota whisper excitedly as they walk toward us. That's when I notice the golden band glittering on Damian's finger. My eyes narrow as they approach.

"You're married?" I say, my brows disappearing into my curls.

"Uh—Surprise?" Lani says, her lips pursed. She holds up her left hand, a simple band resting on her ring finger. Damian shoves a hand into his pocket, his free hand held up to show us a matching gold band.

"I didn't see that one coming," Dakota says under her breath.

Sterling looks at me, her eyes wide as she shoves a whole strawberry into her mouth.

"I guess what happens in Vegas, *doesn't* stay in Vegas." I tease, locking eyes with Damian.

This is about to get interesting.

THE END...

Read Lani and Damian's Story in Sin-Bin, book three of the PuckHeads Series

Goal-Suck- Book One
Dirty-Dangles- Book Two
Sin-Bin- Book Three

ACKNOWLEDGMENTS

Wow, that was definitely a journey. I am so excited to be able to finally share this book with all of you. It's about damn time, am I right?

As always, I'd like to acknowledge my faith. Writing is something that I've always loved and without my faith, I don't think I'd be here today.

To Bae, thank you for everything that you've done for me before during and after this book reaches people's hands. You sat on the phone with me for hours while I cried to you about how I wasn't sure if I could continue writing and I'll never be able to thank you enough for that.

To Hazel, thank you for all of the brainstorming sessions you sat through, and for being my ultimate hype-woman. I appreciate you endlessly.

To the Trash Bin, y'all are the shit. I love all of you. Thanks for being my besties and for supporting me through this journey.

To my family, I love all of you more than I can say. Thank you for being supportive of my journey and for not judging me for writing smut. Also...maybe just skip to the acknowledgements. I don't know if I can face all of you after you read the sex scenes I wrote... whoopsie.

To my dad, you are my biggest supporter and I'll never leave you out of my acknowledgments. Thanks for telling every person you encounter that your daughter is an author and for all the free marketing you do for me, lol. I love you so much. You're my hero.

Last, but not least, thank you to my street team and to my readers for being amazing as fuck. I've loved meeting you all and sharing my stories with you. I can't thank you enough for being here.

ALSO BY GABRIELLE DELACOURT

Beautiful Danger

Goal Suck: Book 1 in the PuckHeads Series

CPSIA information can be obtained
at www.ICGtesting.com
Printed in the USA
LVHW020204180423
744642LV00013B/686